LURED INTO LOVE

LURED INTO LOVE

MELANIE MARTINS

Melanie Martins

BLOSSOM IN WINTER

BOOK TWO

Melanie Martins, LLC
www.blossominwinter.com

First published in the United States by Melanie Martins, LLC in 2021.

ISBSN ebook 978-1-7333564-4-2

ISBN Paperback 978-1-7333564-6-6

Printed and bound in Great Britain by Clays Ltd, Elcograf S.p.A

This is a 1st Edition.

DISCLAIMER

This novel is a work of fiction written in American-English and is intended for mature audiences. Names, characters, places, and incidents are either the product of the author's imagination or used fictitiously. Any resemblance to actual persons, living or dead, is entirely coincidental. This novel contains strong and explicit language, graphic sexuality, and other sensitive content that may be disturbing for some readers.

To all of you, my dear readers.
Thank you.

"It's a nasty kind of love.
The kind you can't escape from
even if you want to."

—Petra Van Gatt

PROLOGUE

Rotterdam, August 20, 2020
Tess Hagen

"Tess, they are ready to start," Carice announces from the doorway of the terrace.

Standing alone in the living room, I check my appearance once more in the mirror as I stretch the hem of my beige blazer. I'm not sold on the color though—with my blonde hair, I don't think it suits me. Nevertheless, Carice kept insisting that Von Der Leyen—the European Commission president—was wearing beige on TV and she looked flawless. Well, in my opinion, Carice spends too much time watching the news and flattering politicians. But that's her thing—Carice is an observer, picky to the bone with details, and the best lawyer we have at my nonprofit. She is also my friend, my adviser, and the shoulder I lean on to cry when days are too hard to handle. "I'll be there in a minute," I reply before she returns to the terrace.

Turning fifty-three in ten days is no easy task, but it's even worse when your only child has been in a coma for nearly six months, while you are here living—or surviving—on the other side of the Atlantic.

Oh, my little angel…

It's hard not to give up, not to fall into a deep state of depression like the one I was in after I found my daughter in March, lying in bed, unconscious, somewhere between life and death. The steep pain I felt in my chest is still there—and it's just as intense, raw, and merciless. Since then, I've been able to visit her in Bedford Hills only once a month, and under close supervision of the two men I despise the most. Mind you, from the global pandemic to the riots, they've tried all the excuses in the world for me not to travel there. But a deal is a deal: I've flown private and have managed to see my daughter at least once a month. Despite it all, I don't lose hope. One day, my little angel will wake up. One day, I'll see her big blue eyes again. And one day, Van Dieren will be gone. Petra will live a happy, healthy life—a life far away from him. But for now, I can't let my depression come back to haunt me. Advocacy and politics are good distractions—and interviews like this one too. Taking a deep breath, I leave the living room and head to the outdoor terrace where the TV crew, Kenneth—the reporter—and Carice are waiting.

It's a warm, bright summer afternoon, and the natural light is fantastic, but I don't see any fans around to bring a much-needed breeze. Although the sun keeps beaming on my face, I take a seat in front of Kenneth, while an assistant pins the small microphone onto my blazer.

Oh, he is only wearing a shirt. Maybe I should ditch the blazer. I look at Carice briefly, but her face tells me nothing. She likes this blazer so much though. Trusting her as I do, I decide to keep it on.

"Are you still sure about this?" Kenneth asks me once more, appearing more anxious than I am.

"Yes, of course." I disguise my torment with an assertive tone and find myself smiling at the glass of water sitting on the table.

Kenneth grins too. But I know it's because of the interview. After all, he hates Julia and the Van Dieren family as much as I do. Kenneth is one of those rare souls that isn't corrupted or impressed by money, status, or power. In fact, he couldn't care less about those things. I wish Petra would be more like him—less impressionable. As an investigative journalist, Kenneth has uncovered pretty scandalous stories and brought many influential people to account for their crimes. Let's just say he's our country's version of Ronan Farrow. Now his focus is on the Van Dierens and everyone surrounding them. Needless to say, I couldn't wait to give him a hand.

"It's recording," informs the man behind the camera.

And here we go…

"Ms. Hagen, many thanks for having us on your beautiful property."

"Thank you, Kenneth. It's a pleasure having you here."

"As one of the most—if not *the* most—influential activists in the country, you've recently been in a court battle advocating justice for Leonor De Vries—wife of the prominent industrialist, Jan De Vries—who was victim of marital rape. Thanks to your help, the court sentenced him to two years in jail, but unfortunately the penalty is now suspended as he appeals to the court of second instance. Given the fact that this case is now in the hands of the most conservative judge in the country, do you believe we will still get justice for the victim?"

"To be honest, I'm particularly worried. It's definitely not a good idea to give such cases to judges who have a tendency to overlook facts and to conclude that there isn't enough evidence. I just hope Julia Van Den Bosch won't withdraw the penalty imposed on the assaulter. This is a serious case of domestic violence, and the judiciary system cannot take it lightly."

We both smile at each other. Yes, I did it. I just called out the judge I despise the most on a TV interview that will be broadcasted nationwide this evening. And while it seems like a small thing, no one in this country has ever done that before. Judges like Julia are untouchable, protected by their powerful families and allies. They are also unknown to the public eye—they live in the shadows, in total anonymity.

"Indeed, the country is in shock. With elections coming up next year, would you urge the next government to make reforms to the judiciary system? Especially when it comes to cases related to domestic violence and violence toward women in general? After all, you've been the most prominent voice in this field."

"I'd definitely urge the future government to elect, first and foremost, a Minister of Justice and Security who understands the society we live in and the need for reforms," I tell him. "According to a report conducted by *AD*, suspects of rape are rarely prosecuted, and those who are often get away with a low sentence. On average, a convicted rapist spends one year and five months in prison. This is living proof that we urgently need to bring new policies in force."

"Wow." Kenneth does a quick fact-check on his iPad. "That's disturbing. Do you have someone in mind to occupy such a position?"

I ponder his question. "I don't have anyone in particular, no. But it has to be someone who protects the victims rather than the assaulters to begin with."

Kenneth lets a smile escape at the corner of his mouth. "If I may, why not you, Ms. Hagen?"

MELANIE MARTINS

CHAPTER 1

Bedford Hills, August 27, 2020
Alexander Van Dieren

"So…" I let the word trail off as I look at Petra's left hand and then at her flushed cheeks. "How does it feel?"

Sitting up in our bed and nestled in my arms, Miss Van Gatt keeps staring at her hand in absolute awe.

"Feels fucking amazing," she states bluntly. "But it's not a discreet ring."

I can't help but chuckle. "Definitely not discreet. The whole world will know you are engaged from miles away." Then, my smile getting wider, I add, "And just in case you forget to whom, my family name is engraved inside."

She lets out a quick giggle before resting her head on my shoulder, her joyful expression switching into a thoughtful one. "Are we gonna have an engagement party?"

I press my lips together at her question; I've got no idea. "Would you like one?"

But Petra doesn't reply immediately. I hear her sighing loudly instead. "I'd love to, yes, but does it make you or Dad uncomfortable? I know everyone else sees us, like, um, like, differently."

After kissing the top of her head, I look into her big blue eyes and say, "I don't give a damn. If my fiancée wants an engagement party, then we'll have one."

We keep quiet as we smile at each other.

I recognize that smile. It's my favorite one—it's the one she has when she's happy, and the one she had when I said *yes*. Her entire face glows beautifully, and her eyes are even brighter than the sapphire she's wearing. God, how many nights I've wished I could see her big blue eyes again. And despite everything I went through this year, here I am looking at them. Nothing else matters. She is here. And she is finally awake.

"Petra?"

"Yes?"

"Thank you," I tell her.

Her brows crease in confusion. "For what?"

"For giving us a second chance." But before I can say more, we are promptly interrupted by three knocks on the door. "Come in," I say. And as soon as the women enter, I introduce her to them. "Petra, this is your physician, Dr. Nel, and your nurse, Cynthia. They've been taking care of you since you came back from the hospital."

Born in the Netherlands and residing in New York for the past five years, Dr. Nel Van Djik was recommended—or imposed—by Tess to supervise Petra and her medical care.

But I must say, she has indeed been the perfect fit: with a specialty in neurology and well-known experience with patients in comas, Nel started monitoring Petra very closely upon her transfer to my estate. And after five months, she's become part of the family. Not sure if I can consider her a friend though. After all, she seems to be quite close to Tess. And why wouldn't she be? A sixty-five-year-old mother of three, she looks at me with some caution and ick in her eyes.

"Good morning, Petra. It's so good to finally see you awake. How are you feeling?" Nel asks, her voice unusually warm and welcoming. "And you may just call me Nel."

"Hi, Nel," Petra mumbles, her tone still weak. "Actually, my entire body hurts. I can't even move my legs."

"You are most likely suffering from atrophy. After being motionless for so long, you'll need physiotherapy to get back on your feet and walk."

"Oh…" Petra can't hide her disappointment. "I haven't tried to stand up yet. But… does that mean I can't walk at all?"

"Do you want to give it a try?" I ask, seeing her so alarmed.

"I can't even bend my legs. They feel like stone." She lets out a sigh, quite tormented. "In my dreams, I could jump up from bed and trot."

"In your dreams?" Nel and I repeat in surprise.

"Were you having dreams?" I ask. "What kind of dreams?"

But Petra doesn't reply immediately. It seems my question has left her a bit troubled as her eyes drift away for a second. "Um, mostly nightmares."

As I'm about to ask further questions, Nel steps in. "Mr. Van Dieren, Cynthia, would you mind if I have a talk with Petra?"

"Not at all." I place a long kiss on my fiancée's forehead—still barely believing we are engaged—and whisper, "I love you." Then I stand up and leave the room.

***

Petra Van Gatt

If my mother introduced me to her best friend, she'd most likely look like Dr. Nel—big glasses, short gray hair brushed over to the side to feign some originality, petite figure, red lips, and a big, friendly smile on her face that only the biggest hypocrites can pull off. Now that I'm alone with her, the room falls into an uncomfortable silence. She might be my physician, but she's still a stranger to me.

Nel waits a few more seconds before moving toward me and sitting on the side of my bed. I don't feel like talking, though. "I know you don't know me," she begins, keeping her smile just as big. "I've been monitoring your medical state for the past few months. The MRI showed your brain was quite active, but surprisingly, you didn't move or even blink. Can you explain to me what kind of nightmares you were having?"

No, not really. But instead I say, "Um… They were scary."

"I see…" She pauses for a beat while studying me. "Did it feel like you were trapped in some sort of reality you couldn't escape from?"

My eyes widen in surprise at how accurate that is. "How did you know that?"

"I specialize in brain activity on patients in vegetative states. Those who wake up keep telling me they felt like they were trapped while in the coma, and there was nothing they could do to escape."

While her words resonate with me, it's quite hard to open up about it. After all, I don't know much about her, or her relationship with my mother... Nevertheless, I ask, "Are you gonna repeat our conversation to anyone?"

"Of course not," she asserts. And as she sees me hesitating, she leans closer, putting a hand on top of mine. "Everything you tell me stays between us, Petra." Her tone is warmer than baked cookies; it sounds fake but so reassuring at the same time. Her eyes darting down for a second, she adds, "That's a beautiful ring. Congratulations on the engagement."

I look at it instinctively, my lips curving up. It is indeed a beautiful ring. I love sapphires. They are my favorite gems. I guess I started loving them back when I was a child and Alex used to compare the color of my eyes to sapphires. He knew I loved that word. I'd always giggle hearing him pronounce it. After all, it sounds so different from the boring word *blue*. "Thank you," I tell her.

After some consideration, I decide to open up, but very cautiously. "I only remember one nightmare. But it felt way too real." I pause, searching for the right words. "I woke up from the coma, but in Manhattan with Mom by my side, stroking my hair and telling me everyone had abandoned me. She and Emma were the only ones left."

Dr. Nel nods as she reaches for her notebook and pen from her briefcase. "Emma? She's your best friend, isn't she?"

"Yes. She's like a big sister to me. We basically grew up together."

Dr. Nel keeps nodding and starts writing something down. "And what about Mr. Van Dieren? Where was he?"

I frown at her question, closing my eyes for an instant. Despite that nightmare not being real, the pain I felt, oh jeez, I felt it quite sharply. "He was gone," I mumble, my eyes still shut. "He was married, and he was gone."

"Hey…" I feel her hand pressing mine. "Petra." My eyes open wide. "He's here. And he's not going to leave you." Somehow, as I look into her gaze, I can't help but feel my heart tightening. Her words don't reassure me. They sound fake, just like those sweet little lies you tell someone in order to not hurt them.

"My mom said Alex promised her he'd leave me." I take a much-needed breath. "Abandon me and move on with his life."

"Your mom doesn't like him, huh?"

"She hates him," I correct. "She hates the fact we are together, and she's firmly against our relationship."

"It's not easy for her, I imagine. Your mother has been coming here every single month. Each time she leaves, she cries. She loves you a lot."

"You know her?" I ask, feigning my surprise.

"Yes. My parents are also from Rotterdam. She's a very strong lady."

"Yeah… And very stubborn too."

Nel lets out a quick chuckle. "She told me the same about you." I mirror her laugh for a moment, but we keep quiet afterward.

"I can't live without him." *Shut up, Petra!* "I mean, in my dream," I amend after seeing the astonished look on her face. "It was not the reality I wanted."

"You mean, you... you ended your life in your dream?"

I nod, not wanting to admit it to myself. And I even confessed it to her. *Damn it.*

"That's okay. It means your brain was trying to somehow escape a reality it felt trapped in. I have patients who jumped from bridges in their own dreams. It might have been the reason why you woke up."

"Please don't say a word to my mom," I plead. "She can't know I'm awake. She can't know anything."

"Relax. It's not up to me to do so. I'm just here to help you." Nel looks over to the cardiac monitor and continues taking notes, then she reaches for her briefcase again, taking something from it. "Now, let's check your blood pressure. Shall we?"

* * *

Alexander Van Dieren

When I told Roy over the phone that his daughter was awake, he not only said he would cancel all his meetings for the day but told me in a sobbing voice that he would be here in thirty minutes. I also told him that she was in a consultation with Dr. Nel and to pass by my office before going to see her. While he agreed without hesitation, I have no idea how I am supposed to tell him I'm engaged to his daughter. I know I can't marry her, and I know perfectly well that I've got to move to Singapore now that she is awake.

And yet…

Here I am, a pen between my fingers, trying to figure out how to tell him otherwise. After all, despite what I should or shouldn't do, being engaged to her feels exactly how it should—so right and natural.

Glancing briefly at my watch, I expect Roy to arrive anytime. Thirty minutes seems quite implausible if he's coming from Manhattan, but just forty minutes after our call, I hear a knock on my office door. And as I order the person to come in, I see Maria opening the door wide, and then Roy smiling at me with a twinkle in his eye. I mimic his smile and good mood before inviting him to the sitting area. There I take a seat in the armchair, while he sits on the sofa beside me. And as he observes me rolling a pen between my fingers, his glowing face switches into a stern one. "What do I have to know before seeing her?"

He knows me so well. "It's not that easy…" I tell him.

Blowing out a loud, exasperated breath, Roy starts ruminating. "Did she lose her memory?"

A bit astonished by his question, I say, "Um, no, I don't think so."

He nods pensively and then asks, "Can she talk, see, and hear?"

"So far she seems okay…"

But Roy doesn't stop there. "What about walking? Does Dr. Nel know if she will ever walk again?"

"Dr. Nel is still in there. But I believe after intensive physiotherapy, she should be able to walk again, yes."

Roy exhales quickly in relief. "So what are you so worried about?"

Knowing there's no escape, my heart keeps thundering as I look him in the eye and decide, for better or worse, to tell him the truth. "We are engaged," I announce. "And before you say anything, she's the one who proposed." Then I remain silent as Roy draws in a deep breath, and, in a failed attempt to calm himself down, starts rubbing his eyelids tiredly. "That is not what we agreed upon," he snaps back in a strident voice. "Engaged or not, you will have to leave."

I observe the distress written all over his face, and as I do so, I realize how easy it is for him to lose his temper when his reputation is at stake. "There must be another way," I tell him. And leaning over, I ask in a low tone, "Did they find anything against Tess?"

Roy glances around before leaning closer to me and saying, "They searched quite a lot, but no. They could find neither the files, nor anything against her. Not even a damn traffic ticket." He exhales once more, his gaze darting down for a moment, before looking back at me. "As it said on the report, she's the apogee of a law-abiding citizen."

I can't help but chuckle at his comment. "What a good, obedient woman she is," I tease. "I'm surprised she didn't share your lifestyle."

But Roy is not in the mood for jokes. "You will have to leave," he says once more, his tone unusually grave. And since I don't reply, Roy keeps observing me. "You know that, right? We've discussed it many times." But I'm not convinced, and as he reads my answer in my gaze, his torment keeps growing and his voice rises. "I thought we had an agreement!"

The fear I might break it is something we both share. "I know."

As I ponder my next words, Roy asks, "When are you going to tell her?"

"I don't intend to tell her anything." And before he can yap or get physical, I add, "Tess is coming back in three weeks. We have some time ahead of us."

"And what do you intend to do until then?"

Leaning back in my chair, I observe him for a second more before saying, "I intend to invite my family over and have an engagement party."

Roy doesn't hide his bewilderment. "Oh, I see..." he mumbles pensively. "An engagement party? But of course!" His sarcastic tone is now borderline offensive. "Have you lost your fucking mind or what?"

"Petra would like one. It's the least I can do before—"

"Before you leave?"

Leave. I hate the meaning of that word, and I hate even more the fact that Tess is anxiously waiting for me to do so. Maybe even Roy. But for now, I just nod at him in agreement. Today is a great day. A day I'll never forget, August 27, 2020—the day Petra woke up, the day we got engaged, and the day my life made sense again.

"Very well. I guess having a farewell party before your departure seems appropriate."

I ignore his nasty comment and say, "One more thing: be nice to her."

Roy looks at me with raised brows. "Of course I'll be nice to her! Why on earth wouldn't I be?" He might look outraged, but he knows very well why.

"And no remarks about the engagement," I add as Roy mutters something under his breath. "You might not approve, but don't scold her about it."

* * *

I've never seen Roy shed a tear. Not even the day he found his daughter in a coma. His face might have gotten unusually gloomy and somber, but I never saw him cry.

Until now.

Until he met his daughter's blue eyes for the first time in nearly six months.

"Hey, darling," he greets softly, before plunging Petra into a hug. "I missed you so much," I hear him saying in a broken voice.

"I'm sorry…" she mumbles, sniffling against his shoulder.

"Hey, it's not your fault. You are finally awake. That's all that matters." I've never seen Roy being so soft, compassionate, and friendly. It's good to see this side of him for once. Then, with a contemplative smile, he asks, "How are you feeling?"

"Um, I'm okay… A bit dizzy, but I guess that's from the medicine." I notice how Petra tries to hide her left hand as Roy releases her from his embrace. "Dad, I…" She then glances over at me. "I have to tell you something."

"I already know."

"Oh…" Her eyes widen in surprise. "You do?"

"Well…" He presses his lips against her forehead, swallowing the bitter remarks he might hold against the engagement. "If that's what you want, I'm happy for you."

My lips curve up at his comment; it's a decent one. One that makes my fiancée smile at him and give him another hug.

"Thank you so much. It means a lot to me," she tells him, her eyes closed as she rests her head on his shoulder.

What a pity that Roy doesn't mean it.

I remain leaning against the doorframe of my bedroom, observing the dearest person of my life as she talks to her father about the engagement party. There are no words to describe such a miracle. Petra is alive, so alive.

Seeing Dr. Nel ready to leave the bedroom, I discreetly ask, "May we have a word before you go?"

She cringes at the question, knowing all too well the subject of the conversation. Nevertheless, she agrees, and we leave the bedroom in a frigid silence, making our way to my office.

There, I open the door, inviting her in. "Please, make yourself at home." Dr. Nel enters the room, already on guard, her face unsmiling as I close the door behind us. The air between us is as cold as her glare. "Have a seat." But she just looks at the armchair and sofa with suspicion. "May I offer you a drink?" I ask still, trying to warm the atmosphere.

She lets out a breath while I open the decanter and pour some Macallan in a glass.

"I won't be telling Tess about the engagement, if that's what you are worried about."

Ah, I forgot how direct she is. "I'm not worried about the engagement," I say, adding an ice sphere to my drink. "Because you won't tell her anything." I take a first sip, my lips curving up at the taste. "Not even that Petra is awake."

"Tess has the right to know that!" she barks immediately. "She's her mother."

"And a fucking threat," I reply just as fast, glaring at her.

"She pays me the same as you. I owe her the truth."

"You don't owe her anything. The only person you owe the truth to is to your patient—to Petra." Dr. Nel drops her gaze to the floor, pondering my words. "She's the only one who has to decide if she wants to see Tess or not."

"Petra needs to start physiotherapy," she announces, most likely to switch the subject of our conversation. "At least thirty minutes a day to make sure she recovers as fast as possible from her atrophy." She then opens her briefcase, taking a business card out. "This is the doctor I told you about."

"We'll do as you recommend. You may call her now."

Despite my instruction, she keeps studying me behind her big frames. "And she needs her mother." She draws in a breath before exhaling loudly again, this time her head shaking. "Not an engagement party." The room falls into a twitchy silence at her unsolicited comment. "I'll make the appointment with the physiotherapist today," she says.

"Perfect. Many thanks." I brush her off.

Then Dr. Nel finally leaves, taking her disapprobation away from my sight.

CHAPTER 2

Bedford Hills, August 27, 2020
Petra Van Gatt

It's a strange feeling to be alive again, especially because when you are in a coma, you don't even realize you are no longer a part of this world. When I close my eyes, though, all I can see is the reality of my nightmare—being in Manhattan, but only with Mom, while Dad and Alex are gone… Jeez, I remember absolutely everything about it as if I were still there. Despite Dr. Nel saying it was just a way for me to escape my subconscious, I'm pretty sure I didn't have that nightmare out of nowhere. After all, nightmares and dreams do tend to mean something.

"Is there something troubling you? You seem worried."

My gaze lands on Dad, who is still sitting on a chair, softly stroking my hair. He hasn't left the bedroom since he arrived, but he's been quiet for a while, doing nothing but contemplating me with a twinkle in his eye.

But my attention shifts toward the sound of a knock on my door. And after Dad orders the person to come in, we are welcomed by a bunch of new faces. Accompanied by Dr. Nel, my nurse Cynthia, and Alex, my new physiotherapist and her assistant are introduced to me.

"Petra, this is Dr. Jade, your new physiotherapist, and her technical assistant, Kylie," Nel explains.

"You may just call me Jade. How are you? Nel told me you are suffering from atrophy, especially in your legs. Have you tried to stand up yet?"

"Hi, Jade. No, not yet," I reply. "My lower body feels like stone."

"Let's take a closer look. May I?" Dr. Jade pulls down the sheet and starts pressing her fingers into my legs. "Do you feel anything?"

"Yes." And I'm quite relieved I do.

She then moves to my knees and does the same. "And here?"

"Yep."

Then she moves to my feet and squeezes them. "And here?"

"I do."

Afterward, she takes my right leg and bends it. "If I bend your leg like this, does it hurt?"

"Nope."

With a smile on her face, she says, "Good. It seems your muscles are just very weak. We'll start today with electrical stimulation on your legs so you can at least bend your knees and do some basic movements. It's fundamental that you do daily workouts and trainings to develop your muscles. I also recommend you do aquatic rehabilitation at least three times a week and eat a diet rich in protein." Dr. Nel nods and adds everything to her notebook. "If you follow everything, you should be able to walk within a week or two. Not run, not jump, but at least walk."

"Do you think I can start back at Columbia this fall?" I ask her. "It'd be great if I could get back to a normal life as soon as possible."

Dad, Alex, and everyone else in the room fall into a weird silence, as if I said the craziest thing in the world. They even look at each other without saying a word.

"Did I say something wrong?" I ask, my gaze landing on Dad.

"Petra," Alex starts. "Um, did anyone tell her?"

"Tell me what?" My question goes to everyone, but no one seems to want to answer.

"I didn't," Dr. Nel says.

"Neither did I," Dad replies.

My heart starts thundering as I observe everyone remaining mute, their faces grave like at a funeral. "What's going on?" Yet no one answers. "I got expelled from Columbia?"

"No, of course not," Dad blurts out instantly. "They are aware of your situation."

"So what's going on?"

"Normal life will be a bit different this year," Alex says.

"I know I'm gonna have to work harder, but I can do an intensive program and pass last spring's exams this year," I tell them. The last thing I need is to be treated like a fragile little girl. Since no one seems convinced, I add, "I'll spend more time at the library, and I'm sure my friends will help me out."

"I don't think you can go back to Columbia this year," Dr. Nel says. "Given your current state, you should remain at home and do online learning."

"No," I snap back. "I want to have a normal life. I don't want to stay here alone. I want to go back on campus and meet my friends. And have lunch with them, and…"

"You can't do that anymore," Alex interposes. "Even if you wanted to."

My heart freezes, and my brows furrow instantly. What are they planning against me? "Why? Why not?"

"The world has changed," Alex says. And my brows continue to crease, wondering if they are playing some prank on me. "And not for the better."

"What do you mean?"

"There's a global pandemic out there," Dad finally announces. I can't help but chuckle at the absurdity of it, but they remain just as serious.

"What kind of pandemic?" I ask.

"Let me show you." Dad pulls out his iPhone, types something on it, and gives it to me. It's a PDF file from the Rockefeller Foundation—aka one of his go-to sources of info to know which stocks and securities to buy next—with the title "National COVID-19 Testing & Tracing Action Plan."

I start reading it, and the more I read of the report, the more the words *pandemic*, *economic losses*, *social distancing*, and *facial coverings* become regular vocabulary. "Is this some sort of prank?"

"No," Dad snaps as he takes his iPhone back. "And we've made three times more than in a normal year, our best year yet, actually. We switched most of our investments into pharmaceuticals and consumer tech. It was challenging, but a great strategy for the coming years."

"Three times more? That's impressive," I tell him, sharing the same enthusiasm. I wish he could've been just as excited for the engagement party. But when I announced it, Dad couldn't even feign interest in it. As I suddenly recall something, I ask, "By the way, um, did you end up buying an island in the Pacific?"

Dad's jaw drops at my question. "Um, yes, I did. For my birthday. How do you know that?"

"I... I of kind figured it out. You've always wanted one," I lie, as there's no point in telling him the truth. That nightmare must stay between Dr. Nel and me. "How is Emma? Is she here?"

"I think so," Dad replies before looking at Alex. "Is she already out of jail?"

"What!" I can barely believe it. "Jail? She was in jail? Why?"

"From what her dad told me, she was caught at an underground party, violating safety measures, then non-compliance with police and incitement on social media. She refused to put a mask on and shouted the f-word at a cop."

Despite Dad's serious tone, a smile settles on my lips, and I try hard not to chuckle. *Oh, my Emma.* How much I've missed her. "Can I invite her over? She could have lunch with us."

"Let me check if she's out." Dad walks a few steps toward the door, and after pressing the call button, he puts his phone against his ear, waiting for Emma to pick up the call.

"Meanwhile, we will start your physiotherapy," Dr. Jade announces. "Today's session will only be thirty minutes. Is that okay with you?"

* * *

I might have done only thirty minutes of electrical stimulation, but the real struggle came after—when Cynthia gave me a walker and helped me go to the bathroom and shower. My legs feel heavy like stone, and despite the first session, I can barely bend or move them. It's a real hassle to take one single step, let alone walk. Nevertheless, being my first lunch with Dad and Alex, I've decided to be as presentable as possible. Wearing nothing but a bathrobe, I walk into Alex's closet with Cynthia's help, and I'm surprised to find so many clothes of mine in it. Most of them brand-new.

"What about this dress?" she asks as she takes one out of the wardrobe. "Not bad, huh?"

I smile at the color; it's the same as my engagement ring. The dress is vintage, fresh, and summery, with a blue-and-white porcelain print. It looks like Alex did some shopping in that vintage shop, and I wonder if that was his way to cope with my being in a coma.

"Looks good," I tell her. Cynthia then opens another drawer. As I peer over, I see many different shapes and colors of bras and panties, all matching sets and perfectly folded and aligned like on a store shelf. Letting out a quick chuckle, I can tell they are all brand-new. They seem to have come straight from a catalog of a fine, high-end lingerie store. I don't see any basic cotton knickers though—which is what I use the most at home. Here, all I see are delicate thongs and G-strings made of sheer tulle or lace, some with bows and others with embroidered floral details.

"Beige is okay with you?"

"It's perfect," I reply.

They all look so thin and fragile that Cynthia takes out the matching beige set with just the tips of her fingers as if it were some sort of invaluable masterpiece.

And I can't help but say, "It's just lingerie, Cynthia."

"Well, I checked out this brand online after it was delivered. This set is made in Italy from a brand created in the fifties. I was not even born back then." Her discovery makes me laugh. She then leans closer to me and whispers, "And it's three-hundred and ninety dollars."

"Three-hundred and ninety dollars for *this*?" I repeat.

"Yes, ma'am. I'd never heard of this brand before. But damn, I can go down the street and get something similar for thirty bucks." A quick chuckle escapes me as I observe her. "Oops," she utters, reaching for her mouth. "Sorry, ma'am, I know it's none of my business. I…"

"It's all good, Cynthia." And with curiosity tingling on my tongue, I ask, "Are you from here?"

"Yes. Born and raised in this great state."

I glance around, making sure we are all alone. "Um, can I ask you something else?"

"Sure."

Keeping my voice just as low, I do so. "How he has been doing?"

"You mean your fiancé?"

"Yes…"

Her head cocks to the side as she ponders my question. "Well, um… I'm not sure if I can talk about it."

"I won't tell him," I assert. "I promise."

Considering me for a few more seconds, Cynthia leans closer to me and, adjusting her tone to mine, says, "He was very, um, gloomy, most of the time, very serious. I don't think I ever heard him laugh. And he tends to drink every day."

My brows lift in surprise. I know Alex enjoys drinking a glass of whiskey every night, but is it more than that? "Really?"

"I mean…" I see Cynthia hesitating, her gaze going down.

"You can trust me," I remind her. "I won't tell him."

I know it's hard for her to open up. After all, she doesn't know me. Yet I keep my eyes pinned on her. Cynthia finally looks back at me, and, keeping her voice just as low, she says, "Your dad had to move in, you know. He was afraid Mr. Van Dieren had become an alcoholic or something."

My heart tightens at her words, and, matching her tone, I ask, "And, um, did you hear him speaking with my mom?"

"Not much, no. When Ms. Hagen comes here, they barely talk. Most of the time it's only Maria who lets her in." She pauses, thinking something through. "Oh, but they had a fight once."

"About?" I ask immediately.

"Um, I think it was regarding someone leaving you in peace, not sure who though."

The more I hear Cynthia talk, the faster my heart seems to beat. "Was it my mom who said that?"

"I'm not sure, ma'am. I just heard a few words here and there. It was a long time ago. But I think so."

I feel so tense and nauseous at the idea of it that I simply say, "Thank you," and leave the conversation at that. After all, Cynthia has just confirmed what I already knew—my nightmare was not only an unconscious fear but also a glimpse into my future reality if I don't prevent it from happening.

Then she walks me slowly back to the bedroom, where I sit on the bed. There she helps me put on my beige bra and thong. After I raise my arms, Cynthia pulls the dress down and closes the zip on the back. To my surprise, she brings me a pair of flat camel sandals, the type I love, the type that goes well with everything. Once I'm fully dressed, she asks, "What do you usually do with your hair?"

"Um, I just let it dry."

"Any makeup? I'm not a certified artist, but I've followed many tutorials on YouTube."

I laugh at her comment. Cynthia is such an amazing woman. No wonder they chose her to be my nurse. "I'm all good. Just gloss if you have any."

She goes to the bathroom and comes back with the exact same gloss I used to have. "Here." This one, though, hasn't been opened yet, but it's exactly the same.

All of a sudden, we are promptly interrupted by a knocking on the door and Maria coming in. "Miss? A certain Emma is downstairs waiting for you."

Oh my God! I gasp instantly. "Emma?" I repeat, barely believing it. I try to stand up, but my body holds me back just as fast. Cringing, I look at Cynthia, who takes me by the arm and helps me up again. "Dr. Jade said you'll need a couple of days before you can walk on your own," she reminds me.

Holding the walker, we leave the bedroom, and as we slowly cross the corridor, I can't help but wonder how I am gonna walk down the stairs if I can barely bend my legs. But Cynthia stops in front of two glass doors instead. "Oh," I utter. "That wasn't there before."

She presses the button and smiles at the little ding when the doors open. "It's nice, isn't it?"

As we get into the lift, she presses the button for the ground floor, which is where the dining room, kitchen, lounge bar, and outdoor terrace lie. Jeez, I can't believe Alex installed a lift here. The idea that he has been so obsessed with all these details, from clothes, underwear, and shoes to the medical treatments and the lift, brings a wave of unanticipated emotion, leaving me almost on the verge of tears. He never gave up on me—even after so many months in a coma and with little to no chance of ever waking up again. And that's something I will never forget.

"Babe!" I hear as the doors open. "Fuck! I can't believe it!"

A big grin settles on my lips upon recognizing the familiar voice. "Emma!" As soon as we step out of the lift, Emma plunges me into a hug that nearly leaves me out of breath, but it feels too good to say something. "Oh, Emma…" With my head resting on hers, I close my eyes, treasuring this moment as much as I can.

"I missed you so damn much," she whispers in my ear.

Matching her low tone, I say, "I missed you too."

Once she releases me, Cynthia helps me walk toward the lounge.

Emma promptly asks, "Um, what happened? You can't walk?"

"Not much, no. My muscles are still very weak," I tell her. "But in a week or two, I should be fine. I've got an intensive training including aqua gym and electrotherapy." And as I look at her, I can't help but ask, "What happened to your long hair?" I realize she is now sporting a short bob with bangs. "Why did you cut it so short?"

"It's been a rough year," she confesses before pressing her lips against my cheek and embracing me tightly in her arms again. "I'm so happy you're finally awake."

"Thanks," I reply, reveling in her hug. "I'm so happy to see you."

Afterward, I observe her for a moment and notice how she has started to cover her chest, neck, and shoulders with new tattoos. A big butterfly with open wings now covers her décolletage, and as we reach the lounge room, I can't help but also ask, "So your parents are finally okay with them?"

"Yeah… A small reward for me getting out of jail."

"Always the same, huh?" I tease.

She gives me a big, bright grin. "Always the same, babe."

"What have you been doing this year?" I ask her as we sit on the sofa. "Dad told me about the pandemic. I might not be able to go back to Columbia because of it."

"Yeah. The world is going nuts. I just came back to New York two weeks ago," she tells me. "Fucking cunt I was. I should've stayed in Saint-Tropez. But Laura was planning an underground concert for her birthday party, and I wanted to attend. As soon as I landed, those motherfuckers started asking me to wear a mask. Heck, even on the street, and then someone at her party called the cops! I've got no idea how they found out."

"And the police put you in jail because of that?"

"Well," Emma lets out a quick chuckle, "I also told them to fuck off and shove their masks up their—"

"How was Saint-Tropez?"

"Oh, it was great. The beach clubs, the vibe, the food, everything was dope. I'm thinking of flying back there ASAP."

"Do you mind staying until my engagement party?"

"What?!" Emma finally looks down at my left hand and grasps it. "Fuck! I can't believe it! Damn, girl." She then observes the ring more attentively. "That's a beautiful ring. When did he propose?"

"Um, actually, I did it when I woke up."

"Oh, wow. You don't waste time."

"I don't want to," I tell her. "I... I had a terrible nightmare..." As I look her in the eye, I announce, "I've got a feeling he's gonna leave me sometime soon."

Her jaw drops just as fast. "Huh? Why? Like, after everything you went through? Why on earth would he do that?"

"Mom told me Alex promised her that he'd leave me and move to Singapore."

Her eyes widen like a startled owl. "You already spoke to her?"

"In my nightmare, yes." Then her brows crease in confusion, so I add, "And I don't think this is a coincidence."

"Then why did he accept your proposal if he intends to leave you?" she asks, perplexed. "That doesn't make any sense. And why would he even promise that to your mom? I don't see Van Dieren making such a promise to her."

"Neither do I, but I'm sure this nightmare didn't come out of nowhere."

"You guys have to talk. I've always told you that. You must confront him, and you need to have an open conversation with each other," she lectures, even though she's right. "Hiding that pregnancy was fucked up."

"I know…" My gaze goes down to my lap at the embarrassing truth. "Well, now it's gone."

Emma presses her hand to mine. "I'm sorry for your loss." Her voice is unusually low and serious. "I know it meant a lot to you."

"It's alright." I take a deep breath, silencing the sadness that my heart can hardly bear. "I'm sure she is in a better place looking after me." As I close my eyes, I recall the loud honk of the truck I was about to crash into and the moment I pressed the brake as much as I could. But it had been too late. "I…" My head begins to pound, my heart speeds up, my breathing becomes fast and shallow as I remember the impact that made me lose her. "I just loved her so much already…" A sob bursts from my lips, and I reach to cover my mouth before it gets worse.

"Hey…" Emma wraps me into a hug as I try to recover from my unwanted emotions. "I'm sure she is." Her thumb goes to my right cheek, where she wipes away a tear. "I'm here for you, alright?" I nod at her, trying to prevent further tears from falling. "Look, I will stay here for the engagement party, but make sure you speak to your fiancé about your nightmare. You guys need to clear up all of this."

A knock on the terrace door brings our attention to Cynthia. "Ma'am, sorry to disturb you, but lunch is ready." She emerges into the lounge and helps me to stand again and get back to my walker. Then she escorts me at a turtle pace to the terrace. I feel pathetic walking so slowly and making Emma wait for me as she walks at my pace, but each movement feels like climbing a mountain. My muscles can barely support my body weight, and I couldn't imagine myself without Cynthia or this walker.

As we reach the outdoors, I let my eyes take in the beautiful setting Maria has prepared: green plants and white lilies bloom in a milky glass vase at the center of the table. I love the white linen tablecloth she's chosen—it gives a great summery vibe to the table. Closing my eyes for a second, I take a deep breath, inhaling the fresh air of the gardens. Sunshine is on my face and eyelids, covering my cheeks with heat as I listen for a moment to the familiar birds and grasshoppers singing. Ah, summer in Bedford Hills truly has a special aroma. "Janine?" I call, recognizing the familiar voice I hear.

Standing beside Maria, Janine looks over at me, a big grin on her face, and promptly walks over in my direction. "So good to see you back, Ms. Van Gatt." She gives me a warm embrace, although not too strong so as not to hurt me.

"Ah, here they are!" Dad and Alex stand up from their seats to welcome us. Dad greets Emma with a friendly smile followed by two cheek kisses. "Glad to have you back among us."

"Thank you, Mr. Van Gatt."

"Emma," Alex mumbles when she turns to him.

"Van Dieren," she replies just as dryly. "Congrats on the engagement. You won the jackpot."

Smiling back at her, Alex gives me a quick glance and says, "I know."

While they are already pulling out their chairs and sitting, I'm still slowly making my way toward the chair beside Emma's.

"I hope they treated you well in jail," Dad prompts to change the subject. "I'm sorry you had to spend a week there. The judge was not really the most sympathetic. But as you may understand, sharing live videos of an illegal concert and tagging the singers was not really the smartest move."

Emma grabs a slice of bread from the basket and starts dipping it in olive oil. "It's okay. It was not smart, but it was fun. I'll be leaving New York soon anyway."

"Any place in mind?" Alex asks as they wait for me to sit.

"Um…" Emma garbles around her bite of bread. "Saint-Tropez was dope. I'm thinking of going back there. Jean-

Pierre is a longtime friend of my parents, so I should be fine. He said he'd give me diplomatic entry if needed."

"Who's Jean-Pierre?" I ask as I proudly sit down without Cynthia's help.

"The mayor," Dad replies. "A fine gentleman indeed."

My eyes go directly to Alex, who's sitting in front of me. It looks like he's finally gotten some sleep. I notice he's changed clothes, sporting a slim white shirt, sleeves rolled up to his elbows and three buttons wide open at the collar, leaving his sun-kissed neck and upper chest exposed. Oh boy, I miss running my hands over his chest so much, tasting, kissing, and nibbling his smooth skin...

"Have you guys thought about a date yet?" But Emma's question shuts down my fantasy, bringing me back to earth.

"A date?" I ask.

"Yeah, for the party. Like, no pressure, but the earlier, the better. I don't want to stay in New York for much longer."

I can't help but chuckle at her comment. "Um, it depends when his family can come over."

"Mom and Julia suggested in two weeks," Alex replies. "It might be better to wait until you get back on your feet though."

"Oh, wow. They already know? I see news travels fast."

A smile settles on our lips as we look at each other, and I can't help but feel the heat on my cheeks rising. This time, though, it's not from the sunlight. Jeez, I still can't believe I'm engaged to him. And Dad being okay with it? It feels almost too good to be true. "I think in two weeks I should be fine. Who's attending?"

"Everyone," he says.

My eyes widen at his response. "You mean *everyone*?"

"Yes, everyone you saw at Christmas is attending."

"You can also invite your parents," I say to Emma. "They have always been so kind to me."

"Alright, I will."

Alex starts checking his iPhone and asks, "Should we host the gathering on the eleventh, around six p.m?"

"Sounds good to me," Emma mumbles as Maria puts some grilled vegetables on her plate.

"Dad?" I ask, looking at him. "Is the evening of the eleventh okay for you?"

"Huh?" Dad looks back at me a bit dazzled, as if he was somewhere else, engrossed in his own thoughts. "Yes, the eleventh is perfect." After taking a sip of his sauvignon blanc, he adds, "Don't forget the eighth is the beginning of the fall semester at Columbia."

"Does that mean I will have classes on campus?" I ask instantly.

"No, unfortunately. I just received an email from the president, and there won't be classes on campus this year. Everything will be done online."

"But what about my group? Does that mean I won't see them the entire year?"

"Do they live in Manhattan?" Dad asks.

"Hmm, I think so."

"Well, why not invite them over to our place so you can attend the online courses together? Might be better than spending your entire college year studying alone."

Our place? So does that mean I will have to return to Park Avenue once my classes start again? I can't believe after everything Alex and I have gone through, Dad wouldn't agree for me to live with my fiancé. After all, Alex also has a condo in the city.

"It's a great idea. I can pick you up once you're done," Alex replies, which basically confirms what I was thinking. And the fact that he doesn't even suggest to my dad for us to remain living together shouldn't surprise me. "What do you think, Miss Van Gatt?"

You know exactly what I think. But instead I say, "That would be great. Thanks." After all, this lunch is not the right place to talk about it.

"Do you guys have anyone in mind to plan the event?" Emma suddenly asks.

I take a sip of water before saying, "Um, no, not really."

With a big grin on her face, I know exactly what she is about to say. "Perfect. I'm in charge of it, then."

Alex drops his jaw like he's about to unleash some sort of comment, but I manage to speak first. "Are you sure? What do you intend to do?"

"I can arrange the setting, the flowers, the music, the invitation cards, like, all that stuff, you know. I've organized plenty of parties in my life. Fifteen days is short, but I can manage."

And with a hint of naughtiness, I look at him and ask, "What do you think, Mr. Van Dieren?"

"Sure," he mumbles, returning the smile. His eyes then go to Emma, but now they are more formal. "What *exactly* do you have in mind?"

"Hmm…" Emma takes out her iPhone, and after checking something, she shows us a picture on Pinterest of an elegant dinner with candles, white tablecloths, live music, and an impeccable setting. "Something like this. What do you think?"

"Oh, wow." My lips curve into a broad smile, picturing our engagement party in such a classy setting. "That looks fantastic."

"Perfect," she says. "And how many people are gonna attend?"

"Thirteen adults," Alex replies. "Including you and your parents."

As I watch them discuss the details of our party, and how they can arrange the terrace to include live music, a soft smile quietly charms my lips, warming my heart. Being engaged to him tastes better than anything I could've dreamt of. And I make the conscious effort to keep it in my memory for as long as I shall live. To me, having lunch surrounded by all those I love is the exact definition of happiness, and my mouth starts watering at the delicious smell of the sautéed mushrooms Maria is now putting on my plate. Ah… what a beautiful day to be alive.

* * *

After lunch, Emma, fully empowered in her new role as the event planner, goes around the terrace, taking pictures and jumping from call to call to prepare the decor and setting. Meanwhile, Cynthia brings me my iPhone so I can check all the emails and messages I've missed. To my surprise, I find many unread texts from my group at Columbia, and in particular from Matthew: *Prof Chilnisky told us you got into an* accident and are in a coma. I hope one day you will wake up and see this. Columbia is not the same without you. We miss you so much, Petra. Please call me once you see this. That one is dated all the way back in March.

Then another one from him, this time for Easter: *Happy Easter!!! I know you are still in a coma, but if you ever wake up, I want you to know you are in our thoughts. The group had lunch at my place, since a lot of restaurants are closed due to the current pandemic. But in your memory, we tried matcha lattes with seven spoons and soy milk just like you like. I must say, though, it's absolutely disgusting (sorry). But hey, at least Sarah loves it! Xx*

Oh boy, I crack a laugh imagining him tasting a matcha latte for the first time. What a pity I wasn't there to see it.

Then another text—this one, though, is really long:

Well, today I just took my last exam. With the current pandemic, we're doing everything online. And we didn't even know if the exams would ever take place. It was such a big mess. I swear, what a terrible time to be alive. You're kinda lucky that you don't have to witness any of this. The mood is pretty bad; everyone is kinda depressed. Suicide rates are skyrocketing. Our group is having some friction, and Katrina and Sarah had the biggest fight ever because of the face coverings. Anyway, sorry for the rant, but I miss talking to you. I hope one day you will see my messages and call me.

Wow. My heart feels tight as I finish reading his text. Scrolling farther down, I notice that Matthew kept sending me many, many more messages, the latest one sent just a week ago. Without waiting any longer, I press the FaceTime button and call him.

My anxiety grows as I wait for him to accept my call.

Oh! Finally! "Hey, good afternoon, Mr. Bradford," I tease with the biggest grin.

"WHAT?!" he screams, before covering his mouth. As I wave at him, I see him getting overly emotional and his eyes watering. He starts sniffling, looking up to prevent tears. "Thanks for the messages," I tell him. "They were really amazing. I felt like I was still there with you guys."

After breathing in and out, and getting used to seeing my face, Matthew gives me one of his goofy laughs. "Good afternoon, Ms. Van Gatt," he jokes back. It feels amazing to see him again. He looks happier, heck, even tanner, like he just came from vacation or something. "I can't believe you're finally awake. I'm so sorry I didn't visit you, but with the current pandemic, like, I didn't think it would've been prudent."

"Don't worry, I understand. How are things with the group? Is everyone alright?"

"Yeah, things were a bit tense, ya know, some arguments here and there, but friendship always wins," he confesses. "I haven't seen David or Katrina all summer. I think they went back to their home states to visit their families."

"Are they coming back to New York for this semester?"

"Yeah, they should be flying back next week. Very few people managed to get a dorm room, ya know. They got very lucky. Campus this year is pretty much closed. Most people are staying in their home states and will do everything online," he says.

"Oh, wow. And Sarah, how is she?"

"She's great. We went to Hawaii for my dad's birthday. We stayed there all summer. You don't see my tan?"

I laugh at Matthew's failed attempts to try different angles of light that will enhance his bronzed skin. "Yeah. You look great," I tell him. "Look, um, the first day of classes is the eighth. What if we meet at my place on Park Avenue and we attend the classes together?"

"Um." Matthew seems confused. "So you also decided to switch to economics-philosophy?"

"Huh?" My jaw drops at his question. "What?"

"You didn't read my last message?" he asks.

"No," I confess. "What was it about?"

"Well, the group and I have decided to major in economics-philosophy instead of finance."

My heart freezes at the terrible news and I'm left totally speechless. Then, after a few moments of processing his words, the only thing that comes out of my mouth is, "But why?"

"Well, a major in finance means we'd be part of the system that's destroying our economy, our planet, and pretty much everything we stand for. But with a major in economics-philosophy, we can challenge the current status quo and present new solutions and alternatives," Matthew explains.

"Oh, wow." That's the only thing I manage to say. "So you guys changed your minds just because of the pandemic?"

"It's pretty serious, Petra." Matthew's tone is indeed just like that. "I'll explain to you once we meet. But it's not only about the pandemic, no. It's much deeper than that. It's always the same folks doing the same shit, and I'm tired of it."

For some reason, I've got the impression that those "folks" include my dad and Alex. Indeed, I had forgotten for a minute how much Matthew hated everything about Wall Street, politics, and the tech industry. He has always been a dreamer, an idealist, a utopian. I was like him when I was younger—the idea of wanting to make the world a better place by fighting the evils of capitalism. But growing up with someone like my dad, you drop those ideals as fast as you get them. "So, what kind of career do you intend to pursue with a major in economics-philosophy?"

"There are many to choose from, like economist, academic, heck, even adviser to politicians. There's a lot we can do."

I'm still in shock at the group's decision, so I remain mute, digesting the horrible reality that I might have to spend the next few years completing my major in finance-economics all by myself from home.

"You know me," he mumbles, breaking our sad silence. "You know finance wasn't the best fit."

"Well… you like fancy cars," I tease. "So I thought it wasn't such a bad idea."

Matthew chuckles. "I can still appreciate brands and beautiful things."

"So does that mean you're gonna have different classes than me from day one?"

"Why don't you attend some of them and see if you like it?" he asks. "Maybe you would prefer philosophy over finance."

Not even in a million years would Dad accept such a switch. I chuckle at the simple idea of asking him. I think he'd choke on his food if I did. Surprisingly, though, I say, "Yeah, I'd love to give it a try. Which course do you recommend?"

"Hmm, definitely Public Economics. It's about exactly that debate you had last year with Prof Chilnisky, remember? About the role of the government in the economy? I swear, it's pure intellectual porn. You're gonna love it. The online class starts at ten a.m. or so."

The invitation seems quite tempting. I remember perfectly well the dissertation I had to do last year. This course indeed seems right up my alley.

"Alright, I'll attend that one, then," I tell him as I wonder how I'm gonna persuade Dad. "I'll send you the address and we'll meet at nine-thirty, okay?"

"Amazing!" Matthew gives me a big, bright smile. "I'm sure you're gonna love it. See you on the eighth, then."

"See you on the eighth," I reply back before ending the call.

Wow. That was such a big blow. It's hard to believe they decided to switch majors so suddenly. But I guess the heated arguments and the current pandemic must have been the deciding factors. I look briefly at the courses that Columbia offers for a major in economics-philosophy. I must confess, all the subjects seem really interesting. But as Matthew just said, they are pure intellectual porn. They won't teach me asset management, financial markets, portfolio allocation, or even entrepreneurship. They seem to be more about theory than practice. Nevertheless, attending one class with them to keep up some sort of social life seems like a pretty good compromise.

Decision made, I now have to persuade Dad to let me enroll in Public Economics. When you can't walk, your phone becomes your best ally, so I decide to call him.

"Hi, Dad," I greet upon hearing his voice. "Um, can I talk to you for a sec?"

"I'm pretty busy now. What's going on?"

"Well, I just spoke to my friends at Columbia…" I say, carefully choosing my words.

"And?"

"Well…" I know I won't convince him by phone. Dad seems to be in a rush, and he never takes time to think about my requests when he's hurrying up a conversation. It's better to go and talk to him in person. "May I speak to you in person?"

"Um, sure. I'm with Alex in his office."

"Oh, alright, I'll be there soon, then." And I hang up.

For a second, I'm about to stand up on my own, but just as fast, my weak legs prevent me from doing so. They are not ready to support my body weight by any means. Then I call Cynthia, my tone laced with distress at my constant dependence. As she helps me walk back inside the house, I can't help but curse under my breath at my own fate. To be dependent on someone to do things as basic as walking, showering, and dressing can cause even the nicest person to become annoyed pretty quickly.

As I stand in front of Alex's office door, I knock before Cynthia can, and upon hearing an approval, I reach for the handle just as fast so I can open the door on my own. A small victory among an ocean of things I can't do alone.

"May I?" I ask.

I find them sitting on the sofa as they analyze some sheets spread over the low table. Oh, Alex has his glasses on. He looks so damn hot with them on—it gives him that intellectually serious vibe that suits him so well. But he removes them upon seeing me. I should tell him he looks great with them on—but not in front of my dad.

"Hey," Dad greets me. "Sure. Have a seat."

I notice the empty armchair beside them, and I instruct Cynthia to help me over. As I slowly make my way toward them, I feel a bit embarrassed that Alex has to witness this. But as I glance over at them, they have already returned to their conversation and don't seem to be paying attention. *Good.* I'd have hated to see their eyes filled with pity or impatience as they waited for me to sit.

With Cynthia's assistance, I sit quietly in the armchair and wait for them to finish their talk. As I peer over at the sheets laying on the table, they seem to be about portfolio performances. From what I can see, the graphs are quite positive. Dad didn't lie—it looks like it has been a really good year for them.

"So..." Dad looks back at me and I put on my best smile —the one I give when I need to be convincing. "What's going on with your friends?"

"Well, they have changed their majors to economics-philosophy," I tell him.

"Really? But didn't they want to do finance like you?"

"Um, I thought so. But they said it makes more sense for them, ethically speaking," I explain. "Do you think you can have a word with the dean so I can enroll in Public Economics? It's one of their courses, and I'd like to enroll so I can see them from time to time."

Totally caught by surprise, Dad asks, "You want to take even more classes than you have now?"

"Well, PE is similar to the dissertation I did last year, so I'm sure I'm gonna be fine."

But he doesn't look convinced. "You already have so many courses to take this year. Don't you think it's going to be too much?"

"Just that one is fine." Letting out a sigh, I tell him, "They are the only friends I have at Columbia. And now, since we are doing everything from home, I don't see how I'm gonna make new ones."

Dad keeps quiet as he ponders my request. "Okay, let me have a talk with the dean and see what we can do."

My mood lightens up immediately. I never thought I'd manage to convince him so easily. "You're the best. Thank you," I praise with a big grin.

"Roy, we have the Zoom call with management in ten minutes," Alex informs my dad. "Should we go to the lounge?"

"Oh, I can leave," I interpose just as fast, looking at my fiancé.

His striking blue eyes land on me, and with a smile on his lips, he gets up from his seat. "There is no need," he replies, heading in my direction. Then, as he stands in front of me, he crouches down to be at my level. "There are a couple of books that you might enjoy here in the library," he says in a low voice, his eyes never leaving mine. The fact that he is whispering while so close to me makes my heart go wild. His cologne invades my nostrils, and my body heats up at his scent. Jeez, lust invades me, and I feel totally powerless at my growing arousal. "Cynthia will show you." His gaze drops to my parted lips, and I wonder if he'd dare to kiss them in front of my dad.

"Alright, let's go," I hear Dad saying as he stands up.

And my much-wanted kiss lands on my forehead instead.

CHAPTER 3

Bedford Hills, August 27, 2020
Petra Van Gatt

Alex was right—the great thing about his home office is that there is a library with a wide selection of books dedicated to finance, money, and banking. As I take one of the paperbacks, I wonder if he got these books especially for me, since they appear to be brand new and without any creases on the spine. With the whole afternoon pretty much available, I start reading the ones Matthew recommended to me in order to get ready for the exams in the fall.

But just as I am about to finish the first book, I'm interrupted by a knock on the door and Cynthia comes in. "Ms. Van Gatt, sorry to interrupt, but Dr. Nel advised that you should go to bed no later than nine p.m."

What? I glance at my watch, and I can't believe the time has gone by so fast. Jeez! Despite her medical advice, I feel like a freaking child when someone tells me it's time to go to sleep. It reminds me of when Janine would usher me into my bedroom while I was in the middle of a good book. I hated it so much that I'd take the book with me to read it in bed—well past the twenty minutes' allowance. But at that time, I was seven, not eighteen! Janine hasn't bothered me to go to bed since I was fourteen or so.

Once we get into the bedroom, Cynthia helps me into a red silk nightgown with laces on each side that falls above the knees, and a quick giggle escapes me as I observe myself in it. At my house on Park Avenue, I'd have worn cotton pajamas or shorts instead. Heck, I don't even have any nightdresses there. Afterward, Cynthia helps me to the bed and tucks me beneath the sheets. I can't help but wonder how long this childish routine will continue. "This is just until I can walk, right?" I ask her, my tone defiant as I lie in bed with my book resting on the nightstand.

"Miss, sleeping is very important," Cynthia lectures. "If you were in a hospital, you'd have a nurse escorting you back to your bed, just like I'm doing now."

She didn't even answer my question, so I ask again. "Once I'm able to walk, you won't have to stay, right?"

"Correct," she replies. "But until then, I will be here."

Having someone telling you what time you have to go to bed when you are an adult is an absolute nightmare. And for some strange reason, my thoughts go to seniors living in a retirement home and to anyone physically incapacitated who needs assistance. Are they being infantilized like me? I never thought that one day I'd be paying attention to such a small luxury. But the truth is, I can't wait to walk again so I can go to bed when I feel like it. Then I wonder if Alex will come anytime soon and if he's gonna sleep with me. Jeez, I can't possibly imagine spending my nights here alone when we are both living under the same roof. I already miss him way too much.

Once Cynthia closes the door behind her, I take my iPhone from the nightstand and text him: *Are you gonna sleep with me tonight?*

Then, impatient, I text again: *Forget it. It was NOT a question! When are you coming?*

Afterward, I sit up in bed, switch the light on, and keep reading. To my greatest surprise, I hear three knocks on the door not even ten minutes later. Instructing him to come in, I put down my book upon seeing him. "Hey..." I greet in a soft and mellow voice, my lips already curving into a smile as I observe the most handsome man stepping inside my room.

"Hey," Alex replies, matching my tone. After closing and locking the door behind him, he strolls over in my direction, and as he sits beside me, his delicious scent takes over me. And just like in his office, it awakens all my senses, causing a flood of wetness between my thighs. Regardless of my current medical state, I hope he's not too tired to make love.

"How are you feeling? Did you take your medicine already?" he asks, keeping his voice so calm and caring.

"Yeah, I did," I tell him, licking my lips. Then I pull down the sheets, revealing my nightdress. "Um, Cynthia got me new pajamas," I tease. "What do you think?"

Letting out a quick chuckle, his eyes gleam like jewels at the view, and a smile laced with naughtiness and desire settles on his lips—one that makes my cheeks blossom with heat. His gaze remains fixed on me, like he's mentally undressing me. He then leans down and gives me a peck on the mouth. "Thank you for wearing it," he whispers. We keep quiet as we stare at each other, my heart already beating so damn hard. "I love it."

Warmth surges through me at his presence, and the more I look at him, the wetter I become. It's so painful not being able to move as I'd like, but I do my best to bring myself closer to him. Just inches from his chest, I run a hand inside his open collar, fondling his smooth skin. "Now that we are alone…" Letting my words trail off, I keep my eyes on him as my fingers go to his shirt and start unbuttoning it. Alex seems to revel in it as he keeps silent, watching my every move. Returning the smile, with contemplative eyes, he brushes some locks of hair out of my face, then leans over to plant another quick peck on my lips. But I want much more than that.

"Petra?" His tone is neither sensual, nor playful. It feels like the beginning of a painful conversation.

"Yes?" I reply apprehensively.

"Can I ask you something?" His voice sounds so heavy that my heart gives a little jump.

With my lips flattening, I mumble a quick, "Sure." And I do my best to tame my growing nervousness.

His eyes remain pinned on me. They are tender but also curiously troubled. "Why did you lie to me?"

His question is enough to make my gaze drop to my lap and my body freeze in utter embarrassment. I know exactly what lie he is talking about. "I… um…" Still dazzled by his question, I tuck some hair behind my ear, thinking how this evening is not going as expected, but apart from that, nothing else comes to mind. "I don't know," I tell him sincerely. "It just felt right."

"Right?" he repeats in confusion.

"I mean, that we were doing it naturally." Oh jeez, I must sound so pathetic right now. I decide to look up at him, and as I do so, my cheeks must've turned a thousand shades of red. Searching for a better answer, I say, "I… I didn't want to use a condom." But it turns out to be just as bad as my first one.

"That doesn't explain the fact that you lied about taking the pill." Despite his soft and caring tone, he can be so pushy sometimes. As Alex sees me completely wordless, he adds, "Did you want to get pregnant?"

That question is like a reality check. Pressing my lips tightly together, I look down for a few seconds before mumbling, "Maybe."

He lets out an exasperated breath, the one you make when you can barely believe what you just heard. After glancing around the room, his gaze lands again on me. Yet he takes a blatant moment to ask, "And did you think about me? Don't I get a say in it?"

Rolling my eyes, I can't help but chide, "Oh, relax. Would it have been so bad to have a child?"

He blinks twice, his jaw dropping at my statement. "I'd have wanted to be informed first, yeah. See, unplanned pregnancies are not really my thing." He pauses, observing me. I'm not sure if he expects me to say something more or not, but I've got nothing else to add. "I… I can't believe how careless and selfish you were." Another rush of air, and this time, he runs a hand through his wild hair as he keeps ruminating. "You didn't even think about it, did you?"

But I remain mute, devoid of any will to speak.

"I'm talking to you, Petra."

"What do you want me to say?"

"The truth," he answers just as fast. "I want to understand what was going through your mind to lie about something so damn important." His expression is so serious that I shiver. "Having a child is a life-changing decision," he scolds. "It's not like buying a new dress that you can return if you don't like it."

"I don't think Dad's life changed that much after he had me," I snap back. "You were just scared."

"Scared?" he repeats, sounding offended. "Scared of what? I nearly raised you." Since I'm not answering back, Alex keeps going. "I know how to give a bath to a toddler, how to put him to sleep, how to play—"

"So what's your problem?" I cut him off, my tone higher than usual. After calming down, I add, "I knew you would've been a great dad. I just… I just didn't mind if we'd have been parents that soon." And for some unknown reason, everything just starts flowing out of my mind and then out of my mouth. "Yeah, I didn't think much about it, but I was cool with the outcome anyway. That's the truth for you. Good enough?"

As we glare at each other, our expressions cold and unsmiling, an uncomfortable tension rises between us. And it's not pretty to witness. Alex breaks eye contact, his eyes lowering. "Wow," he utters, his voice filled with disappointment. "Sometimes you have such an attitude."

Creasing my brows, I ask, "What attitude?"

"You lied to me," he reminds me before standing up from the bed. Then I hear nothing but silence as he lets the weight of his words sink into me. "And yet you make it seem like it's okay if it's to get what you want. Don't you see it?"

This time, I roll my eyes at his comment. I just can't help it.

"I never *ever* had sex without using a condom, and you knew it. And despite that, you lied. And instead of apologizing and being humble, you make it seem like it's my fault."

"And the fact that you're making such a big fuss about it is even more concerning," I reply back. And then, as I look him in the eye, I ask, "Or was it Dad who sent you to lecture me?"

"I'm tired of this discussion." Avoiding answering my question, Alex walks back toward the door. "I will sleep in another room."

My heart drops at his decision. And I can't possibly fathom spending my first night alone without my fiancé. "Wait," I plead. Alex does so and stands near the door. As I look at his expression, I realize my words were rude, and deep down, I know they truly hurt him. Blowing out a breath, I swallow my pride and say, "I'm sorry I lied." I try to sound as sincere as I can, but I'm not used to having arguments and having to apologize. "I know I broke your trust, and I should've told you the truth. It was selfish and immature. I won't do it again." My lips twitch into a smile at his stiff expression loosening up. "And, um, I'm not on the pill."

Alex lets a quick chuckle escape as we look at each other. "I kind of figured that out."

Feeling more at ease, I then tell him, "It was selfish, I know."

"You used me," he adds.

Rolling my eyes, I quickly protest, "Don't exaggerate. I'm already apologizing."

"I never thought you were so proud," he comments, and not in a good way. As I keep observing him, his hands in his pockets, I do a quick victory dance in my head once he returns to sit beside me. "Thanks for apologizing." He then leans down, pressing his lips against my forehead. "Now it's time for you to sleep."

"Huh?" My eyes widen, and I gape instantly. "No…"

"Petra, Dr. Nel said—"

"I know…" Cutting him off, I take his right hand, and switching to a more sensual tone, I mumble, "But I'm not sleepy…" Then I guide his hand slowly down under my nightdress and between my thighs, pulling him closer. "Can't you feel how wet I am?" His lips part in surprise, and after he blows out a breath, his fingers start gliding around my clit while his smoldering gaze travels down to my crotch, reveling in the view. I do the same, and as I look at his erection pressing against his pants, the naughtiest thoughts perk up in me, and I lick my lips.

But in a sudden move, his hand leaves me. "Petra, we should take it easy," he utters in a low voice. "You just woke up. It's better we have a medical—"

"Oh, stop it…" I pull his head toward mine to claim his lips. His mouth slams into mine, silencing everything but us. Intense and hot, his kiss causes a rush of heat to stream through me, and I'm left breathless at my growing desire. My hands move from his neck up to his wild hair, tugging on it and inviting him to lean over me. But his lips part from mine, and as I reopen my eyes, I find him taking his shirt off, revealing his muscular torso. Oh fuck… My eyes linger on his perfect pecs, his biceps, his wide shoulders, and my jaw drops at the view as I blow out a breath.

Then he comes over and grips my legs, opening them wide, and yanks me against him. His piercing blue eyes tease mine as he starts tracing warm kisses up my inner thigh, moving all the way toward my center, where he buries his head. I shudder at his presence, my wetness intensifying, my pussy desperate to be eaten.

"Ah…" A quick gasp escapes me as he flicks his warm tongue over my clit and starts sucking my tender flesh, making my pelvis arch instantly. Oh fuck, a rush of adrenaline starts flowing through my veins, and my fingers run through his tousled hair, clutching it in my fist and pushing myself into his mouth even more. I feel his tongue now entering me, and I can't help but moan at the intrusion. "Oh my…" His mouth is taking every inch of my cunt, his lips on my clit, his tongue exploring inside me. "Ah…" And it takes everything in me not to yell at the intensity of my pleasure. Holy fuck… His hands hold me tightly against him, and his intensity speeds up, the suction on my little nub bringing me to the edge of ecstasy. It feels so damn good that my hips start moving in slow waves against his mouth, and I can hear him groaning while he's eating me hungrily. "Ah," I whimper, overwhelmed with all the sensations, and my thighs tense against his head at my growing rapture. Fuck, I'm so damn close… My entire body is tingling, my head a hazy mess. I'm soaking against his mouth as I feel him licking and lapping every bit of me. My back arches, and I throw my head back as my hips roll into his greedy mouth. Dear Lord! I moan louder as I come from his vigorous tongue circling my swollen clit. "Oh God…" The climax is so great I could cry from it. Alex reaches up and presses his mouth to mine in a much-needed kiss filled with so much fervor and passion that I skip a breath, and, tasting myself on his lips, I moan in the back of my throat, letting him know how much I want him. Then I hear a little grunt from him as our tongues dance and swirl with vivacious tenacity. Our kiss becomes more urgent, without holding back. My hands go down to his belt, and I start unbuckling it. Alex breaks our kiss, and with a ragged breath and parted lips, he lets his eyes travel down to watch me unzip his pants. My moves are hurried, my hands shaking at the urge to feel him.

"Are you sure you're okay?" he asks softly, his voice laced with concern. "You can barely move your legs."

Oh gosh, who cares? I'm burning with desire, and the urge to feel him inside me is unbearable. "Don't worry…" I breathe as I shove his pants down his hips and below his ass. Wow. I gape at the thick bulge straining against his boxers. I might have seen him naked countless times, but it always feels like the first time. My pussy is drenched, and I feel the first fluids dripping down my thighs. "I'll be fine." Then I reach for his neck, pulling him down and kissing his swollen lips hard. His lips leave mine as Alex stands up from the bed to strip off his pants, giving me a wide view of his delicious body and erection.

As I remain sitting in bed, the sight of his naked body leaves me in total awe. Oh gosh… I'll never get enough of it. He's almost too sinful to look at.

"It should be a crime to have a body like yours," I tease, licking my lips.

He chuckles in return but doesn't say a word. Then he straddles me, my legs between his knees and my eyes inches from his striking abs. He reaches down, takes my hand, and presses it against his pec. A loud gasp parts my lips at the touch of his warm skin. I missed absolutely everything about him, and after so many months in a coma, this feels just like my first time seeing and touching him. He guides my fingers over his chest, and the sensation of his skin, his energy, his warmth deepens my breath, which becomes loud and ragged. Then he brings my fingers down to his abs, and my mouth remains wide open to breathe.

"You like it, huh?"

I think that's a question, but I'm too high to reply. My gaze follows my fingers tracing all the way down to his pelvis, and a little gasp escapes me once he guides my fingers to wrap around his length.

"You have no idea how much I missed this…" he says just above a whisper.

Keeping my hand around his cock, I start stroking him from the tip to the base. First slowly enough, before increasing the pressure as he likes it. Then my other hand moves under him and starts gently cupping his balls and playing with them. Little grunts of pleasure come from his mouth, and he leans forward, holding himself against the head-board. His length becomes hard as granite, and a small drop of precum emerges from the tip. A rush of dopamine takes over me at the sight of it, and without waiting any further, I start licking and sucking the head, before moving to the sensitive underside of his cock, where I place wet kisses with my tongue. "Fuck..." he breathes out.

Heat bursts through me at his growing arousal, and, determined to give him as much pleasure as he gave me, I take him deeper into my mouth, going as far I can until the tip of his cock nudges my throat and I withdraw a bit. Alex grabs the back of my head, entwining his fingers in my hair, and gently starts moving me back and forth to follow his rhythm. But any time he thrusts his hips, he hits the back of my throat, causing my eyes to water.

"Oh, yeah..." I hear him groaning in satisfaction as he keeps going. "Just like that..."

Then sloppy sounds start erupting from my mouth while my tongue keeps licking the shaft, already soaked with saliva. There is something extremely satisfying about pleasing him like this. It reminds me of when I was on my knees by the fireplace, and I sucked him until I was sore.

I look up at him, meeting his gaze filled with lust, before his head tilts back and his lips part to growl. I shut my eyes when they become too blurred to see and let myself revel in his guttural sounds. I keep sucking him with more insistence and enthusiasm, and little moans vibrate in my throat at the throbbing sensation of his cock. Losing himself in the heat of the moment, he forces his cock all the way down, filling my mouth completely, then Alex holds me there, long enough that I start to gasp for air. He retracts a bit before thrusting in and out again, his cadence increasing faster and faster as he approaches his climax.

"Fuck yeah…"

I can feel my saliva dripping down my chin and my jaw starting to ache. As I hear him grunting, he starts pulsating intently, and I can taste hot cum pumping inside my mouth. "Keep sucking…" I follow his command and remain focused on sliding up and down, his shaft getting wet from his cum. Once I realize he's done, I pause for a moment and swallow all at once. His breath is shallow and quick, and it seems like he's exhausted. His cock leaves my mouth as he bends forward to catch his breath, his forearms resting on the headboard.

"Jeez…" he blurts out. "I really missed that."

A quick chuckle rolls off my lips at his comment. But my attention remains lower—his new position gives me a better angle to his balls, waiting for me to take them. I trace a line of wet kisses from his shaft all the way down to his sack. There I hold it in my hand and start licking and sucking a ball before putting it into my mouth. Since his ball is too big to get it all in, I keep kissing and caressing it in my palm.

"That feels so good…"

The sensuality in his tone catches me off guard, and a little whimper escapes me while my tongue lingers around his flesh. I feel his hand now stroking the back of my head in appreciation. All of a sudden, though, his bent legs switch position, and my head falls down on the pillow as he lies on top of me. His eyes are on mine, searching for something. "I still can't believe you are here."

A smile plays on my lips, and I wrap my arms around him. "And I can't believe you are here either."

His gaze drifts down to my mouth, and he closes the small gap between us with a kiss filled with so much passion that a flush of pure bliss hits me hard. Oh my... His warm tongue slides inside my mouth to meet mine, setting my body on fire. This is the perfect position to make love, so I reach down between us for his cock, but Alex breaks our kiss, casting a quick glance at the nightstand. "Let me grab a condom first."

I retain him before he can move. "You can just pull out..." And I take his length in my palm, bringing it toward my entrance. I can barely bend my legs, but thank God, the electric therapy I did earlier today is finally having some results.

His eyes are burning with desire, his breath shaky, and I know he's yearning for so much more. "I won't be able to control myself," he growls, his crotch pressed against mine. Oh gosh, neither will I. "Ah..." I hear him groaning as I push the head inside me. His eyes shut down and his brows crease as he fights to keep control. "Fuck, why are you doing this?"

"Because I want you." I seal his lips with a kiss and start twitching my pelvis to accommodate his girth. "Just like this." Then a quick moan escapes at the feel of him entering me so smoothly. "Ah..."

But in a sudden move, he withdraws himself from me, and his rejection leaves a bitter taste in my mouth. "Don't you see how selfish you are?" His tone is so cold that it stabilizes me. "We just had an argument about birth control, and you still don't give a shit."

I can't believe how stubborn he is about this! Fuck! I'm left in total awe as he gets off of me and rolls to the other side of the bed.

"I'll ask Dr. Nel to prescribe you the pill tomorrow." And he kisses the top of my head before turning his back to me and switching off the lights. "Good night."

CHAPTER 4

Bedford Hills, August 28, 2020
Petra Van Gatt

"Good morning, Miss." Despite having my eyes closed, I immediately recognize Cynthia's voice as she walks into the bedroom. "Did you sleep well?"

"Mmm…" I mumble as I slowly stretch my arms. I try to do the same with my legs, but my muscles hurt like I ran a marathon. Jeez, they are so tense! I try to bend them, and although it's slightly better than yesterday, it's still impossible to get up without help. Turning to my right, I'm not surprised not to find Alex there. He's the type of person who wakes up at six in the morning, hits the gym for one hour, showers, eats a quick breakfast, and by eight, is already working. I look at the alarm on the nightstand: it's nine-thirty a.m. Yeah, I'm not crazy like him. Even during the school year, waking up at seven-thirty was still a big hassle for me.

Cynthia is already pulling on the bedsheets and dragging my legs to the floor. "Do I have aquatic gym today?" I ask, impatient to get all these muscles functioning again.

"Yes, later on today," she replies. Great! I'll have at least some semblance of a summer day as I do my workout in the outdoor pool.

I hold on to her arms and lift my body up, then I switch over to the walker, and with Cynthia's help, I drag myself to the bathroom.

After getting showered and dressed, Cynthia tells me the program for the day. "Dr. Nel is waiting for you on the terrace, then you have two hours of reading, lunch at one o'clock with your fiancé and your dad, one hour of reading, then an hour of aqua gym, then electrotherapy for fifteen minutes, and a full-body massage session."

"Wow. That's pretty filled up," I blurt out. But it seems like Cynthia is not even finished.

"Then you have nineteen minutes to read, and dinner with your fiancé at seven thirty."

"Oh," I utter, quite surprised to have a romantic dinner with him and only him. That must mean he's not mad at me for my insistence yesterday. As we take the lift down to the ground floor, I wonder if, once I'm married, I'll have Maria telling me my schedule every morning like this. I kinda like it, waking up and having someone tell me what my day will be like. *That's what assistants are for*, I think to myself. But assistants don't walk into your bedroom and wake you up, only household staff can do that. Might be something to tell Maria to start doing.

As I reach the terrace, I see Dr. Nel sitting at the table having an espresso. It's a beautiful, bright morning in Bedford Hills, blue sky, warm weather… What more can I ask for?

"Good morning," Dr. Nel greets me, a big grin on her face, before standing up.

I return the smile and take baby steps to get to the chair beside her. "I'm sorry for taking so long," I tell her once I'm finally seated.

"Don't worry, it's normal. How are your legs?"

I wish I could tell her I'm all good, but unfortunately, I've got to tell her the truth. "They are very tense from yesterday's workout." Then I glance toward the doorway and see Maria carrying a tray with a matcha latte, grilled mushrooms, and avocado toast. Oh, wow! It looks so delicious! To my surprise, Maria greets me in Dutch as she puts the food on the table. And I hear Dr. Nel replying back in the same language.

After she leaves, Dr. Nel is the first to break our silence. "Your fiancé asked me to prescribe you the pill," she informs me. "Were you already taking it before your coma?"

"Oh," I utter as I taste the grilled mushrooms. *I see my fiancé doesn't waste time.* "Um, no, I wasn't."

"Were you using any other form of birth control?" she asks again, and her question makes me squint at her.

"Why do you need to know all that?" I ask her as I take a sip of my matcha latte.

"Well, it's normal. You might have used patches, injections, implants…"

"No, I've never used anything before."

"Alright." Dr. Nel starts writing something in her familiar notebook. And I start to wonder if this is just for her, or to share with my mom. "Is your menstruation cycle regular?"

"Um…" The question makes me twitch in my seat. I've never given much importance to what my body does. I kinda trust that it's doing its part, so I don't really know. But for the sake of answering, I say, "I think so."

"Do you have any pain before or during your periods?"

The avocado toast is so tasty that for a second, I forget Dr. Nel is still beside me asking questions. "No, I don't even notice when I get it."

"Oh, that's great," Dr. Nel says as she keeps writing in her notebook. "Alright, I'll ask Cynthia to get you a box. Please keep me updated if you notice any side effects." As she writes the prescription, I keep eating my toast. "You have to take one pill every morning with breakfast for twenty-one days," she explains. "Then you stop for seven."

"Is it immediately effective?" I ask, already full of hopes for tonight.

"No, you have to take it for seven days first."

Seven days?! The idea of sleeping with Alex and not doing anything for seven more days seems terrifying. I already miss him so damn much! "Can I start today?"

"Only tomorrow morning," Dr. Nel says. "Maria will give it to you every morning with breakfast, so you don't forget it."

My heart squeezes a bit hearing her. I wish I didn't have to move back to Park Avenue once my classes start again. After all, just like Dr. Nel thought, I should be living permanently with my fiancé. Except I'm not. In nine days, I will have to live at Park Avenue during the week with Dad. How ridiculous! I hope I can change his mind before classes start, because I have no intentions of sleeping at Park Avenue again. And why would I? Alex has a condo in the city, and we can perfectly well stay there during the week.

*** *** ***

Bedford Hills, August 28, 2020
Alexander Van Dieren

With the current social distancing protocols in place, most of our meetings have been done through Zoom calls. Today's no different; Roy and I are sitting in the dining-room-turned-boardroom, getting ready for our next call. As I flick through the report we'll be discussing, Roy shatters the silence with one single question. "Did you talk to her?"

And I can't believe he's asking me that. I wish I could tell him that my life with my fiancée is none of his business, but I need him on my side more than ever, so I swallow my pride and say, "Yes, I did." I keep it short, not even bothering to look at him as my gaze remains on the report Paulo sent me an hour ago.

"And?"

Fuck! He's going too far. I squint my eyes, looking at him with annoyance. "Well, it's between her and I, don't you think?"

"No, I don't," he answers without any bother, sounding like an arrogant asshole, his stare defying mine as he patiently waits for all the details.

Shaking my head in disapproval, I ponder if I should tell him to fuck off or not, but I remind myself I need his support against Tess, and despite the anger creeping up my neck, I reply as friendly as possible, "She just lied to me about the pill to get pregnant, that's all." And I cut eye contact just as fast, my gaze drifting down to the report.

"That's all?" he repeats in outrage. Since Roy sees me being indifferent about the matter, his indignation keeps rising, and he asks louder, "That's all?"

"I already asked Dr. Nel to prescribe her the pill. Problem solved. Can we move on?" My attention falls back to the sheets I have in my hand, but something tells me Roy has more to say.

"And is she really gonna take it?"

I hold my breath for an instant. Roy is really testing my patience today. I hate sharing details of my intimate life with him, let alone those involving his daughter so I just mumble, "I believe so."

"You *believe* so?"

Tired of his inquisition, I put down the report, take off my glasses, and, holding his stare, I tell him once and for all, "Look, Petra and I are together. You know that and—"

"And you'll be gone to Singapore very soon." His reminder is like a hammer crashing into me. "I just want to make sure you won't be leaving a single mother behind."

What a fucking asshole he can be. If I didn't have so much self-control, I would punch him right now until he was lying on the floor in tears. "What a disgusting remark," I snap, shaking my head. "Don't you see how Tess is destroying our friendship?" Since Roy doesn't say a word, I add,

"Before Tess knew about Petra and me, everything was fine. Don't you miss it?"

"Alex, we've spoken about this a thousand times," he says, the lines around his eyes pulling tight as his jaw subtly shakes. "There's no other way around it, and you know it. My remark might have been crude, but my concern is nonetheless pertinent."

My pulse intensifies at the idea of breaking up with her. It's impossible for me to do so. That I am sure of. But time is passing, and very soon, Tess will be flying back here to visit Petra. And since she is now awake, I'll have to... *leave.*

Or at least that is what I promised her I'd do.

The easiest option seems to be to take Petra with me to Singapore before Tess travels here, but I know the pilot and crew will recognize her instantly and call Roy. Even if she flies separately, sooner or later, Roy will find out and won't waste any time telling Tess. There is nothing he wouldn't do to protect his little reputation. The truth is, our friendship is now solely based on the premise that I'll leave for Singapore and break up with his daughter. If I don't, Roy and I will most likely become... *enemies.*

Wow. Enemies? A shiver runs down my spine thinking about it. Having Roy Van Gatt as an enemy is the last thing anyone would want, including me.

Especially me.

"Maybe she should go back to Park Avenue from tomorrow on," Roy suggests. "It's a safer option."

"You know it's better for her to stay here than in an apartment. Even Dr. Nel told you so," I remind him. "Maria will make sure she takes the pill every morning," I add to appease him.

Roy seems satisfied—or at least silenced—with my answer as he draws in a deep breath, his eyes falling down to his copy of the report. Then my laptop starts ringing, and I know it's time for Roy and me to jump on our Zoom call.

* * *

As I reach the terrace, I see Petra from afar, sitting at the table and watching the last rays of light as the sun slowly sinks beneath the horizon. Cynthia is a genius—she knows Petra hates to show her physical incapacity in front of me, so she has been mindful enough to seat Petra before I arrive. Not that it bothers me, but I've noticed that Petra hates to display her limited mobility around other people. I guess it's a matter of pride—I'd have probably felt the same.

"Hey," I greet her, giving her a peck on the lips.

As I sit in front of her, her gaze remains glued on the scenery behind me. "You missed the sunset." And her tone tells me she knows exactly why.

I turn to look at the horizon. True, the sun is already gone, resulting in rich hues of red blended with orange, purple, and crimson in the sky. "Ah, well, there will be many more." I find myself drawn to her exposed collarbone and the pendant she is wearing. A quick sigh escapes me, remembering when I put it on her. Damn, I'm the luckiest man alive. "You look absolutely stunning today."

"Only today?" she asks in a tease, her brows raising in amusement.

Her humor twists my lips into a smile, and, playing along, I say, "Yep, only today."

And I manage to get a laugh from her. "You look nice today too."

Petra doesn't waste any time telling me all about her aqua gym and deep-tissue massage session. She always has something interesting to share, and, despite the fact I'm still in total awe that she is here, all I can do is smile as I try to focus on what she is saying. I guess I will need some time to get used to the idea that she is finally back. Then, Maria comes in and places our starters on each side of the table. Once she leaves, Petra falls silent, probably engrossed in her thoughts as she stares absently down at her plate. And I'm like an idiot, observing every inch of her face, her hair, her lips...

"Once my classes start again," she says in a low voice, "um, maybe I could move in with you to your condo." With an ounce of timidity in her voice, her gaze goes up to meet mine as she waits for my answer.

"You know that's not possible." It hurts like hell to smash her hopes and watch her smile fade away. "Your dad is looking forward to you going back to Park Avenue."

Blowing out a breath, Petra doesn't hide her discontentment, and her eyes drift away, staring past me at nothing. "Why is Dad so insistent about that?"

"He just wants to spend some time with you," I tell her. "After six months in a coma, you can't blame him for that." But Petra is not naive. She can see through me like no one else, even if she doesn't say a thing about it. In an attempt to reassure her, I add, "We can spend the weekends together."

"We are in the twenty-first century. Couples live together even before getting married," she points out. "I can see him from time to time."

The last thing I need is another fight with Roy. After all the arguments we've already had since Petra woke up, my friendship with him is within a hairsbreadth of falling apart. "Look, once we are married, we'll live every single day together," I tell her, sounding as confident as I can. "Just enjoy your last months there."

Petra takes a mouthful of her food and keeps quiet while chewing. Then she drinks a bit of her juice, still considering my advice. "Alright," she mumbles, her gaze on mine. "I guess I can survive a few months there."

We exchange a quick smile, and I reach for her hand, giving it a kiss. "I truly appreciate the sacrifice, Miss Van Gatt." My tone is sarcastic, and she plays along.

"I hope so."

The sound of her laughter is enough to fill me with joy.

Regardless of what the future holds for us, a part of me still believes I will marry her.

Fuck, what a fucking mess I've gotten myself into…

But my critical thinking and rational mind pull me back to reality—they know very well my time with her is limited. And the more I look into her big blue eyes, the more I know I've got to accept it—with Miss Van Gatt, there's only a present, not a future.

CHAPTER 5

Manhattan, September 8, 2020
Petra Van Gatt

After over ten days in upstate New York, I find myself stepping into the hallway of my home on Park Avenue. And without Cynthia's help or a walker. Nope. I can't really do much more, and it still hurts when I bend my legs, but being able to put one foot in front of the other on my own is already a big victory for me. Although I love Bedford Hills, especially for its fresh air, green scenery, and quiet surroundings, being back in the house where I grew up brings a wave of memories that feel so old and distant, and yet some are no older than a year. With twenty minutes left before the beginning of my first online course, I can't help but sneak into my bedroom to have a look. The place is immaculate— Janine must come here often to clean the dust. Then I step into my closet and find all the clothes I wore the past year, perfectly stowed. Even my white dress is here too... A quick sigh escapes me at the sight of it.

"Hey, Miss Van Gatt," Janine greets me, entering the room. "So good to see you here."

"Hey, good morning," I reply. "I see you've been taking great care of this place. Thanks."

"This place, Miss…" She lets her words trail off as she steps closer to me. Then Janine glances around, taking in our surroundings. "…is your bedroom. And no matter what happens, it will always be yours." Her tone carries some sort of nostalgia that I know all too well.

Her expression becomes melancholic as she ruminates about something. And I can't help but ask, "Are you alright?"

Janine dips her head in embarrassment, and she quickly wipes something away. "I… Oh, it's nothing, Miss. Don't worry," she mumbles, twisting her apron.

Holding her arms, I try to meet her gaze and insist, "Of course not, tell me."

Her eyes lock with mine for a second before they survey the room once more. And I've got the sensation she's hesitating whether to open up or not. "It's just… it's just so weird that you're engaged and no longer living here. I never thought the day I would no longer wake you up and prepare your avocado toast would come so soon."

A quick laugh rolls off my lips, and I say, "If it reassures you, Dad wants me to stay here until I'm married, so you might have more avocado toasts and matcha teas to prepare."

Janine throws me a grin full of empathy that warms up my heart. "Oh, well, I don't think Mr. Van Gatt is ready to see his daughter leave him so soon. Who can blame him?"

"I know…" My lips curving up, I recall everything Dad has done for us and how he even agreed to come to the engagement party. And while I'd rather have moved in with Alex, we both need my dad's support more than ever. "Dad's been so incredible and supportive," I tell her. "I never thought he'd be like that."

"He loves you a lot." Janine has such a sweet, friendly voice that I can't help but smile again. "Not many parents would've done the same," she says. "I know my dad for sure would've kicked me out of his household if I didn't end the relationship."

Wow, that sounds quite excessive. But I guess in a way she's right—not everyone is as lucky to have a dad that is so tolerant. I know if I had been living with Mom, things would've been pretty different. Then, curiosity getting the best of me, I ask, "Did you, um, did you know about us from the beginning?"

"Since the day you spoke to your dad, yes," she admits.

"Oh…" My brows lift instantly in surprise. "Nothing escapes you."

"Not much, I have to admit."

After a brief silence, I decide to invite her to the engagement party Alex and I will be hosting. "It'd mean a lot if you could come," I add.

"It'll be a pleasure, Miss," she replies just as fast. And I'm positively surprised at how easily she accepted. "I'll be there, *but* I want to give a hand to that Dutch lady." Janine steps a bit closer to me, and, lowering her voice, she says, "She is so kind, but so shy. Jeez, that woman barely speaks."

I chuckle briefly at her comment. "Yeah, Maria doesn't speak English well, I think."

"She's so discreet," Janine blurts out. "You can barely hear her breathing."

I couldn't agree more with her. Since the day I met Maria, I've always thought how different she is from Janine. "Yeah, Margaret's staff is like that too."

"Margaret?" Janine asks.

And I remember I never told her who Margaret is. "Alex's mom."

"Oh, you've already met her?"

"Yeah, I spent Christmas with his family," I tell her, even though it's not usual for me to be so open about my future in-laws.

"And how is she?" Oh, the question! How does someone describe Margaret Van Dieren? Damn, Janine can be so curious. The differences between her and the silent Maria couldn't be more obvious.

"Um… I guess, interesting…" I tell her, keeping it short.

Fortunately for me, we are startled by the ring of the main doorbell, bringing an end to the inquisition.

"Looks like your friends have just arrived," Janine says as she walks back to the entrance to invite them in.

Then I check myself briefly in the mirror—it looks like I've gained a pound or two during my stay at Bedford Hills, and maybe, dare I say, a semblance of a summer tan thanks to my aquatic classes in the outdoor pool.

Once Janine opens the door wide, I smile, seeing the joyful faces of Sarah, Katrina, David, and, of course, Matthew.

"Hey," I greet them, my voice coming out a bit too low, maybe apprehensive at their reaction.

Sarah trots over in my direction and takes me into her arms, squeezing me so tight that I gasp. "I'm so happy to see you."

I try hard to restrain the rising tears. I don't feel comfortable being so sensitive and emotional in front of them, but it's one of the side effects Dr. Nel cautioned me about when she gave me my new meds. There's also something comforting about knowing your friends missed you. It could be fake, but my heart feels it straight to its core. After Sarah releases me, Katrina also gives me a hug, followed by David, and at this point, it feels like a ritual to welcome me back on planet Earth and among humans.

"How are you doing?" David asks me. "Did you recover well?"

"Um, yeah, I've been doing therapy, and I'm taking a lot of meds," I tell them.

Seeing how they are nodding at me, I'm not surprised when Katrina asks, "Did you lose your memory or anything?"

"No, but I had atrophy of my legs for, like, ten days, and I could barely move."

"We understand. It must've been so tough," she replies, her tone always so kind.

But the truth is, they can't understand, no. Regardless of the amount of empathy and compassion they have, no one can understand what it's like to be practically dead for so many months, when your own life is put on hold by an awful car accident—an accident I could have avoided.

Not even Alex, Dad, or Emma can understand. And I know I'm beyond blessed to be here again, to have woken up six months later without my brain damaged or my memories wiped away. After all, I could've simply... died.

I *could have.*

But I believe God decided otherwise for a reason, and nothing from that day on has ever felt the same—every breath, every laugh, every smile, every moment I spend with those I love will never be taken for granted ever again. I've admired and cherished every single one of them as if they were the last.

And, as I smile at my engagement ring, I think precisely about that. *Never take anything for granted, Petra. Him either.*

"Wow! Look at this ring!" Sarah shouts, taking my hand. "That's a huge sapphire, and it's so beautiful."

"I can't believe you are engaged." Katrina hugs me again, before whispering in my ear, "I'm so happy for you."

But my eyes dart instinctively to Matthew. He doesn't look as enthusiastic; he feigns happiness with a polite smile, and I try to compose one back. But looking at him standing right in front of me feels awkward—to my surprise, his disappointment is overly palpable. I thought he had moved on after I'd been in a coma for so many months, and especially after telling him before Christmas that the man standing in front of the car he liked so much was my future husband. Well, I just hope we can remain friends.

"Alright, everyone, enough," Matthew chides. "Petra can barely breathe with so many hugs."

"Oh, c'mon," Katrina ripostes just as fast. "We have double reason to celebrate today." I tuck some hair behind my ear—half blushing, half embarrassed with so much attention.

"Congratulations on your engagement," David says, patting me on the back. "Your fiancé is a very lucky man. Is he studying at Columbia?"

"Her fiancé is way older," Matthew interposes. "At least fifteen years, if not more."

I frown at his unnecessary comment. *What is that? Jealousy? What the heck, Matthew?* I censor him with my glare, but he doesn't give a crap, apparently.

"It doesn't matter," Sarah snaps, coming to my rescue. "He's super handsome, and you guys look great together." I smirk at Matthew; Sarah is such a great ally.

"Okay, time to get serious now," I say as I glance at my watch. "The course is gonna start soon." I lead them into the dining room, which is the best place to attend Public Economics via Zoom. My laptop is already plugged in and connected to a projector, which will display the class on the white screen stretched in front of us. Once the video call starts, Sarah praises my idea to watch it on the "big screen" like we are in a theater. So far, though, all we can see from the classroom is an office desk and an empty chair, a whiteboard on the wall behind it, and a closed door beside that. After a few more seconds, the door finally opens wide and a gray-haired man steps in. My brows lift, and my lips spread in a wide smile as I quickly recognize him—it's Prof. Reich, one of the funniest and most fascinating teachers I had last year. Unlike Prof. Chilnisky, Prof. Reich has always managed to entertain us—most of the time involuntarily, but his short stature and sympathetic gaze, combined with his oversized jackets and cringeworthy expressions, make him all too funny and adorable. My eyes move discreetly to my right where Matthew is sitting, trying to gauge his reaction. After all, he considered Prof. Reich, like, his idol last year. But my curiosity is then startled at the sound of Prof. Reich's quirky voice. "Is it working?" I hear him asking. And we giggle like children seeing his face and neck in full screen as he double-checks his laptop cam.

"Do you think he can hear us?" I ask Sarah.

"I can hear everyone," Prof. Reich shouts at his laptop. And I try my best to contain a laugh, so I just chuckle inwardly. "But I can't see anyone though." And he narrows his eyes, trying to figure out how to make it work. "Ah! I think I can see you guys now. Oh! There are a hundred people attending?"

Matthew puffs into his palm, but I can hear him all too well.

"Very well, so…" Prof. Reich reaches into his briefcase sitting on the chair and takes out a pen. Then he starts writing something on the whiteboard: *Wealth is not money. So what is it?*

I feel Matthew leaning toward me, and he whispers something in my ear. "And here lies all the beauty of philosophy."

My eyes travel in his direction, a smile already hanging on my lips, but Matthew doesn't notice me as he's already taking notes on his MacBook. I observe him for a few more seconds, my smile just as big, and, for some stupid reason, it just crosses my mind that he's the only one who didn't hug me at the entrance. Not even to greet me. Nothing. Why didn't he show any affection like the rest of the group? I thought he cared about me; at least, during our video call when he nearly cried, he seemed like he did.

Then, as my attention falls back to the screen, I realize Prof. Reich is already engrossed in his introduction speech, and I'm slightly annoyed that I missed part of it. "So, in order to preserve some social interaction between students, each group of five will prepare a study of an ideology as applied to economics. It can be anything, from liberalism to Marxism. The idea is that you deeply analyze the ideology and how good or bad it can be when applied to public economics, including governmental policies, equity, welfare, and the role of the government itself."

He looks again at the whiteboard and writes:

Title and ideology of the study to be assigned by Sept. 15.
Study to be delivered between Nov. 15 and Dec 5.

I take note of the deadlines and what the study should include. For the next twenty-five minutes, Prof. Reich starts forming groups of fives, and since there are one hundred people attending, he just groups us alphabetically. Fortunately, he makes an exception for our group, recognizing us from last year. Then, he develops the concept of wealth in a capitalist society and explains it with the same energy and fun that he always has, and we all take additional notes at every opportunity.

Once the class is over, the obvious question pops up. "Any idea which philosophical system you guys would like to choose?" Matthew asks.

We all glance at each other but remain mute. Since no one seems particularly chatty, I say, "I think objectivism is one of the most underrated philosophical systems in history. Maybe we could explore that."

"How cute…" Matthew tries hard not to chuckle, but his facial expression gives everything away. What's wrong with him today? "Given the fact that you haven't opened a decent book for the past six months, I'll let this go. Any other suggestions?" I crease my brows, absolutely baffled at his inconsiderate and careless comment.

Before anyone can suggest something else, I hold his stare and ask, "What's wrong with objectivism?" Which translates to *What's wrong with you?* And I give a glance toward the rest of the group, trying to read the answer on their faces, but they are totally expressionless. "It's the opposite of intellectual conformism. It's precisely about taking risks and choosing the least traveled road…"

"Rand's a very shallow philosopher, Petra." His harsh criticism about something and someone that I admire greatly makes my whole body tense up. But Matthew doesn't seem bothered that I shake my head in disagreement with his statement, and he proceeds, "I understand the appeal given your young age, but it's painful to hear your comments endorsing it. If you are into classic liberalism, you might just read the classics instead."

His tone is condescending, making me think less of him at every interaction. Nevertheless, I say, "If I'm not mistaken, scholars such as Gotthelf considered the philosophy as a unique and intellectually interesting defense of classical liberalism worth debating."

"Too bad he is dead," Matthew snaps back, before drifting his attention to everyone else. "So any other suggestions?"

What a fucking asshole he can be sometimes! "What's so wrong with objectivism?" I ask again, aiming for a straight, clear answer for once. "Just because it's not mainstream doesn't mean it's a juvenile philosophy not worth exploring."

"It's useless intellectual garbage." Matthew doesn't go soft on his words. "We can do something more contemporary."

"It's contemporary; Allan Gotthelf, one of her scholars, died in 2013," I tell him.

"Guys," David intervenes, his voice steady and most likely searching for a peaceful compromise. "I know nothing about objectivism, but if you both know enough about it, then maybe it's a good idea we do the study about it."

"David," Matthew snaps again, his tone dismissive. "Petra gave one of the worst suggestions in human history," he rebukes with a smirk. "It's like saying Hitler had a point to do what he did."

"What?!" I gape instantly at his absurd comment. "What does Nazism have anything to do with objectivism?"

"It's a right-wing philosophy that defends selfishness and capitalism. It's just as bad," Matthew snaps back.

"*Ethical* selfishness," I correct. "It's about pursuing your destiny, what you believe in…"

"That's something Hitler would say," Matthew keeps teasing. Or at least I hope he is, because I'm hating him to the core with every new word coming out of his mouth.

"Any ambitious person would say so. Any entrepreneur likes objectivism," I tell them.

"Oh yeah, Wall Street and tech titans must love it," Matthew chides. Then he looks at David and says, "It's a philosophy that basically defends classic liberalism and laissez-faire."

"And individual freedoms and rights," I add. Grasping my iPhone, I quickly search for one of my favorite quotes by Rand and read it out loud, "Throughout the centuries there were men who took first steps down new roads armed with nothing but their own vision." Then looking at my group, I ask, "Isn't it heroic and noble? Something we should all want to aspire to? Objectivism rejects social and intellectual conformism. It's like the slogan of Apple, 'Think different.'"

"It's like the philosophy of the greedy when applied to the economy," Matthew interposes, having none of it. "That's why Prof. Reich and so many scholars rightfully dislike it so much. I'm disappointed that you even like it."

"So we're screwed?" David asks, his tone filled with fear. "I feel like we're gonna get such a bad grade. And I can't have bad grades. My scholarship depends on it."

"No one is gonna get bad grades," I reassure him. "We will work methodically and decompose objectivism first as a philosophy, and then how it applies to different branches of PE…" I stop before saying, *Matthew is just being an ass.* And looking at the asshole sitting beside me, I say, "For someone studying economics, you should be a bit more open-minded."

"It's *because* I'm open-minded that I don't like objectivism. I studied it, and I found it very juvenile and shallow."

"Enough, you two," Sarah interjects, her loud voice startling everyone. "I've never seen you guys like this," she points out, looking at Matthew and me. "You guys used to be great friends." As she lets out a sigh, we look at each other, knowing Sarah is right, but not acknowledging it. "I couldn't care less about objectivism, but I *do* care about our group." Then she pauses, thinking something through. "Since you guys are so crazy attached to this philosophy, Matthew will say one good thing about it, and Petra one bad thing."

After assessing Sarah's request, Matthew is the first to speak. "Hmm, the fact that objectivism believes hedonists and whim-worshippers are living sub-humanly sounds good to me."

"And you, Petra?" Sarah asks.

"That's exactly what I don't agree with when it comes to objectivism. I think hedonism can be pursued as a sustainable and ethical lifestyle."

"What the fuck? Ethical hedonists?" Matthew huffs, trying to brush off my opinion. "Sounds like a PC way to describe spoiled brats who have never worked a single day in their lives."

Squinting my eyes like lasers, I focus them on Matthew like I could zap him. "Just because some people don't need to work doesn't mean their lifestyles are less honorable," I find myself saying, as if the attack was personal.

Mercifully, our heated argument gets interrupted by a knock on the door, and Janine comes in. "Miss Van Gatt? Lunch is served," she announces.

Glancing at my watch, I realize it's already midday, the time I told her to have lunch ready. "Thank you, Janine." As I look at the group, I say, "Um, Janine prepared some food for us all." I pause for a beat, gauging their reaction. "I thought it'd be great to have lunch together to celebrate the beginning of the new school year." A smile escapes me, seeing how everyone but Matthew is praising the idea. And as I quickly glance at him standing up, I never thought, not even in a million years, that the sweet Matthew I met last year could become a total dick when discussing philosophy.

"Thanks, girl," Sarah says, patting me on the arm. "That's really nice of you."

I lead them to the terrace where lunch is being served. And we are all caught by surprise at the beautiful setting Janine has prepared. *A well-arranged table always makes lunch a bit more special*, I remember her saying.

As we start eating, courses and professors quickly monopolize the conversation. And, not unexpectedly, Sarah then asks me, "So you also switched majors?"

"Not really. I'm still doing finance, but I'm taking Public Economics to be with you guys," I tell her, keeping it short. After all, it's not usual for students to do that, and I know the dean is making an exception due to the current social distancing rules. Nevertheless, the more we talk about Public Economics, the more they seem to enjoy the idea of the study. Then, as Sarah starts talking about their other courses, I notice Matthew remaining unusually quiet. In fact, he hasn't said a single word the whole lunch and his gaze remains vacant, starting at nothing, like merely a zombie. Something must be going on with him—something he isn't telling me. Then I remember the texts he sent me when I was in the coma. And despite our heated argument this morning, I do believe he still cares about me. So, leaning a bit closer to him, I say in a low voice, "My dad introduced me to objectivism." His eyes widen in surprise, a bit taken aback by the revelation. After all, it's not usual for me to open up and say something so private. "A first edition of *Atlas Shrugged* has been on his nightstand since I can remember. I know he'll be quite proud of this project." I see a faint smile settling on his lips, but he remains still, carefully listening. "Dad said it was Rand's philosophy that inspired him to move to New York and start his own company." And I also smile as I recall the first time he told me about it. "You know, he was the first person from his family to emigrate and the first to become financially successful."

"Wow. I didn't know that."

"Yeah, we even went to pay tribute to her grave in Valhalla. So believe me, it's a bit like a religion for him."

Matthew seems to ponder something, and, after seeing my hand resting on the table, he reaches for it and says, "Look, I promise we'll work as hard as possible to do the best study we can on objectivism. Even if I hate it to its core."

I feel the urge to ask him why he hates it so much, but since he didn't bring it up, I decide to bite my tongue and close the subject once and for all. "Thanks," I tell him, keeping my smile just as big. "It means a lot."

After lunch, as I see everyone getting ready to leave, I can't help but ask, "Where are you guys heading now?"

"Matthew and I are heading to the library. We've reserved two seats there," Sarah replies.

"Really? The library is open?" I ask instantly.

"Yeah, but you have to book a spot in advance to get in." And my hopes are crashed just as fast.

"And I booked a table at the cafeteria," David adds, a big grin on his lips. "You wanna join us?"

Looking at my watch, I see I still have two hours before my next class, so why not? "Of course. I miss the smoothies they used to serve."

***

Matthew Bradford

Damn it! My feelings toward Petra are more serious than I thought. As soon as I saw her welcoming us into her house with her beautiful wavy black hair, her big blue eyes, and the cute little smile on her face, I knew I had never stopped having feelings for her. But how come she woke up from the coma just ten days ago and is now engaged?

I try to focus on page fifty-four, analyzing the supply and demand market and governmental intervention in the seventies, but I can't. After all, I've never thought getting engaged was something Petra had in mind. I mean, she's not even nineteen! Why the hurry? Maybe it was the coma that gave her boyfriend the courage to get down on one knee so fast...

And who is her fiancé, by the way? She's never given us any info about him. What's his name? What does he do? How old is he? I said he's fifteen years older than Petra, but it might be even more... Is he that superficial and shallow that he needs to pick her up in a Rolls-Royce? Jeez, if I knew it had belonged to him, I'd never have looked at it.

One thing is for sure: after my terrible douchebag attitude this morning, Petra won't be sharing any info about him with me anytime soon. But she might have shared some with Sarah and Katrina… Looking at Sarah, who's right in front of me, I ask, "Sweet Sarah, how are you?"

She suspiciously raises an eyebrow as she stares at me from behind her big, rounded glasses. "What do you want to know?" Putting down her book, she leans back in her chair, folding her arms. "Who's the man behind Petra's engagement ring?" She knows me so well.

"Yes, pleaaaase," I assert instantly, rubbing my hands together.

"Not happening." And she dives back into her book.

"Why?" I lean forward, lowering my voice. "Did she tell you who he is? At least his name?"

"Not even his name, no. You know her. She's closed up like a shell. Katrina and I have nicknamed him Mr. No Name. I just know he works on Wall Street, a hedge fund manager like her dad."

"Impossible to find out with so little…"

Sarah sighs loudly. "Matt, for your own sanity, forget her, alright? She is into someone else."

"It's not that easy." I pause for a beat. "Petra is perfect for me. She's really my type. She is smart, kind, funny, humble, modest…" I let out a breath, probably sounding pathetic as I look at Sarah's unimpressed face. "She is just confused, I'm sure. No one gets engaged after waking up from a coma."

And before Sarah can say a word, I ask, "Did she give you any details about how he proposed?"

Sarah chuckles at me like I just said the stupidest thing in the world. Did I? "She proposed to him."

"Oh…" I feel utterly dumb now.

"They had decided before her coma to get engaged, but the proposal didn't happen until she woke up and took care of it." I blink twice, but my jaw remains on the floor. "Now that you know it was Ms. Van Gatt who rushed Mr. No Name into engagement, move on, and let me finish my book."

But I've got more to ask. "Do you know why it didn't happen? I mean, why he didn't propose before?"

Sarah rolls her eyes just as fast. "Oh boy. No, I don't know. I'm not the gestapo. Why don't you ask her? She doesn't bite."

"Um, after our argument this morning, I'm not sure…"

* * *

The truth is, there's no point in staying in the library if I can't focus. I have to talk to Petra. We can't stay mad at each other forever, especially because of my attitude this morning. Our friendship is too dear to me. After leaving the library, I find her entertained in the cafeteria with Katrina and David, a straw between her lips, drinking a strawberry smoothie. She looks all sweet and adorable with them. Not sure how she'll be with me though. One thing is for sure: I've got to apologize first. Taking a deep breath, I glance at the vitrine on my right to check my reflection, and, seeing that I look presentable, I walk toward them.

Removing my mask, I ask, "Petra, may I talk to you?"

She takes a sip of her smoothie, while Katrina and David look at me with a WTF face.

"Outside, I mean."

"Um, sure."

A grin of joy warms up my face.

Petra takes up her backpack without even letting the straw fall from her lips, and follows me outside, where we decide to stroll around the campus.

She smells exactly like before—jasmine flowers. Ahhh... Petra's scent, I've missed it terribly. It's delicate, elegant, young, and feminine.

We finally stop walking. She looks at me, wondering what I will say or do next. My first impulse is to kiss her, taste her beautiful glossy lips, and tell her this engagement is total nonsense. But I'm sure I'd get a slap in return, so instead I say, "I really wanted to apologize for my attitude this morning. I was behaving like a total ass." I pause, carefully pondering my next words. It's not easy for me to open up about my feelings. And it's not like I intended to, but I owe her an apology and at least some sort of explanation. "I'm not gonna lie, I... um, I got pretty pissed off as soon as I saw you with your ring on."

I feel bad for talking about it, but she doesn't seem put off by the conversation. Petra keeps listening, her vibe so kind and affable, like the friend she has always been. I break eye contact, my eyes staring at nothing. Jeez, the reality that she's now the fiancée of anyone but me is devastating. "I was angry and sad, but if it makes you happy, then I'm happy," I lie, but she smiles in return, so it's all good. That's all that matters anyway. "I hope you are really sure about this engagement. I mean, you're very young. I was just worried about you, as I found it quite odd…"

To my surprise, she hugs me tight in excitement. Wow. Finding her arms wrapped around my neck, her hair itching my nose, her heart beating against mine is way more than I ever thought it would be. I do my best to remain insensitive to it, but I'm only human.

"Thanks," she says in relief. "I'm so glad we can continue to be friends." Well, what choice do I have? After she releases me, Petra looks down at her iPhone and says, "Well, my next class is starting soon. I've got to go." And she gives me a quick peck on the cheek before leaving me.

CHAPTER 6

Bedford Hills, September 11, 2020
Petra Van Gatt

The week went by pretty fast, but regardless of that, I counted every single day until Alex would finally come and pick me up to go to our engagement party. Respecting my dad's wishes that I only see Alex during the weekend so I can focus on my studies during the week has been harder than I thought. I think his demand is total bullshit, but since Dad has been so supportive, I've been going along with it. Plus, Alex and I text every day and even FaceTime, so it's not like we don't talk to each other. But obviously it's not the same. As the car crosses the gate and goes into the driveway of his estate, I feel my heartbeat accelerating with every second—tonight we will finally make our engagement official to his family. And I only hope everything will go smoothly and that Emma managed to arrange something decent to amaze the guests. As I am engrossed in my thoughts, I feel Alex's hand pressing against mine and his attention never leaving me. "Are you alright?"

His low voice makes my gaze travel from the outdoors to his blue eyes. And as our eyes lock, my lips curving up, I tell him, "Yeah, I'm just so happy to be here with you." I lift his hand, giving it a kiss. "Thanks for believing in us."

As Alex and I arrive in the roundabout, I'm surprised to see the one and only Emma Hasenfratz waiting for us, standing on the front porch. She's already sporting a black lace evening dress, which reminds me I still have to get dressed before the guests arrive. "Hi, Emma," I greet her as soon as I get out of the car.

"Oh, finally!" I notice Emma was just finishing smoking as she drops her cigarette on the ground and smashes it with her high heel, then she promptly walks over in my direction, and, after briefly greeting Alex, she takes me by the arm and drags me in a rush inside the house.

"What's the hurry?" I ask as we go upstairs.

"You need to get dressed," Emma replies just as fast. "Guests are gonna be here in twenty minutes." And I'm surprised at how comfortable she is walking me down the hallway and into my fiancé's bedroom like it was hers. There, I see three different dresses lying on the bed, and Emma takes the first one before saying, "Janine brought three different dresses for you to choose from, but I think this one is gonna suit you the most." The one Emma's holding is a long, white mesh dress embroidered with red flowers and green stems. I let a small smile escape at seeing how similar it is to the dress I wore in Aspen. I glance at the others, but this one is definitely the most beautiful and unique to me.

"Alright, this one is fine." I take off my sneakers, then my jeans and shirt, and Emma helps me get into the dress.

As she closes the zip on the back, I hear her asking, "Did you speak to him already?" And I know exactly what she is talking about.

A tense silence settles between us as I ponder for a moment. "Not yet," I tell her quietly. With the dress on, I start observing my figure in the mirror. "Looks good, no?"

"Babe," Emma mumbles, her expression laced with disappointment. "You guys have to talk. That nightmare was—"

"I know," I cut her off. "But this evening is definitely not the right one to talk about this." Then I see a pair of heels standing by the mirror, and after putting them on, I ask again in an attempt to change the subject, "Do you think these heels go well with this dress?"

But Emma is not giving up, and as she stands beside me, she looks at me in the mirror and forces me to face reality with one single question. "What are you afraid of?"

Letting out a sigh, I break eye contact, my gaze darting down for an instant as I consider if I should tell her the truth or not. "I have something else in mind besides confronting him."

And as I look again at the mirror, I can see Emma raising her brows. "Really?"

"Yes." Before she can keep inquiring, I turn, and, holding her stare, I say, "Look, I really appreciate all your advice, but he's the one who has to be honest with me about my mom. I'm not supposed to know they had a talk. Alex is the one who must come forward and tell me about it. Not the other way around."

Emma contemplates my answer for a second. "And what if he doesn't?"

"Well, then, I'll assume he handled the situation." And trying to leave the subject behind once and for all, I ask, "What time are they arriving?"

"Around six p.m.," Emma replies, glancing at her watch.

"You look very beautiful today," I blurt out. "I mean, you're always beautiful. But that black dress looks really nice on you." After all, it's not every day that Ms. Hasenfratz dresses up in a fancy lace dress with high heels.

She gives me a big smile in return, brushing my arm in gratitude. "Thanks. You look great too," she praises. "Alright, we should go out to welcome them. Where's your fiancé?"

But a text pops up before I can reply. "Oh, Yara is here. Let's go." I take a clutch, shove my iPhone into it, and drag Emma with me as we go back to the entrance to welcome Alex's youngest sister.

Standing on the porch, we notice Yara's car coming around the roundabout and stopping right in front of us. The valet opens the rear door and extends a hand to help her.

As she gets out of the car, neither Emma nor I can help but gape. In our defense, Yara has this very enigmatic expression, with her dark brown eyes always so stern yet mysterious. Her posture is just as straight as the last time I saw her. Not surprisingly, she's wearing her usual equestrian attire, with black boots, beige breeches, and a white shirt buttoned up to the neck with a dark blazer. Her hair is brushed back in a high ponytail, giving her a sense of finesse that fits her so well.

"Who's this woman?" Emma whispers nearly out of breath. "Fuck…" she blurts out. "She looks like a model coming out of a Ralph Lauren ad."

"Let me introduce you." I grab Emma's arm, and we walk in Yara's direction. "Yara!" I greet with a big grin.

But Yara first glances to my right, where Emma is standing.

"Petra," she finally greets back. "So good to see you again." Her voice is more formal than usual though. Not sure if it's because there's a stranger standing beside me.

After giving her three cheek kisses, I introduce her to Emma. "Yara, this is Emma, my best friend."

"Emma Hasenfratz," Emma adds with an ounce of snobbish formality as she extends a hand. The fact that she wanted to add her surname leaves me a bit troubled, but I guess she must have her reasons for doing so.

Yara observes Emma's hand for a second, considering it. Then her stern brown eyes meet Emma's. "Yara Van Lawick," she replies, shaking her hand. "Pleasure meeting you, Ms. Hasenfratz."

Wow. Such a formal introduction—not what I expected, to say the least. Yara used to be so casual in the Netherlands. And what happened to her sense of humor? This seems to be a totally different Yara from the one I met last year.

"Mrs. Van Lawick, please just call me Emma."

What? I've never heard Emma being so refined and polite to anyone in my entire life. What happened to her casual manners? Emma seems like a totally transformed woman as she stands in front of Yara. Is that because she is from nobili-ty? No freaking idea. But it's weird to see Emma talking like a posh lady.

Yara smiles back at Emma and says, "And you may just call me Yara."

They keep their voices so contained that I can't help but roll my eyes. What's going on?

"Ah! Elliott!" I say in relief as I glance at Yara's husband.

"Petra!" He offers me a warm, friendly hug. "Congratula-tions on the engagement. I'm so happy for you and Van Dieren. You guys deserve it."

"Thank you so much," I tell him, still perplexed that Yara didn't say the same. "Where are the kids? They didn't come?"

"Nah," he answers, patting me on the back. "We love you guys too much to bring them. They are with the nanny." As Elliott looks around, he then asks, "Where is your fiancé?"

"Oh, I think he's still inside with my dad. Let me check." I grab my iPhone out of my clutch and call him, but as I hear the door opening behind us and Elliott shouting, "Alex!" I hang up.

"Elliott! So good to see you!" My fiancé welcomes him with a hug and a pat on the back. "Where's everyone else?"

"They should be here in a minute," Elliott replies. "We were just a bit ahead." In fact, as soon as Elliott finishes his sentence, we see three more executive black cars entering the roundabout.

As the first car parks in front of us, a big grin lands on my lips upon recognizing Alex's oldest sister, Julia. This time, though, I go to greet her on my own. "Julia!"

Julia reciprocates with a warm grin and opens her arms wide to welcome me into a hug. "I'm so happy to see you alive," she whispers in my ear. "You have always been in my prayers." Oh, wow. Her words were not expected but they are just as welcome, bringing a wave of emotion through me.

"Thank you," I say discreetly. At least her kindness and warmth are just as I recall. "I'm so happy to see you again."

"How are you doing?" she asks in a low voice, observing me. "Have you been eating properly?"

"Yes, I have," I tell her, feeling quite self-conscious about my struggle to do so. "I'm, um, on medication for anxiety and PTSD." I haven't opened up about this to anyone, but I guess with Julia it's a bit different.

She doesn't seem surprised; rather, she keeps her expression just as serious and attentive. "Of course. After everything you went through, I can imagine." Then she takes my hands unexpectedly, her seriousness deepening. "I'm sorry for your loss, Petra. If you need anything, you know I'm here, right?"

"Oh…" Now that was unexpected. "Alex told you?"

"Petra…" She cocks her head to the side. "I knew before anyone else." And my gaze drops to the floor just as fast. Of course she knew before anyone else. Who was I trying to fool? "I don't want you to blame yourself for anything, alright?"

I frown at her request. "Um, what do you mean?"

"The accident, the baby… It belongs to the past. You have to focus on healing now." Her tone is so empathetic and caring that I can't help but revel in it.

"Thank you, Julia." I plunge into her embrace again, a bit devastated at the memories. And I know I will need time to heal from all of it, but her energy and words have such a healing power that I can only be grateful to have her in my life.

"My brother loves you a lot," she says in a whisper. "Those five months without you were not easy for him."

I'm about to answer, but we are promptly interrupted by another female voice. "Can we say hello?" His mother, Margaret, asks, stepping in with his other sister, Maud.

"Margaret," I greet as we exchange three kisses. She looks just as radiant as last year, sporting a black jumpsuit and a gray silk shawl over her shoulders. My attention then goes to her second daughter. "Hi, Maud." And I also give her three kisses.

"Alex told us about your coma," Margaret informs me. And I wonder if he also told her about the baby, but I'm definitely not the one who's gonna bring that up. The fewer people that know, the better. "What a miracle you are awake. Doctors thought you'd never recover," she says, taking my hand between hers.

"Thank you." Pausing for a moment, I then add, "I'm really lucky."

"Damn right." She gives me one of her warmest smiles, and, before either of us get emotional, she asks, "Well, shall we?"

As we step onto the terrace where dinner will be served, everyone marvels about the setting Emma has prepared, and my eyes fill with joy as I take in my surroundings—strings of fairy lights are cascading overhead, creating a wonderful romantic vibe with a gold-colored glow, then at the center lies a long dining table covered with candles, lanterns, and bouquets of white jasmine. My heart flutters in excitement at seeing those flowers; after all, they are my favorite. I see Julia already recording the setting on her iPhone and asking her husband, Sebastian, to take a picture of her and Maud. "It's so beautiful," I hear her praising. Then a bit farther down, I see a live band, including a violinist and a pianist. They start playing the beginning of a new song, and after a few notes, I smile, recognizing it—"Everlasting Love" by Jamie Cullum.

"Do you like it?" Emma asks.

"Oh, Emma, it's perfect." I pull her into my arms and squeeze her tightly. "You're the most amazing friend I could ask for," I whisper in her ear.

With tears in her eyes, Emma clears her throat and does her best to keep them under control. "Alright, let me show you where I placed everyone." She brings me to the table, and, showing me the names written on each placement card, she explains, "So, I have you here. Alex on your left, me on your right, Julia in front of you, her husband in front of Alex."

Before she can finish, Julia and her husband Sebastian are already taking their seats, followed by Yara and Elliott, and everyone else does the same. "Oh, I see that everyone likes to seat quickly."

"I think everyone is hungry," I tease in a low voice. "You did a fantastic job."

As we sit, I notice how Emma keeps gazing discreetly at Yara, which is understandable as she's the only one sporting equestrian attire for an evening event. And for those who don't know her, it might come off as a pretty weird fashion statement. A side smile escapes me at thinking I was not supposed to see that.

"I'm so glad you guys could come," I praise as I look at Julia now sitting in front of me.

I notice how a waiter is already behind them, filling Sebastian's glasses with red wine and water.

"Me too," Julia says, before declining the wine.

"It was really perfect timing," Sebastian points out. "We were about to come here to New York anyway."

"Oh really?" I ask in surprise. "For what reason, if I may ask?"

As Julia looks at her husband with a twinkle in her eye, she says, "Well, it's our twentieth wedding anniversary, and since Sebastian has always wanted to go bear hunting…"

But my joyful expression switches into a perplexed one. "Bear hunting?" I repeat, nearly out of breath. "What do you mean?"

"Um," Sebastian mumbles, glancing at Alex. "I mean, tomorrow is the opening season in the Hudson Valley. You know, for black bear hunting. We don't have bears in the Netherlands, so I'm really looking forward to tomorrow."

Tomorrow? What is he talking about? I look at Alex, trying to understand what the hell is going on, but he's talking to Maria. And just like me, Emma can't stop glaring at Sebastian as he casually tries to justify the killing of animals for pleasure.

"So you came here just for the sake of killing black bears?" Emma unleashes.

"We came here first and foremost for the engagement, of course," Julia interposes in the sweetest and most polite tone to rescue him. "Black bear hunting is not illegal; it's actually an extremely regulated sport."

"Sport?" Emma repeats, nodding sarcastically, but I know she is doing her best not to enter into a bloody debate against them. One thing is for sure: if this were happening at Loyola, she would've gotten really aggressive, maybe even violent. Meanwhile, Alex avoids eye contact with me by keeping himself engrossed in conversation with Margaret and Dad. Well, if my fiancé thinks he's gonna kill a black bear tomorrow with Sebastian, then he's in for a big surprise. But I'll take care of him and his hunt later. For now, and for the sake of a good evening, I try to lead the conversation to a lighter subject. "So, it's your twentieth wedding anniversary?" I ask Julia, my tone enthusiastic. "Congratulations. You guys are such an inspiration."

And keeping her smile just as big, she says, "Yes, unbelievable how time flies so fast."

"Wow," Emma utters, playing along. "That's impressive. And you look so young…"

"Well, I'm just thirty-nine."

Emma nearly chokes on her wine. "Wait, what? You got married at nineteen?" Then she looks at me and says in a lower voice, "I understand now why you like her so much." Still under a wave of shock, Emma seems to be thinking something through. "But, like, you dated other guys before him, right?"

"Nope. I knew he'd be my husband the day I met him," Julia replies, her tone laced with pride as she gazes for an instant at Sebastian. "I was sixteen at the time, and we dated until I finished high school. Then he proposed, and a year later, we were married."

Emma makes a mental effort not to gape again, but her expression says it all. "So, Sebastian was your first and only boyfriend?" she asks, nearly in outrage. And we can't help but giggle at her astonished face. It feels like two worlds discovering each other.

"Yes," Julia replies amid the laughter. "When it's the right one, one is enough."

"Oh…" I swoon as Julia gives her husband a quick peck on the cheek. Sebastian then takes her hand and gives it a kiss. Letting out a sigh, I picture Alex and I doing the same after twenty years of marriage. Then my gaze goes to Emma, who is still blinking in total shock.

"I think Julia had more important things to do than fooling around," I whisper in her ear for the sake of teasing her. Then I reach for her hand, and, imitating Sebastian, I give Emma's hand a kiss.

"And what about your friends? Were they like you?" Emma continues inquiring.

"My friends, yes," Julia replies with a big grin. And my amusement keeps growing. "But some girls at my school were obsessed with boys, like everywhere else."

To my surprise, Margaret jumps in. "I've always said to my daughters, if you find yourself in a group of friends who only speak about boys, then you are in the wrong group."

"I couldn't agree more," Dad interposes, and I'm not surprised by his statement.

"With all due respect to these fine gentlemen who are here, my daughters had better things to do than waste their mental energy on a bunch of dicks."

"Mom!" Julia exclaims. "What was that?"

But we all break out in laughter. I've never in my entire life imagined Margaret saying the D-word. Oh gosh, this must be the funniest dinner I've ever been to.

"I totally agree, Margaret," Emma replies. "Dicks are a waste of time. At Loyola, girls were constantly swooning over a bunch of jerks. It was pathetic. Right, Petra?"

I huff at her blatant sarcasm. After all, Emma knows I had a crush on James since the first day he spoke to me. And it was, as she said, pretty pathetic.

"Right," I mutter.

Then my attention goes to Julia, and, after exchanging a look, she asks Alex and me, "So, do you guys have a date in mind for the wedding?"

Alex doesn't waste time saying, "We haven't—"

But I cut him off just as fast. "Yes, we do."

"We do?" he repeats, squinting at me.

"Yep," I tell him. And putting on my most innocent face, I add, "I've been thinking about it, and, um, I've got the perfect date for our wedding."

"Oh…" Alex is left speechless. "And what date is that?"

Then I look at Julia and announce, "The fifth of December, on my nineteenth birthday."

"What?!" Dad blurts out. "Are you sure?"

"Are you sure about that?" Alex asks me in a discreet, low voice, repeating my dad's question.

"Why not?" I match his low tone, and, wetting my lips, I add, "Don't you think it's a meaningful date?"

His lips part in astonishment, and I know he's picturing exactly the same as I. "Of course it is."

As we smile at each other, his gaze drops to my lips, and I wish for once he'd kiss me in public.

"That's a wonderful date," Margaret praises, breaking our intimate moment. "A winter wedding is perfect. We have less than three months, but I'm sure we can manage."

Alex's attention shifts back to his mother, and, letting out a sigh, I do the same. At this rate, I guess he will only kiss me in public at the altar.

"We can speak to Bishop De Korte and have the ceremony at St. John's Cathedral," Sebastian suggests. "That's where we got married. It's the most beautiful cathedral in the Netherlands."

"That's a great idea," Julia praises. "I'm sure you're gonna love it. We can organize the whole wedding for you if you want."

My eyes widen instantly. "Really?"

"Of course. We will hire the same people who planned ours. They are super professional—you just have to tell them what your preferences and wishes are, and they'll make it happen."

"Um, as long as the groom attends, I'm good," I tease, looking at my fiancé.

"Not sure if they can make it happen, but they will try," Sebastian replies back.

A quick laugh escapes us, and, thanks to Sebastian's comment, my fiancé puts an arm around me and gives me a kiss. I just wish it would've been on the lips, not on the head.

CHAPTER 7

Bedford Hills, September 11, 2020
Emma Hasenfratz

Over the past nineteen years, very few people have managed to make an impact on my life. When you have a fifty-million-dollar trust fund, believe me, most people you meet are quite shallow, boring, clichéd, and devoid of any interesting personality. All they care about is your money or the lifestyle you can provide. Petra was the exception. She's always been weird and reserved enough to keep me—and everyone else at Loyola—interested in getting to know her.

Today, though, I've met someone else: a noblewoman.

A *married* noblewoman.

Yara Van Lawick.

She's stern and formal, like a general in the army. And unlike her sisters, I haven't seen her either laughing or giggling during the whole dinner. Her presence is unmistakable though, and her pale face is as immaculately cold as the marble walls standing in my parents' house.

"How did you two meet?" Yara asks. And her Dutch accent makes my lips curve up.

"Oh, we went to the same school together," Petra tells her.

"I kind of figured that out. But how did you become best friends?" she insists. "You two seem to be quite the opposite." Petra and I share the same complicit smile as we recall memories that only we know. "Who spoke to whom first?" Yara asks again.

"I did," I tell her. "Petra was always alone with her books and so quiet. After a couple of months in the same class, she had, like, zero friends. She was such a weirdo that I had to introduce myself."

But Yara doesn't stop there. "And then?"

And then I fell in love. "And then…" I mumble, looking at Petra. Words remain stuck in my throat as we smile at each other. "And then she was like a mystery that I wanted to solve." I'm sounding cheesy as fuck, but Petra seems to like it. Choosing my next words more carefully, I add, "And the more I knew about her, the more I liked her." Blinking twice, my focus remains on Yara, and I aim for a steadier tone. "She used to talk about shit I couldn't care less about, but she was so passionate about it. And that was"—*hot*—"dope," I say instead.

"Like what?" Petra asks with her big blue eyes pinned on me.

"Oh jeez, from artists to philosophical bullshit. You always had something weird to talk about," I tease her. "She wanted to drag me to every museum and gallery in the city, I swear," I tell Yara, before taking a sip of my Primitivo.

Petra giggles and says, "Okay, I plead guilty on that one."

But Yara remains just as serious. "So Emma is your only friend?"

"The only one I trust enough to invite here," Petra replies, putting a hand on top of mine. Her touch squeezes my heart, reminding me of the deep shit I'm in. "She's even the one who organized this beautiful gathering."

And I smile at her answer. It feels good to know I still hold a special place in Ms. Van Gatt's heart, despite the fact that in three months, she will no longer be Ms. Van Gatt…

Fuck, feeling the urge to smoke, I excuse myself and leave the table.

The only safe place to do so is by the front porch, near the roundabout. There, amid the darkness of the night and few outdoor lights, I stand against the wall and bring a cigarette up to my lips.

But a voice stabilizes me just as fast. "It's tough, huh?"

"Sorry, what?" I ask, jumping a little, my cigarette locked between my lips.

"Being in love with someone who is not in love with you." Yara's imposing figure emerges from nowhere, and I'm surprised to see her holding a metallic lighter. Opening the clasp, she rolls the spark wheel down, igniting the flame, and brings it up to burn the tip of my cigarette. Once the tip is burning brightly, I take a long, steady inhale of smoke. This woman knows her shit. That's why she was asking so many questions.

"Is it so visible?" I ask, puffing the smoke out of my lungs.

Yara takes a cigarette from my pack and puts it between her lips. It's a simple move, yet extremely sensual coming from her.

"Not for everyone." And she brings her lighter up. After burning the tip enough, she quietly pulls the smoke in before exhaling it out. And I notice how classy she looks doing so. "But enough for me." With her cigarette stuck between her long fingers, she keeps observing me with squinted eyes. "Does Petra know?"

"Not really..." I confess. "Friendship over feelings, ya know."

"I see..." Yara replies, her eyes meticulously studying me. "And how do you cope with that?" she asks, before bringing the cigarette up to her lips.

"Well, to put it bluntly, I fool around..." I tell her, taking another puff of smoke. "And I pursue many other endeavors..."

"Such as?"

"I'm also an equestrian." That's a bit of a stretch, but who cares? "I have a stable at home and ride from time to time."

"Oh, that's interesting," she says with a side smile, her mind still ruminating. "Do you play polo?"

"Polo?" I repeat, a bit perplexed by her question.

"Mm..." she utters as she takes another inhale of smoke.

"I've never played polo, no. Do you play?"

"A bit..." She lets her words trail off as her dark eyes linger on me.

And her tone is suggestive enough for me to ask, "Would you like to teach me?"

Giving me nothing but a smirk, Yara seems to revel in the calculated silence that fills the space between us. Then she finally says, "I like to teach." But I've got the feeling we are not talking about polo. "Would you like to learn, Ms. Hasenfratz?"

I swear, her question gives me goosebumps. No idea if it's polo she's talking about, but it doesn't matter. There's something about her that draws me in, something I can't really put my finger on—maybe it's her sternness, her formality, her impeccable posture, and manners. I don't know, but I'm keen to go down the rabbit hole to find out. Looking straight into her brown eyes and trying to discern the underlying meaning of her question, I offer, "I'd love to."

And her smirk grows. "Great. I'm staying here until Monday."

"My parents are out this weekend," I tell her. "You could come to my place on Sunday."

She reaches into a pocket inside her blazer, and after taking her iPhone out, she asks, "What's your phone number?" And now my heart gives a little jump. She seems to be dead serious. But what should I expect? A polo lesson? Or something else? Well, there's only one way to find out.

Taking her iPhone, I type in my number. "Here. Saved as Emma Hasenfratz."

CHAPTER 8

Bedford Hills, September 11, 2020
Alexander Van Dieren

Three months. That's the time left before we get married. Wow. It feels even more real now that there is a deadline. I knew this day would eventually come, but I never thought it'd come so soon. My thoughts instantly go to Tess and her threats. I wonder how she will react once she knows the wedding is taking place just an hour's drive from her house. But my gaze remains on Petra, who is engrossed in conversation with Julia, and I can only hope her mother will restrain herself from interfering with the ceremony. I know how much Petra is looking forward to a perfect day. One she can remember with a smile on her face, not tears. But knowing Tess as I do, this is nothing more than wishful thinking. Then my attention goes to Mom, and as our eyes lock, she beckons to me, and I know it's time for our tête-à-tête. After all, dinner has already been served and we are now finishing coffees and digestifs.

"I'll be right back," I whisper in Petra's ear before standing up.

Mom does the same, and we quietly leave the table, the guests, and the outdoors in the direction of my office.

Opening the door, I invite her inside. "Make yourself at home." And Mom does so, removing the shawl covering her shoulders and sitting comfortably on the sofa.

Closing the door behind me, I go to the bar and ask as I take the decanter, "Macallan Thirty, one ice sphere?"

"Where does your ice come from?"

Is that question a temperament check? Few questions could be as insulting to me as this one. And Mom knows this perfectly well. In fact, I don't think anyone has ever dared to ask me that. She thinks I'm what? Fifteen? I'm tempted to scare the hell out of her and say it comes from the fridge, but instead I politely bring her the glass and say, "Wintersmiths. Anything else?"

She observes the crystal-clear ice sphere sitting in her glass, half covered by the single malt, and her lips curve up. "We can never be too prudent. Thank you." Then, as I sit on the armchair beside her, I realize it's the first time I've received her in my house. We've always met on the family estate in Dieren, but never in a house that is only mine. After taking a sip, she announces, "Tess attacked your sister on a TV interview."

"Which one?" She cocks her head to the side, which means Julia. I then ask, "And how does that have anything to do with me?"

"Tess intends to become Minister of Justice if her party wins next year. And reform the entire judiciary system, most likely to get rid of your sister."

"That doesn't answer my question."

"It's your sister's *life* we are talking about, Alexander," Mom chides. "Tess is attacking her because of your fiancée."

"Tess never liked Julia," I snap back. "This has nothing to do with Petra."

"But Tess never attacked Julia on TV before. Her name has never been exposed in the media," Mom interposes. "Look, Julia can handle a few remarks, but I don't want my daughter to be her next target because of your relationship."

"Tess won't do shit, and you know that."

"Unless you don't move to Singapore."

And there we are. The real reason Mom wanted to hold the engagement party so quickly and was so keen to come here. Furrowing my brow, I ask, "You are here to make sure I'm really moving, aren't you?" And I wish I wouldn't have asked this question in the first place. Sometimes there are things I prefer not to know. Mom doesn't answer. But there is no fucking need. Her expression says it all. "Fuck…" I huff, head shaking, my heart taking a goddamn blow at the realization. "When I thought for once you had no agenda," I tell her, my tone laced with disgust and disappointment. I can't help but feel sick to my stomach at her move. "We were so happy to welcome you here." Regardless of what I tell her, Mom takes another sip, remaining just as serene and unbothered. "So all that talk about the preparation of the wedding for Petra's birthday was bullshit, wasn't it?"

She presses her lips tightly together, considering me for a moment, and mumbles a mere, "I'm sorry."

I chuckle at the blatant charade. Sorry? That's the only thing she has to say? "Get the fuck out of here."

Mom creases her brows, finally leaving her indifference behind. "Alex—"

"Get. The. Fuck. Out."

Since Mom is not moving, I'm the one to leave.

As I reach the door, she says, "There is another option, you know."

Turning back to look at her, I ask, "What are you talking about?"

"If you move to Singapore and break your engagement, you'll be doing the right thing, and everyone will be happy. Well, except the two of you," Mom explains. "On the other hand, if you stay and move forward with the wedding..." She lets her words trail off, while studying me attentively. "There might be some painful consequences," she says, finishing her whiskey. "You might lose your friends, your reputation, your hedge fund—"

"I know that."

"And that's all fine," she keeps going. "If that's what you want... But if Tess presses charges against us for what happened twenty years ago, repercussions are to be expected." I frown at the word *repercussions*. "At the end of the day, the real question is..." She leans back and waits a morbid second before asking, "How far would you go for love?"

And I know at that moment that if I choose to marry Petra, this marriage will come with a hefty price tag. I could always sell my part of the company and resign. Roy might never talk to me again, but the repercussions against her own mother? Could I really live with that? Damn it... I promised myself no more deaths. What if Petra finds out and never forgives me? And worse, what if, after her mother's death, someone tells her the whole truth about what happened twenty years ago? Would she forgive me?

"So if I marry her, the price to pay is what I think it is?"

"If you do really intend to marry her..." Mom leans forward, looking me straight in the eye. "I'd suggest you ask your future mother-in-law to drop whatever it is she has against us before it's too late."

CHAPTER 9

Bedford Hills, September 11, 2020
Petra Van Gatt

Everyone is gathered in front of the female singer and her musicians, who are now playing "The Look of Love" by Diana Krall. As the singer starts crooning, I remember how much I love this song. It's so damn romantic! Looking around at the strings of fairy lights and how everyone seems to be happily enjoying the evening, I can't help but feel so much gratitude for the outstanding job Emma did. Julia and Sebastian are already slow dancing, along with Maud and her husband. On my right side, I find Elliot and Dad, glasses in hand, engrossed in conversation, and on the other, Yara and Emma. But I don't see either Margaret or Alex. They have been gone for over half an hour though. Why are they taking so long?

Instead of sitting here alone, I decide to turn to Emma and Yara. "Hi, Emma," I say, putting a hand on her shoulder. "Are you enjoying the evening?"

"Very much, and you?" she replies for the sake of politeness, but I can see by their faces that I'm disturbing them.

"Um, sorry to ask, but have you seen Alex?"

As I notice them looking over my shoulder, I turn around and see my fiancé smiling at me. "Were you missing me already?"

His question brings a grin to my lips, and I instantly put my arms around him, saying, "Finally!" Then I drag him to the dance floor. "This song has to be the one for our wedding dance."

"Do we have to hire Diana Krall too?" he asks, most likely teasing.

"If you can manage it…" I reply before wrapping my arms around his neck as I finally manage to get him only to myself. He puts his hands on my waist, and we start swaying together to my favorite song. "We haven't had one single minute to ourselves the entire evening."

He gives me one of his charming smiles that makes my heart go wild. "Get ready, because that's most likely how our wedding day will be." And I can't help but bite my bottom lip as I hear him speaking about our wedding.

"Do you mind if we get married on the fifth like I said to Julia? I had the idea at the very last minute," I tell him. "But if you don't like it…"

"It's the perfect date," he reassures me in a low voice. "Bishop De Korte is part of Sebastian's family, and my mom knows him very well. I'm sure they can make it happen."

"Great," I reply before we lapse into silence as we revel in the dance and the beautiful music. But after a few more beats, curiosity takes over me, and I have to ask, "Um, I know it's none of my business, but what did you and your mom speak about?"

Alex doesn't reply immediately. I see him pondering his words before cautiously saying, "Just details about the wedding."

As I observe the nervousness written all over his face, I can't help but insist, "Are you sure?"

An awkward silence fills the space between us as we keep pace to the sound of the jazzy melody. "Yes, of course," he replies, barely keeping his eyes on me.

But not even our dance and his irresistible smile are enough to reassure me. I know there is something troubling him. I can feel it. And I've got the feeling it has to do with my mom. "Is there anything you want to tell me?" I ask again, searching for his gaze.

When his blue eyes finally lock with mine again, I look for a hint of what he could possibly be hiding from me, but he presses his lips together before they land on my forehead. "Are you enjoying the evening?" His question is not what I was expecting, to say the least.

"Alex…" I mumble, bringing my mouth to his ear. "You know you can trust me."

"I know…" He answers me with contemplative eyes, his lips curving up as he softly strokes my long hair. "You are so beautiful tonight."

I swallow dryly at his words. His voice carries a heavy melancholia that doesn't match the mood of our evening. "What's going on?" I keep insisting. "Alex, tell me."

"Do you trust me?"

"Yes, of course. But—"

"One day, I'll tell you," he interposes.

"When?"

"When the time is right." And he seals these words with another kiss, this time on my head.

Secrets. I never thought they would become a thing between us. From the moment we got engaged, I had hoped we would be a couple with open, honest conversations, with no secrets, and no bullshit. But the truth is, I fucked up. I should've told him about my nightmare, and I didn't. I didn't confront him like Emma told me to, and I know I'm a coward for not doing so. But I'm scared of his reply. I'm scared as I ask him, "Are you gonna leave me?" Fuck! The question left my mouth without any warning!

An uncomfortable emptiness fills the space between us before he says, "Your mother is planning to come next week."

"I don't want to see her," I snap back. "She's nothing but trouble."

A little chuckle escapes him before he nuzzles against my hair, reveling in it. "I know."

Then, as I rest my head against his, I breathe slowly in and out to prevent tears, but one silently rolls down my cheek. After all, Alex didn't answer my question.

* * *

After our dance, and while Emma seems to be in love with Yara's chitchat, Alex and I decide it's time to start saying goodbye to our guests. But before my dad leaves, I ask him to take a quick walk around the gardens with me. Taking my dad by the arm, we stroll around the country yard, immersed in the tranquil night, lit only by the stars and moon above us. After some small talk, and once we've gotten far enough away from the crowd, I ask, "Do you remember when I was seven? I used to play here with Alex."

"I do, yes," Dad mumbles, keeping it short and formal.

With my mind already wandering as I recall such memories, I say, "No matter how cloudy or sunny the day, I loved to play hide-and-seek with him. One of my tricks was to lie on the grass and remain quiet. I always thought he wouldn't find me like that." I let out a quick giggle, but Dad remains silent, replying with just a polite smile. Switching to another subject, I say, "Did you enjoy the evening?"

"It was wonderful. Emma did a great job. I never knew she was so talented at event planning," he replies, just as calculated as before.

"Yeah, she's great." After a few more steps, I decide to cut the bullshit and get straight to the point. "Dad, I need to ask you a favor."

Dad stops walking, and, looking me straight in the eye, he asks, "What's going on?"

There aren't a thousand ways to say it, so I make my request as straightforward as possible. "Can you fly to Rotterdam and let Mom know I don't want to see her? Like, ever again?"

Dad twitches his head to the side, sighing in exasperation, and maybe also disbelief. "Petra…"

"Please?" I insist. "Can you do that for me? Alex told me she's planning to visit me soon. Can you go before that?"

Dad's eyes widen in shock. "You mean, you want me to go to Rotterdam *this week*?"

"Please tell her I don't want to talk to her anymore. I wish her well, but I don't want her in my life."

But Dad shakes his head, not even bothering to consider my request. "I've got a lot to do here."

"Please," I plead once more as I take his hands and confront him face-to-face. "It's really urgent."

"Petra... She's your mother. She loves you a lot. I can't tell her that. She's going to be devastated."

"Then tell her to leave me and my fiancé alone," I press on. "If she does so, I might even invite her to the wedding."

Dad drops his stare to the ground, drawing in a breath. I know it's not easy for him to be in the middle of such a fight, but I need him on our side more than ever. His eyes meet mine again, and, after noticing the distress laced in my gaze, he says, "Alright. I will talk to her."

My brows lift in surprise. "Really?"

"I can't promise anything," he admits. "But I will do my best."

Jumping into his arms, I whisper, "I'm sure you'll manage. I trust you."

CHAPTER 10

Bedford Hills, September 12, 2020
Petra Van Gatt

Mornings have always had a special scent in Bedford Hills, especially when I have to spend the week on Park Avenue and can only be here during the weekends. I've noticed there's always a trace of Alex's cologne left on the pillows and maybe all over me when I wake up. Slowly stretching my arm over to the left side of the bed, I find nothing but emptiness. *Oh God! The hunt!* Gasping, I open my eyes wide, my heart already pounding anxiously fast. There is no way I'll let him kill a poor bear! In a quick move, I leap out of bed, grab my iPhone from the nightstand, and call his number. Since he doesn't answer, I've got to find him and fast. I put on the first pair of jeans and sweater I can get my hands on, no bra—there is no time for that—and after running down the stairs, I start looking around for him while shouting his name. But I get no answer. Nope, nothing. *Damn it!* I rush to the kitchen in the hope of finding Maria there.

"Ah! Maria," I call as I find her chopping vegetables. "I need to know where Alex is."

But Maria doesn't even bother to look in my direction, and, keeping herself just as focused as always, she just says, "I have no idea, Miss."

"Of course you do," I press on. Seeing how she keeps ignoring me, I put my hand on her shoulder, turning her to face me. "Maria…"

"Okay, maybe I do," she confesses. "But I can't tell you." She tries to dodge me, walking toward the fridge to take something from there. Too bad I'm the most stubborn between the two of us.

"Look, the hunt starts in an hour. Please, I need to talk to him."

"I'm not allowed to tell you where he is," she admits. "I'm sorry, Miss."

I'm so furious at the instructions he gave her that I just want to strangle him, but instead, taking a deep breath, I try to keep my temper in check. "Please," I insist. "It's really urgent. I won't tell him you told me." Despite my serious tone, Maria continues to ignore me as she tastes the soup simmering on the stove. "I promise, I will make it seem like I just found him."

"Why is it so important?" she finally asks.

"An innocent life is at stake," I reply just as fast.

But Maria immediately rolls her eyes. "He will fire me if I tell you," she says. "He gave me clear instructions."

"Huh?" Fire her? I cannot possibly believe it. "Of course not, no one's gonna fire you. I promise." Maria shakes her head in denial. "Maria, I will never let it happen."

The gravity in my tone makes her ponder my words more seriously. She then frowns and, a bit skeptical, asks, "Are you sure?"

"Yes. I will protect you. No one will fire you. I give you my word."

After some hesitation, she finally looks again at me and says, "He's with Sebastian, getting ready."

"Sebastian? He's already here? Okay... Um, where?"

Maria twitches her lips, thinking twice, but finally blurts out, "In the trophy room."

"*What*?!" I snap in total disbelief. "A trophy room?" I ask again, making sure I heard her properly. Maria just nods at me in return. Oh God, my heart thunders at a thousand miles an hour. "What kind of trophies are we talking about? Don't tell me it's what I'm thinking."

"I'm afraid it is."

"Where is the room?" I ask, ready to kill *him* instead and expose him as a trophy among those innocent lives. Maria's attention shifts back to the stove, ignoring me. My nerves are boiling under my skin, and my patience is vanishing. "Where is the room?" I demand louder.

Startled, Maria finally stops her little game, and after cleaning her hands on her apron, she leads me out of the kitchen. "This way, please."

After walking all the way to the end of the hallway, we take the stairs and go down to the basement. I knew there was an old winery here, but that's all. Alex has never bothered to show me all the rooms occupying his basement. Once we reach the wood-paneled corridor, she switches on the light, and looking ahead, she says, "The last door on your right." But before I can walk farther, Maria holds me back and adds, "Don't tell him I told you." There is genuine concern and fear in her voice, which makes my heart squeeze.

"I won't. Thank you, Maria."

Speeding up my pace, I finally stand in front of the infamous room. I can even hear people talking on the other side. I think twice about knocking, but fuck it! Taking a deep breath, I open the door wide and go inside the room, asking, "May we have a word?" But my mind goes wild as I look at the walls lined with stuffed animal heads. "Oh God!" I see the heads of dead deer (some with antlers, others without), rhinos and gazelles. Then, placed on the wall in front of me and above the fireplace, is the head of an elephant. I try hard not to cry at the sight of it. This is the most disturbing place I have ever been in my whole life.

"Petra! What are you doing here?" I hear Alex scolding me, and his tone is enough to bring my attention back to the duo in the room.

Alex and Sebastian are both already in full hunting attire, with brown ankle boots and rifles in hands, Alex sitting slightly on a dark wooden desk that stands behind them. Needless to say, the view is vomit-inducing.

"Good morning, Sebastian," I snap for the sake of politeness.

"Hi, Petra." He looks at Alex and says, "I will wait outside." Afterward, Sebastian puts the rifle sling over his shoulder, takes his jacket hanging on the wall, and leaves the room, closing the door behind him.

Now that we are alone, Alex barks, "What the fuck was that? Where are your manners? You don't even knock now?"

But I'm having none of it. Walking over in his direction, I say, pointing my index finger at him, "You're not gonna kill anyone! That's horrible!"

"How did you—"

"You know perfectly well that I'm a vegetarian!" I cut him off.

"How did you get here?" he asks.

"That doesn't matter. Please don't kill a poor animal."

"I'm sorry, but Sebastian is looking forward to the hunt," he replies without any bother. "Plus, he's helping us with the wedding—"

"Promise me you won't shoot," I interpose with my sweetest voice.

Alex lets out a rush of air, displeased, and his gaze goes down to the floor. But I keep mine pinned on him and my expression just as virtuous. Then, meeting my gaze again, he says, "Petra, it's just a bear."

"No! It's a life. A bear has the right to live just like you."

He frowns instantly at my comment and snaps, "It's a sport. Our families have been doing it for centuries. Stop with your nonsense."

"Taking an innocent life is not a sport. It's barbaric—"

Alex blows out a breath and asks, "You're not gonna stop, are you?"

"I can't. It goes against everything I stand for. I can't let you do it," I keep insisting. And since he doesn't seem convinced, I plead, "Please, do it for me."

We stay quiet as he thinks something through. "And what do I gain in exchange?"

My jaw drops at his audacity. "How dare you? You're saving a life and want something in exchange for that?"

"I'm doing you a favor," he snaps. "Killing a bear doesn't bother me, so yeah, I do."

I keep gaping at him in total awe. "You don't deserve anything in exchange for being a decent human."

But Alex just shrugs his shoulders in return. "Then, I'm afraid I can't help."

I'm so disgusted by his attitude that I slap his arm. "Fucking monster."

"Ouch," he utters at the blow as he massages the area with his palm. "That hurts."

I roll my eyes because I know he's lying. "Yeah, right. Don't you dare kill that bear," I threaten. "I'm dead serious about it."

But before he can reply, we are interrupted by three knocks on the door.

His attention shifting to above my shoulder, he orders, "Come in."

"Alex, um, sorry to bother you," Sebastian says as he stands in the doorway, "but it's time to go."

"I'll be there in a minute," he tells him before Sebastian closes the door again. His eyes drift back to me, and with his expression just as severe, he says, "We'll continue this talk once I'm back." Then Alex stands up, places his rifle sling over his shoulder, and, without me expecting it, leans down to claim my lips. And damn it, his kiss shouldn't feel that good. He slightly opens his mouth and I do the same, and our kiss becomes fire, waking every part of me. He pulls my body to his, closing the small gap between us, and I let a little grunt escape at the feel of his torso pressed against mine. My hands go around his neck as our tongues dance with each other's in blissful harmony, my cheeks radiating with warmth, and, losing myself in the moment, I become unaware of my surroundings. Lust travels through me, causing a rush of wetness to coat my thong. Jeez, I should be mad at this asshole, not thinking about his body and all the wonders he can do with it.

Breaking our kiss, I can't help but say, "Your lips taste so good." I blame this impulsive praise on the hormones. Even though I should be mad at him, the need for his touch and to be so close to him overpowers everything, and I succumb to his demand for another quick peck on the mouth.

With very light pressure, Alex starts stroking my cheek, and his lips twist into a smile laced with pride and satisfaction as he observes me with contemplative eyes. His proximity keeps my heart asking for so much more. And I'm pretty sure he knows that. "You owe me one," he says. Then he gives me a quick peck on the top of my head and makes his way out.

Yeah... I just hope he will keep that in mind during the hunt.

CHAPTER 11

Alexander Van Dieren

I glance quickly at my watch as I speed up to get outside. Reaching the front porch, I look both directions and find Sebastian standing against the wall. "I'm sorry for the wait," I tell him. "I didn't think she would find us."

"No worries," he replies, half smiling. "She's got quite an attitude, huh?"

"Yeah… And she's stubborn," I tell him as we make our way toward the car.

Sebastian lets out a quick chuckle before patting me on the back and saying in a low voice, "I'm sure you're gonna take care of it later."

His comment makes my stomach twitch. After all, Sebastian and I have always been quite close, and he knows perfectly well how I used to handle this type of situation with Amanda. As we put our rifles and jackets into the truck, I ponder my next words.

"With Petra, it's different," I tell him to avoid any mis-understandings in the future. "We are not into that."

"Why not?" After being so open with him for the past twenty years, his curiosity doesn't surprise me. "You were quite into that before."

Once we get in the car and close our respective doors, I reply, "I promised Roy I wouldn't…" But the rest of the sentence gets stuck in my throat—I just can't bring myself to finish it. "You know…"

"Discipline her?"

Jeez, that simple question is enough to make me grow hard. And for a brief moment of pleasure and guilt, I let my mind wander to what I could possibly do to her bare bottom later on. Petra's got such a beautiful butt, her rounded cheeks are so firm, pale, and soft to the touch. My pulse ticks up picturing her buttocks blotchy and deeply red. Fuck, and no one has ever done that to her before… Closing my eyes for a second, I hear the song of her whining as she endures every swat. Then I imagine the burning sting left on each cheek as she tries to reach back to alleviate the pain… Fuck… What I wouldn't do to see her so chastened like that… Before my erection gets too visible, I snap, "That part of me belongs to the past." And shutting down those thoughts, I draw in a deep breath and exhale before turning on the engine of the car. Pulling out, I leave the parking spot and focus on driving.

"Are you alright?" Sebastian's inquisitive eyes are all over me, but I keep mine straight on the road. Then I press the brake as we wait for the gates in front of us to open.

"Yeah..." And smiling at him, I say, "It's good to see you."

Once the gates are wide open, I look down at the GPS and start following the road in the direction of the land located in Sullivan County that we leased for the hunt. After a few minutes of silence, though, I hear him asking, "You want to talk about it?"

Does it look like I want to? My first instinct is to snap back a resounding *no*, but I know that Sebastian is just trying to understand me better. I can't blame him for worrying about my sudden change. Apart from Roy, Sebastian has always been someone I can trust and confide in. He's my brother-in-law after all. But unlike Roy, we've got the same upbringing, the same education, the same background, the same connections in the Netherlands, and the same title. And while I love Roy as a friend, Sebastian is like the older brother I never had. And I must confess, I couldn't have imagined my sister getting married to anyone but him.

"It's better if I don't," I tell him more politely as I turn left, following the GPS route.

But Sebastian can read me like no one else. "Did you speak to her about it?" I can't find the will to answer his question though. And Sebastian knows it. "I mean, she's gonna be your wife. Don't you think she should know about your previous lifestyle?"

"I told you—it belongs in the past."

"Van Dieren..." he teases with a smile. "I know you better than you do."

"I've changed," I lie. But it's better to tell him that. "I can live without it."

"Alright. If you say so… Good luck with that." He turns his head to his side, observing through the car window the many trees covering miles and miles ahead on either side of the road. Letting out a sigh, Sebastian seems to be engrossed in his thoughts as he starts shaking his head.

Curiosity getting the best of me, I ask him with a chuckle, "You sighing at the view?"

"It's just…" Turning his face to me, he observes me quietly for a moment before fessing up, "Man, I can't believe you're getting married. It feels weird, ya know. I never thought you'd ever settle down."

"Oh," I utter, not expecting such a direct answer. "I always told you I would."

"Yeah, but she was seven at the time." We share a laugh, recalling the day I told him about the incident at Roy's house.

"Well, I promised her I'd marry her, and I like to keep my promises. You know that." Keeping my hands on the steering wheel, I turn right, and, according to the GPS, we should be nearly there.

Sebastian presses his lips together, considering me. "What if she'd have fallen in love with someone else though?"

The idea sounds terrifying at first, but I tell him, "That's actually what I hoped for."

Cocking his head, Sebastian looks at me with deep furrows creasing his brow. "I don't get it…"

"I love her in a way I can't explain." And I have no idea why on Earth I just confessed that to him. Maybe it's the privacy of the car, and the fact that it's just the two of us here, that makes me feel so at ease. "If she had met someone else—someone in her league—then I'd have just remained her godfather and stood by her side, protecting her as I promised I would." I pause for a beat, observing his expression. "But I had to be present in her life. I had to at least come back." I sound cheesy as fuck, and we both know it. Clearing my throat and switching to another subject, I ask, "By the way, um, what's the name of that castle where you held your wedding reception?"

Giving me a quick smile, Sebastian promptly answers, "De Haar?"

"Ah, yes, um, do you think it's available on the fifth of December for ours?"

His smile keeps growing, and his face beams with joy. "Of course it is. I will take care of it myself."

Looking at him, I can't help but give him a big grin in return. "Thanks." And as he continues observing me, I know there's something else tickling his fancy. "What?"

"That's where you want to turn her into a woman?"

My eyes widen in shock, and I can't help but chuckle at his question. Of all the questions he could've asked, this seems like the weirdest of all. Does Sebastian really think Petra is still a virgin? Does he think we don't sleep in the same bed? Didn't Julia tell him about the miscarriage? My heart squeezes simply at the memory of it, making it difficult to even breathe. I press the brake as I close my eyes for a moment, focusing on my breathing.

"Are you alright?"

I swallow hard, taking a few more beats to breathe. "Julia didn't tell you?"

"Tell me what?" he asks with squinted eyes, waiting impatiently for an answer. "You know Julia. She's full of secrets."

Looking at the GPS, I see we are finally arriving at our destination. "Nothing. It belongs in the past…" I tell him as I turn right again, before driving straight ahead for the last mile.

"C'mon, you're really gonna keep secrets from me? After everything we've gone through?"

"I'm sorry, it's really personal," I say, having no desire to discuss any of it. It's too soon for that.

"More personal than what happened twenty years ago?"

I twitch at his question. Not even your family and best friends should know the darkest side of you. And for an instant, I forgot how deep Sebastian's been in my whole life—him and everyone else. That's one of the reasons why I decided to leave the family office and start my own hedge fund with Roy. I ponder if I should tell him the truth or not, but if I don't, he will most likely ask Julia and she'll tell him anyway. It's pointless hiding it from him.

"Petra and I lost a baby." I pause for an instant, but I can't control the gravity of my voice. "She had a miscarriage in the accident."

"Fuck," he blurts out instantly. "I didn't know that." Sebastian glances out the window and remains speechless for a while. In situations like these, there are indeed no words to be spoken. Then he turns his attention back to me, and I hear him say, "I'm sorry. Um, I knew about the coma and the accident, but not the miscarriage."

"It's alright." Another lie. But this one hurts more that I'd like to admit. Finally, I can see Mark, the landowner, as he stands in front of his big fence, waiting for us to arrive. "Well, here we are."

As Mark opens the fence, we drive into the open yard, and I park the car where he instructs me to. After shutting off the engine, silence fills the space between Sebastian and me. I close my eyes for an instant, rubbing tiredly at my eyelids to get rid of all the gloomy thoughts haunting me. But I know he's witnessing all of this, which makes it even worse.

"Alex, you're like a brother to me, you know that." He puts a hand on my shoulder. "What's going on? You know that whatever you tell me, it stays between us. You've got my entire loyalty."

I never talk to anyone about my fiancée or her medical state. This is not only private, but also very personal to me. Especially when it comes to her mental health. I don't discuss it, not even with Roy. But keeping such heavy secrets inside can be quite a burden and even damaging to one's health. So, taking a deep breath, I tell him, "According to her physician, Petra hasn't been able to move on yet. She has what's called survivor guilt." And I see the change in him as my words sink in. "And, um, we've had a few arguments because of the pill. She's been trying to skip days, and I couldn't figure out why, but it's probably to fill the void of our loss." Talking about something so damn personal is hard, but it feels incredibly satisfying and liberating to do so. As I see the landowner looking in our direction, I nod at him, and say, "Alright, let's go. Mark is waiting for us."

"She's also very skinny to get pregnant," Sebastian comments before I can open my door. "Does she eat properly?"

"Um, from time to time," I disclose, a bit surprised that he would touch on such a delicate matter. Although one would have to be blind not to see that she's lost a few pounds. "Petra has agoraphobia," I tell him. "She can keep it under control with Xanax, but this kind of disorder can also affect eating habits."

"Oh... And is this curable?"

"It's like any mental illness," I answer. "Treatment helps you to get better, but it can come back and get worse."

"Thanks for telling me all this." Sincerity fills his eyes and voice, bringing a quick smile of appreciation to my lips. "We haven't had a proper talk in such a long time," he points out.

I know Sebastian perfectly well. And I know the hunt was just a pretext to have a "proper talk" and cover all the delicate subjects we couldn't discuss by phone. Subjects like those my mom brought up yesterday...

I put a hand on his shoulder, returning the gesture before getting out of the car in a quick move. Then we go and shake hands with Mark, who gives us a map of his five hundred acres of land along with a brief explanation of the trails and fauna.

"We've spotted a male bear right here." He points on the map where a red dot is. "It's near the stream. There is plenty of food around, and he tends to go there at this time of the day. I suspect there is a den nearby too."

"Thank you, Mark. I really appreciate it."

"Good luck. And if you manage to catch him, don't forget to call me."

"Will do." I shake his hand once more. "Thanks."

We go to the truck and grab our rifles and jackets. And without further ado, we head into the woods.

After a couple of minutes marching through the trees and following the path Mark had indicated, Sebastian asks, "Did your Mom tell you about the interview?"

Ah, I was starting to wonder when he'd bring this up. "Yes, she did," I reply, keeping it short.

"And, um, did you see it?"

"I haven't, no. She just said that Tess made some remarks about Julia."

"And the media is loving it," he confesses. "They are following every bit of the case."

"The case?" I feign my interest in it.

"Margaret didn't tell you?"

"No…" Although I didn't even bother to ask her.

"Jan and his wife are divorcing," he announces. "She's being represented by a lawyer that works with Tess."

And I stop walking for a moment. Jan is a longtime friend of our families, a member of several clubs we are part of, and a close friend of Sebastian and me. Needless to say, knowing he's going through a divorce makes me want to call him straightaway. "No way? Are you serious?" As he nods, I add, "Fuck… They used to be so in love."

"It's a messy divorce." Sebastian stops walking too, and, as he looks me in the eye, he says, "He's been convicted of marital rape, and Julia is now reviewing his appeal."

I gape in total awe. "What?" Talk about a messy divorce… "You can't be serious. How do you even prove that?"

"No idea. I think the judge just wanted to make a point. It's most likely political. But if Julia doesn't do something, Jan will serve two years in prison."

"I can't believe it," I tell him, shaking my head as I draw in a breath. "Well, I'm sure Julia will take care of it." In an effort to close the subject, I start walking again.

Sebastian replies with a smile and follows closely beside me. After a few minutes of silence, I hear him ask, "Um, does Petra still talk to her mother?"

The question makes me squint my eyes. "Not that I'm aware of. Why?"

"Well…" He pauses for a beat, considering me. "I just wanted to know what kind of relationship she has with her…"

Ah, the real reason why he mentioned Jan's case. "Petra doesn't talk to her, since Tess is against us being together."

"Good…" He nods, and as I look at him, I notice a faint smile settling on his lips. "Very good."

My brows crease together as I can see that Sebastian is engrossed in thought. "May I ask why you wanted to know?"

"I just…" He lets his words trail off as we keep walking through the woods. "I just wanted to make sure she won't miss her."

But I grab his arm, stopping him immediately. "Hey, there is no need for that."

With an inquiring look, his attention goes first to his arm, which I release at the realization of my impulse. "I'm not saying I will do something," he replies, his tone just as calm as before. "At least, not for now…" But this time it comes out heavier, carrying a darkness beyond what I could have imagined.

"Sebastian," I snap. Despite facing each other, our expressions remain unreadable, the tension between us palpable. "Tess might be a threat, but she hasn't done anything."

"Until you marry her daughter," he ripostes, his eyes never leaving mine. "You know what's at stake, right?"

"I know…" Breaking eye contact, I have to empathize with his concerns. I'd have done the same if I were in his position. "I'm still hoping I can dissuade her before that."

Sebastian cracks a quick chuckle. "Right, that woman won't stop until we…" But he stops before unleashing the rest—and I'm grateful that he does so. "Anyway, let's keep moving. We need to find that bear."

While Sebastian keeps walking, focused on the hunt, the idea that he would actually do something to Tess has left a bitter taste in my mouth and a terrible knot in my stomach.

"Look!" Sebastian shouts in a whisper, bringing me back to reality. He points his index finger at the black bear standing on the other side of the river, casually drinking from the water. The animal is still far away from us, although maybe ten more steps and Sebastian will be good to shoot. We are approaching the feeding area that Mark pointed out, and with some luck, we might even see some more bears around. The excitement running through him makes me smile as we silently move closer to our target. "Isn't he majestic?" he asks, marveling at his prey. "It's gonna make a great addition to your trophy room." He pats me before jokingly adding, "But I want my name on it."

I see him quietly pointing his rifle and inspecting the target through the riflescope. He's too far away though. There is at least seventy-five percent chance he will miss it if he tries to shoot now.

"We are too far," he says, lowering the rifle. "We have to hide behind that tree."

Looking in my riflescope, I briefly check the target, adjusting the magnification. It's a mature male for sure, suitable for harvest. And while I don't see any issue with that, Petra's voice is now haunting me. It's a life! A bear has the right to live, just like you! I remember her shouting. We silently get behind the trunk, where Sebastian lies on the ground. From where he is, the view to the bear is unobstructed, and he should make it with a broadside shot.

"Perfect," I hear him saying as he looks through the riflescope. But a flash of Petra's angry expression travels through me again, and I know if I don't do something right now, she will be utterly devastated.

Standing behind Sebastian, I take my iPhone out and simply press the ring bell. The sound breaks through the woods, ending with our perfect silence. The bear's attention perks up instantly, and his eyes drift in our direction, searching out where the noise came from, and a second later, our target runs away.

"Fuck," Sebastian chides. "What was that?"

"I'm sorry—I thought my phone was on silent."

"He's gone now," he rebukes, standing up from the ground. Drawing in a breath and exhaling, he observes me quietly and asks, "She asked you to do it, huh?" He knows me so well. And I'm not even sure my expression says otherwise. "Wow. And you're not even married," he says, head shaking, before he starts to walk back to where we came from. "Alright, I don't want you to be punished if you bring a carcass home."

"Don't exaggerate," I brush him off.

"Really?" He stands still, observing me for a second. "And what about our duck hunting in the winter? Are you gonna need her permission?"

"I…" As much as I know it's gonna hurt, I've got to tell him the truth. "I don't think I'll be able to hunt anymore, Sebastian. I can join you, but I won't be able to shoot."

"But you used to love hunting. We used to do it every year." His stare goes to the ground, as he seems to be thinking something through before it drifts back up to me. "You spent ten years with Amanda, yet she never prevented you from hunting."

"I know, but Petra is a vegetarian. This goes against everything she stands for."

"Yeah, but you aren't," he replies just as fast. "She's imposing her views on you. Soon enough, she'll dictate what you can and cannot eat."

I must say, his bewilderment is pretty fun to watch. And just to horrify him a bit further, I say, "Actually, when it's only the two of us, we just eat vegetarian."

He blinks twice, containing the urge to gape, and his expression is as amusing as I expected. "Are you serious?"

I force myself not to laugh, and reveling in my little game, I keep going, "I don't mind. In Aspen, I spent a week eating vegetarian, and I survived."

"Oh boy," he mumbles, rolling his eyes. Then a rush of air leaves his mouth as he shakes his head. "See? With Amanda, you always remained yourself."

"Amanda and I had a different arrangement," I remind him once more.

"And that arrangement was good for you," he presses on. "You were always in control, but now? Sorry, buddy, but not anymore."

"Well, Petra and I don't have any arrangement to begin with," I riposte as we keep strolling through the woods.

"Oh, she definitely has one with you, even if you know nothing about it," Sebastian unleashes. I frown at his comment. "She knows she can control you with her sweet little voice and smile. Petra is not stupid—she knows how to get what she wants."

"C'mon, Petra is not controlling me." But I know I'm just fooling myself.

"Well, she proposed, she decided the date of your wedding, she doesn't want you to hunt, she dictates what you eat in your own house…"

"The things one does for love…" I chuckle. And while Sebastian seems to be utterly outraged, I'm pretty okay with everything he mentioned.

"My relationship with Petra is different from the ones I had before. And that's exactly what I like about it," I tell him, hoping to close the subject once and for all. Damn it, I shouldn't have opened up to him in the first place.

But Sebastian doesn't seem to get it. "And how did she even find out about the trophy room? You told me no one knew about that place."

Letting out a sigh, annoyed at his insistence, I mumble, "Most likely Maria told her."

"And now your own employees are loyal to her? Soon enough, she'll be like Margaret, and you will be Hendrik."

"Enough," I bark. "Dad deserved it. I will never cheat on my wife."

"That's not what I—"

"Look, I appreciate your concerns. But don't ever compare us to my parents again."

I've never raised my voice to Sebastian before. And I hope I never have to do it again. With so much friction between us, we leave the woods in a painful silence, and, even worse, we are both too proud to apologize.

CHAPTER 12

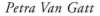

Petra Van Gatt

There is one thing I'm getting pretty used to in this house, and that is the comfy sofa in Alex's office. I've started a habit of lying there and reading while listening to a jazzy playlist or just spending time on the phone with Emma, which is what I'm currently doing. All of a sudden, though, I hear a few knocks on the door and I put my call on mute, right before Maria walks in. "Miss?" she says as she stands in the doorway. "Mr. Van Dieren would like to talk to you. May I escort you?"

Oh! He's finally back? "Um, sure." Putting my iPhone back to my ear, I say to Emma, "I've got to go. I'll call you later."

"Good luck," she says before hanging up.

To my disgust, Maria escorts me again to the most horrible room in this house—the trophy room. I'm enraged simply at the idea that he wants to meet me there again.

She knocks out of politeness and, at the sound of his approval, opens the door, inviting me in.

As I walk in, I see him leaning against the antique wooden desk, his head slightly down as he looks absently at the floor. At least he had the decency to change his attire to a casual one.

"Where's the bear?" I ask, moving closer to him.

His eyes travel up to my face, and, to my surprise, his expression is unreadable. "Sebastian missed it," he replies.

"And you?"

"I didn't shoot." I smile immediately, but not him. His tone and face are unusually grave. He paces slowly in my direction and then stops right in front of me, glaring at me for some unknown reason. "And I hated not being able to, Petra."

Oh, he's still annoyed because of the hunt? I do my best not to roll my eyes at his comment. "Sorry," I brush off. But in my mind, I'm doing a happy dance at the idea that I saved a poor bear.

"Look me in the eye." Not that I want to, but I do so to avoid a useless argument between us. "Now tell me, how did you find this room?"

Uh, oh. "I found it by myself."

"I'm gonna repeat the question."

Jeez, my heart starts thundering, and my gaze drops to the floor. "Look at me," he demands.

I meet his frigid glare again, but it's becoming quite uncomfortable to do so. "How did you find this room? Last chance to tell me the truth," he warns.

My breathing becomes heavy, and I'm sure I'm blushing a sharp shade of red as I keep staring into his blue eyes. Nevertheless, I swallow my anxiety and say, "I told you, I found it by myself."

But he knows I'm lying. Studies have shown that liars' pupils often dilate when they're telling a lie, and mine must have betrayed me a long time ago.

Blowing out a breath, he moves his hands behind his back and his gaze drops to the floor for a moment. Then, as they raise up again to meet mine, he says, "Miss Van Gatt…"

Wow. He hasn't addressed me so formally in such a long time that it feels weird and awkward hearing my surname out of the blue.

"You've really crossed the line this time." Oh gosh! I swallow dryly at his statement. What does that even mean?

His voice is calculated, cold, yet laced with so much disappointment that I feel tempted for a moment to apologize and tell him the truth. Then I can't help but wonder if he's gonna cancel our engagement just because of a little lie. No, he wouldn't do that!

"Very well…" he mumbles as he ponders something. "Take off your clothes."

My heart freezes at his request. "What? Here?"

"Yes, here."

His answer has my blood boiling, and I snap, "Or else what?"

"Or else Maria is fired."

"No!" I implore. "You can't do that."

"Then do as you are told."

Such a fucking asshole, I think to myself. But I will never let Maria get fired. That woman and her family have dedicated their whole lives to serving the Van Dierens, and I know it'd break her heart if she had to leave because of me. "Okay, I… I'll take them off."

With shaky hands, I first reach down to my All Stars and remove them. Then I unbutton and unzip my jeans, quite self-conscious at the embarrassment I feel. My fiancé keeps watching without an ounce of enjoyment. And for some odd reason, I was expecting some sort of appreciation for the show I'm giving him. I don't know, maybe a smile? But no—his expression remains just as severe. The same as he had when he found Emma and me behind bars. Taking a deep breath in and out, I push my jeans down, until I lift one leg and then the other to remove them completely and drop them on the floor. After that, I reach for my sweater and pull it off. And here I am standing in my knickers in his cold, disgusting trophy room and the thought of it makes me hate him even more. But instead of cursing him, I ask, "And now?"

Without an ounce of joy, he says, "Your panties too."

Fuck you! I want to protest, chuckle, tell him to fuck off, but I don't. Maria's employment is at stake, and I will do whatever it takes to keep my promise to her.

I leave my sweater on the floor before reaching for the waistband of my cotton underwear. It's not even a sexy lace thong. Nope. Just a comfy pair of knickers that I brought from home. I push them slowly down my legs, and I'm pretty conscious of the fact that he is watching me do so.

Once they are in my hands, I put them on top of my clothes and say, "Done." But I don't even dare to look at him. My gaze goes to the floor—it feels safer.

And I wish I were deaf, so I didn't hear him say, "Bend over the table."

Not a fucking chance! I look in front of me at the rustic dark wood table, and then at the elephant head right behind it.

For a moment, I forget to breathe, but honestly, I would rather faint than have to look at the dead animals surrounding me while I'm bent over that table as he does God knows what.

Since I'm still conscious and alive, I've got no option but to obey. My heart is stuck in my throat, but I slowly walk toward the table, bending over as he asked.

In that moment, I'm expecting maybe the sound of his zipper opening, but after waiting a few more seconds, I hear only his footsteps walking in my direction and then him standing still at my side.

"Bottom up," he demands.

My ass up? Fuck... I want to cry at the most horrendous moment in my life. Sticking my bare bottom up in the freezing air of this room, I keep my legs straight and my arms stretched out on the surface. There are no words to describe how vulnerable and exposed I feel with my bottom presented to him in this manner. I wonder if I will hear his pants unfastening now. But again—no zipper, no belt, nothing. As one of his hands rests on my lower back, I only feel warmth coming from his other palm as he rubs my buttocks in a circular motion.

"You've got such a beautiful ass," he praises in a low voice, carrying the same severity in his tone. Alex keeps caressing them with such a gentle touch that it starts to make me drenched. Oh jeez, arousal starts rising between my legs at the feel of his presence, his energy, his body, and the fact that we haven't made love for such a long time is becoming unbearable. "Mmm..." I quickly lick my lips while he massages me. Heat keeps spreading, but so does the sexual tension between us. My heart is thundering, and I wonder what the hell is going on. As I'm about to ask him just that, I suddenly feel his palm leave my right cheek, only to smack it a second later.

"Ow!" I chide at the blow.

No one—literally no one—in my entire life has ever dared to spank me! What the fuck is wrong with him?! Then there's nothing but a light caress over my buttocks to soothe the sting. This feels really good though. But then his hand leaves my butt again, only to strike it a second later, this time on my left cheek. "Ow..." I wince, the sting rising on the other side, but so does my wetness.

"You're gonna get ten swats for lying and eight more for your attitude this morning," he explains, his voice strident but not angry. "Do you understand?"

But I don't answer. I can still barely believe what's happening, and my heart is hammering nonstop, my body sweating.

"Petra?"

"Yes," I tell him, knowing if I don't comply, Maria will get fired, and that's definitely not an option for me. "I do."

"Yes, please," he commands.

"What?!" Another blow. "Ouch!" I cannot for the life of me believe he's asking me to answer him with "please."

"You heard me very well," he scolds. "I want you to say 'yes, please' before you take the rest of your punishment with grace and composure."

I'm left speechless at his statement. What happened to him? Was it Sebastian who told him to do this? How am I even supposed to take this with grace and composure? Saying "please" would make it seem like he's doing me a favor. Thinking a bit more, though... okay, maybe he is since Maria won't get fired. Swallowing my pride, I simply repeat those words for the sake of having it done. "Yes, please." Another swat. "Fuck!"

"Stop swearing," he snaps back.

Four have landed already, but I can't fathom how to endure fourteen more. "Eighteen is a lot." That's the only thing I manage to say. Then I realize it's my own age, and I wonder if he did it on purpose.

And I feel another strike landing on my right cheek. "F —!" I say the rest between clenched teeth.

"Did you say something?"

"Five," I shout, making it seem like I'm counting them.

"Good." Another smack, this time in the middle of my backside, and I can't help but bend my knees at the blow. "Do you want to start again?"

"No," I whine.

"Then keep your legs straight." And as much as I want to disobey, it seems wiser to do what I'm told.

Smack! Smack! Smack! Smack!

Alex delivers four blows across my cheeks in such record time that my brain doesn't even have time to fully process the impact. I whine at the pain, but I think my butt has become numb by now. I feel like the quick strikes hurt less than those he takes more time to carry out. Maybe because of the anxiety that anticipates each blow. After ten swats, his hand rubs warm circles on my cheeks, soothing me and getting me ready for what is yet to come. His touch shouldn't drench me though. I should be mad at him, not getting wetter! He then stops for a moment, and I feel his fingers glide between my thighs while I'm panting from the pain and the heat.

"You're wet," he says, letting me know that it isn't a secret.

"I can't help it," I tell him in a whisper as I realize that this punishment has been more erotic and intimate than I thought. Then I feel his fingers parting my labia and entering me. I part my legs a bit, welcoming the insertion of first one finger, then two. "Mmm…" I chew my bottom lip, closing my eyes at my growing rapture as he pushes his two fingers farther in and then out. It's hard to stay still as he fingers me. My hips start following the rhythm of his thrusts, and I know I'm not the only one enjoying it. "Ah…" The sound of my moans seems to incite him even more as he keeps his fingers pressed inside me, reveling in my moisture. Then his two fingers leave my pussy, but only to move up to my clit, where he starts rubbing it. "Ahhh…" A whimper of pleasure escapes my lips, and I feel myself getting more and more drenched. Jeez, I can't control the climbing orgasm, and my legs bend at the stimulation. His other hand fondles my chest before cupping my right breast. My nipples tighten, my body shivers, and my thighs tremble at the electrifying sensation of his fingers owning my swollen clit. "Oh gosh…" I'm gonna come at any moment if he keeps going. And Alex does keep going, increasing the pressure and friction on my flesh to leave me in a trance. "Oh my…" My heart is pounding against my ribs, my parted lips pant, and I'm feeling close, so damn close…

"Come for me," he growls. The sensuality of his demand catches me off guard, turning me into a hot mess, and a flush of ecstasy hits me hard. My legs quiver, struggling to hold still at the imminent orgasm. My fluids have probably dampened his whole hand by now, but I couldn't care less. A burst of electricity explodes from within me, and I fall onto the surface of the table, my legs melting, no longer able to hold my weight at the immensity of my gratification. Regaining my breath, I can't help but say, "That felt so damn good…"

Alex takes me by the hips, putting me back in position. "Eight more to go."

A shiver rolls down my spine at his sharp tone. And I'm brought back to reality at the smashing sound of his palm against my right cheek. *Smack!* "Ow…"

Either he added intensity to this swat, or my skin has become more sensitive, leaving the sting to feel like a blaze! Knowing there is more coming, I brace myself for the next one and shut my eyes. *Smack!* This one lands on my left cheek, and it's just as merciless as the previous one. Damn it! My bottom feels on fire, and I'm panting. I resist the urge to reach back because I know it'd be worse. Fortunately, Alex starts gently massaging my skin around the redness, relieving the pain a bit while I recover my breath and calm down. My heartbeat keeps hammering, apprehensive for the next blow. *Smack!* Alex delivers another strike, this time landing across both cheeks. "Ow…" My body twitches, but I make a conscious effort to stay in position as much as I can. My eyes remain shut, but the tears are resting on my eyelids. Five more to go, I think to myself.

Smack! Smack! Smack! Smack! Smack!

"Ow!" I whine and curse at the intensity, but I'm glad he delivered them so quickly. My butt must be covered in a sharp shade of red by now as it burns like hell, and I slide a hand behind my back to relieve the sting.

"Your punishment is done," he announces, but I don't dare to stand up without permission. I focus on my breathing instead. And although I can't see it, I've got the firm sensation that he's taking off his shirt. "But you still owe me one."

And for some obscene reason, I decide to remain still and bent over, curious at what he'll do next. Regardless of my burning butt, if it's to make me come again, I'm all for it. Then I hear his belt unfastening and his zipper going down. Knowing he's undressing makes my heart thump wildly against my chest and my breath quicken. Then I feel his hands lingering on my back and going all the way down to my ass, his thumbs stroking me softly like a feather. "You have no idea how hot you look."

Oh my goodness… I part my lips, drawing a gasp at his praise. Then his thumb goes in between my buttocks, where he starts rubbing the most intimate part of me in a circular motion. "Mmm…" Pressing my lips tightly together, I shut my eyes, reveling in it.

"Do you remember in Aspen?" he asks. "In the shower?"

Of course I do. His question makes me picture everything we did there. "Yes…" I breathe, my hips twitching as they follow his rhythm. It had been so wild and intense, how could I forget? At that moment, though, I no longer feel his thumb rubbing me, but his palms spreading my cheeks wide apart, leaving my hole exposed. "Alex!"

"Stay still," he orders softly. And before I can say anything further, he sticks his tongue right there and starts licking me. SWEET LORD!

A moan leaves my throat at the unexpected intrusion. "Ah…" He has never been there with his mouth before! And my heart is about to explode at all the mixed emotions consuming me. I try hard to stay still, but damn, how can I not shiver with him eating me like that? Each deep, luscious lick sends my head spinning. My pussy is dampening again at his depraved actions, and pleasure overpowers me. "Oh gosh…" I cry out as his tongue delves deeper, lapping and tasting my hole so sensually that I rotate my hips in a wave against his mouth, drunk on every sensation he's making me feel. Frantic with need, Alex doesn't hold back, and his hands cup each side of my hips, pulling me tight into his face. A low grunt escapes his throat as he keeps eating my ass with unparalleled devotion. Holy shit! His tongue on me, licking and sucking every inch of my flesh, is sending me into a deep state of pure ecstasy.

"Oh yes…" I push my butt into him even more while his wet tongue digs deeper, making slurping sounds as he keeps licking me. Fuck, there is nothing more powerful and satisfying than a man worshipping his woman like this. I drag some precious air into my lungs as my body is a blazing fire, ready to erupt. Desire takes over me, and I feel the urge to feel so much more than his tongue. My breath comes out in short gasps, so I simply mumble, "Please…" Taking another breath, I say, "I need more…"

His mouth leaves my hole, but not without leaving traces of saliva on my flesh first. As he leans over me, his lips go to my ear while his hands cup my tits, before he asks in a whisper, "What do you want? Tell me…" His voice is filled with lust, and I know he's just as hungry as I am. But I feel too shy to be crude and blunt, and somehow, I can't find the right words to tell him.

"You." That's all I manage to say.

"Be more explicit," he commands, before nibbling the shell of my ear. "What do you want me to do?"

And I know he's playing with my timidity and my lack of bluntness. "You know…"

"You want me to fuck your tight little asshole, huh?" His breath is ragged, and I can taste the sexual tension in his words. "You miss it, don't you?"

I can't help but moan at his question. His disgusting vulgarity and attitude shouldn't make my body simmer with rapture. "Yes…"

"Then say it."

"I can't…" I grow desperate at his insistence.

"Of course you can. I need to hear it," he insists. His lips go to my cheek, lingering on my skin, and his energy is burning with desire to do exactly what we are both thinking.

Then his lips come close, so close to tasting mine that I know he's teasing me just to drive me to the edge. His right hand leaves my breast and moves up to my neck. "Petra, say it." Oh jeez, I feel like the lamb trapped by the big wolf.

Armed with some audacity and throwing all manners out the window, I say very slowly, "I want you to… fuck… my tight little asshole."

"Fuck," he mutters under his breath, but loud enough for me to hear it. His right hand leaves my neck and travels all the way down to between my thighs.

"Ahh…" A little moan escapes me at the feel of his fingers now exploring me.

"Jeez, you're soaking." Well, that's a bit obvious. His hand lingers around my opening, and I know my fluids are all over his fingers. He then goes back to my ass, and I feel a greasy finger penetrating me. I can't help but gasp at the intrusion. "Look at that, it's already in."

My pussy spasms in response to his words while his finger starts pushing in, slow and deep. I bounce forward at the pressure, but his other hand puts me back in position. "Oh my…" I press my lips tightly together, feeling quite sharply his finger going deeper inside me.

"You like that, huh?"

I'm panting, barely able to reply, but I breathe a feeble, "Yeah" between moans filled with pleasure.

His finger leaves me, and I know exactly why. My heart is thundering, a bit anxious and apprehensive to feel him. After all, we haven't done this since that night in Aspen. And while I can't see him, I've got the firm sensation that he's now palming his cock. To my surprise, though, he drags the tip up to my wet pussy.

"Oh gosh…" I shiver, feeling his tip rubbing around my lips. But he doesn't push himself in; nope, his tip, now fully coated with my juices, travels up to the other hole. And I wince, feeling a bit of the head pushing inside me. Fuck, he feels so damn big, and this is so much more painful than last time. I always feel so weak, fragile, and defenseless in this position, but I'm also impatient for him to take me entirely.

"Ssh…" he utters, soothing me as he rubs my back. Alex remains still and motionless, giving me some time to adjust to his girth. "Relax…" He then thrusts a bit farther in, and I'm amazed how smoothly it goes. I guess my fluids are a good lube. "See how easily I go in…" He hovers over my back, and I feel his warm lips placing kisses on my spine. My teeth bite into my lip, reveling in every second of his touch, and dragging some air into my lungs, I shut my eyes in blissful rapture. "You're so damn tight…"

I chuckle at his comment. "I can feel that."

With parted lips, I unleash another moan at feeling such a big part of him buried inside me. "I missed fucking your ass so much," he shamelessly states. His right hand grabs my neck from behind, while his left hand keeps holding me at the waist. He then fills me completely by rocking inside me straight and deep. Fuck. And I can't help but whimper a bit. "Ow…" By now, I not only feel the sting on my butt, but also his length gaping my hole. My body is shaking under his, and I'm too drunk on a mixture of pain and pleasure to fully process everything he's doing.

He adjusts himself inside of me and positions his cock at a deeper angle. "It's all inside now." His fingers tighten on my neck and waist while his hips keep thrusting back and forth in quick, shallow moves. Each one of his thrusts leaves me on the brink of pure bliss. His passion is all-consuming, his energy so raw, intense, a force that drives me to the edge of erotic madness. "You're such a good slut."

"Oh my…" My face goes red hearing his words, and a rush of heat takes over me. I sigh in euphoria. It sounds like a compliment, and I take it as such. "Don't stop…"

His cock twitches at my comment, and I hear him groaning behind me. I know he liked it, and at this precise moment, all I really want is to feel him coming inside me. After all, he hasn't done that since I woke up. He keeps ramming in and out, leaving me a hot mess, my orgasm building inside me.

"Ah…" There's nothing hotter than hearing him moan, especially knowing I'm the reason for it. This man drives me crazy, and I love how he takes full control of me and my body. There is something extremely sensual about it. Something I can't explain. Maybe it's wrong, shameful, or immoral. But it feels so natural to give myself entirely to him. Holy fuck… I'm so close…

"Ah…" Alex keeps banging me repeatedly against the desk. His thrusts are hurried, impatient, and more bestial than our first time. His pelvis taps against my buttocks, and I'm reminded of the sting at every touch. My body is so used to having him inside by now that I let myself go, consumed by nothing more than the insanity of the moment. Holy fuck. I hear him groaning again, and a massive smile fills my face as I can feel his orgasm unloading inside me. And the simple thought of it makes me reach new highs. I cry out as I explode from the inside in a thousand little pieces and then collapse on the desk, totally exhausted by the immensity of my pleasure. I hear nothing but our heartbeats, pulsing hard inside our chests. At this moment, nothing else matters, just us. I breathe slowly in and out, taming my unsteady pulse.

After we both calm down and recover our senses, Alex removes himself from me very slowly. I feel a bit sad for it to be over. I can already feel his cum dripping down my ass, and once I stand up, it only gets worse. As I turn to kiss him, he seems to be in another galaxy, his face devoid of any expression as he simply orders, "Now go to your room." And he starts rubbing his eyes tiredly with his fingers.

I blink twice at his coldness. Why is he behaving like this? I feel the urge to ask him what's wrong, and to reassure him, let him know everything was fine. But I don't do any of it. Sometimes it's better just to leave and give him some space. So I just gather my things, walk out the door, and rush to the bedroom.

There, I make sure to lie in bed on my stomach and have nothing covering my burning butt. And as I close my eyes and try to sleep, my mind ruminates nonstop about what I just went through. I'm beyond perplexed at Alex's behavior, and I don't even think the spanking was the worst part. No, the worst part was seeing his expression afterward. Like he was angry and disappointed at himself. Then, I hear two knocks on the door, but I can't find the will to answer.

"May I come in?" Oh, it's Maria.

"Not today," I mumble back without even turning. But instead, I hear Maria close the door and walk over. As she sits beside me, I see that she's holding a tube, and before I can ask her about it, she starts applying something on my redness. I twitch at the cooling effect. But the relief it provides is truly appreciated. It feels like those after-burn gels. Nothing but silence can be heard as she keeps applying more. Should I be surprised that she knows I got a spanking? I imagine Alex told her. And to be honest, I'm not in the mood to even ask her. The idea that she's taking care of my red bottom is humiliating enough.

"Thank you," she says in a whisper before standing up.

I know exactly what this thank you is for. And while Maria will keep her job, I know Alex won't trust her as much as before. And I'm not sure how I feel about it.

Then I hear the door opening and closing again, but instead of it being followed by silence, I hear someone else's footsteps walking in my direction. And by their pace and the cologne that starts invading my nostrils, I know perfectly to whom they belong.

As I feel another cooling texture being gently applied on my skin, I say half sleepily, "Maria already applied some."

"This one is better." An uncomfortable silence grows between us as he keeps rubbing my skin. "In a few hours, the redness will be gone." I don't feel like saying "thank you" or anything else though. "Petra?"

"Hmm?"

"I'd like to tell you something." He keeps his husky voice low, despite our being the only two in the room. My attention goes to his face, and I realize his expression is just as serious, grave, and laced with disappointment as before. But I can't understand why. His brows creasing together, he takes a morbid second before muttering, "I loved spanking you." His tone is laced with shame, and it seems like the truth is hurting him somehow. "I've pictured that moment many times in my mind—how it'd feel, how much you'd whine, how your ass would look afterward…" He closes his eyes for a second, letting out a breath while shaking his head. Then he looks at me again, his piercing blue eyes glued on mine, and says, "But reality turned out to be so much better." I blink twice, gaping at him, but I'm so stunned by his revelation that I remain speechless. "Your attitude at standing up for what you believe in, regardless of what others think, is truly remarkable." Okay, so Sebastian or Maria must have made some remarks about me. Alex pauses for a beat, considering me. And I see a faint smile settling on his lips. "I'm madly and terribly in love with every side of you, Miss Van Gatt."

Everything in me drops upon hearing this. My heart feels so tight right now that I jump on him and kiss him hard. Alex welcomes me with a little gasp as I press my lips to his, devouring his mouth. Then I look him in the eye and say, "And I'm just as madly and terribly in love with every side of you, Mr. Van Dieren."

He gives me one of his charming smiles—the one I'll never get tired of seeing. "I want to ask you something," he starts. "And before you say yes or no, I want you to think about it as long as you need to."

My brows raise, and I'm completely taken aback by his statement. "Um, okay."

Alex draws in a breath before saying, "I'd like your permission to discipline you from now on."

But my jaw falls again just as fast. "My what?"

Chuckling at my expression, he repeats, "Your permission—"

"I know," I cut him off as I close my eyes for a second, trying to find the best words to articulate what I'm thinking, but the only thing I manage to say is, "And, um, how do you intend to discipline me in the future?"

His smile twists into a racy one. I guess he was not expecting such a question. "Depends… If you do something really naughty, I might use the belt." Fuck, I nearly moan at his words, and I don't think I'm supposed to feel like that. "But you have to misbehave very badly for that…" Somehow it sounds like an invitation for me to do so. "I'll never do anything out of anger though. I want you to know that."

Before I can say something more, he presses his lips to my forehead. "Now get some sleep and let me know your decision when you have thought this through."

I close my eyes, reveling in his kiss as much as I can, and as I lie in bed, the sting feels nearly gone.

CHAPTER 13

Hudson Valley, September 13, 2020
Emma Hasenfratz

I've never looked forward to a polo lesson like I am today. With my parents and the housekeeper out, Yara and I will have the entire house to ourselves. Cameras are disconnected, and I've made sure the housekeeper stays in the city long enough, buying shit I don't need. As Yara gets out of the car, I notice she's already wearing a marine blue polo shirt, white breeches, and boots. Well, she truly lives for her passion. Her chauffeur goes to the trunk and takes out two big brown leather bags, which must contain her polo gear.

"Good morning, Ms. Hasenfratz." Her formal, icy tone is enough to make a flood of emotion erupt inside me and a dark desire in my pussy ache to come out.

Jeez, I feel soft like a marshmallow when she is around, and I'm pretty sure this bitch knows it. "Hey, Yara," I reply casually, trying to feign indifference to her charms.

"Where should I put the bags, Miss?" the chauffeur asks me. And judging by his tense shoulders, they seem pretty heavy.

"Oh sure, this way, please." I lead them to the changing room beside the stables. Yara enters first and takes a quick glance around at the modern and spacious design of the place, while her chauffeur is already headed toward the bench that sits in the center to put the bags there. Curiously enough, I notice she smirks once her eyes alight on my brand-new polo apparel resting on a chair beside the Italian shower, and I wonder what she's thinking.

"Thanks," Yara says as the chauffeur leaves. My breath quickens at the realization that there is only the two of us in the changing room. Fuck, I'm with Yara Van Lawick, alone in my changing room. Thank God for that engagement party. As I see Yara opening the first bag, I ask, "Um, what did you bring?"

She turns to face me, and as our eyes lock, she says, "Everything we need to have fun."

I let out a quick chuckle at her serious statement, but not her. Yara opens the first bag wide and takes out two polo sticks, two mallets, two pair of gloves, two helmets…

"Helmets?" I ask, nearly in outrage. "I've never fallen from a horse before. This is ridiculous." But I take my words back upon seeing her turn again, her squinted eyes dangerously censuring me as she holds a long leather whip.

"There are whips in polo?" I ask, my voice slightly shaky. I must sound like a dumbass right now, but my heartbeat is speeding up like crazy. And I can't seem to look away from the instrument between her hands.

"Yes," she says simply. "Don't you have riding crops in your stables?"

"I guess I do." The truth is, for the sake of horseback riding, I've never thought about using it. And I don't remember Petra using one either.

Yara is checking me out from top to bottom with a resting bitch face. "Get dressed. You have five minutes." And then she leaves the changing room, her order hanging in the air.

What? Bitch, no one tells me how long I have to get dressed! But at this point, I'm just batting my eyelids at the door she just crossed through. Well, she seems just as authoritative as her older brother. Must run in the family. My thoughts then go to her poor kids who have to deal with a mother like her.

I take my clothes off and put on the polo shirt, beige breeches, and brown boots I bought yesterday, while cursing under my breath at her attitude and praising my parents for being her precise opposite.

Stepping outside, I see Yara smoking a cigarette as she waits for me. Enjoying one without me? I huff at how rude that is.

"Ready," I snap.

She throws the cigarette away, not even bothering to ask me if I want one. My face is as angry as it gets, but she gives me a polite smile and brushes past me, returning to get her gear.

And I thought *I* was a spoiled brat—damn, this woman is the worst! Since I still have some manners, I ask, "Need some help?"

"Yes, please, you may put your helmet on, and get your gloves and polo stick."

Since she said "please" for once, I swallow my bitterness, put the idiotic helmet on, and follow her to the stables. Wait —why is she even leading the way in my house? "Do you know the way?" I ask her.

"I know where the entrance to the stables is, thanks."

* * *

"Your left thigh is not tightening enough in the saddle. That's why you can't turn properly and miss your offside shot," Yara explains right after my failed attempt to hit the ball at twenty yards. It seemed so easy though! Fuck, we've been here for at least thirty minutes, and I haven't been able to hit the ball once! Meanwhile, Mrs. Van Lawick did some gracious demonstrations of what an offside and nearside shot look like. Well, at least I had the pleasure of admiring her sculpted body in action.

"This is way harder than I thought," I say in my defense.

But Yara doesn't give a shit, and she is already showing me once more how to do the rotation. "See my thigh?" My eyes are again on her thighs, and I must have checked them out a thousand times by now. "It's tightening in the saddle, and my right one is gripping and pushing in. This gives me a strong, firm base on the saddle. And I'm confident enough to lean out, turn my shoulders wide, and make my shot without feeling like I'm gonna fall off." I nod, following every inch of her moves as she executes her shot and the stick head hits the ball.

Wow. It's pretty dope to watch, and from afar, it seems effortless. "Now go and repeat!"

I get back into position, and when Frodo starts trotting in the direction of the ball, I follow her instructions exactly. My left knee goes into the saddle, then my left thigh tightens into it, my right one grips and pushes in, and with a firm base, I lean out, turn my shoulders almost parallel to the horse, and my mallet goes up and then straight down to hit the ball. Damn! It worked! My eyes glow with excitement seeing the ball soar away, like, super far away.

"Finally!" I shout with joy at my small victory.

Her horse gallops in my direction, and she makes him stop inches from mine. "There is nothing like persistence and training. Good job."

I lick my lips at her praise. Just to hear another compliment from her, I'd be keen to spend the whole afternoon training.

"Now try to do a nearside forehand shot."

"Okay, but first, can you show me again how you move your thigh?" I ask with a hint of humor.

Without further ado, she does just that. But Yara is so focused on the demonstration that she doesn't even understand my underlying intention.

"Sure, so my right knee digs into the saddle, my right foot pushes into the right stirrup, and my left thigh grips the saddle and pushes in. This gives me more freedom and stability in order to reach out on the nearside."

My lips curve up as I let myself picture her body, this time completely naked in my Italian shower.

"Now go!"

But her loud voice is enough to startle me, and Frodo starts trotting by himself, following her command. *What the fuck, dude? You have to obey me, not her!* Since I wasn't focused, and this is a nearside shot, which needs more concentration to execute the rotation, needless to say, I miss the ball terribly.

"You're not focused! Repeat!"

Jeez, I'm getting tired of her shouting commands. I'm not a polo expert, for fuck's sake! Give me some time!

"Remember, you don't have to hit it hard! Keep your shot to twenty, thirty yards!" I hear her saying as I trot again in the direction of the ball.

My position seems stable enough, so I lean out and my mallet goes down and strikes the ball at around twenty yards.

"Yeah!" I say just above a whisper as I see the ball rolling away.

Then I push the reins and instruct Frodo to gallop toward Yara. As I reach her, I notice there's a smile on her lips. "Well done, Emma." And mine just gets bigger. "When you focus and follow my instructions, you can do wonders." I know she's talking about polo, but my eyes are drawn to her lips, and I imagine her saying that but for another reason. "Alright, let's take a break," she says, getting off her saddle.

I do the same, and we take our horses to tie them up at the entrance to the stables. Then I invite her inside the house and into the kitchen. After I take my helmet and gloves off, I open the fridge and grab two small bottles of water. "You want one?"

My question is hanging in the air as I observe Yara taking her helmet off carefully enough not to disarrange her ponytail. If there's a ladylike manner of taking a helmet off, Yara surely is the best representation of it. Then she removes her gloves with the same elegance, and, as my eyes fall on her hands, I squint upon seeing that she's got a tattoo on each wrist. Oh, I didn't expect Mrs. Van Lawick to be tattooed. I don't think I've seen them before, but I recall she was wearing a bracelet and a watch when she arrived, covering her wrists. I look a bit closer as she extends her hand to take the bottle—there's a black *X* inked in the center of her inner wrist. It's not too big, but visible enough to notice it.

"Thanks," I hear her saying, before she drinks a bit of her water.

"Nice tattoos."

She gives a quick glance at her left one, then her eyes land on mine and she just says, "Yours too."

I thought she would open up and tell me the meaning behind the letter *X*. After all, when it comes to mine, they all have a reason for being on my skin. So I ask, "I've never seen that type of tattoo before. What's the meaning behind it?"

Yara just replies with a side smile as she keeps observing me with her dark brown eyes. Then she takes another sip of her water, letting an awkward silence settle between us, like I asked a question I shouldn't have.

"It means I'm different," she replies, keeping it way too short for my liking.

"Oh, I've got one that says exactly that." I show her my left inner forearm, where it says, *In our differences lies our strength*, the quote written in italics on one single line. It's one of the first tattoos I got, but it's still my favorite one.

"You got that because of her?" And it doesn't take a genius to know who the *her* is that she's referring to.

"Yeah," I utter vaguely. "And you? You got them because of someone?"

Another question that Yara wishes I wouldn't have asked. She lets out an exasperated breath that makes me feel like I stepped over some sort of boundary.

"No," she replies back. "I didn't get them because of someone."

"So you just woke up one day and thought, 'Why not get the letter *X* tattooed on each of my wrists?'"

At this point, I know Yara is getting pretty pissed off by my insistence. All of a sudden, she steps closer and stands just inches from me. Then she meticulously observes every feature of my face, and, to my greatest surprise, the back of her fingers go to my cheek and she starts stroking it. Her touch is exciting and petrifying at the same time. It reminds me of one of the Bond villains stroking his white cat. "You know curiosity killed the cat, don't you?"

Fuck, I freeze on the spot as she says that. Not that I'm scared, but because I didn't see it coming. Playing along, I lock my eyes on hers and tell her, "I enjoy taking risks."

There is a trace of a smile filled with pride that lands on her lips. By now, this feels like a test. Yeah, she's testing me, my character, and my audacity.

"Don't play a game you can't win, Emma."

Oh boy, she's really testing me. My heart feels stuck in my throat, but I remain as stoic as possible. If there is one thing I'm pretty good at, it's games. And whatever is happening between us right now, it's electrifying, bizarre, and pretty exciting. The more I look at her, the more I want her mouth on mine, to taste her lips and feel her tongue tangle with mine. But the fucking truth is, I'm just too nervous to take the plunge, so instead I just lean over and whisper, "I may surprise you."

Her lips part slightly in astonishment, and her eyes drift down to my mouth. I swear, the tension shifts at that instant—it's sexual, visceral, and my heartbeat feels like it's about to jump out of my chest. She licks her lips. I swallow at the sight, and I'm this close to kissing her.

"The break is over."

But Yara's frigid voice crashes all my hopes, and the air between us cools down just as fast.

She turns her back on me like the bitch she is and leaves the kitchen. And while I'm left wet and hanging like a dumbass, I've got no options but to blink twice, mentally slap myself, and follow her. If this is a game, then we are at Yara one, Emma zero.

We take our horses again to the vast green field on my estate, and once Mrs. Van Lawick is back in her saddle, she's also back in polo trainer mode, or yeller, or whatever she is.

After another half an hour of training, my skills have truly improved, and despite the fact that she annoys the hell out of me, I must say, I feel way more confident as a horseback rider than before. Once Yara announces we are done for the day, we put the horses back in the stables and quietly return to the changing room.

There, Yara starts putting her polo gear into her bag, and as I watch her do so, it's clear to me that this day was just about polo, and nothing more. Jeez, when I thought for a second that the training was just an excuse for something else… What a fucking dumbass I was… She is married after all. What was I expecting? To get laid? I huff at how naive I was.

"Undress."

Huh? Did I hear her say something? My eyes land instantly on her as she's standing right in front of me. And I wonder if I'm not hearing voices in my head. "Did you say something?"

"Yes." Her tone carries the same authority it did during our polo session. "I want you undressed."

And her words feel like they settle in my stomach and catch fire. She demanded just like that, no explanation given whatsoever. It seems like just another command, like during our polo training. Fuck, Yara is playing again just like she did in the kitchen, and I'm not sure what I'm supposed to do. Play along and stand naked in front of her? She knows she's getting under my skin. She fucking knows that. Should I obey? I have never wanted to undress so damn fast, but I'm not in control of the situation and she knows it. If I decline, it means I lose—as simple as that. Why? Because Mrs. Van Lawick will retract herself, leave my house, and I'll never have another opportunity to play. My pussy is drenching at her words, my heartbeat pounding, and my mind wondering what she will do next. So I take my helmet off, my gloves, my boots, and the rest just follows. Yara doesn't flinch, doesn't move, or even blink. She remains observing me attentively as I strip my clothes off. And I must say I never imagined myself stripping for anyone's pleasure. When I think of a striptease, I think of those accompanied by idiotic dances and songs. And to me, it's ridiculous and lame.

My clothes are on the bench, and I'm barefoot and naked in front of her. Yara is still in full polo attire, and the contrast makes me feel exposed, and so damn anxious.

She inspects me like a general would inspect her troops, and I wonder for a second if she attended military school or something. Then she moves behind me, and I hear her breath approaching my ear, and then asking, "You wanna play?"

Her question gives me goosebumps, and my nipples harden at the tension that is emerging again.

There's not a thousand ways to say yes, but I don't want to sound desperate either, so I just mumble a lazy and nonchalant, "Yeah…"

All of a sudden, though, her hand is on my throat, and she pushes my head backward. "Don't talk to me like that ever again." Her voice is not loud, but it's steady and firm enough to make me freeze on the spot. "Try again." Okay, she definitely attended military school. Who in her right mind would take someone by the throat?

But, swallowing my pride, I stand straight, and, playing along, I give my answer in a more composed manner. "Yes, I do."

And while I can't see it, I've got the feeling that Yara is smiling at me, reveling in her little game. "Better." She brushes my hair to the side, leaving the nape of my neck exposed, and, leaning down, she presses her lips to my skin.

Jeez, I try not to shiver at her kiss, but it's harder than I thought. "Let's play, then…"

She turns me around, and, before I can say or do anything, she slams her mouth down on mine. *Oh my…* A flood of heat pulses through my body, and I whimper into her. This kiss is exactly what I imagined it'd be like—intense, raw, visceral, aggressive… But I want more than that, and as if she knows it, she reaches up and grabs the back of my head, pressing us closer together. Then, once our lips part, I hear her saying in a low voice, "Bend over the bench."

My body is simmering with rapture, and I can barely process her request. "What?"

"Didn't you say you want to play?" Her tone is filled with desire and lust, but I'm still not used to her blunt commands. Jeez, what does she have in mind?

"Yeah, but—"

"Your lesson is not over," she says, cutting me off. My eyes open wide, and as they lock onto hers, she adds, "So do as you are told."

For someone who spent her entire youth defying authority, it's hard to swallow her passive-aggressive tone, and while I'm curious enough to see how far she will go with her little game, I still have the tenacity to ask, "You gonna punish me, huh?" I pause, gauging her reaction. "Are you gonna do it with that whip?"

Yara doesn't hide her annoyance as she keeps glaring at me. And a smirk escapes me as I observe her anger rising. It doesn't seem like she enjoys being unmasked and her intentions called out. My provocative tone turns her expression into a stern one, and as she reaches down to unfasten her belt, I hear her saying, "I'm no longer using a whip." My eyes fall on the leather belt that is now between her hands folded in two. And as I look at it, I can already feel the sting on my ass. No one has ever dared to go as far as Yara. But today, boundaries have been thrown out the window. And no one would've ever imagined me asking, "How many swats?"

"Five strong ones."

I'm not sure what strong is gonna feel like, but five seems bearable. And as I keep thinking something through, I ask, "If I do it, then you'll undress and shower with me?"

My question makes her lips curve up with a naughtiness I haven't seen before, and after she presses her mouth to mine for a peck, she whispers, "There's only one way to find out."

CHAPTER 14

Emma Hasenfratz

I watch not-so-discreetly as Mrs. Van Lawick puts her hair up into a new ponytail as she looks at her reflection in the mirror above the sinks. Then she takes her toiletries bag, opens it, and applies some spray on her hair. There is something captivating about looking at Yara do her beauty routine after a shower. It feels intimate. Afterward, she uses three creams, one for her face, one for her eyes, and one for her neck. I recognize the brand—my mom uses the same one, which makes me wonder her age, but I'd never dare to ask her.

"I've never met someone like you," I tell her as I'm still recovering from the incredible orgasm she gave me.

"Someone like me?" She turns around, her dark brown eyes landing on me as I light up a cigarette. "What do you mean?"

Before answering, I take my time enjoying the view as she takes a new polo shirt and puts it on. This one is white and marine blue on the shoulders, but it fits her just fine. Then, taking a puff on my cigarette, I say, "Yeah, I mean, someone into... um..."

"Someone into sadomasochism?"

Her blunt answer makes my stomach squeeze, and the word "Yeah" barely leaves my lips.

Yara lets out a quick chuckle in return while applying her creams. "Oh, you have definitely met someone like me."

I squint my eyes at her insinuation. Does she mean Van Dieren? Of course she does, they are so alike. And before I can even ask her about it, Yara is standing right in front of me and takes the cigarette I'm holding before putting it between her lips. Then she takes a steady inhale of smoke and puffs it out.

"My chauffeur has just arrived. See you soon in Amsterdam, Ms. Hasenfratz."

Without further ado, she exits the changing room, leaving me baffled. And before I can even cover myself, her chauffeur steps in and takes her bags with him.

Resting the back of my head against the wall, I exhale loudly, ruminating over everything I've gone through today. Jeez... I've experienced a lot of crazy shit in my life, but having an affair with a married noblewoman who happens to be a sadist is by far the craziest of them all.

Not even ten minutes later, my iPhone beeps, and I jump a little when I see that it's Petra calling.

"Hey, how are you?" I greet as I pick up the call.

"Hi, I'm outside. Your housekeeper is not here. Can you come out and open the door for me, please?"

What? Did I invite Petra to come over today? I don't think so. "Yeah, my housekeeper is out. Alright, gimme a sec."

I grab the clothes I was wearing this morning and head outside to the main entrance. There, I find Petra standing on the front porch, wearing a linen shirt and a pair of denim shorts. Her long hair is pulled up in a high ponytail, and I must say, she looks really cute like that. "What's up?"

"Hey," she greets me with a full-tooth smile, her eyes gleaming. "I'm sorry for not calling back yesterday. Um, I need to talk to you. Do you have a minute?"

"Yeah, of course. Do you wanna go upstairs?"

"Sure."

I invite her to my room and close the door behind us. Since it's a sunny, warm day, Petra and I go to my private terrace and sit on the lounge chairs. "Alright, what's up?"

Petra seems pretty anxious as she says, "First, you've got to promise me you won't tell anyone."

I raise my brows at her statement. Like, doesn't she trust me enough? "Alright, I promise."

But Petra doesn't seem pleased. "No, it has to be more serious. You need to make an oath."

What the fuck? "An oath?" I repeat, squinting my eyes.

"This is super serious. I need you to make a solemn promise first." Petra reaches down and takes my left hand, laying it flat and palm down. Then she puts hers under mine and says, "Raise your right hand."

Oh boy. I do so, enjoying her little show.

"Emma Hasenfratz, do you solemnly swear not to repeat, under any circumstance, what I'm about to tell you? And that you will honor your oath until the end?" The way she says it sounds super serious though.

"I do, babe."

"You are under oath," she reminds me. "Are you sure?"

"Yes, Ms. Hasenfratz will keep her mouth shut."

"Perfect." She takes a deep breath, like she's pondering how to even start. "Do you remember when we hung up yesterday?"

"Yeah…" And I also remember she didn't call me back like she said she would.

"Well, afterward, I met Alex in the trophy room I told you about, and he…" Words seem hard for her to get out as Petra becomes mute, her eyes darting down to her lap.

"He?" I repeat.

"He did something I'm very confused about."

"Such as?"

Her cheeks bloom with heat, and I raise my brows at the sight. "He…" Blowing out a breath, Petra finally fesses up. "He bent me over and spanked my butt."

"*What*?!" I shout, at the verge of breaking into a laugh. "Oh gosh, you can't be serious."

"Oh wow. You find it funny?"

"Yeah, like…" I'd love to spank her ass, too, but she doesn't need to know that. "Alright." Clearing my throat, I aim for a steadier tone. "And why did he do that?"

Her eyes keep going down with embarrassment as she twists her lips. "To punish me for my behavior."

Her behavior? I can't believe Petra could have done anything bad. But even if she did, it must have been cute to watch. "And how was it?"

"It was painful."

"Yeah, I imagine your butt must have been on fire. But how did you feel about him doing it?"

"I felt… weird."

"Weird?"

"Wet," she corrects.

"Ah. That's not the same thing."

"I just… you know, no one has ever done that before."

This has to be the naughtiest confession I have ever heard. Picturing Petra getting a spanking is too delightful to be true, and I feel the urge to prepare a joint to smoke while she gives me all the dirty details.

"Where are you going?" she asks, seeing me leave the terrace.

"I'm just getting a little something." Yeah, and since Yara took all my cigarettes, I just have weed left.

When I come back with a sealed bag, rolling papers, and filters, Petra rebukes, "Weed? Really?"

"Why not?" I sit beside her again, grab a joint filter, and start rolling it. "Okay, so what's next?"

"He asked permission to discipline me in the future."

"Oh," I say, staying focused as I now drop some herbs on the paper. "That's interesting." Then I pinch and roll it before licking the edge like an envelope to seal it. "And what did you say?"

"I have to give him my answer after thinking it through."

I look around for a lighter, and a smile escapes me when I remember Yara's metallic one is in the changing room. I stole it when she was getting dressed so I could keep a little something of hers until we meet again in December.

"Gimme a sec." I run back inside, leaving Petra behind, asking where I'm going as I rush to the changing room to grab the lighter. Then I return to the terrace just as fast. After burning the tip, I take one deep puff and ask, "And how many swats did you get?"

"Um, eighteen."

"Was he very hard on you?"

"Well, some were quick and soft, others more intense and harsh, but I didn't cry. He was also rubbing me, and it felt good."

"So it was like a gentle punishment?" I tease, because if she had gotten one like I did with Yara's belt, she wouldn't be sitting on her ass.

"It was not that gentle either."

Petra keeps her eyes glued on me, like she's waiting for some unparalleled wisdom to come from me. Extending the hand that's holding the joint, I ask, "Do you wanna try it?" And then with a dash of naughtiness, I add, "Or do you need permission?"

She huffs at my comment. "You're very funny."

Knowing Ms. Van Gatt has never been into smoking, I keep it to myself, taking another inhale of smoke before asking, "What is your gut telling you?"

Petra doesn't reply immediately. She seems to be on another planet as she thinks something through. "Well, I kinda liked it. It was so… intense and… different," she mumbles, a dash of embarrassment in her tone. "I never expected something like that to happen between us. But what if he stops respecting me because I accept being punished in the future?"

Hmm… I take another puff on my joint, pondering her words, and then ask, "Did he kill that bear?"

"Um, no."

"And Sebastian?"

"Not that I'm aware."

"So Alex stood by your side even though he was looking forward to killing one."

Petra creases her brows in confusion. "And?"

"And that means he does value your opinion and respect you a damn lot." Since Petra keeps considering me, I add, "Look, you can grant him permission and see how it goes. If you enjoy the dynamics, keep going; if not, have a talk with him." I take another puff, quite proud of my answer. It seems like a balanced one. Smoking a quality joint kinda helps though.

"That's why I love talking to you."

"Huh?" Her praise is a bit unexpected.

"Yeah, everyone else would've judged me, or called me names, but you've always been different."

Her statement warms my heart. And it's in these moments that I remember why we are best friends. We've never judged each other's lifestyles. After all, we have always been two freaks with our own issues. "Well, I'm the one and only Emma Hasenfratz." We share a quick laugh, and, after pausing for a beat, I say, "Jokes aside, I just know life's short. So don't waste your time living a life you don't want to. If this can bring you guys closer to each other, why not?"

"You're the wisest person I know." Petra leans forward and embraces me tightly, her head resting against mine. "Thank you for everything, Emma," she says in a whisper.

"Always, babe."

After she releases me, she lets out a sigh of relief, like a huge weight has just dropped off her shoulders. "Um, when are you leaving New York?" And suddenly the subject is closed.

"Next Sunday," I tell her.

"Already?" Petra doesn't hide her bewilderment.

"Yeah, some wild nights are waiting for me in the Mediterranean."

"Oh, wow. And when are you coming back?"

Her question makes me tense up; I've got no idea. "Um, I don't know."

And her jaw drops instantly at my answer. "Really?"

Seeing the disappointment in her eyes, I come up with a quick solution. "You're staying at Park Avenue during the week, right?"

"Yeah…" she mumbles, keeping it short. And although she's never opened up about it, I know she'd rather live with her fiancé than with her dad.

"Well, I might pop over, and we can do something."

"Deal." Petra gives me another hug, and I can't help inhaling her jasmine perfume. This time, though, my heart tightens a bit. Despite the best friendship we could have, this will never feel like enough.

CHAPTER 15

Manhattan, September 14, 2020
Petra Van Gatt

I should be paying attention to Sarah's fascinating debate with Matthew about the best movie ever made, but my mind has been replaying the sound of every swat landing on my bare bottom and the terrifying anxiety and chills I had anticipating every single one.

You're such a good slut...

A shiver runs down my spine as I recall the insanity of the moment when he said those words. Everything about that night was hot, scary, and left me wanting it over and wanting more at the same time. Like a roller coaster—it's frightening at first, and we know we are gonna scream, but we do it anyway for the rush of adrenaline and excitement. Then I remember his expression once I turned around, and how his eyes were laced with disappointment, like he was regretful for what he'd just done. It reminds me of the night at his family estate when he bent me over to satisfy his urge and asked me if I was okay with it. There's a part of him that yearns for that kind of control, that intense feeling of possession, while the other seems to try to avoid it at all costs. My heart speeds up as I imagine being punished again, but this time with his belt. It must hurt like hell, for sure I'd cry. But the idea is more alluring and enticing than it should be…

"By the way, do you mind if we postpone our next meeting from Friday to Saturday morning?" Matthew asks me.

"Um?" I blink twice, returning to planet Earth, and find the entire group staring at me.

"We've got some extracurricular stuff to do on Friday," Sarah adds, before taking a mouthful of her spaghetti.

"Oh, um, okay," I tell them, a bit sad as I was planning to go to Bedford Hills Friday evening.

Taking my phone, I text Alex very quickly: *Hey, my classmates have just postponed our next meetup to Saturday morning. Can you pick me up Saturday instead? X*

"Petra," Matthew says. "I'm sorry, is this cheese?"

Looking at the spaghetti dish sitting in front of him and then at mine, I say, "Um, I think so. Why?"

"Do you want mine?" he asks, showing me the cheese he put aside. "I don't eat cheese."

"Really?" My brows lift instantly. "But I recall you used to, no?"

"Matthew wants to become vegan," Sarah teases as she takes his plate and puts the cheese on hers.

"I don't want to," he protests. "I am." And he looks back at me and says, "It's the least I can do to save the planet."

A quick laugh escapes me, but the curious side of me has got to know more. "And how hard has it been saving the planet?"

"Super easy, actually. You've got substitutes for everything. There's vegan cheese, eggs, milk. Like, everything can be switched."

Sarah rolls her eyes as she eats his slices of mozzarella.

"I'm really impressed," I tell him as I reach for his hand. "That's very brave of you."

"I'm not being brave," he looks at Sarah, "just not being a selfish bastard."

"Watch your mouth, boy," Sarah yaps. "I'm sacrificing myself to eat your mozzarella."

I lean back in my chair, my eyes on the mozzarella, and assess whether I should eat mine or not. "You know what? I'm not eating mine either," I tell him. "Janine?" I call, my gaze searching for her.

"Yes, Miss?"

And for some odd reason, maybe because of the traumatizing experience of the trophy room and the hunt, I say, "From now on, we'll eat only vegan food. Vegan cheese, vegan eggs. We're gonna support Matthew in saving the planet and the animals."

While Matthew claps his hands in excitement, Janine gapes and blinks twice. "Um, I'm not sure your dad wants to ditch his meat and fish, Miss."

"Your dad eats meat?" Matthew asks, like it is a crime.

"Yeah…"

"But you're vegetarian, no?"

"Since birth," I tell him. "Mom is too, and Dad respected her choice to raise me vegetarian."

"Wait—you've *never* tasted meat?" David asks, matching Matthew's judgmental tone.

"Nope."

"Not even bacon?" he asks.

"Ugh…" I cringe at the image. "No."

"Wow. Your mom seems awesome," Matthew praises.

Not really, no.

"I wish mine were like that too. It's disheartening when not even your friends or family support you."

Sarah rolls her eyes, teasing him. "Oh, poor baby."

"Sorry, mate, but bacon is life," David chides.

"I support you," I tell him with my biggest smile.

"Finally! After the bloody battle over objectivism, you guys have found some common ground," Katrina points out.

And as my eyes fall on him, I pinch his arm for fun, and say, "Yep, we might be philosophical enemies, but now we are also vegan besties."

"Vegan besties…" Matthew repeats a bit nostalgically, his gaze still pinned on me. "Sounds great to me."

CHAPTER 16

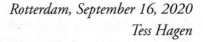

Rotterdam, September 16, 2020
Tess Hagen

My nonprofit has been growing into something beyond what I expected. Since my interview was broadcast live, I have gained many new donors and, a bit surprisingly, many women have reached out to me with very similar cases to the one of Leonor—wives of powerful men who would like to get a divorce but don't know what to do or how to do so. I wonder why they haven't hired a lawyer from a top firm, but it seems like my message resonated with them and they feel safer with me to open up about their lives.

Today, Carice and I are signing on a new client, a friend of Leonor, Allison. The poor woman is around my age, but unlike me, she seems to be devoid of any confidence or self-respect, and despite all the money her husband possesses, she is the quietest, most discreet and humble woman I've ever met. Her clothes are so modest and simple that I'd have never imagined her husband is the owner of two big factories in the region and a member of Dutch nobility. After hearing her entire story, Carice finishes preparing a report with the main points for the divorce.

"What is this?" Allison asks.

"This is your statement," I say, giving her the papers and a pen. "Read it, and afterward, just sign below. We will give it to the prosecutor and use it for the press."

Allison starts reading it carefully. "Um…" she mumbles, hesitating. "It states that my husband raped me."

Based on the entire story she just told us, I'm surprised she's even inquiring about it. "Yes…" I answer. Seeing her hesitating, I take a chair and sit beside her. Leaning closer to her, I say in a low voice, "Allison, you are safe now. You don't need to be afraid or ashamed to say what he has done to you."

"But…" She looks down, thinking something through. "I'm not really sure about this."

"What do you mean?" I ask, confused. Before she can reply, I add, "Look, the defense will use your hesitation against you, so you can't vacillate. When the defense attorney asks you if your husband raped you, you have to be strong and say, 'Yes, he did,'" I explain. "It's hard to recognize it. I totally understand that. But I'm here to help." I lay my hand on top of hers. And as I see her looking down at her lap, her mind ruminating over everything she's been through, I can't help but feel my heart tightening. Every woman who comes here reminds me of how I was nineteen years ago. I was just as naive, but above all, I was deeply in love with a man I held too high in esteem. A man I was also too emotionally and financially dependent on. A man who, without me even noticing, saw me only as his mere possession.

Allison takes a deep breath, her face just as tormented, and finally looking at me, she says, "I'm just not really sure if he did what you are saying he did."

I try hard not to roll my eyes—I've heard this so many times. "If you are not sure, it's because it was rape," I assert. "You were just not aware of it at the moment it happened."

"I just want a divorce, a settlement is okay…"

"No." My tone comes off a bit more aggressive than I intended. "A settlement is not okay. The law *must* be enforced, and he *must* be sentenced." I'm tired of laws that are just written for the sake of being on the books. It's time to apply them properly.

"But the kids…" Her voice remains barely audible, and she tucks some hair behind her ear, while her body tenses up in her seat. "I don't want him to go to jail."

I try my best not to huff at her comment. After everything he did to her, she's still worried about him? Instead, I just say, "Allison, you are doing what is right."

Then I hear a knock on my office door and order the person to come in.

"Tess, there is someone here… Someone, um, you aren't really expecting," my assistant announces with some uneasiness.

"We will talk later," I say to Allison, who takes her purse and makes her way out. As Carice does the same, I stand up and go back to sit in the chair behind my desk. Before I can ask who, my assistant opens the door wide and invites him in. I recline back with a sly smile, and, crossing my arms over my chest, a quick huff escapes me. "Roy," I mutter as he enters. "Well, when I thought I had seen everything from you, you still manage to surprise me."

Carice closes the door behind her, leaving us alone.

"Tess…" he greets under his breath as he takes a few steps in my direction, his face already unsmiling. Roy seems to be quite uncomfortable to be here alone with me in the office of my nonprofit, which only makes my amusement grow. "I apologize for the unexpected visit, but we need to talk."

I gesture for him to have a seat, but instead Roy starts pacing around my office like a tormented and unsteady child. Then he stops in front of my bookshelves, observing a frame of Petra and me—it's a picture we took on the twenty-fourth of December last year before our heated argument.

"That is the last time I saw her alive," I tell him as I walk over in his direction. Standing beside him, I take a closer look at the photograph. I smile seeing my daughter glowing, happy, her arms wrapped around my neck and her cheek touching mine. I can't help but feel a squeeze in my chest each time I look at us.

"It's a beautiful selfie," Roy says, sounding unexpectedly honest and warm.

I study his face attentively and then ask, "What's going on, Roy? What brought you here?"

He lets out a sigh, his eyes still pinned on the frame before they look up to meet mine. "I want the best for our daughter, just as you do." Oh dear. I instantly roll my eyes.

He's got something up his sleeve. "Petra is awake," he announces.

"What?" I reach for my mouth immediately, covering my gape. My mind is so astonished by his announcement that I can barely breathe. I close my eyes and let the first tears of joy course down my cheeks. Those three words are the ones I have hoped to hear the most. Oh, my little angel... What a miracle. Then I draw in a breath and quickly wipe the tears, trying to regain my composure. "When?" I ask, barely containing all the emotions. "When did she wake up?"

"Around two weeks ago."

I let out another gasp, my eyes and mouth wide open as a wave of shock overtakes me. "And why am I only finding out about it now?" I bark instantly. "Why didn't Dr. Nel inform me?" This time, I'm the one pacing around, digesting all this news. "It was her duty to do so!"

"Petra asked her not to," he informs me. "Dr. Nel just respected her choice."

Before I can fall on the ground, mercifully there is a sofa behind me to sit on. "I can't believe it," I mumble, my mouth remaining wide open to breathe, and I try to drag some precious air into my lungs. "But why would Petra do that?"

Roy walks slowly in my direction, sitting in the armchair beside me. He leans forward, supporting his elbows on his knees, his hands entwined. "Tess..." he says gently. "Because she doesn't want to see you, or to even talk to you." His words squeeze my heart so much that I can barely breathe.

"She knows you asked Alex to leave her again." He pauses for a beat, his eyes darting down for a second. "As I said, I want the best for our daughter, just as you do. And that is why I came here… to ask you in person to accept the fact that they want to be with each other."

I can't help but chuckle at the absurdity of his request. "How dare you, huh?" I glare at him in disgust. "How dare you!" And I leap off of the sofa. "We had an agreement. A deal is a deal! He's nothing but a—"

"They are engaged." From absurdity to atrocity… I sit again to avoid dying in between. "And before you curse him once more, she is the one who proposed."

"She is sick." That's all I manage to say. "Petra needs therapy."

"She is undergoing therapy, but she loves—"

"This is not love, Roy," I snap back. "He is manipulating her. Grooming her." I take a much-needed breath before standing up again. I walk a few steps and stand in front of the glass wall, looking absently at the gray sky. After calming down, I turn to face him, and with a steadier tone, I say, "Your friend is a predator. A dangerous pervert hidden behind good looks and a gentle smile."

"I know him very well. I don't share the same—"

"Look," I cut him off. "Letting our daughter be alone with that man for one week in Aspen was already a huge mistake and miscalculation on your part."

"But they love each other, for God's sake," he interposes.

"Stop it!" I say louder. "What a disgraceful and immoral man you have become…" I shake my head once more. "He's luring our daughter into becoming someone we do not want her to become." I hope Roy will now finally understand me.

"Do you really think he will tame his domineering nature once they are married? Once she has his surname?"

Roy looks at me with squinted eyes. "Is that the reason you never wanted to take mine?"

"We are not here to talk about that," I snarl back. "Do you want to wake up one day and learn our daughter is... dead? Choked by that man?" I reach for my mouth, containing the urge to cry at the simple thought of it.

"Oh, Tess," Roy stands up, walking toward me. "We all know it was an accident, and it was twenty years ago."

"Accident or not, make sure he keeps his promise and goes to Singapore," I tell him, my tone threatening. "You know what's at stake."

And Roy does know what's at stake—maintaining an immaculate reputation in New York has always been a priority for him and his business. It takes a lifetime to build a reputation, and one story to destroy it, I remember him saying every time there was a scandal about his peers on the news.

He drops his gaze, exhaling loudly. "Petra will never forgive me if I let him go. She'll be devastated."

"One day she will. When she's cured, she'll forgive us and thank us for doing the right thing." Roy seems uncertain, so I proceed, "Our job as parents is not to say yes to her every wish. But to make sure she is safe. I prefer her to be mad at me and alive than happy and dead the next day." His expression remains just as thoughtful, probably assessing my words. "She will meet someone else—trust me. Someone of her age. We are doing the right thing."

My office falls into a twitchy silence as I observe Roy, his face severe, looking out the wall of glass at the horizon ahead. "What an ugly day to be in Rotterdam."

CHAPTER 17

Manhattan, September 17, 2020
Alexander Van Dieren

Roy has been out for the past two days. Not that I'm bothered at not seeing him, but when your best friend tells you he's taking two days off without any reason, you kinda expect some sort of explanation once he comes back.

I look again at the text message he sent me earlier today: *Meet me at midday at The Knick, at 2 East 62nd Street. We need to talk.* And I keep wondering why he's chosen this place to meet up. After all, I've never been to that club before. Despite my dad being an active member, he never brought me there, but I guess there is a first time for everything. As my chauffeur drops me off right in front of Two East Sixty-second Street, I look at the clubhouse architecture—it seems like an average Neo-Georgian building in Manhattan. After pressing the doorbell, I see a gray-haired majordomo come and open the front door.

Before I can even introduce myself, he bows his head slightly and says, "Good afternoon, Mr. Van Dieren." *Wow.* My brows lift instantly, and I'm left quite astounded at how quickly he recognized me. "Mr. Van Gatt is waiting for you. Follow me, please."

"Um, thanks," I reply as I enter the hallway. Taking in my surroundings, I must admit the entrance is pretty elegant, with its white walls, chess tile marble floor, and white marble staircase covered with red carpet. We go up to the next floor. There, I follow the majordomo, who crosses the hallway and stops right in front of a closed wooden double door, which he knocks on three times.

"Come in," we hear from the other side.

"May I take your jacket, sir?" he asks me before leaving.

"I'm fine," I tell him.

Then he opens the door, inviting me in. "Please."

"Thank you." Stepping into the room, I'm left speechless as I take in its immensity. It's actually a two-floor wood-paneled room linked by a staircase—upstairs I can see walls covered with books, while on the current floor, where Roy is standing afar by the window, lies a typical lounge with a bar, sofas, a low table in the center, and a fireplace, surrounded by gilded gold frames of classic portraits hanging on the walls.

"Would you like a glass?" Roy's question brings my attention back to him.

"No, thanks. I no longer drink before lunch."

"Oh, that's wise," he replies, his tone contained as he walks in my direction. "Have you been here before?"

"No," I admit, my eyes still taking in the surroundings.

Stopping in the center of the room, Roy says, "Only your father and I have the key to this room." His face carries some sort of nostalgia as he starts pacing around and observing the portraits on the walls. "This room means a lot to me." He pauses for a beat, a trace of a smile settling on his lips. "It's here that Hendrik gave me the opportunity of a lifetime." And I know exactly what he means by that. "It's here that I became a portfolio manager for your family office." I can see a twinkle in his eye as he recalls such memories. "Boy, I was young and tenacious. Driven by nothing more than hunger to win." Roy lets out a quick chuckle, looking pensively at the floor, and then at me. "Proving to your dad that the boy from Rouveen he helped get an education could manage billions was all I wanted."

"And yet, just two years later, you resigned," I tease him.

"You know why I did it."

"You did the right thing. My offer was better," I remind him. "And my dad was disgraced and fired once Mom found out about his bastard, so I saved you from a big mess."

Blowing out a deep, long breath, Roy starts shaking his head. "I'm still astounded that your family managed to vote him out."

"Mom can be very convincing," I tell him, keeping it short.

"I have nothing but the utmost respect for your dad. The fact that he had to leave the country and never return, well, that was quite unexpected, but I guess he had his reasons."

"Why am I here, Roy?" I ask, cutting through the bullshit. "To talk about my dad's fate?"

"No," he says, and it's exactly the answer I expected. As Roy stands in front of me, just inches from my face, he adds, "We are here to talk about yours."

Looking him in the eye, I warn, "I'm not Hendrik. And I'm not leaving."

"Even your dad knew when it was time to leave."

"I'm not resigning," I insist.

Roy draws in a breath, his eyes drifting down for a moment, before he says, "If you don't resign, Tess will press charges against us and everything we've worked so hard for will be gone. That is not an option for me." And he turns his back on me, slowly pacing toward the sofa.

"We have to be found guilty first."

"Enough!" he shouts, spinning around, his glare now censoring me. "It takes a lifetime to build a reputation, but only one goddamn story to destroy it." We keep staring at each other, and the same tension as when we play chess becomes palpable. "Guilty or not, I won't risk it. Even if you're engaged." I let out a rush of air, irritated with his obsession to maintain a perfect reputation. "It's my daughter's heritage we are talking about. Have you thought about her? What will she think about us once she finds out?"

"I'm sure Petra will understand and forgive us."

Head shaking, he chuckles again. "You're so delusional. She can't even cope with the killing of a bear, but you think she will with that of a girl?"

The reality hits me hard, and I remember how mad she was just for the sake of an animal. But I know deep down Petra will forgive me if she ever learns the truth. Or at least I want to believe she will. "Accidents do happen. It was not intentional."

"And yet we hid the body like it was."

His concerns are clear and understandable. If Tess unleashes the story to the media, Gatt-Dieren Capital will go down in history not as a reputable hedge fund firm founded by two Dutch social-capitalists, but as a disgraced company started by two murderers of a young virgin at a depraved party. And Petra will ultimately inherit such a reputation. Her health is already so fragile that I can't imagine how she'll cope with the media bashing her as the daughter of a killer and all the investigations that will ensue. At least it's a good thing we've never made our relationship official to anyone except our families and close relatives. "You spoke to Tess, didn't you?" I ask him.

"I did," he replies calmly as he takes a file laying on the low table. "She's ready to move forward with the case and a story in the media if you don't leave Petra alone."

Roy walks back in my direction and hands me the file. As I open it, my eyes land on a photograph of Petra hugging a college boy in the hallway of Roy's penthouse. I knew his place was fully equipped with surveillance cameras, but I never knew Roy actually checked the footage. "You have been spying on her?" I ask, although not that surprised now to find out he has. And I close the file just as fast, giving it back to him.

"His name is Matthew Bradford," he informs me. Opening the file again, he takes out another photograph. This time it's in the dining room where they are having lunch. Matthew is smiling with a twinkle in his eyes while Petra is laughing at him. "They have been friends since last year. And from what I know, he also went to her birthday dinner at Emma's."

"What's your point?"

Roy starts pacing around, engrossed in thought. "Matthew is from a good family. He's currently studying economics, he doesn't smoke, drink, or do drugs…" He pauses, looking downward and then up at me. "This boy deserves a chance with her."

"You are fucking insane, aren't you?" I shout. "Forget this bullshit!" Now I'm the one who starts pacing around the room—an attempt to keep my rage from consuming me. Looking back at him, I snap, "Petra made her choice. It's her fucking damn choice. She loves me. This boy is just a friend. Forget this nonsense."

Roy, with his face just as serene, walks over and, standing behind me, puts a hand on my shoulder. "Alex," he utters quietly. "I went to Rotterdam personally. I tried to reason with her. Believe me, I even told her it was Petra who proposed…" He sounds defeated, like a beaten dog. "As hard as it is, this relationship has got to end." And before I can punch him with all the anger boiling in me, Roy casually goes back to sit in his armchair. Once comfortably seated, he says, "You'll have to do as you promised and go to Singapore."

Leave Petra? My fiancée? The woman I nearly lost? No fucking way. "I'd prefer to go to court and face that evil bitch than leave Petra. If she wants to press charges against us, she can go ahead and—"

"Enough!" He punches the low table, making his glass tremble. "I should've never supported this relationship in the first place! It was such a fucking mistake."

"You know perfectly well that I love her. I'm not perfect, but—"

"My decision has been made," he interposes. And I have never hated him and the air he breathes more than now. Roy looks me in the eye and adds, "You'll announce your departure and the new CEO at our annual dinner. You have a month to pick either Paulo or Mike. Tess will be watching your speech on livestream, so you better not screw up."

"I can't do it," I snap, but Roy remains stone-faced and expressionless. "Petra's health is so fragile. If I leave her—"

"She's got an entire team of physicians to take care of her," he barks. He pauses for a beat to regain his composure. "Petra has to get used to this new reality—a reality without you. It'll be painful at first, but there is nothing time doesn't cure." And a sly smile escapes him as he adds, "Or a new love interest."

At that instant, I clench my fists tighter to contain the urge to beat the hell out of him. But it's not only my fists that are tight—my stomach is in knots, and my breathing is shallow too.

Then we are startled by knocking on the door and someone coming in. "I'm sorry to interrupt, Mr. Van Gatt, but your driver Anthony is waiting outside."

"Ah, yes. We are leaving now." Roy gets up, fastens the button on his blazer, and walks toward the door. Once he passes by me, I put a hand on his shoulder, making him stop.

"Roy…" I stare at him, utterly baffled, my heart heavy, trying to find what is left of the man that is—or was—my best friend. "You can't do this to us. We can fight back."

"I'm sorry." His eyes finally meet mine. "But this is the end of it." And before I can say anything else, he adds, "You've got a plane to Singapore tomorrow night."

"What?" That's the only thing I manage to say. He can't be serious! "You want me to leave now?"

"The sooner the better." Before I lose all remaining self-control, Roy gives me a quick pat on the back and says, "Now let's go have lunch." And he leaves the room and our unbearable talk behind.

CHAPTER 18

Manhattan, September 17, 2020
Matthew Bradford

There are few things I despise as much as having lunch with Pops. We could have a great relationship, though, if he'd stop behaving like someone stuck in the past century. We've tried many times to get closer, but each time we talk about politics, my social activism, my YouTube channel, or anything related to his job, we get into conflict. We are so different that the only thing in common we have is our surname. But in an effort to keep a semblance of a relationship with him, I've accepted an invitation to have lunch with him at one of his favorite restaurants. Upon entering, I briefly check the place and see only replicas of him—formal and boring dudes. He waves at me from afar, his short gray hair and fancy suit couldn't blend any better with the rest of the crowd.

"Hi, Dad. How are you?" I greet mechanically as I sit across from him and drop my backpack from my shoulders.

I then glance around the posh restaurant and realize I'm the only one in jeans and sneakers. "I hope they have vegan options."

"Yes, they do," Pops replies, handing me the menu. "After waiting for you for half an hour, believe me, I had time to double-check."

"Good," I snap, and start checking the menu.

Leaning over a bit, he then asks with irritation, "When is this phase gonna end?"

And I can't help but sigh at his comment. Putting down the menu, I say, "This is not a phase. This is the future." Displeased by my answer, Pops lets out an exasperated breath and starts shaking his head. I'm already regretting having come here. "Look," I start. "If we are just going to argue, it's better that I leave."

"How is your girl doing?" he asks to avoid an argument.

"First, she is not *my* girl," I correct. "And this is stupid. No one belongs to anyone."

Rolling his eyes, he says, "Sorry. How is your friend doing? Petra, right?"

"Yeah…" And I let myself dwell briefly on my thoughts. "She's not doing well, unfortunately."

"Really?" Pops asks with shock in his eyes. "You told me she was finally awake."

"Yeah, but she is mentally ill." As he gives me a confused look, I decide to open up. "She is engaged."

He raises his brows in total disbelief. "At eighteen? To whom?"

"That's the million-dollar question. I just know he's got a hedge fund company."

He rolls his eyes again, but this time I like it. "Oh, dear. Don't tell me she fell for one of those assholes?"

"Yeah… That's what I'm afraid of." Leaning over, I say, "Petra has a good heart, like, really, I can't explain it. When I told her I was starting a vegan diet, she was the only one who supported me all the way. So much so that she decided to do the same. We have this thing, you know, like, this connection." Pops nods in perfect harmony with my words. "That dude once came to pick her up after exams," I explain. "He was so full of himself. He even came in a Rolls-Royce. A Rolls-Royce, can you imagine? What a show-off," I blurt out, my head shaking as I think of it. "She is just being lured with some cheap talk."

"And I guess you're going to save her…" Dad might sound like he's teasing, but I take his words seriously.

"That's what friends do," I tell him. "She seems to like him a lot though. But that dude is gonna break her heart." I take a sip of my water, and proceed, "It's not healthy. I swear, he's at least thirty-five. You have prosecuted people on Wall Street for decades. You know them, right?"

"Of course I do." Pops leans closer to me, and in a lower voice, he says, "But that's not enough to find out who her fiancé is."

"I know…" Yeah, I kinda figured that out. And Petra is definitely not gonna tell me who he is out of the blue. She is so secretive about that, and I can't help but wonder why.

"Good afternoon," the waiter greets as he stands in front of us. "Are you ready to order?"

"Yes, please. I'll have the filet mignon with potatoes," Pops says. And as he orders his favorite wine, the sound of laughter breaks through the restaurant, and my attention goes to the table behind him.

To my surprise, the more I look at the dudes sitting there, the more I think I know one of them. I can't really pinpoint from where, since I can only see half of his face, but his figure seems familiar. Suddenly, I see one of his middle-aged friends paying the bill and inviting the group toward the cigar lounge. As he stands up, I can finally see his entire face and—

Jeez!

My heart tightens at the view. That's Petra's fiancé!

"I'll be right back," I say to my dad, leaving the table as fast as I can.

"Excuse me…" I call out. But only the host and the doorman look at me, while Petra's fiancé and his friends cross the double doors into the lounge.

As the host accosts me, I say, "Hi, I'm Matthew Bradford and—"

"Sorry, son. They are not recruiting," the host brushes me off.

"Oh, no. Um, is that man that just entered the lounge Petra Van Gatt's fiancé?"

At that instant, the host narrows his eyes and takes one step closer to me. "And may I ask why are you asking?"

"Um, I'm a close friend of hers. We are in the same class at Columbia. I remember seeing him once. I need to talk to him. It's really urgent."

He seems to be considering me attentively, and I already feel stressed as I observe him doing so. "What's your name again?"

"Oh, Matthew Bradford, sir."

"Very well. I will call him."

I think twice about trying to get into the cigar room too, but the tall, bulky doorman glares at me in refusal. I guess I'll have to wait outside. After a few moments, though, the host comes out, inviting me in. To be honest, it's my first time in a cigar lounge. I hate the smell of smoke. It reminds me of my pops's friends, and they are all boring and lame. As I step inside, I glance around out of curiosity. And it's exactly what I thought it would be—a darker, cozier room, featuring leather Chesterfield sofas and armchairs, low marble tables, maple-veneered vitrines displaying different types of cigars, and an old-school vibe. Everyone here sports suits, some with ties, others without. I feel like an imposter in my jeans, white sneakers, and T-shirt. For some stupid reason, my right hand goes to my tousled hair, trying to make it more presentable among these middle-aged dudes. Then my eyes land on the man sitting in an armchair, talking to two other guys, one on each side. He seems to be the oldest, and from the way those dudes are looking at him as he speaks, he must be their boss or something. And as if he feels my eyes on him, his attention swings in my direction, his blue eyes landing on me.

"Mr. Bradford?" And here he is—the mystical fiancé of Petra Van Gatt. Just from his voice, he sounds like a criminal—a criminal of Wall Street.

Typical.

My dad has prosecuted many of his kind.

As he stands up to greet me, my eyes can't help but dart down to the smoke curling from the cigar between his fingers. He gives me a warm, welcoming smile and holds out his other hand. "Alexander Van Dieren."

I usually never memorize names when people introduce themselves. But his… I'll never forget it.

As I take his hand, I'm not expecting such a strong grip. Fuck! Did he do that on purpose or what? I try to appear unaffected, but damn it, it hurts like hell!

"Pleasure meeting you, sir." What? Why on earth did I say "sir"? My tone is low and shaky. Not what I wanted. Clearing my throat, and aiming for a steadier one, I ask, "Um, may I speak to you alone?"

He looks behind him and beckons to the other two men to leave, then his gaze goes over my shoulder, and I hear him say, "Roy, do you mind?"

Wait! Roy? Isn't that the name of Petra's father? No, it can't be. They wouldn't be hanging out like besties. It must be someone else. I do my best to contain the urge to take out my iPhone and Google "Roy Van Gatt" and check out what her dad looks like.

As Roy and the other guys leave the room, the sound of the door closing behind me is enough to make me swallow dryly.

Before an odd silence settles between us, he takes a steady inhale of his cigar, then asks, "Do you smoke?"

"Smoking is not my thing," I snap, trying to feign indifference. In reality, the smell of it is vomit-inducing! Jeez, how can anyone enjoy that shit?

He gives me a side smile. "That's something Petra would say."

And I smile, too, at the thought of it. "Yeah, she would." Yeah, Petra would totally say that. She understands me like no one else.

He invites me to sit on the sofa beside him, and, taking his glass, he asks, "May I offer you a drink, at least?"

"I'm good," I tell him, trying not to sit too close.

"Not even a glass of wine or champagne? A mojito perhaps?"

"I don't drink alcohol."

He chuckles, observing me attentively. "Of course you don't." He takes a sip of his drink, which seems to be whiskey. Reclining in his seat, he heaves a quick sigh, and starts considering me to the point that it's uncomfortable. "So, Matthew Bradford, if you are not here for a job or an internship, then what are you here for?"

I'm here for way worse than that. And yet how am I supposed to tell him to leave Petra alone?

There is no other way around it. If I love her, I've got to do it.

Taking a long, deep breath into my lungs, I look him straight in the eye and say in my most confident tone, "I don't think Petra should be with you."

There! In your face, dude.

"Of course she shouldn't," he replies without any bother. As I sit there batting my eyes and digesting his words, he takes another inhale of smoke before puffing it out. "In fact, she should be with you. Or another pal her age. Don't you agree?"

I'm so astounded by his question that I don't even know what to say. "Um… yeah, I guess so."

"Great," he says, before glancing at his watch. "I'm gonna have to go." Then he finishes his glass and stubs out the cigar in the ashtray.

"So…" My word trails off as I think of another way to approach this. "What do you intend to do about it?"

We get up from our seats at the same time, and he gestures for me to go first as he continues thinking something through.

"Matthew," he says, putting a hand on my shoulder. And as he does so, we stop walking. "I need your help."

What?

"Can you do me a favor?"

Another question I barely know how to answer. "Um, sure."

"Can you convince her not to marry me?" My jaw nearly drops at his request. Is he joking? Is that some sort of Dutch sarcasm?

"Um, what do you mean?"

A side smile tugs at his lips, and he says, "What about putting a plan in place to get her to forget me?"

Squinting my eyes, I examine his face, fixedly trying to detect any traces of sarcasm, but his expression is dead serious. "A plan?"

"A plan," he repeats. "What do you think?"

"A plan to convince Petra not to marry you?" I ask again, making sure I heard him properly.

"Exactly." His hand goes down to his pocket, and he takes a business card from there. "Think about it. Here is my phone number. If you are interested, let me know, and we can discuss further tomorrow."

Holy shit. He's not joking!

"Well, that's great. Um, thanks for your understanding." I shake his hand wholeheartedly. "By the way, this talk stays between us, right?"

He pats me on the back. "Of course. Now, if you'll excuse me, my driver is waiting outside."

"Sure. Um, it was a pleasure meeting you, Mr. Van Dieren," I say again, floating on cloud nine.

My eyes look absently at the double doors he just crossed through, still digesting everything that just happened.

Well, one thing is for sure: that was the weirdest talk I've ever had with someone. An old dude asking me to convince his young fiancée, whom I love, to drop him… Who would believe it?

***

Manhattan, September 18, 2020

Of course, I called Petra's fiancé straight after classes the next day. And while I was expecting to meet him at a similar place like we were at for lunch yesterday—you know, at a restaurant with a cigar lounge—I was positively surprised when he invited me to his condo. Maybe it's a trap, I thought when he did so. But, after all, he seems to be civilized enough, and I assume he just doesn't want anyone to see us together. Before leaving for his place, I decide to call Pops out of precaution and give him the address. I've also got an alert ready to send to the nearest police station if anything goes wrong. Plus, with the psycho boyfriends my female friends used to date, we can never be too prudent. I never understood the appeal of those assholes, but then again, what do I know?

"Here we are," my Uber driver announces, dropping me off at Mr. Van Dieren's address. As I exit the car and head into the building, I'm greeted by a doorman who holds the door for me, just like at Petra's. And, damn, this lobby is fancy as fuck! There is even a reception desk like in a hotel!

"Good afternoon," the receptionist greets me with a pleasant voice. "How may I help you?"

"Um, good afternoon. I've got an appointment with Mr. Van Dieren," I tell him.

"Sure." The receptionist takes a sheet of paper and a pen and puts them on the reception desk. "Write your name and signature here," he says, pointing to blank spaces on the paper. "And I also need an ID card."

"Sure." Damn, this is security to a whole new level.

"Very well. This way, please." I follow the receptionist to the lift, where he presses the button that says "PH."

I get in and wait patiently, while listening to the chill elevator music, before arriving at the PH floor. My breathing is faster than usual though. And I'm not sure why.

As the doors open wide, I see another hallway with only one door at the end. I guess that's where he lives, since I see "PH" written on the wall beside the door. I press the doorbell and wait, my anxiety rising. After a few seconds, someone finally unlocks and opens the door.

My eyes land on a woman dressed in a dark blue uniform with a white apron—she must be the housekeeper. "Please come in," she says with an accent.

As I step in, my eyes can't help but widen in surprise. *Wow.* What a vision this place is! The interior design is so clean, minimalist, and contemporary that it's surely won some kind of award. A female French singer is crooning from the speakers. Her dramatic voice, full of suffering and grief, gives me goosebumps, and it makes this place kind of scary.

"Follow me, please." I follow the lady through the immaculate open space to the outdoor terrace. "Wait here," she says as I'm about to cross the doorway onto the terrace. Looking up, I smile at the impressive skyline this place offers. Talk about a million-dollar view.

Then my eyes land on the back of a tall man standing afar, his hands on the steel railing as he contemplates the view. He looks at the lady, who whispers something to him, and then his head turns to the side, looking at me with a smirk. I do the same before I see he's holding a cigarette. Oh, great! Does Petra know he smokes? I shake my head in displeasure. What a bad influence this guy must be.

"Matthew," Alex greets. I didn't even realize he's now standing right in front of me. He looks younger today, maybe because he's also sporting a pair of jeans and a slim Henley shirt. His brown hair is just as unbrushed as mine. He shakes my hand, but not as strongly as last time. "Great to see you."

Keeping a steady and firm voice, I say, "Mr. Van Dieren."

"Are you hungry?" he asks rhetorically, inviting me into another room. "Maria made a vegan tortilla for you."

I squint my eyes immediately. "How do you know I'm vegan?" I ask, annoyance thick in my tone. I follow his pace and find myself in a spacious, bright room with lacquer-paneled walls and floor-to-ceiling windows, a big glass dinner table at the center.

"I did a little background check on you," he casually says, taking a seat at the table.

Of course he did. "And did you find anything exciting?" I ask, also sitting down as Maria places the famous tortilla in front of me. And I must confess, it looks really delicious.

"Not much, so either your dad cleared your record or you're really a saint."

"Not everyone is a criminal, you know…" I say as I start cutting a bite.

"Not everyone has a dad who's the attorney general of the state of New York." But I put the cutlery down just as fast. We remain mute as we stare at each other. His eyes study me meticulously, ready to catch any missteps. "If there is anything I should know, you better tell me now, 'cause I've got a pretty good flair for finding things people don't want me to."

I'm starting to understand why Petra likes him. He seems smart. And I like smart. "Alright, um, I drank a beer at a party last year, and the cops came 'cause of the neighbors. Needless to say, we got in trouble."

"Anything else?"

"I don't think so," I reply, containing the urge to attack the tortilla.

"Who is Sarah Leniski?" he asks. And my jaw nearly falls. Did he spy on our entire group or what?

"Eh, she's a friend of ours. She's part of our group at Columbia, which includes her, Katrina, and David. Why?"

"You spent the entire summer with her. Is she your girl-friend?"

"I, um… well…" Damn it! Did he check my credit card statements? Might be the flights I booked to Hawaii with her. "She is a friend with benefits," I tell him.

"So you guys just fuck?"

"It's over now," I lie. Crap! I shouldn't. I'm actually seeing her tonight. What if he finds out? "I mean, we do see each other casually. But it's just sex, you know."

"And how does Sarah feel about it?"

"Oh, she is cool with it. She's actually the only one who knows about my feelings for Petra." I bite my tongue. Fuck, I don't think I've admitted that to him before.

Her fiancé obviously heard me very well and asks bluntly, "So you love her?"

"I… um, well, that's quite a private question…"

His chin slowly dips, and he gives me a solid stare. "Matthew, cut the bullshit."

"I've got strong feelings for her, yeah," I confess, throwing all secrecy out the window. "Not sure if I can call it love, but yeah, I care about her." Letting out a sigh, I then add, "No one knows except my pops and Sarah. To everyone else, we are just vegan besties." I can't help but crack a smile remembering when she gave us that nickname. "But why are you asking me all this?"

"I'm moving to Singapore in a few hours," he announces. And his tone is enough to make me freeze in my seat. "So I need to make sure she'll be alright once I'm gone." I put down the cutlery and take a sip of my smoothie, trying to disguise my smile. Is he really leaving? Damn!

"Um, sorry, but why are you leaving?"

"That's beside the point," he snaps. "She'll need friends around her. Friends that are a good influence and will keep her on the right track."

"So, wait, does that mean you guys are gonna break up?" But he doesn't reply. Instead, he just observes me as I finish the tortilla. Did I leave him mute? "Is she gonna be single or not?" I ask him again, my tone steadier. But Alex keeps looking at me. It seems like the question bothers him—maybe even more than he thought. After waiting a few more moments for his response, I ask, "Are you okay?"

He finally blinks, and as if it hurts him, he mutters, "Yes. She will."

CHAPTER 19

Manhattan, September 19, 2020
Petra Van Gatt

"Petra..." I hear someone whispering in my ear. Then I feel soft kisses on my face and forehead as I mutter something under my breath. "Petra, wake up."

"Mmmm..." I say in response, my eyes still closed as my body remains under the warm blanket.

"I need to talk to you," the voice murmurs to me. "Please wake up."

My mind slowly starts processing those words. *I need to talk to you.* And then the voice...

Jeez! It's Alex! I wake up with a jump, startled by the revelation. Opening my eyes, I find him sitting beside me on my bed at Park Avenue.

"How did you get in?" It's the first question that comes to mind.

"Your dad opened the door for me," he replies, keeping his voice just as low.

Sitting up in bed, I turn on the lamp, which gives a cozy and gold-colored light to the room and see it's *2:30 a.m.* on the digital clock lying beside it. Then I look at my fiancé, who's sporting a slim white shirt, and I can't help but notice how tight the sleeves are around his toned biceps or the way his chest flexes under the material. His face is overly serious though, his expression laced with severity and concern as he observes me.

"What's going on?" My tone comes out a bit shaky, but my heart is already pulsing anxiously fast. The more I look at him, the more alarmed and worried I am.

"I'm moving permanently to Singapore." His announcement is enough to make my heart fall to the ground. "I'm leaving in two hours."

"Um…" I bat my eyelids twice, totally speechless. Then, after processing his words, I ask, "So… should I start packing some clothes? We're going together, right?"

Alex gives me a quick smile, looking tenderly at me. "Oh, Petra…" His voice is loaded with sorrow, but he doesn't say anything further. Instead, he takes my hand, giving it a long kiss that squeezes my heart even more. "Your life is here, in New York."

But I pull it back immediately. "My life is with you!" Then I take a deep breath, thinking something through. "This is because of my mom, right?"

"And your dad," he confesses.

And my dad? So he's also against us? I shouldn't be surprised. If anything could destroy his reputation, Dad would automatically stand against it, including us.

"Why did you accept my proposal, then?" I ask, confused. Dazzled. Lost.

"Because I do want to marry you," he replies, his eyes locked on mine. "I just can't." As if he's ashamed to have said so, he breaks eye contact, looking downward.

Those three words, as sharp as a knife, have just perforated me, my soul, my heart, my dreams… And, worst of all, I saw this coming. The nightmare I had was not just a nightmare, but a glimpse into my new reality—a reality without him.

I close my eyes in a failed attempt to control the pain. "Why?" I mumble, knowing all too well the answer. "Why can't you?"

He lets out a sigh, pondering his next words. "Your mom has some dirt against my family, your dad… and me. And she is ready to press charges if I don't leave you alone."

"What kind of dirt?" I ask just as fast.

"The kind that could land me in jail for a long, long time," he says, keeping it short. "I can't tell you exactly what it is, since it involves other people, but I can't take it lightly." He pauses, observing my distress. My mind must have shut down, as I'm totally unable to speak. "Your father tried to talk to her, I also tried, my own mother tried…" His face and voice are filled with disappointment and pain. "I'm so sorry to have started this relationship," he says, sounding defeated. "I should've been wiser."

This is it. He's really breaking up with me. My jaw must've dropped a long time ago by now, and as I process everything he just said, my eyes start watering, and I can't help but sniffle. "So this is how it ends, huh?" Wiping the first tears coursing down my cheeks, I add, "My mom wins, and you let her get away with it?"

"Petra…"

"No!" I shout as I release myself from his embrace. "I thought you'd fight for us. That you'd face anything and beyond for us!"

"I'm doing what is right…"

"For them!" I snap back. "Not for us. Not for me."

"I know it hurts—"

"I hate you," I tell him. "And I'm beyond…" I tilt my head back, trying to contain the tears that are already falling. "I'm beyond disappointed with your attitude and cowardice." I take a deep breath, and, looking him in the eye, I say, "If you give up on us, then you are not the man I fell in love with."

"I know," he replies, his voice just as calm. Then he wipes my tears with his thumbs, pulling me again into his arms. "I love you so damn much. Never forget that." I huff, barely believing his words. "One day you will understand, trust me."

But I push him away. Then I reach for my engagement ring and say, "I guess you might need this."

As I'm about to remove it, he stops me immediately. "No, keep it. This ring is yours. It always will be. Please," he insists. "Keep it as… as a keepsake of the time we spent together."

I feel so empty inside that even death doesn't seem like such a bad option. How can he do this to me? To us? What does my mother have against him, my dad, and his family that is so serious he doesn't even try to fight back?

Before I can think any further, he presses his lips against my forehead in a never-ending kiss. "If you leave for Singapore, I will never forgive you, Alexander," I tell him, my tone threatening. "Never. Do you hear me?"

We look in each other's eyes as if it is the last time.

"Promise me you will take good care of yourself," he asks.

"I won't promise you anything," I snap back. Despite my anger and sobs, I plead once more, "Please don't leave me." I sound pathetic, but my despair is too great to even care. "You can't leave me. Please."

"Hey…" he whispers, soothing me. "You'll be fine. You've got Dr. Nel taking care of you." I close my eyes, trying to force myself to wake up from this nightmare. It must be one. It can only be that. "You're destined to do great things, Miss Van Gatt. I'm sure you'll be fine."

But as stubborn as I am, I keep insisting. "Let me go with you. We can leave everything and everyone behind."

"Petra, they won't even let you in." He pauses for a beat, smiling at my tenacity. "The pilot and crew know very well that you are not supposed to fly with me."

"I will fly commercial, then."

"If you go to Singapore, your parents will find out and bring you back," he explains. "You know that."

"Even by force?" I ask.

"Even by force," he replies. And knowing them as I do, I know they are capable of doing so. "It wasn't an easy decision. I thought about it for many months. I contemplated every possible solution." He stops for a second, as if talking was hurting him. "If I could do something more, I would."

"I'll never forgive you," I tell him again. But the truth is, I'll never forget him either. I'm doomed to love him until the end. I gave him not only my heart, but also myself in a way no one can understand.

"I know," he says under his breath before kissing me on the cheek. "Good night, Miss Van Gatt."

But I instantly grab his arm and ask, "Can you at least kiss me like before?" He doesn't say or do anything, so I ask again, "Just one last kiss."

"Petra…" he mumbles. "I don't think I should."

"Just one," I insist.

He keeps looking me in the eye, hesitating for a moment. "I can't. I'm sorry."

His rejection fills me with shame. As Alex stands up and walks slowly toward the door, I don't try to call him back. I don't even want to. After all, he is the one who has decided to leave me, to abandon me… again.

And the truth is, while Alex has chosen to settle for peace with my parents, I'd have chosen war.

I don't know much about breakups. The only time I ever experienced one, I ended up at the hospital in a six-month coma. Surely this time, I'm staying safely at home, surviving in the darkness of my bedroom, curled up in my big, empty bed. I don't even know what I hate the most about him, the fact that he broke up with me to protect us—me, him?—or the fact that he's not telling me what my mother has against him and everyone else. Is it that bad? I know Dad will never tell me. After all, if there is one thing my father truly cherishes, it's maintaining a perfect image of himself in the public eye and in mine. And now that Alex is out of the equation, Mom won't bother telling me either. I shut my eyes, breathing slowly in and out, wishing somehow I could escape this life—a life I can't even choose for myself.

CHAPTER 20

Manhattan, September 19, 2020
Petra Van Gatt

Morning comes faster than I would have thought. Janine, as punctual as always, opens the curtains wide, allowing the sunlight cast into the room to wake me up. But I don't hear her usual "good morning" to finalize her daily ritual—she most likely knows it's not a good one for me.

I hear nothing but Janine's footsteps walking in my direction. After she sits on my bedside, she lets out a rush of air, softly stroking my head. "Miss," she murmurs. "I'm so sorry about your breakup." My eyes remain closed, but a tear escapes. I remain mute, devoid of any will to even talk. "I wish I could let you stay in bed," she says, her tone just as low and soft. "But your dad is waiting for you to have breakfast."

I sniffle, and, opening my eyes slowly but surely, I mumble, "Oh, Janine." I swallow through my sobs and add, "Please tell my dad I'm not feeling well today." Not that it matters anyway, but at least I can stay in bed a few more minutes.

"Alright, I will let him know."

Janine stands up and leaves my bedroom, only to come back five minutes later. She sits on my bedside again, and, with her voice just as calm as before, she says, "Your dad is demanding your presence. He'd like to talk to you. You can even stay in your pajamas if you want to." Wow. In my pajamas? *What an honor*, I think sarcastically.

I knew Dad would insist. He's such a fucking narcissistic and egocentric man. Trying to sit up, my head feels dizzy like it has been hit by a hammer. "Do you have something for headaches?" I ask her. "My head is hurting so much."

"Of course." Janine stands and gives me a hand to help me up, then takes my robe and helps me put it on. As she does the same with my slippers, my mind and body can barely believe what I went through last night. Just twenty-four hours ago, I was a happily engaged woman, looking forward to spending a romantic weekend with my fiancé. But twenty-four hours ago, I was also a very naive dreamer.

Janine keeps supporting me with an arm around me as I slowly walk out of the bedroom.

Once we reach the terrace where Dad is having breakfast, I say a quick "thank you" to Janine, who then goes to get some medicine for my headache. As I observe my dad from afar, I can't help but despise him even more. Whoever said parents tend to sacrifice themselves for the wellbeing of their children lied. Dad would gladly sacrifice me to keep an immaculate reputation on Wall Street.

"Good morning," Dad says.

I sit down in front of him, barely alive after going through the worst night of my life. "Good morning."

Putting down his newspaper, he observes my gloomy expression. "Look, the smartest way to survive a breakup is to keep yourself busy," Dad advises, his tone devoid of any empathy. "You'll be fine, don't worry."

So easy for him to say, right? Of course, when it's not you, it's always easy to say.

"I hate you," I casually reply as Janine puts my matcha latte on the table and gives me a box of Xanax. "I asked you to go to Rotterdam to support me, not Mom."

"Petra," he snaps, although not too loud. "Watch your mouth. You still live under my roof."

But I reply just as fast, "I'd gladly move out, believe me."

"Let's stop this nonsense, shall we?" he asks, his tone tired and hurt. "You know I tried to convince her."

As I take a Xanax, I say, "You didn't try hard enough." Then I put it in my mouth and drink some of my matcha to swallow it down.

"We are organizing a corporate dinner next month," he informs me. "It'd be a great opportunity to raise some capital to grow your fund. Our clients will be attending, and I've spoken greatly about its performance, you know."

"Are you gonna take a cut if I raise money from your network?"

"No," he promptly replies. "It's the least I can do after everything you're going through." But of course—Dad trying to buy his forgiveness with a capital injection. Does he really believe he can buy me like that?

As Janine brings me avocado toast with vegan cheese and cherry tomatoes, I say, "Okay, thanks." And I take a first bite.

But Dad doesn't stop there. "Petra," he says again, this time with a tone more empathetic. And my attention goes back to him. "Unlike your mom, I know how much you love him. I myself loved your mother just as much."

I raise an eyebrow in total disbelief. "And yet your parents never prevented you from marrying her."

"If I could make things different, I would." Since I don't reply, he adds, "Despite hating it, I supported you and Alex from the beginning. Not many parents would've done the same."

"Yeah…" And as we keep staring at each other, I add, "Until Mom stepped in and threatened your precious little reputation." Dad lets out a sigh, irritated by the blatant truth I've exposed him to. "I might be young, but I'm not stupid," I remind him. "I know there is a lot at stake."

"Did Alex tell you?" he asks suddenly, his voice laced with anxiety and fear.

"He didn't tell me the crimes you committed, no." As I keep looking him in the eye, I can see that the more I remind him of his past crimes, the more inner bruises and cuts I create. Even if he tries to appear unaffected, I know him pretty well. So I decide to say, "But I want you to know that whatever they are, I can handle the truth and forgive you." He breaks eye contact, most likely out of embarrassment. "But I won't forgive you for asking my fiancé to break up with me." And because I want to hurt him as much as he hurt me, I announce, "After that corporate dinner, I'm moving out."

Then, as I stand up, ready to leave the table, Dad asks, "Are you really gonna leave me here all alone?" His voice carries a heavy sadness—a sadness I was looking forward to.

"You've got Janine, no?" I ask, reveling in it.

Immersed under a wave of shock, Dad takes a second to reply. "Yes, but it's not the same." His voice is unusually shaken—he seems so lost and destabilized by my statement that I can't help but rejoice in it.

"Oh, and you've got your precious reputation too," I tell him. His expression remains just as tormented, afraid of losing me once and for all. "Have a great day," I mumble, making my way back inside the house.

"Petra!" Dad stands up, his sadness switching to anger. I stop walking and look back at him. "If you want to become my estranged daughter, then by all means, but you can forget your inheritance."

WHAT?! I cannot for the life of me believe that he's threatening me and my inheritance. "Wow," I blurt out. Now I'm the one in shock. "You would go so far as to disinherit me?"

"If you intend to leave..." he starts, observing my distress, then as our eyes lock, he says, "Yes."

Shaking my head in disgust, I look upward, trying to prevent tears from falling at the blow I just got. After being the perfect daughter for eighteen years, this is what I get in return? Very well, if he is making his moves, so am I. I feel the urge to call Emma's attorney and ask her if Dad can do that. But knowing Dad as I do, he must have already checked it out. Then my mind goes to Julia, and I feel the urge to ask her instead, but I'm not sure if I should. After all, her brother just broke up with me.

"Wow." That's all I manage to say in return. I keep gaping at him, barely believing how our argument has escalated into threats of disinheritance. What a wake-up call this is! Ice water has just been thrown on me, and I feel so sick to my stomach about his intentions that I shout, "What a monster you are!" To my surprise, Dad remains mute. Vexed maybe? I can't tell. But the air is so toxic between us that I can barely breathe. "I, um, I've got to go."

Mercifully, he doesn't try to stop me. When I get to my room, I close the door behind me and call Emma.

Upon hearing her voice, I ask, "Hi, Emma, how are you?"

"I'm good, but by the sound of your voice, I'm not sure if you are."

Lowering my tone, I say, "I got into a big fight with Dad."

"Ooh la la…" Emma replies. "Alright, I get it. You need a place to stay."

I can't help but chuckle. She knows me so well. "Not for now. But we need to talk. Um, do you still have that lawyer of yours?"

"Yeah, of course I do. But what's up?"

"Well, long story short, Alex broke up with me, and Dad threatened to disinherit me if I move out."

"Holy shit!" she shouts. "Are you serious right now?"

"Of course, I'm serious!" I whisper, looking around as if I'm being spied on. "Do you think I'd call you if I wasn't?"

"Damn!" Emma seems to be just as shocked. "That's fucked up. Like... super fucked up. Alright, I'm calling my driver, and I will be there in an hour."

"Can you just call your lawyer first and ask her about inheritance laws in New York, please? I just want to know if he can really do that."

"Yeah, of course. So, should we meet for lunch at your place, then? I mean, your dad's place?"

I huff back at her, knowing all too well that she's teasing. "Ha ha. Thank you for the reality check..."

"Be careful with your moves, babe," she warns.

"I know..."

"Look, take a deep breath, and, um, we'll talk later. I've got you, okay?"

"Thanks Emma."

"Love you," she says before hanging up.

And I smile because love is not something I've experienced very often in this house.

* * *

Once I finish getting dressed, I realize Dad left the house without even apologizing. Not that I was expecting him to anyway, but I thought he wouldn't leave before calming down and at least withdrawing his threat. The ringing of the doorbell brings me back to earth, and, as I glance at my watch, I know it's my group from Columbia. We meet twice a week to work on the analysis of objectivism applied to economics for our study. Today, though, I'd rather be left alone than meet with them.

Janine is already on her way to open the door as I leave the dining room, where we'll be studying, to welcome them. Before they even notice me, I glance over at the mirror to check my face. I look horribly gloomy, sad, and tired. My face is blotchy, and my eyes are swollen from crying.

"Are you alright?" Matthew asks in a low voice as he reaches me.

"Hey," I greet as I see Matthew, followed by Sarah, David, and Katrina. I nod at him, swallowing everything I've gone through the past twelve hours. "Shall we?"

I lead them into the dining room, where I've got my laptop and a few books lying on the table. Once we all sit and everyone has their laptops out, I make the conscious effort to focus on what matters for the hour, and say, "So, I've been working on the impact of objectivism on the individual, the economy, and, consequently, our country," I tell them. Then I give each of them a printed copy of what I wrote. "The idea is to look over what I've done and fact-check if anything is wrong or could be improved."

Matthew is already diving into my dissertation, and everyone else follows. I hope it's decently written though. Jeez, I'm so glad I did it last week. I'm not sure how I would have managed to do it after the breakup.

"Well, it's a pretty classic elaboration of American liberalism," Matthew points out. "Strangely enough, though, you don't mention the wrongdoings that come with it."

"And I'm not surprised by your observation," I tease him with a smirk. "Anything factually incorrect though?"

"Not that I can see," Matthew replies. "You explained everything about how self-interest is an ethical point for objectivism, which in turn is what drives our capitalist society. That is correct."

My smirk turns into a quick laugh. I love how he knows I did a good job, but he can't praise it, because objectivism is something he hates. And, reveling in it, I say, "You know that objectivism, because it's strictly linked to individual freedoms, was actually a driving force of progressivist ideas?" Matthew blinks twice, a bit troubled by my statement. "What? Don't tell me you forgot that Rand was a liberal, from the word *liberalism*, which advocates for individual freedoms and rights, and how the government shouldn't censor and limit anything that goes against the interest of the individual? Many individual rights have been conquered over the years thanks to liberalism, which you claim to hate for some reason."

"I don't hate *that* part of liberalism," he finally admits. "I hate the economical part of it. Big difference."

"So you agree that objectivism is important socially but not economically?" I ask.

"I agree objectivism and liberalism play a big part in human rights, and we are all good there. But when it comes to the economy, it's a big disaster."

"Guys, seriously, *again*?" Sarah chides, letting out a sigh. As I look at everyone else, I see how bored they are at our debate, and I wonder why, because I was really having fun.

"Sarah, this is what this study is all about," Matthew tells her. "We are meant to debate objectivism. Why aren't you guys participating?"

"I couldn't agree more," I emphasize as we glance briefly at each other.

"It seems like a Twitter war," she ripostes.

But Matthew is having none of it. "Petra doesn't even have Twitter," he snaps back. "Philosophy is about debating ideas and concepts. What's wrong with you today?"

"Well, maybe you guys could talk to us instead of just looking at each other," Katrina interposes. "Honestly, we are always excluded. I think it's better if just the two of you go forward with the study."

"Yeah, it only takes two to tango," David adds. "Or, in this case, to debate objectivism."

"And I've got the feeling you'll both end up agreeing with each other at the end," Sarah tells us. "You guys most likely think exactly alike, and you just don't know it yet."

"What?" we both say at the same time, looking at Sarah.

"We don't think alike *at all*," Matthew presses on, nearly in outrage. "Petra is into objectivism, and I'm not."

"Matt, you know more about objectivism than I know about my own self," Sarah points out. She draws in a breath and adds, "Like, I wanted to do this study to help my grades, but this is just becoming a pretext for you guys to talk to each other."

Before I can even fully assess her comment, Matthew takes over. "Petra has already done at least half of the study, and you're complaining?"

And I can't help but smile at the way he's defending me. Trying to offer a compromise, I say, "Alright, what if we explore objectivism as applied to financial markets and the economy?" Which was basically the goal from the beginning.

"Exactly," Matthew replies just as fast. "That's where I think the self-interest goes too far. We know laissez-faire capitalism does a lot of wrong and hurts a lot of people, especially the working class."

"Now you sound like Prof. Reich," I tell him.

And Matthew seems to like it—his lips twitch into a smile full of pride. "Thanks."

Sarah, on the other hand, just rolls her eyes. "See? That's exactly what I said. You both will just end up agreeing about exactly everything. It's inevitable."

"Well…" Matthew keeps his eyes pinned on me and his smile just as big. "Great minds think alike."

I shake my head at his teasing, but a quick chuckle escapes me. When Matthew said this course was pure intellectual porn, I guess he couldn't have been more right. "Okay, so what if we include the negative aspects of objectivism in the study?" I suggest. "I enjoy objectivism for the social aspect, which gave us individual freedoms—including freedom of expression, which, as an artist myself, I truly value—but I'm sure it's not a perfect philosophy."

Matthew nods, agreeing with me. "I think it's a great analysis. I'm in." He takes something from his backpack and hands me a bunch of papers.

As I read the title of the first page, I can't help but laugh. "'Ten Reasons Why Objectivism Sucks'?"

"No need to thank me," he teases. And as he watches me flick through the pages, he adds, "I couldn't help it."

Instinctively, a smirk tugs on my lips, but the sound of my iPhone ringing startles us. And as I look at it, I see that it's my alarm to announce the end of the meetup. *Wow.* It went by so fast. As we all stand up, I see that Sarah, Katrina, and David are the first ready to leave, while Matthew seems to take his time.

"You coming? Our Uber is here," Sarah asks him as she's about to cross through the doorway with the rest of the group. But by his stare, I guess he wants to talk to me.

"I'll take another one…" And once we are left alone, Matthew stands in front me and, in a voice quite humbling, says, "I'm sorry for Sarah's attitude today."

"It's alright…" And I give him a soft pat on his arm. "You have to admit, though, we kinda monopolized the discussion about objectivism."

A trace of a guilty smile lands on his lips. "Well, we're just two people very passionate about it. If anything, we're giving them free entertainment."

I crack a laugh at his observation. *Fair point.* "Thanks for everything," I blurt out a bit unexpectedly. "Um, it's nice to have you around." I'm not the best at expressing myself, but I want him to know he matters.

"We are vegan besties after all." Without expecting it, though, he drags me into his arms, giving me a hug for the first time since I woke up from the coma.

With the current pandemic, hugs have been few and far in between, but some empathy and compassion feels too good to pass up. And, reveling in his embrace, a wave of emotions goes through me as I realize Alex won't hug me anymore. In fact, after this meetup, my fiancé was supposed to come here and pick me up, which is what I set up the alarm for. But thanks to the worst parents in the world, he's now most likely in the air on the way to Singapore. The realization brings tears to my eyes, and I can't help but sniffle.

"Hey," Matthew whispers, looking at me. "What's wrong?"

Oh jeez, what a freaking embarrassment. I wipe the tears and take a deep breath, as I think about whether to tell him the truth or not. Matthew keeps observing me, most likely wondering where this emotional breakdown is coming from. Our eyes lock for a second, but then I look down instantly. And, for better or worse, I decide to open up. "Sorry, um, my fiancé just broke up with me…" I never thought I'd say those words. And yet here we are.

"Wow…"

I thought Matthew would crack some dry joke about how dumb I was to get engaged so young, but nope. He actually just gives me another hug to soothe me. For the first time, I notice how good he smells, but I resist the urge to ask him about his cologne.

"What an asshole he is. I'm so sorry."

I know at this point that my face and mind are a big mess. I'm tired from crying, tired from the pain, tired from everything.

"When did he break up with you?" he asks, releasing me.

My heart feels stuck in my throat, but I bring myself to say, "Um, at two o'clock this morning."

"Damn…"

I sniffle, and trying to prevent more tears from falling, I make the conscious effort to calm down. "Yeah, it sucks."

"If I may ask, why did he break up with you?"

"He moved to Singapore," I reply, keeping it short. There's no need to tell him the whole truth anyway. "And it seems he doesn't want me there."

To my surprise, he brings my chin up, and says, "Well, he's a fucking idiot." Matthew holds on to me, rubbing my arms and giving me strength.

"Thanks. I really appreciate it." And I release a deep breath.

"Do you want to do something later tonight? We could go for dinner or—"

"I'm okay…" I give him a smile as we stare at each other for a few heartbeats, and then say, "For now, I need some time alone." The truth is, I can't find the will to do anything. If I could just go to bed and sleep, I would.

"Alright…" Matthew can't hide his disappointment, but he also smiles in return, and, after putting his backpack on his shoulder, he adds, "If you need someone to talk to, I'm here."

CHAPTER 21

Petra Van Gatt

Just twenty minutes after Matthew leaves, the doorbell rings again. This time, though, I rush to open the door, and when I find Janine in the hallway, I say, "It's alright. I'll take care of it."

As I open the door, I see the one and only Emma Hasenfratz, slaying it with perfectly styled bangs, red lips, and an all-black outfit—extra-large D&G T-shirt, denim shorts, ankle boots, and big black sunglasses on her face.

"Babe, Emma Hasenfratz is here to save the day, don't worry," she says, stepping in. "I've got you."

Shaking my head in amusement, I inwardly chuckle at her comment. And after giving her two cheek kisses, I notice Emma's holding a file in one hand and a bottle of Dom Pérignon in the other. "Um, are we celebrating something?"

"I'm saving you from misery, so yeah, we are."

I can't help but roll my eyes. "Jeez! Don't exaggerate. I still have my own fund and some savings."

"Babe, I'm not talking about misery in a financial sense, duh." But my eyes squint in confusion. "I'm talking misery as in emotional misery."

Oh, emotional misery. Yeah, that pretty much sums up how I'm feeling right now. But does she think a bottle of Dom Pérignon is gonna fix it?

Emma follows me into the kitchen and, after greeting Janine, puts the champagne in the fridge. Then we stay quiet as we wait for Janine to leave us alone. Once we hear the door close behind us, Emma hands me the file and says, "Your dad needs to sign this, and you'll be fine." I start reading the contract, and I can't help but be impressed at how protective it would be of my inheritance. "My lawyer and I already signed it as your witnesses. Your dad just has to do the same, and he won't be able to disinherit you. Even if he wants to."

The more I read the contract, the more I wonder if Dad will ever agree to sign it. If he did, that would be perfect. "So, as long as I talk to him once in a while, he can't disinherit me, right?"

"Yeah. Basically, as long as you talk to him once a month, it's fine. You cannot become an estranged daughter though, which means never seeing him again." The contract is everything any heir would ever want—it protects my inheritance without letting my parents control me. From what I read, as long as I text Dad once in a while and meet with him once a year, he cannot disinherit me from the shares of Gatt-Dieren, the penthouse on Park Avenue, or any accounts that belong to him or any trust that he's the beneficiary of. There's even a clause that says he cannot sell his shares or his penthouse without my written notarized consent. "This is a really good contract."

Then I realize Emma must have a similar agreement with her parents. "You have the same thing with your parents, huh?"

Ms. Hasenfratz gives nothing away but a smirk. After a few seconds, though, she says, "Babe, there are two things in life you always have to watch out for: your ass and your assets."

Wow. It feels like she just described objectivism in one sentence.

"What?"

Oops! I must have said that out loud. "Nothing…" I say, as I don't feel like explaining to her an entire philosophy focused on self-interest, at least not now. "Thanks for everything, Emma. You are the best."

"And you?" she asks, looking me in the eye. "How are you coping with the breakup? And, like, why did he break up with you in the first place?" She sounds irritated and angry simply at the thought of it. "That's crazy. Everything seemed to be fine."

For a second, I barely remembered that I had told her about my breakup. And I'm glad I only have two friends that I talk to on a regular basis—each time I hear the word *breakup*, there is an uncontrollable wave of emotion that emerges within me and brings me down. But enough tears. I already gave a pathetic show in front of Matthew; I'm not going to do the same with Emma. I take a deep breath, and I mentally crave a hole in the ground to bury these depressing thoughts deep down and leave them there once and for all.

"It's just like my nightmare. It's crazy. Mom threatened Dad and Alex with something she's holding against them, and Alex just left," I tell her. "He didn't even try to fight back, you know."

"Jeez…" Her eyes widen in shock, and her mouth even gapes. "Do you have any idea what it can be?"

After pondering for a few seconds, I say, "I just know it's a crime serious enough to land them in jail."

"Holy shit…" Emma blinks twice, dazzled by my revelation. "Your dad and Alex in jail? Are you serious? Even if they *did* commit some serious crime, I can't see them behind bars."

"I know… It sounds impossible. It must be something really bad."

Emma looks downward as she thinks something through. "Do you want me to hire some people and see if they can find out?"

A few days ago, I'd have called Emma crazy and declined straightaway. But now…

"How much does it cost to hire those people?" I ask.

"Don't worry about it, babe, it's on me…" she says, brushing my arm. "But they are known to find things no one else can."

The more I assess her offer, the more I realize that if those people are capable of uncovering those secrets, they'd be a weapon they can use against Dad and Alex and threaten them with, just like Mom is doing. And that doesn't sit well with me. "No, I better not. I don't want anyone else involved," I tell her. "If anyone is going to find out, it's got to be me and no one else."

Emma seems a bit disappointed about my decision and says, "Alright, as you wish. How are you gonna find out, then?"

"I'm gonna ask those who know," I tell her.

But Emma chuckles at my overly simple and naive tactic. "Good luck with that." After drawing in a breath, she looks me in the eye again and asks in a low voice, "Do you think it's really over?"

That's the question I've been asking myself since he left. And the truth is…

"I don't know… Alex explicitly said it was. But it's not like he wants to—he's just being forced."

"Yeah, that sucks big time." Emma lets out a rush of air, shaking her head, her expression becoming serious. "Fuck, I wish I could do something for you."

"It's not you who has to," I tell her, putting my hands on her arms. "It's him. *He's* the one who decided to leave." And as we stare at each other, we exchange a small smile. "You are the most amazing friend I could ask for, Emma. Thank you for everything." And I plunge her into a tight hug. Then, as I release her, I give her a kiss on the cheek, filled with gratitude. "You'll have lunch with me, right?"

"Yeah, of course," she says, her eyes gleaming with joy. "Should we drink this bottle?"

"When Dad signs the agreement, we will."

And for some unknown reason, her face becomes grave again. "You know, my flight is tomorrow."

"Oh," I utter back. Damn, I had totally forgotten about her trip to Europe. "Well, when you come back, then. I think Dad is having another gala dinner next month. You have to come, you know that, right?" And since she seems to be hesitating, I add, "It's in our friendship agreement. You signed it."

We break out in laughter, and, as she bites her bottom lip, she says, "Alright, text me the details when you can."

After lunch, and since I've got homework to do, I escort Emma back to the entryway. There, we hug each other again, and, before I can open the door, she asks, "You sure you don't want me to stay until your Dad comes home?"

"It's alright, don't worry." All of a sudden, though, my iPhone starts ringing, and, as I grab it from my pocket, my eyes widen in surprise as I see the name of the caller.

"Who's calling?" Emma asks as she sees me not picking up.

"Um, my mom." Well, of course she's calling me. Now that she knows I'm awake and that Alex and I broke up, she's gonna try to get back into my life. Too bad—I've got no intension of ever talking to her again.

"Are you gonna reply?"

"Nope." And I mute the call just as fast. "Not even in a thousand years." Then I put my phone back inside my back pocket and give Emma another hug. "Thank you so much for everything."

"Always, girl," she whispers, her head resting against mine.

I open the door and say, "Enjoy your time in Europe."

"You sure you don't want to come? After a breakup, there is nothing better than traveling with your best friend, you know."

The idea sounds really inviting. But there is no amount of travel, alcohol, or fancy villas that will fix my heart. And, unfortunately, I know that all too well.

* * *

I glance once more at my watch. It's nine p.m., and, since Dad usually comes home around this time, I remain patiently waiting for him in his study-library, the contract lying on his desk. I text him: *Are you coming home tonight? I'm in the library. I think we should talk.* Then, lying on the sofa, I pick up my book and keep reading. Fifteen minutes later, Dad texts me back: *Alright, see you there soon.* I wonder what he means by "soon," but as I hear the front door opening and footsteps walking in, there's no need for more guessing. A knocking sound then startles me, and as I see Dad open the door, I pray we can have a civilized conversation that doesn't end in tears and name calling.

"Hey," Dad greets quietly as he steps inside. "Are you doing okay?" At least this time, he sounds calm and serene. That's a good sign.

I invite him to sit beside me, and, as we look at each other, I decide to start. "Um, look, I don't want to become your estranged daughter. But, as you might understand, you've contributed greatly to my unhappiness, my emotional instability, and my breakup." I might sound overly formal, but I won't let my emotions drive me mad again. I have an inheritance to protect, and that's what I'm gonna do. "Can we at least agree on that?"

Dad winces at my observation but doesn't deny it. And to my surprise, he nods and says, "We can agree on that."

"Great." I stand up and take the contract from his desk. Then, as I sit beside him again, I continue to argue my case. "I never thought in my entire life that you'd want to disinherit me. Honestly, I don't think I deserve it. I'm getting a degree in economics just as you wanted, I did the internship last year as you suggested, and I've always tried my best not to disappoint you." As I say these words, he nods pensively, his focus on me. "So, um, I spoke to Emma's lawyer, and she drew up an agreement for us that will ensure these kinds of threats don't happen again." I hand him the contract, and his eyes widen in surprise; nevertheless, he takes his glasses from his inner pocket and starts reading the first page. Instinctively, though, my pulse starts rising as I watch him do so.

"Well, I see she's really got your back," he comments as he turns to the second page. A smirk escapes me, but I lower my head to hide it. "Very well…" Dad removes his glasses and looks down pensively. After some more pondering, his eyes land on me, and he says, "I want to include something else in it." My heart hammers against my ribs at the realization that he wants to make changes. "If you want to inherit everything stated here, you have to graduate in economics, *finance*-economics," he corrects. "And I want you to see Dr. Nel at least twice a week for a month."

"See Dr. Nel? For what?" I ask instantly.

"For therapy to recover from your breakup."

Does he really believe I will get over it in one month? Jeez, not even in a year, let alone a month. "Um, alright."

"And," he starts again, "as long as you live in the state of New York, I'd like to see you once a week, preferably on Sunday."

What? From once a year to every Sunday, that's a big difference. Fuck... Well, I guess I'll have to move to New Jersey, then.

"Oh, and, eh, once a month if you live outside of the state." Did he hear my thoughts or what?

"Okay. Deal. But if I live outside of New York, you have to travel."

"No problem, it'll be a pleasure to visit you wherever you live."

I take a deep breath, assessing all his requests. I have to graduate, which I intended to, see Dr. Nel for a month, and then visit him once a week if I live in the state of New York. Alright, I think I can manage that. "Okay, I'm gonna make the changes and will give you a new contract tomorrow."

A satisfied smile tugs at his lips, and, as I'm about to stand up, his words make me fall back again in my seat. "I'm not the monster you think I am, Petra."

For once, he sounds empathetic and caring. But I can never be too prudent with him. After colluding with Mom to destroy my relationship with Alex, Dad is, and always will be, the enemy. No matter what he says, no matter what he does. There is no amount of inheritance that can buy his forgiveness. At this point, this is purely me saving my ass and my assets, just like Emma told me.

"I know," I tell him for the sake of making him feel good about himself. "Thanks for everything." I lean over to give him a kiss on the cheek. "Good night, Dad."

He seems to rejoice at my affection and gives me one on the forehead. "Good night."

CHAPTER 22

Manhattan, September 21, 2020
Petra Van Gatt

Few things in life are as useless as paying a visit to Dr. Nel. But since it's in the inheritance contract that Dad, his lawyer, and I just signed this morning, I've got to play my part and spend one hour twice a week lying on her couch and looking at the white ceiling in her minimalist office.

"Petra?"

"Mm?" I turn to my right side and see Dr. Nel sitting in a black armchair, glasses on, legs crossed, holding her notebook and a pen.

As she glances at her watch, she says, "You've been here thirty minutes, and you've barely spoken."

I let a little smirk escape. Talking was not part of the contract. Just my presence here was.

"Oh," I mumble for the sake of saying something.

"Alright…" She closes her notebook and grabs something from her briefcase. "If you don't want to open up, then I'm gonna have to cancel all our meetings."

"What?!" Now I jump from the couch and say, "There's no need for that." Her lips twitch in a smile at my fearful expression, and she keeps tapping her pen on the notebook like a drum—most likely for me to hurry up. Knowing there's no escape, I draw in a breath and ask, "What do you want me to say?"

"I told you," she pauses, gauging my reaction. As I cock my head to the side in confusion and squint my eyes, she repeats her question. "What have you been dreaming of?"

"I don't dream," I tell her just as fast. "I haven't been able to sleep properly since he left."

"Nightmares, then?"

Nightmares. Of course I have nightmares. When I'm alone in the darkness of my bedroom, all I think about is him. I can even feel his presence as if he were there. When I close my eyes, I can feel him squeezing me tight in his arms, his fingers lingering on my bare skin. I can see his full lips and the way they curve up to smile at me, his piercing blue eyes and how they gleam. And I can even smell his scent as if he left it all over my bed. Everything about him is power and beauty at the same time. Jeez, all these memories… They're a mix of remembering the past, crying for the future I will never have, and hoping I'm wrong about all of it. But I can't tell her that. Nope. I know she'll tell my dad everything after the session. I have to tell her something that won't raise any alarms. "I don't have those either. Now that he's gone, I only have insomnia."

"That's easy to fix," she answers, writing something in her notebook. "I will give you a prescription for a pill you can take before going to bed, and you'll sleep like a baby."

I highly doubt her meds will work, but I give her a sugary smile and say, "Thanks."

"Have you been eating?" Another annoying question that makes me cringe. "You look skinnier."

"Um, I do have some trouble with that," I tell her, embarrassed at the reality she's exposed me to.

"Why don't you eat?"

I shrug my shoulders in return. "If I knew…"

"Does the food you have at home taste bad?

"Oh, no," I reply just as fast. "Janine is a great cook. I'm just never hungry."

"Your body is. It's your mind that prevents it from getting the nutrients it needs to survive." The more she talks, the more self-conscious I feel about the whole thing. I've always had issues with eating. It's nothing new, yet it's usually due to stress, which is easily manageable with Xanax. "Why are you doing this to yourself, Petra?" Her voice is soft, yet her question goes right through me. She sounds disappointed, like a mother to her child.

I press my lips tightly together and close my eyes, no longer courageous enough to face her or the present reality. "When I close my eyes, it's like I can escape this reality, this life… and everything I can't control," I tell her. "I guess with eating it's the same."

"You feel in control when you don't eat?" I wish I could shut my ears just like I can with my eyes. But alas, for some reason, we haven't been designed like that.

You feel in control when you don't eat? Her question keeps playing in my head like a broken record, or like an intro-spection I should've done a long time ago. "I…" I have no will to answer, no will to face the demons that haunt me and make me do things to myself that I should be ashamed of. "Maybe," I mutter. "I've already spoken a lot for the first session," I rebuke, trying somehow to end the session sooner or just to talk about the weather and nothingness. Since I don't hear any answer in return, I open my eyes and look at Dr. Nel. She's busy writing something in her notebook. Then her head goes up, and she fakes a big, friendly grin. "Is Emma still here?"

I lift my brows instantly, astonished by her question. What does Emma have anything to do with what we were talking about? Well, it doesn't matter—at least this is an eas-ier question to answer. "No, Emma is in Europe. She left yesterday."

"So you don't have any friends to hang out with?"

"I have my group from Columbia, but we just meet twice a week to study." And as I watch Dr. Nel taking notes that will surely be read by my dad later on, I can't help but won-der what does having friends to hang out with have anything to do with me eating?

"So if you don't hang out with your friends, what do you do in your free time?"

"I like to read and paint."

"Paint?" Dr. Nel repeats as she nods, thinking something through. "Petra, I'd like you to paint something that is a re-flection of your own self."

I'm left speechless at her request. "A reflection of my own self?" I repeat, but mostly to myself. What does that even mean?

"Yes, take a white canvas and start painting what you feel represents you and your emotions the best."

I wonder why on earth she is asking me to do this, but having a good relationship with your physician is advisable, so I simply mumble, "Um, okay…" The truth is, I haven't painted since I woke up. I should definitely start again. At least it's a good way to cope with my depression.

In a sudden move, Dr. Nel leaves her armchair and goes to her desk, where she writes me a medical prescription. "Here," she says, now extending a piece of paper to me. "There is everything you need to sleep well and to fight your depression."

And I smile, accepting it. But it's not because of the prescription, no; it's because I know our first session is finally over.

***

Manhattan, September 26, 2020

My new painting has been progressing well. It's dark, melancholic, and… well, a bit depressing. *A reflection of my own self*, like Dr. Nel suggested. At least I've managed to keep myself busy and, most importantly, isolated from Janine and Dad, who've been pretty vocal about my eating habits.

"Petra, get out of here." Dad keeps knocking impatiently on the locked door of my atelier. "You're gonna have dinner with me whether you want to or not. Enough is enough!"

"I'm not hungry," I shout once more as I remain focused on the canvas in front of me. "Leave me alone."

But Dad doesn't give up. "Very well. Janine will lock the kitchen door and there will be nothing for you to eat," he threatens. I shrug my shoulders. If I want to eat, I will order something. "And no food delivery will be allowed to come in."

I turn my gaze to the door at his serious tone, but knowing him as I do, I'm gonna guess he's just bluffing. "Good…" I answer. And my attention goes back to the panting.

I hear an exasperated exhale from him. "Is this some sort of punishment toward me?" His question makes me stop for a second, my heart squeezing a bit at his concern. He sounds worried and genuinely saddened at not seeing me for the past few days. But I kill those thoughts just as fast. Dad is always bluffing, and at this point, I should know better. "Please open the door," he insists, his tone laced with frustration as he keeps pushing on the handle in some hope that it'll magically unlock itself. "I've been very patient with you, Petra. Why are you doing this?"

I ignore his second question just like I did the first one, and, picking up another brush, I take a bit more black oil paint from the palette and softly stroke it onto the canvas.

"Very well, I won't leave until you open this door." He's so pushy, my goodness! "I just want to talk…" And it's either me, or I just heard a quick sob coming from behind the door. "I haven't seen you in days. Is it asking too much to have dinner with you?"

Closing my eyes, I blow out a breath in exasperation. I won't be able to manage remaining focused if he keeps insisting and pushing me emotionally to the edge. It's better to talk to him once and for all, and then come back later to paint. I put my brush and wooden palette down, clean my hands, and go to open the door. "Alright," I mumble as I unlock it.

And to my surprise, his eyes widen in shock upon seeing me. "You are so…" He lets his words trail off as he observes me from top to bottom, disappointment laced in his gaze. "Skinny."

I can't help but lower my head, ashamed in some way by what I've been doing to myself. I've been avoiding Janine and Dad like the plague for the past few days and pretending either to be asleep or to be too busy here to go down and eat.

"Have you looked at yourself in the mirror?" His voice is filled with a sadness that tightens my heart even more. "I don't want to send you to the hospital because you are not eating." I see his eyes water, and he rubs them before continuing. "You are way below your normal weight. You know that, right?"

I nod, not looking at him.

"This hunger strike has got to stop." Dad pushes my chin up, forcing my eyes to meet his. "I won't let this depression kill my daughter."

Tears leak out of the corner of my eyes and roll down my cheeks, and, with a sob of despair, I sniffle them back, forcing myself to behave. I don't want to show him how much this whole situation has affected me, but my expression must have betrayed me a long time ago. "I'm sorry. I just…" I sniffle once more, and my hands go to my cheeks to dry them. "I just can't find the will to get better."

"I'm sorry too," he whispers as he brings me into his embrace. "I'm sorry you have to go through this." And while Dad squeezes me tight in his arms, a hug is something I'd have welcomed from a friend—not from a traitor.

And as he releases me, I remind him just as fast, "I will never forgive you."

"I know." His thumbs go to my eyelids, where he wipes the tears still falling, then, to my surprise, he presses his lips against my forehead. The gesture is so familiar that it hurts and heals at the same time. "But you have to eat."

* * *

There is nothing more beautiful than observing the snow peacefully coating the ground in the gardens of Bedford Hills. I keep my face pinned against the window as I marvel at every snowflake falling from the sky. Alex told me he asked the Snow Queen to send it so we could build a snowman. Letting out a sigh, I wonder when I can have the same powers as her. After all, I was also born in December. If I had them, I'd cover the gardens with snow during the summer. But from what Alex told me, it seems her powers only work during winter, because the Queen hibernates afterward. Maybe there is another way… Oh! What if I ask for a magic wand from Santa Claus? Turning to my godfather, who's lying on the sofa reading, I ask, "Alex?"

"Mm?"

"If I ask Santa Claus for a magic wand, do you think I'd be able to make snow fall in the summer?"

He looks at me with a thoughtful expression, and I keep mine just as serious, before he says, "You know only the Snow Queen has that power."

I dip my head, huffing at his reply, and cross my arms. But he doesn't say anything back and just continues reading. I don't like when he pays more attention to a book than to me. So I walk over, and, standing in front of him, I poke his arm repeatedly.

"Yes, Miss Van Gatt?" He sounds annoyed, and I giggle, knowing I'm the reason for it.

"Why can't you ask the Snow Queen to give me her powers while she hibernates? I could use them during the summer."

Alex lets out a breath in response and closes his book before sitting up on the sofa. I see his lap available, and I resist the urge to sit there. He already told me not to if I haven't asked politely first. But he also told me I'm a princess, and to me, princesses shouldn't ask permission to do anything. My lips twitch, undecided, but if he becomes disappointed with me, he'll tell the Snow Queen, and she might never make the snow fall ever again.

"Because you need to be older first."

My mouth drops because he never told me my age was a problem. "How much older?" I ask, annoyance thick in my tone.

"The Snow Queen only gives her power to adults. You are too young."

I feel tears resting on my eyelids, disappointed at the sad reality. "How long should I wait, then?"

Alex gives me a side smile and lifts me up to sit on his lap. "Those powers require a lot of responsibilities," he tells me. "In ten years, maybe I can introduce you to the Snow Queen."

"Ten years?" I repeat in outrage, thinking about the immensity of what ten years means. "That's a lot of winters and summers."

Alex chuckles in return before pressing his lips tightly together against my head. "Great power requires great responsibility."

I don't know what he means by that, but I know the ground outside is white enough for us to build a snowman.

"Can we go outside and play?" I ask him, my eyes looking upward at his.

"Sure, let's go," Alex replies, setting me on my feet.

"Yeah!" I clap my hands in excitement, my heart pulsing at a thousand miles an hour as I wait for him to stand up. "Let's go!" I shout, rushing to leave his library. Then I go into the hallway and try to grab my coat hanging on the wall. It's a bit too high for me, so I jump, reaching my hand up as high as I can, but it's in vain. I see Alex walking in my direction, and he effortlessly takes my coat and his. Then he leans down to my level and holds my coat wide open for me to put it on.

"Let's go," I press on as he helps me put my gloves on. Then he takes my scarf and my beanie, and I huff, my patience running thinner with every beat. Meanwhile, Alex insists that I wear them. He covers my head with the beanie and then with the hood of my coat. Once we're ready, my godfather opens the front door, and my smile grows wider as I take in my surroundings.

"Wow…" I utter in total awe at the endless snow coating the fields. I rush outside in a hurry to get started and gather as much snow as possible in my hands. Then I lift them up and throw the snow in the air. And I watch, marveling as the snow floats away, taken up by the wind like magic. Wow… "Have you seen this?" I ask, still fascinated, but no one answers. Looking around, I don't see my godfather anywhere.

"Alex?" My smile drops, and I slowly walk back toward the door, searching for him. "Alex?" I repeat, stepping onto the front porch. When no one replies, my heart freezes, not knowing why. "Alex?" Then I hear footsteps, but no one is coming. I hear him saying he loves me, but there is no one around…

My eyes opening wide, I realize it was just another nightmare. Sleeping has become scary to me, and I wonder if this is a side effect of the pills Dr. Nel prescribed me. I keep having the same nightmares, then the same illusions, and the same hope that one day, when I expect it the least, Alex will come back and surprise me. Maybe he will be standing at the entrance of Columbia like last time. And like last time, Matthew will want to take a photo in front of the Rolls-Royce Phantom. This time, though, I'll gladly hold his iPhone and take it. Then I remind myself that there is too much at stake and forgetting Alex is the only wise thing to do. But I can't—my heart is full of hopes.

How foolish of you, my mother would say.

But this sense of hope is beyond my control. Because, after all, hope is what makes the world go round, right?

Hope is what gives us the strength to wake up every day, believing that today will be a better day.

We want to believe it. We need to believe it.

Everything will be alright, the sweet words we hear constantly no matter how bad we feel.

Sunlight is already timidly piercing through the curtains, announcing another day—another day without him…

I know I've got to get up. Since I promised I'd do so without Janine, I push down the sheets and drag myself out of bed, then, moving like a zombie, I head to the bathroom and into the shower. The warm water falls on my tense shoulders as I try to stand steadily, but my body and mind are still asleep, unready for one more day that will just feel like the previous one.

* * *

Manhattan, September 29, 2020

Every day is the same monotonous routine devoid of any meaning. I read my books with a smile, jumping from one online class to another, but it's like living out of boredom, patiently waiting for death to take me.

Then at two p.m., and because it's Tuesday, Anthony is waiting for me downstairs to take me to my appointment with Dr. Nel. Matthew and the group were kind enough to stay with me for lunch—a ritual that makes me eat a bit more twice a week.

"This time, tell her something." Matthew surprises me not only with his caring tone, but by planting a kiss on my temple.

"You shouldn't worry," I mumble, letting a smile escape.

"I want you to be healthy. And happy and alive, just like before." He brushes a lock of hair behind my ear, and I drop my gaze, a bit troubled about how much he cares. "And you should want it too."

His voice brings my eyes up again, but, as I look at him, I've got nothing to say. Giving him a side smile, I just head toward Anthony, who greets me while opening the door.

✳ ✳ ✳

"What was the point of waking up if it's to live like this?" While I remain lying on the velvet chaise lounge, looking at the white ceiling, I feel like Dr. Nel is smiling at me behind her big notebook. I've never initiated a conversation with her before, and I know she wasn't expecting I'd do so today.

"What do you mean 'like this'?"

Keeping my gaze on the ceiling above me, I say, "Without joy... or the will to live..."

"You are going through a depression. It's normal that you —"

"I miss him," I finally tell her. But I don't stop there, no. If I have to "tell her something," then I'll tell her everything. "I miss him every single day. More and more." The sadness my words carry has rendered Dr. Nel totally speechless. "I, um, I don't sleep well, I've got nightmares... Every day the same ones... But who cares, right?"

"I do care." My gaze goes in her direction, and I see Dr. Nel removing her glasses as she looks at me pensively, and I wonder if she can see anything without them. "Tell me about them."

"Well, um, they're always of childhood memories." And my heart squeezes tight as I remember them. "Those of pure joy and happiness."

"You had a lot of those moments with your godfather when you were young?"

"Yeah, my dad was always traveling and busy, so most weekends, I'd go to Bedford Hills." A little laugh rolls off my lips, and I decide to share my thoughts with her. "Alex used to say he knew the Snow Queen and that once I became an adult, she'd give me her powers." Seeing how Dr. Nel is squinting her eyes in confusion, I decide to explain, "Um, the Snow Queen is responsible for snow and winter. It's also my favorite season, and when I was a child, I wanted to play in the snow all the time."

"You don't need him or the Snow Queen to be happy, Petra," she rebukes just as fast. Her patronizing tone is quite revolting though. "You can do it on your own, you know." Dr. Nel starts tapping her pen on the notebook, considering me. "I understand you're associating happy memories with him. But you can build happy memories with your own self."

I'm perfectly aware how pathetic I must sound talking to Dr. Nel about my childhood memories, when I felt understood, loved, and appreciated for who I was by a man that she and my parents despise. After all, why am I even surprised by her reaction? "I'm trying…" I answer her, not even bothering to refute her statements. "I'm taking the pills you prescribed me, um, I'm painting, I'm focusing on my studies, but I still miss him…" Yeah, I'm just human, I guess.

"Yet you barely eat, smile, or talk to anyone," she points out. "Your parents are worried about you. They care a lot about you."

Lies. Clear-cut lies. That's what Dr. Nel and my parents are all about—creating a world where they feed me illusions. The illusion that they care about me, while in reality, it's all about them and the chess game they are playing with each other. I'm just a pawn in the way. Tired of her fakery, I can't help but say, "The truth is, Alex had to leave because Mom told him to." And simply the idea of it infuriates me. "Why? What does she have against him?" I ask once more.

But I know Dr. Nel will never tell me. She might not even know either.

"He is too old for you," she replies, putting her glasses on to write something in her notebook. "It was not a healthy relationship, and it was not doing you any good."

I couldn't disagree more. When Alex was around, my previous doctors told me I could reduce my intake of Xanax, and my agoraphobia seemed to be under control. But there is no point arguing because that's not what matters to Dr. Nel. Her job is to put a smile on my face and to, no matter what, make me forget him. But since the day I saw Alex again at my dad's fifty-fifth birthday, I knew it would be impossible for me to do so. I will always miss him—no matter how hard she tries to cure me.

As she glances at her watch, she closes her notebook, and says, "Thank you, Petra. We have made some good progress today. See you on Friday."

CHAPTER 23

Manhattan, October 2, 2020
Petra Van Gatt

It has been two weeks since Alex broke up with me. And since then, I haven't heard anything from him. Foolishly, I texted him again yesterday and asked how he was doing. But he didn't even see my messages. I then tried to send the same texts to him on WhatsApp and found out, to my greatest surprise, that he had blocked me. Yes, blocked. After everything we've gone through together, I keep wondering how someone I trust and love so much can treat me like this and move to the other side of the world. I've come to the conclusion that whatever my mom holds against him, my dad, and his family cannot justify his choice to sacrifice us and our happiness. The man I love would've never bowed to my parents' threats—he would've fought back. But this is nothing more than wishful thinking. Because the reality is, that Alex didn't fight back. Alex simply left. Then I recall how we were supposed to get married in two months. And I can't help but

feel tears rise. I heave several quick sobs, as I no longer believe that our wedding will still happen. How am I supposed
to forget him? It feels impossible for me to do so.

But my thoughts are instantly shattered by the sound of
my iPhone ringing. As I look at who's calling, I see it's Mom.
Again? Shaking my head, I put my iPhone back on the
nightstand. I can't believe how persistent she can be. After a
hundred tries, she knows I won't pick up the phone. Why is
she still insisting? Should I block her number once and for
all? What if I pick up the call this time and tell her to fuck
off? Or what if I actually try to persuade her to leave me and
Alex in peace? No, she'll never agree to it. My phone keeps
ringing, and the more I hear it, the more my nerves boil.
She hasn't stopped calling me since Alex broke up with me.
What if she wants to tell me the truth? The real reason behind why she is so against us? For better or worse, I decide
to give her a shot at explaining herself, and I answer it.
"Yes?"

"Oh my God!" I hear Mom breaking into tears and sobbing on the other side. "Oh, my little angel, I'm so happy to
hear your voice."

But my anger starts rising upon hearing her joy. "You're
happy, huh? You are such a disgusting bitch!" I can't help it.
The words roll out of my mouth. "You destroyed us! You
have no idea how much I hate you!"

Mom doesn't reply. She takes a deep breath in and then
out, and finally says in the calmest voice I've ever heard,
"Honey, I know you're upset. I totally get it."

"No, you don't. You don't know shit," I snap back. Tears
stream down my face recalling the ugly reality I'm currently

living. "You have no idea how horrible my life has been." Mom doesn't cut me off, and I hear nothing but her breath. "Are you there?"

"I am."

I shut my eyes tight to prevent more tears from falling, and I pause for a beat before asking, "Why did you do that?"

"One day, you will understand," she replies quietly. "I know it has been hard. But he was not the right man for you."

I chuckle at her pretentiousness. "He is perfect for me. Everything about him is perfect."

"You are sick, Petra." Her voice is filled with meticulous coldness, sounding nothing but clinical. Even a physician would've spoken in a more friendly way. "No girl your age would consider a relationship with—let alone get married to —a forty-one-year-old."

"It's not up to you to decide. It's my life, for fuck's sake!"

"My job as your mother is to protect you." She sounds more like a dictator than a mother. But maybe for her they are the same thing. "Even if you are firmly against my decision."

"What kind of dirt do you have against Alex and Dad?" I dare to ask.

Blowing out a breath, Mom ponders for a moment before saying, "It's none of your business, and you know that."

"It is my business, yes. Since my fiancé left me, I have the right to know why."

"I promised I wouldn't repeat it to anyone, including you," she confesses. A short silence settles between us, then Mom adds, "Petra, I know it's hard to understand with so little information why I did this. But trust me on this—I did it with the best intentions."

"I hate you," I tell her, matching her cold and clinical tone. "I hate you, and I hope I never see your face ever again." And I hang up. This must have been the most useless phone call I've ever had. Why on earth did she even bother to call? Was it just to hear me crying over my fate? Was it to make sure Alex was not talking to me anymore? In any case, she's a real bitch.

"Miss?" I hear Janine calling behind the door as she knocks twice.

"Yeah?"

Janine walks in and says, "Um, sorry to bother you, but your friends are here."

"Already?" My brow lifts instantly. And I realize I'm late for our usual meetup at nine o'clock. Despite Janine waking me up an hour ago, I remained in bed, devoid of any will to get up. "Janine, do you mind showing them to the library, please?"

"They are already in there."

"Alright, tell them I'll be there in ten minutes."

"Miss, did you eat something?" But before I can answer, she asks, "Would you like some avocado toast?"

"No, I'm fine. Don't worry."

"Miss, you promised us you will eat."

Drawing in a breath, I say, "Well, it's not that easy." The truth is, the will to eat is never there. How am I supposed to eat when I never feel the need to? I get up, and, as I'm about to take a step, I feel a cold shiver running through my entire body, and another terrible headache seems to take over me. I wince at the pain and sit back down on the bed, waiting to feel better.

"Are you alright?" Janine asks, her voice laced with concern. "You're gonna eat." Now her voice has turned so authoritative that I barely recognize her. "You *need* to eat. Otherwise, you're gonna get sick. And I'm not letting it happen." And she leaves the bedroom just as fast. I grab the glass of water sitting on the nightstand and drink it down all at once. Then I wonder if Alex would come back to persuade me to eat if my health was in jeopardy. Maybe if I got really sick and my weight kept dropping, he would come back. But at that stage, Dad would most likely send me to a clinic to get transfusions. Maybe if Alex knew I was in the hospital, he would come back. My body is tired, like it ran a marathon before I even got out of bed, but I make the conscious effort to stand up and head to the bathroom despite all the pain. Politeness and good manners toward my guests are a good motivation. After a quick, warm shower, I brush my teeth, and, as I face the mirror, I drop the towel and observe myself attentively. My brows crease as I take in the view, then I go back to the bedroom to get dressed quickly. I decide to wear a push-up bra, a large sweater, and a pair of jeans to hide my scrawny physique. Then I head to the library, where I find my group watching a video on David's phone.

"Hey, sorry for the delay," I say as I walk in.

"Hey." Matthew is the first to greet me, and while everyone is still watching the video, he leaves the group and comes to meet me. "How are you doing?" he asks in a low voice.

"Um, I'm fine." I give him my biggest smile in an attempt to disguise my sickness.

As I'm about to walk toward the study table, Matthew asks, "Can I invite you to lunch?"

I raise my eyebrow, surprised by his invitation. It's the second time he's asked me out. And I feel like declining again.

"Matthew, um…" That's all I manage to say. I seriously don't feel like eating out. Actually, I don't feel like eating at all.

"There is a very nice Japanese restaurant nearby. They have vegan sushi," he says. "It's, like, super hard to get a reservation, but I managed to get a table for two."

"Oh…" Now he's left me speechless. "Um, why don't you go with Sarah? I'm sure she'd love it."

"Sarah hates sushi. And she is not my vegan bestie." His cheeky tone makes me crack a smile.

"Well, then… um, alright."

Matthew glows with a full-tooth grin. "I'm sure you're gonna love it." His hand goes to my arm, and he rubs it excitedly. "Thank you."

* * *

I can't deny it—Matthew knows what he's talking about. As soon as we step into Franchia Vegan Café—a small, discreet, and unpretentious restaurant situated on Park Avenue, I immediately fall in love with the place. It's impossible not to with its minimalist and zen vibe. Upon our arrival, we are welcomed by a friendly waiter who escorts us to a quiet table in the back and gives us menus.

As we sit, Matthew asks, "So, what do you think?"

"It's amazing," I reply just as fast. "Thank you for insisting I come."

"I've wanted to try this place for quite some time," he confesses. "But I wanted to try it out with you."

His voice is warm, and I give him a small smile, a bit troubled by his openness. Or maybe I have been the one who hasn't been paying enough attention to my friends, especially to him. After all, he has always been so caring with me. It shouldn't come as a surprise.

"Thanks," I tell him sincerely. "I know I haven't been a great friend lately…"

While I search for the best words to express myself, Matthew takes over. "Petra, I'm seriously worried about you. In two weeks, you've become so thin and bony." Wow. His comment is so unexpected that I lower my gaze in utter embarrassment. "What he did to you is disgusting. But life goes on. You should be mad at him and forget him."

"I agree. What he did is bullshit." After the waiter fills our glasses with water, I take a sip of mine and add, "You have no idea how much it hurts. I feel cheated, you know."

The waiter reappears and asks, "Are you ready to order?"

"Yes. Um, we'll have two vegan sushi combos, please," Matthew answers.

"There are twenty-one pieces in the combo," I tell him in terror. "How am I supposed to eat that much?"

"Did you have breakfast?" he asks me back.

"No…"

"Then you can perfectly well eat twenty-one pieces of vegan sushi. It's not that much, trust me." After the waiter takes our order and leaves, Matthew seems to be thinking something through. "Um, if I may ask, do you know why your ex moved to Singapore?"

"Oh." And now I'm even more surprised that we are still talking about him. It's the first time I've heard the word *ex*. Guess it's a word I should get used to. "Well, he said he couldn't marry me and that my parents are also an issue," I tell him, keeping it short. "It's all bullshit."

"But do you know why?"

And for some unknown reason, I have no issue telling him the truth. "My parents are very against us, especially my mom," I confess. "And since she has some dirt against him and my dad, she threatened them if he didn't leave me alone." Not sure why I decided to tell him all that, but I've known Matthew for over a year now, and I don't think there's any reason not to trust him.

"Wall Street and its skeletons…" Matthew teases, shaking his head. "See? That's why we need Bernie."

"Oh gosh!" I can't help but laugh at his comment. "So that's what you guys have been up to with your extracurricular activities?"

"Yep," Matthew replies with a big grin. "But I know you're not into activism, so that's why I didn't invite you."

"You did well. I'm definitely not into that." I keep my tone joyful and add, "So, what kind of activism have you been doing?"

"Well, we do podcasts, interviews, and YouTube videos teaching people about social rights and stuff," he explains. "It's mostly educational."

As I continue observing him, I decide to ask, "You must be hating our study about objectivism and Rand, no?"

"Hmm, since we are doing an unbiased project, I'm focusing on the bad side of her philosophy."

"Yeah, I read your ten reasons why objectivism sucks," I say.

Matthew smiles at me in return. "And what did you think of it?"

"I think you did a good job." I keep my tone even, but Matthew is already nodding at me. "And showing both sides of the coin will give us a better grade."

"Exactly. And we'll have a good reputation among our profs."

"Here are the vegan sushi combos." The waiter puts our plates in front of us, and I smile at the delicious rolls with avocado, cucumber, and other imaginative combinations.

"Enjoy," he says before leaving.

"So, what do you think?" Matthew beams with joy as he takes his chopsticks and grabs the first avocado roll off his plate.

"It looks delicious," I tell him as I do the same. "Thanks." I mean, each roll is pretty small and seems quite easy to eat. Or at least, easier than I thought.

His gaze remains pinned on me, and his lips curve into a smile I haven't seen before—a smile full of empathy and compassion. Something I don't see very often. "You're welcome."

* * *

I wonder what I did to deserve a friend like Matthew—caring, attentive, empathetic. I'm really blessed to have him by my side during the worst breakdown of my life. With Emma out of town, I was terribly missing the emotional support, and having someone to talk to who has no agenda. Someone that is the precise opposite of my dad. I remember how Matthew has always been present in the hardest moments. Even if I didn't pay much attention to him, he was always there, cheering for me.

"Thanks for lunch," I tell him as we walk back to my apartment.

"I'm glad you enjoyed it," he replies warmly.

And as I think something through, I ask, "Um, what are you doing tomorrow afternoon?"

Surprised by my question, Matthew takes a few more seconds before answering. "I was thinking of studying, but if it's to be with you…" A soft smile charms his lips, and he says, "I can study later tonight."

Shaking my head at his cheeky tone, I give a quick laugh and say, "Um, there is a private exhibit of Borderless by teamLab in a collaboration with Yayoi Kusama happening tomorrow, and I was wondering if you'd like to go with me? I mean, I know art is not your thing, but…"

"I'm sure it's gonna be fun," he replies before I can even finish my sentence. "Should we meet at your place?"

Wow, that was quick. "Um, yep, tomorrow at four p.m. What do you think?"

Matthew bobs his head, unable to hide the smile on his face, his eyes gleaming with joy. "Sounds great."

"See you tomorrow, then."

"See you tomorrow. And don't forget to have dinner!" he reminds me, before giving me a cheek kiss.

"I will."

"And I'm gonna FaceTime you later to make sure you ate."

His scolding makes me laugh, and I can't help but tease him, "Yes, sir."

"See ya."

CHAPTER 24

Manhattan, October 3, 2020
Petra Van Gatt

I don't remember what it's like to get one night of proper sleep. When I'm left alone in the darkness of my empty bedroom, my mind keeps replaying every moment Alex and I spent together... As I touch my pendant, I'm reminded of when he placed it on my neck and when we kissed for the first time. I find those memories so bright and warm that I can't help but find refuge in them. Closing my eyes, I recall the day he said "I love you" for the first time, the moment he helped me choose my white dress, and the moments we spent together in Aspen. Those memories seem so close and yet so distant at the same time. I cherish them as dearly as I can, and I hope one day I'll be able to create new ones with him. The more I think about it, the more I can't accept the fact that he broke up with me. I just can't. Call me crazy, but in my mind, Alex is just on a long business trip to

Singapore. And I pray that one day he will come back. He *has* to come back. Jeez, what a pathetic woman I am for loving him so much. He doesn't even deserve it.

A part of me wants to forget him once and for all and move on. But the other part—the strongest one—simply cannot accept it. I can't picture a life without him, or, at least, a happy one. Unable to fall asleep, I turn the light on and take my iPhone from the nightstand. After seeing it's four a.m., I unlock it and go to check my messages. Nothing new there. Then I go to my image gallery and look at all the photos Alex and I took together.

I smile seeing the pictures taken at our engagement party, especially the ones where we are dancing together under a stream of gold-colored lights. My gaze then goes to my ring, and I keep wondering why Alex insisted so much for me to keep it when I was about to take it off. Something is really off. Surely no man who breaks off an engagement wants his ex-fiancée to keep an heirloom ring on her finger. *Why should I keep your ring on my finger if I'm no longer engaged to you?* I text him, despite the fact that he hasn't seen any of my previous messages. Why doesn't he text me and tell me the whole truth once and for all, for fuck's sake? Damn it! Why so much secrecy? Letting out a breath, I force myself to get some sleep in order to be presentable for the exhibit later today.

* * *

Janine wakes me up at eleven-thirty a.m., and I truly appreciate her for not doing so earlier. Taking my iPhone, I can't help but check to see if Alex replied to my last message. But my heart dies a little more seeing that my texts are only marked as delivered. They haven't been seen yet, let alone answered. And it shouldn't matter anyway. I should focus on myself and leave this asshole alone. Deciding to bury Alex and his memory once and for all, I turn to Janine and announce, "I'm going to an exhibit with Matthew. Do you know what I should wear?"

Janine jumps a little upon hearing me. She looks at me and blinks twice. "You are going out? With Matthew?"

I just shrug my shoulders and say, "Yeah."

To my complete surprise, Janine claps her hands in excitement like a little child, making me raise my brows at her reaction. "I'm so proud of you, Miss." She goes to my closet and tries to find the perfect outfit for the occasion. "Well, I didn't have time to buy new clothes for you, but, um, what do you think about this dress?" I hear her saying from afar. Then she comes out of the closet to show me a black cocktail dress.

I can't really match her enthusiasm, but I force myself to smile before saying, "Looks great."

But Janine knows I'm just faking it, so she walks over and sits beside me. As she draws in a deep, long breath, her gaze remains pinned on me—a gaze that is more tender and nostalgic than usual. It feels like she's carrying some sort of melancholia of her own inside of her. "You know, when I was your age, I was madly in love with an older man."

"Really?" I ask, taken aback by her sincere confession.

"Mm-hmm," she says, nodding at me. "And I know how much it hurts to have to let go."

"But what happened? Why did you separate?"

"Well, life happened. Needless to say, I was left heartbroken. I thought he was my soul mate."

My heart reels hearing her words. It feels like I'm hearing myself from the future.

"But there is nothing time can't heal." Her nostalgia is painted all over her face as she rubs my cheek to soothe me and to prevent the tears from falling from my eyes. But as we share a smile of appreciation for our similar battles, I can tell that Janine never forgot that man—she just learned how to live without him.

"The thing is, I know he loves me. And he knows I love him," I blurt out. "That should be enough for us to be together."

"I'm sure things will get better soon," she says in a low voice, before giving me a wink.

And I'm left a bit confused at her comment. So, looking around the room and making sure there is no else here but us, I ask, "What does that mean?"

"It means just keep the faith, Miss." She takes my hand, holding it between hers. "Look, if love is enough, as you said, then your fiancé has not given up on you. But if that's not the case, you must let him go." Her fatalism makes me shudder, but to be honest, it sounds like the most logical and rational thing to do. After all, if love is enough for Alex, then he will come back sometime soon. But if it's not, I have to move on. I'm not sure how, but I know I must do so.

Standing up, she says, "I'm gonna prepare lunch." And then she points her index finger at me, squinting her eyes. "And don't you dare not eat."

Letting out a quick laugh, I've got no choice but to comply. "Fine, I will eat."

* * *

I've always liked to dress up for exhibits. After all, artists put their hearts, minds, and souls into preparing new collections and then events to present their new masterpieces to the world. I guess it's a matter of respecting their craftsmanship. As I'm finishing putting some gloss on my lips, my iPhone starts beeping with a new text message. And for an instant, my heart wanted it to be Alex, but my mind knew it was Matthew: *Hey! How are you? Sleep well? I'm downstairs. Uber is waiting.*

I text him straightaway: *Coming down. 2 mins.*

But before leaving, I take a Xanax to help me face the crowd—although I know it's gonna be a very small one—and hurry downstairs.

I see his Uber parked right at the curb, and as I get into the car, I'm surprised to see Matthew wearing a face mask.

"Hey," I greet him. "Oh, I should've asked Anthony to take us, I'm sorry…"

He doesn't seem much bothered though. "It's alright, the exhibit is, like, ten minutes from here."

"Do you have a mask, Miss?" the driver asks me.

"Um, I've got a medical exemption." And I take my medical statement out of my purse just in case. "If you want to read it, it's signed by three physicians and a lawyer."

"I'm good," the driver says as he starts the car. "I just don't want to get fined."

"You won't," I tell him. Then, lowering my voice, I whisper to Matthew, "I can get you one, if you want."

He lets out a quick laugh, most likely astounded by my statement. "Are you serious?" And shaking his head, he adds, "Nah, I'm fine."

"Alright."

After our ride, the driver drops us right in front of the entrance of a skyscraper. As we go into the marble hall and to the reception area, we are greeted by an elegant lady who, after checking my invitation, opens the lift for us and presses the button for the fifty-fifth floor.

"Wow, is this in a private apartment or something?" Matthew asks as we wait patiently to get to the floor.

"Yeah, it's an invite-only exhibit," I explain to him.

As the doors open, we are welcomed into a dark open space projecting waterfalls and flowers from the ceiling down the walls and onto the floor like a quiet river continuing its course. Then wind blows through my hair, and sounds of water and nature fill the room. Above us, fake clouds cover the ceiling, while neo-contemporary paintings hang on the walls.

"You can remove your mask here," I remind him.

"Are you sure?" he asks.

"No one is wearing them," I whisper as we both look around. "And no cops are gonna come here to fine you."

Thank God, Matthew finally takes it off and… puts it in his pocket! Don't tell me he's gonna put it back over his mouth afterward? Oh dear…

"It's dope, isn't it?" I ask as we take in our surroundings. "It's called immersive art."

"Wait, you mean these clouds and waterfalls and stuff are art?"

I chuckle at his observation. "Yeah, it's an installation by teamLab, and those paintings over there are by Yayoi Kusama, a Japanese artist."

As we get closer to one of her paintings, Matthew asks, "How much do you think this one costs?"

"Hmm… A painting of hers can cost just twenty grand. But then you can sell it at auction for millions a decade or two later."

"What?" he shouts. "That's insane. From twenty grand to millions?"

"Art can be a very profitable business. Some of her paintings have been sold at auction for seven to ten million dollars," I tell him.

"Damn, that's more than my own apartment! I don't get why rich people would waste millions on this."

I must have heard this remark a thousand times; nevertheless, I say, "It's just like any other investment. The idea is to buy art when there is room for growth and the value can still rise."

"So you think after spending ten million, you can still make more out of a painting?" he asks, even more confused.

"If the value of her art keeps going up, yeah. For instance, there's a six-hundred-year-old painting from Leonardo da Vinci that was sold for four hundred million."

"Jeez, that's insane," he snaps. His attention then goes around the room, like he's looking for someone. "There is a waiter serving drinks. Can I bring you something?"

"Eh, yeah, something without alcohol, please."

"Alright, give me a sec."

As Matthew goes to get some drinks, I keep observing the eccentric painting hanging in front of me. Then I can't help but wonder if Matthew is getting bored with our conversation about art or if he's just thirsty. I hope he's not finding this exhibit boring.

"Ms. Van Gatt?" I hear a male voice saying beside me.

Turning my gaze in his direction, I find a couple I don't recognize. "Um, yes?"

"Mike Steinberg," the man replies as he extends a hand. "We met at Paulo's wedding in Rio." Since I don't seem to be recalling who he is, he then adds, "I'm the COO of Gatt-Dieren Capital."

"Oh, yes, of course." I shake his hand heartily and feel a bit stupid for not recognizing him before. "Pleasure seeing you, Mike." Then I introduce myself to the woman standing beside him.

"I'm so glad you're finally doing well. Your dad and godfather were so worried," Mike says.

"Thank you so much," I tell him, and, to avoid images of my godfather running through my mind, I ask, "Um, what brought you here?"

"Oh, my girlfriend enjoys this type of exhibit, so here we are." I give her a warm smile in understanding, and Mike adds, "By the way, your dad told me you were looking to do a second round for your fund?"

"Oh, yeah, um, I still have to prepare a financial plan and do the math, but yes, I intend to do a second round."

Mike nods for a beat before asking, "And for how much? Any idea?"

My smile grows larger at his curiosity, and after pondering for an instant, I say, "Eh, maybe two or three million."

I see him nod, engrossed in his thoughts. "And are you looking for private or institutional investors?"

"It will depend on the deal, to be honest."

"Well, if you're interested in private investors, by all means…" And he takes a business card from his wallet before handing it to me. "I'd be more than happy to contribute."

"Oh, thanks." I wonder what my dad's told him about my fund, but based on Mike's willingness, he must have made a pretty good pitch.

"Are you planning to operate from a separate entity, or is your fund under Gatt-Dieren Capital?"

"Um, the fund is independent. Gatt-Dieren Capital doesn't own it, but Alex is one of the partners," I disclose. Although it hurts like hell having to mention him.

Mike seems to be quite surprised. "Oh, so Van Dieren is also involved?"

Maybe Dad didn't tell him that part. And as much as I hate to admit it, I say, "On paper, yes."

"Hey…" Matthew steps up, holding two flutes. And thank God for him doing so! "There was only champagne, sorry."

"Oh, thanks." I grab my flute and introduce Matthew to Mike. "Matthew, this is Mike Steinberg, COO of Gatt-Dieren, and his girlfriend, Jenny. Mike, Matthew Bradford, a friend of mine."

"Hey, nice to meet you." Matthew shakes their hands, and after some small talk, we leave them behind in order to see the rest of the exhibit. We then stop walking and stand quietly, admiring another painting.

"Can I ask you something?"

His question breaks our comfortable silence, and, as I take a sip from my flute, I say, "Sure…"

"Um, sorry for my curiosity, and don't feel obligated to reply, but why are you still wearing your engagement ring?"

"Oh…" His question is totally unexpected, but I guess quite legitimate. And as I'm thinking of an answer, I look ahead at the painting and just bluntly say, "I guess a part of me hasn't moved on."

Glancing quickly at his face, I see his brows rising, but he takes a blatant minute before saying anything else in return. "I'm sorry for what he did." Matthew's tone is so caring that it warms my heart, and a small smile curves my lips. But I remain speechless and keep admiring the painting. There is nothing else to say if not agree with him. "Do you think he will come back?"

I can't help but let out a deep, long sigh as I ponder his new question. This time, though, I take a bit longer to an-swer. "Well, technically he's got business in Manhattan, so he has to come back. The question is would he come back for me?" As I look again at the painting hanging on the wall, I add, "I don't want to know. It's better not to." Jeez, it feels so odd to be here with Matthew and have Alex be the center of our conversation. I'm trying to get him out of my system, but it's not easy when someone is reminding you constantly about the person you love.

Matthew continues observing me attentively, before crossing the line and asking, "How did you guys meet?

Tired of his little inquisition, I decide to expose the wicked truth to him once and for all. So, I look him straight in the eye and say, "He's my godfather."

"What?" he gasps instantly at my reply, blinking twice. And his outrage makes me crack a laugh as I revel in it.

"Yep, we met at the church for my baptism."

"You can't be serious…" He is now left totally speechless, and I can't help but keep giggling at his expression. "Oh, wow… Now I understand why you are so, like, into him."

"It's weird, I know," I tell him without even trying to argue my case. "It's a nasty kind of love. The kind you can't escape from even if you want to," I shamelessly admit.

"Do you think he's already moved on?"

"I hope not," I reply bluntly. "I hope deep down he's plotting something against my parents." Then I chuckle at how absurd I must sound. "It's ridiculous, I know… I just, um… I just can't accept the idea that he won't fight for us." I decide to take another sip of my champagne, trying to conceal the nostalgia that is taking over me.

"Well, if what your mom has against him can land him in jail… maybe it's not worth fighting."

"It's always worth a try," I snap back.

"Petra," he begins. My gaze meets his again. "Whatever he does or doesn't do, I don't want you to stop eating because of him."

I wasn't expecting him to say that. Or for him to sound so worried. I break eye contact in shame at what I've done to myself. Self-harm is one of my many demons. Why am I even like this? It's a mystery I can't even solve myself.

"I have been eating," I remind him as a small smile tugs at my lips. "You saw it live yesterday."

Matthew lowers his head in a failed attempt to hide his growing smirk. "And I'm gonna check again today."

The cheekiness in his tone makes me crack a laugh, and I realize as I do so that we are standing a bit too close to each other. I must admit, the closeness feels odd to me, but not totally unwanted.

His hazel eyes drift down for a second, and before our silence gets too awkward, I say, "Um, should we check out the rest of the exhibit?"

* * *

After twenty-five minutes observing and discussing the masterpieces on display, I call Anthony and see if he can pick us up. Fortunately, he accepted and is now on his way. I seriously couldn't stand to see Matthew with that mask on again. Not sure if it's because I was in a coma for six months and don't watch the news or follow anything on social media, but seeing my friend wear it in the car seemed a bit weird to me. Before leaving, though, I don't forget to say goodbye to Mike and his girlfriend. As my father always says, being polite and acknowledging people goes a long way. Once we get into the car, I ask Matthew, "So, did you enjoy the exhibit? It was quite different from your average art gallery, huh?" Since he's about to put his mask on again, I tell him, "It's okay here. You don't have to put it on."

But he doesn't seem convinced and puts it on anyway. I can't help but frown. It was in his pocket the whole time and now he's putting it over his mouth?

"Rules are in place for a reason, Petra," he says.

Rules? What he did is disgusting! But instead I just say, "Okay, but this is not an Uber. It's a private car."

"It's about being respectful to Anthony and you."

"Anthony is not wearing a mask either," I press on. "He only drives my dad and me around."

"The regulations are clear," he insists. "It's okay, really. It's just a piece of fabric. I've been wearing it for months now. I'm used to it."

"Alright. As you wish."

After five more minutes and some small talk about the exhibit, Anthony stops in front of my building to drop me off.

"Well, um, here I am. Thanks for coming," I tell him, wondering if I should give him a hug, a high five, or something else.

"Thank you for inviting me. It was really nice."

Since Matthew neither opens his arms for a hug, nor leans over for any type of physical touch, I'm hesitant to do anything. So I just smile at him and say, "Have a great evening." And I slowly open my door and exit the car. Standing outside, I wave at him until Anthony drives away.

I'm not sure why, but I feel a bit sad at not receiving even a simple hug. Maybe because Emma always hugs me like there is no tomorrow, I don't know, but affection is something I miss. A friendly hug would've been nice. Then I walk back inside, and, as I get into the lift, my thoughts go to

Alex. I remember the hugs we used to give to each other all the time. The first one being when I jumped on him at the Martos gallery where I embraced him so tight he gasped. Instinctively grabbing my iPhone, I check my messages again. Disappointment tightens my chest and emptiness sinks into my stomach as I realize he hasn't seen any of my texts. Why is he ignoring me like this? Why? I can't believe he hasn't checked his texts for the past two weeks. Something is definitely off.

"So, how was it?" Janine surprises me as I walk into the hallway.

"Hey, Janine," I greet back. "It was fine, thank you."

"Great. Um, your dad is having dinner in the kitchen. I made lasagna. You want some?"

"Oh, sure. Is it vegan?"

"Yes, Miss."

As I follow Janine into the kitchen, I find Dad sitting at the table, eating a slice of lasagna. To my surprise, he's dressed pretty casually in a gray sweater, sleeves rolled up to his elbows.

"Hey," he greets me, a welcoming smile on his face. "How was it?"

Why is everyone asking me that? Taking a seat in front of him, I simply say, "It was fine."

Janine puts a slice of lasagna on my plate, and my mouth can't help but water at how delicious it looks. "Thank you." Then a quiet silence settles between us as I start eating.

"Matthew seems to be a nice guy," Dad comments.

As I'm not interested in hearing anything coming from his mouth, I say, "We are friends." And just to make sure he understands that, I repeat the word. "Friends."

"I know. And I'm glad you have friends like him."

"He was a Bernie supporter," I tell him. And, to be honest, I don't even know why I mentioned that. Maybe to scare him? Reveling in his expression, I add, "And he hates Wall Street and big tech."

"I can't blame him." I roll my eyes at his statement. When Dad likes someone, there's nothing anyone can say or do to dissuade him. "The boy has integrity. I admire that."

Letting out a sigh, I say, "I'm glad you like my friend. May I eat in peace now?"

"I'm glad you are eating," Dad says with a contemplative smile. Then there's silence, but his fingers start tapping lightly on the table as he seems to be pondering something. "Why don't you invite him over to have dinner with us tomorrow night?"

"Huh?" That's all I manage to say before swallowing my bite. "You wanna have dinner with Matthew?"

"Why not? You used to invite Emma over, no?"

My jaw instantly drops, and I blink twice. "Um, yeah, but..." But he wants to meet Matthew? Just a year ago, Dad hated anyone of the opposite sex that got close to me, but now he wants to meet Matthew Bradford? What happened to him? A brain transplant? "Alright..."

"When are you gonna call him?" he asks.

What the heck? Can't I eat my damn lasagna in peace? "Um, I guess after I eat?"

Dad glances impatiently at his watch. "Do you mind doing it now? I need to know before going out if we're having dinner together tomorrow or another day."

Blowing out a breath, I say, "Fine." And I grab my phone to call Matthew. I then wait and wait for him to pick up.

"Hey," Matthew greets with a voice warmer than usual. "What's up?"

"Hey," I greet back, and my tone comes out annoyingly sweet. Aiming for a more casual one, I clear my throat and start again. "Hey, um, look, are you available tomorrow evening?"

"Eh… You already miss me that much?"

I crack a laugh at his comment. "Ha ha. So funny…" But then I look up at Dad, who's patiently waiting, and he's not having a laugh, no. "Um, my dad would love to meet you and wanted you to have dinner with us tomorrow night."

"Oh…" Now I'm the one who's left Matthew totally speechless. "Your dad wants to meet me?"

"Yeah, he seems to like you."

Matthew takes a bit longer to reply. "Okay, well, that's great. Eh, what time?"

I look up at Dad, and he shows me eight fingers. "Is eight p.m. okay for you?" I ask Matthew. And before he answers, I decide to reassure him, and say, "It's gonna be super casual. Like, just the three of us at home."

"Alright, sure. See ya tomorrow, then."

"See ya." And I hang up. Then, looking up at Dad, I say, "Done. Tomorrow at eight."

"Great." He stands up and walks in my direction. Bending over, he softly kisses the top of my head. And his affection is totally unexpected. "I'm very proud of you." And his compassionate, mellow voice is too.

"Proud of me? For what?" I ask him.

"For recovering. You're being very strong."

I feel the urge to remind him I shouldn't be recovering from a breakup he insisted on and supported, but instead I do none of that. I'm tired of our toxic fights. So, choosing peace over hate, I swallow all my anger, smile at him, and politely say, "Thanks."

"Don't forget, the seventeenth is our annual investors dinner. So have your financial plan ready by then. Mike and a few prospects might ask some questions about it." I do my best to remain as stoic as possible, and to not roll my eyes at him. Jeez, I had nearly forgotten that event. "You can invite Matthew if you want."

"Nope, not a chance," I snap back just as fast. "But I will invite Emma."

"Emma is in Europe."

"She's gonna be here for the dinner." At least, I hope so. Dad can be so insensitive. Matthew hates everything about Wall Street, but he expected me to invite him to a dinner with bankers and capitalists? How inconsiderate can he be?

"As you wish." He then glances again at his watch and finally shares one piece of good news, "Well, I have to go. Have a good night."

"Good night," I reply as he leaves.

Alone in the kitchen, my gaze goes again to my iPhone, and I open the text app. Curiosity taking over me, I check all the messages I've sent to Alex. Despite none having been seen, all have been successfully delivered. And the more I read the texts I sent him, the more I realize how pathetic and desperate I've been.

How are you feeling today? Happy to have broken my heart? I barely eat because of you! I hate you! I cringe at this one sent just five days ago.

I hope you never come back to Manhattan! Ever again! I hate you! This one is from six days ago. But it's still pretty accurate.

Why don't you reply? Is it too much to ask for one simple answer from you? Can't we even be friends? I read the last question again. *Can't we even be friends?* Well, it seems like we can't. Damn, not even friendship? How disgusting! After everything we went through together? I huff and shake my head. How stupid I was for texting him like that. Jeez, talk about lack of self-respect. I should win an award for the stupidest girl ever. I'd have done anything for this man. My loyalty to him was unquestionable. But what for? Fucking coward he is. I feel tempted to text something to him again, just for the sake of trolling. But I know it's a low blow, and I resist the urge to do so. Then I remember the picture Matthew and I took at the exhibit. I go to my photos and have a look at it. Okay, I can't deny it—we both look great.

Smiling diabolically, I send this photo to Alex instead, and text him something totally unexpected and different from what I have said so far: *Hey, I wanted to apologize for the rude texts I sent you over the past two weeks. I'm slowly recovering from our separation, but as you might understand, it was a very unexpected blow, and I doubt I'll ever forgive you for breaking up with me. I pray one day to be able to forget you though. One of my friends, Matthew Bradford, has been a great support. He's one of my friends at Columbia, and Dad likes him a lot. Dad even invited him to have dinner with us tomorrow night. I won't text you ever again, especially if you don't want me to. I wish you well. Bye.* And I press send.

CHAPTER 25

Manhattan, October 4, 2020
Matthew Bradford

"And you didn't kiss her?" Pops can be so annoying. Damn. "Not even on the cheek?"

But I remain focused on my hair, aiming for a presentable look. And as I glance at his reflection in the mirror, I say, "Nope. I had a mask on. It'd have been so dumb." I'm tired of arguing with him, but quite excited for the evening, nevertheless. "This is a long-term thing."

"You're not gonna wear a mask in their house, right?"

Jeez, I can't help huffing at his question. "Of course not. I just did it because we were in the car."

"You're getting a bit pathetic, son..."

And I sigh again at his comment. Living with someone who is your precise opposite in every way is a total nightmare. No wonder Mom left him a long time ago.

"You're young, you shouldn't..."

"Alright, see ya later." I give him a quick pat on the back before booking an Uber. Then I rush to my bedroom, pick out a new mask, and leave the house. I find my Uber waiting on the curb and get inside.

"Hey, Matthew, right?" the driver asks.

"Yeah, that's me."

As the driver starts his journey en route to Park Avenue, I text Petra: *On my way. See ya in 15 mins.* And I look once more at the selfie we took yesterday when we were waiting for her chauffeur. Yeah, I must've looked at it, like, twenty times by now, but she looks so damn beautiful with her soft pink lips curving up, her pale face contrasting with her dark hair and blue eyes... I look like a complete idiot though, despite Petra assuring me otherwise. All of a sudden, a phone call from a private number pops up on the screen. And since I'm pretty sure I know who's calling, I answer it and put the phone against my ear. "Hi?"

"Matthew Bradford? Alexander Van Dieren." Of course. Who else could it be? His voice is unmistakable. "How are you doing?"

"Oh, hey... Um, why are you always calling me from a private number?" I ask instead.

"It doesn't matter why. It seems you're going to meet Roy Van Gatt this evening?"

I raise my brows in surprise. "Oh, Petra told you?"

"She sent me a text, yes. Did she enjoy the restaurant?"

"Yeah, she loved it. Thanks for the tip and for getting us a table."

"You're most welcome. Did she answer your questions?"

"Yeah, she did." And since I know he's expecting me to delve a bit further, I tell him, "Despite everything you did, she's still hoping you'll come back. And to be honest, I've never met someone so in love."

"I see," he mutters. "Look, if Roy mentions he met you before, don't deny it and don't lie. Petra will see through it. If she asks you about it, just tell her you met him once in a restaurant and said hi."

"Um, do you think Roy will mention we had a talk in the cigar lounge?" I ask, suddenly worried.

"I don't think Roy will bring it up, no." He sounds quite confident of himself. "But he might mention he's seen your face before. Whatever questions he brings up, don't lie, don't shake, and stand your ground."

"Alright, um, thanks for the tip." And before he can hang up, I say, "By the way, um, Petra told me why you broke up with her." I wait for him to comment, but when nothing comes from the other end, I add, "She said her mom has some dirt against you. Not that I'm surprised, but—"

"Good evening, Matthew." And just like that, he hangs up.

Damn it! And since there's no way to call him back, I slip my iPhone back inside my pocket, still a bit troubled by his behavior. Anyway, I'm perfectly aware he is using me to find out how Petra is coping with the breakup. But the closer I can get to her, the better for me.

"Here we are," the driver announces, stopping in front of Petra's building.

"Thanks."

Leaving the car, I smile at the doorman as I walk in.

"Good evening, Mr. Bradford," he greets, holding the door open for me. And I wonder how the heck he even knows my last name. Was it Petra who told him? I shake my head in amusement. After all, she's the only one who addresses me like that.

As I get into the elevator, the mirror reminds me to remove my mask, and, after doing so, my lips curve into a grin as I check my teeth. They look good. I glance at my overall appearance and run a hand through my hair, but it won't behave anyway.

Upon arriving in front of her door, I knock three times, and to my greatest surprise, it's not Janine, but Ms. Van Gatt herself who welcomes me. Her eyes are gleaming like diamonds as she smiles and greets me with her sweetest voice. "Mr. Bradford," she says, as per her ritual of greeting when it is only the two of us. I've always wondered why she enjoys calling me by my surname, but I guess it's to tease me, as she knows I hate it.

"Hey," I greet back. Then I wonder if I should kiss her cheek as my pops suggested. But there is no need for guessing. Petra instantly leans over, and we exchange two cheek kisses. "You look really nice today." Jeez, I sound so cheesy. Why did I even say that?

"You said the same thing yesterday," she points out. But I manage to make her laugh, so it's all good.

"Well, you look great every day, especially now that you have been eating again."

"With someone like you monitoring my meals, it's hard not to."

"Matthew!" I look over Petra's shoulder to where the male voice is coming from. And there he is, Roy Van Gatt. The same man I saw at the cigar lounge. "So good to finally meet you." Roy shakes my hand a bit longer than the norm, but his warm expression and tone feel quite reassuring.

"Pleasure meeting you, Mr. Van Gatt," I reply back.

"Let me check if dinner is ready." Petra leaves me alone with him, and I swear I hate her for a second for doing so.

"Thank you for what you have been doing," Roy tells me in a low voice, a hand on my shoulder, as we walk in the direction of the dining room.

"Oh, that's what friends do." I play humble—it's always the smart thing to do in a situation like this.

"She wasn't eating anything for nearly two weeks," he confesses. And I'm amazed at his ease in telling me that.

"Yeah, I'd noticed that."

As we reach the dining room, I find Petra talking to Janine, and she asks me, "What do you want to drink?"

"Um, I'm fine with a juice or a soda," I tell them.

Petra looks at her dad and says, "See? I told you."

"Fine, I'll try out that juice, then," Roy instructs as Janine goes to the bar and fills our glasses with a green liquid.

"Janine made a green detox juice," Petra explains to me.

Seeing Roy's expression laced with disappointment, I tell him, "You may drink whatever you feel like. I just don't drink alcohol."

But Petra doesn't seem to be on board with that. "He's gonna drink a healthy juice for once." She then takes two glasses and gives me one, while Janine gives another one to Roy.

"Well, cheers," Petra says as we all raise our glasses and clink them together.

After taking a sip, I can't help but praise Janine for its delicious flavor.

Petra does the same and then asks, "What do you think, Dad?"

"You really want to know?"

While I can't help crack a laugh at his reply, Petra, on the other hand, just rolls her eyes. "Matt, please have a seat. Dinner is gonna be served soon."

Oh, did she just call me Matt? That's, like, the first time she's ever called me by my nickname. I try to conceal my astonishment by taking another sip of my drink, and I quietly take a seat in front of her dad.

After we all sit down, Janine starts pouring some soup into my bowl, and Roy takes this opportunity to break the silence and asks, "Petra told me you have been involved in, um, political activism?"

Now that's an unexpected question. "Uh, well, it's more like teaching and promoting social rights through videos and podcasts," I explain. "I'm not campaigning for any candidate. At least, not anymore, since Bernie lost in the primaries." Not sure why I told him all that with such ease, but I just couldn't help it.

"Ah, yes, I have watched some of your videos on You-Tube."

"Really?" Petra and I say at the same time.

"You did?" she asks him again, even more surprised than I am.

"Yes. You're very talented," Roy praises.

And I'm left totally speechless at his statement. He really went to the extent of checking out my videos?

"Are you thinking of pursuing academics or teaching as a career?"

"Um, well, being a professor is a viable option. But first, I've got to finish my degree, and then we'll see."

"That's why you changed from finance to philosophy?"

"Dad!" Petra admonishes.

"What? I'm just asking."

Letting out a quick chuckle, I tell him, "Yeah, I felt like finance was not my calling."

"Why did you enroll in it in the first place, then?" Roy keeps asking.

And I remember Alex advising me to always be honest and not to lie. So I decide to tell him the truth, even if it bothers me to no end having to bring my pops into the conversation. "My dad kinda persuaded me. And since our relationship hasn't been the best, I agreed to give it a try."

"Sounds so familiar…" Petra fesses up. And we can't help but have a laugh at her comment.

"But you like finance, don't you?" Roy asks her.

"Yeah, so far the classes have been interesting."

"The program is excellent," I reassure him. "It's just not what I wanted for me."

"Do you accept donations for your YouTube channel?"

Another question that is totally unexpected. "Um, yeah, I've got a Patreon account."

"Great, then I'll gladly support it."

I raise my eyebrows at his statement, and I try hard not to gape. Petra does the same. Roy, a capitalist of Wall Street, supporting a YouTube channel promoting social rights, progressive agenda, and wealth redistribution? What world do I live in? "Um, that's great. Thank you. But don't feel obligated."

"I don't feel obligated," he repeats, smiling at me. "I admire people that fight for what they stand for. That's all. I'm sure your channel will grow and get millions of subscribers."

"I hope one day that'll be the case. There's a lot of teamwork behind it," I tell him. My gaze goes to Petra, and she gives me a bright smile, her expression glowing with pride. And I try hard not to get fixated on it.

* * *

After dinner, and while Roy goes to his office to make some phone calls, Petra invites me to the terrace to check out the impressive skyline. "It's amazing at night, isn't it?"

"Yeah," I tell her, taking in my surroundings. "I wish my apartment had a terrace, let alone one this big."

Only street noise fills the space between us as we stand together, watching the sights around us. Discretely enough, my gaze goes to her as she seems to be engrossed in her thoughts. And as I contemplate every feature of her face, I can't believe how lucky I am to be here. Damn, I never expected, not even in a million years, that one day, a regular guy like me would be having dinner with the one and only Petra Van Gatt and her dad. Last year, when I first met her, Petra seemed to be a princess of Wall Street, polite to everyone but totally unapproachable and out of my league. But now? Now I want to believe that I might stand a chance.

Not that I expect her to fall in love with me right after a breakup, but maybe in a year or two, once her wounds have healed completely. And I'm okay with that. Petra is a chick worth waiting for.

"My dad likes you a lot," she tells me. "It's the first time he hasn't said anything nasty about a male friend of mine."

"I guess most guys would've jumped on you at the first chance." My tone comes out a bit cheeky, and I then add, "You dad likes me because I've got no interest in getting a slap in the face."

"Smart boy," she teases back.

My phone beeps with a notification from Patreon. And as I check it, I can't help but shout, "What the fuck?!" I can't believe what I'm reading! "Your dad just subscribed to my Patreon for a monthly donation of ten thousand dollars. That's insane!"

While I appear utterly shocked, Petra doesn't even bat an eye. "To be fair, that's probably what he pays in hookers on a monthly basis…"

And now I'm rendered totally speechless at her answer. "Really?"

"Yeah, most likely."

"Your dad pays hookers?" I repeat, making sure I heard her properly. "I mean, he doesn't seem like that type of guy."

She just shrugs her shoulders in return. "Love is too expensive for him."

The more she speaks, the more I need to ask her, "You don't really like him, huh?"

"Nope," she tells me just as dryly. "Dad believes everyone and everything can be bought." And as she keeps looking at the skyline ahead, she adds in a tone deeply concerning, "Whatever stands in his way must be destroyed. Even if it's his own daughter's happiness."

Wow. There's a sadness in her voice that makes my heart tighten. And as I keep observing her, I can't help but notice how deeply she is still affected by the breakup. After all, I know both she and Alex love each other. It's not like the dude doesn't care about her. Nope, it's because he doesn't have much of a choice. Sometimes I'd love to tell her everything I know about her fiancé and the breakup. But I can't. Otherwise, she might just stop trusting me, and that's not an option for me. So instead I say, "Do you think your dad is trying to buy me?"

"For ten thousand bucks?" she asks. "That would be a very cheap price. But if you want a piece of advice, don't take his money." I crease my brows instantly. Ten thousand bucks a month would help quite a lot to grow the channel and reach more people. "If my dad asks you for a favor and mentions what he can or cannot do for your channel, make sure you can send the money back to him if you have to, so you don't feel obligated to do anything for him in return."

"But, like, with ten thousand bucks, we could grow the channel a lot and pay for ads, you know. And this money is from a Patreon subscription, which means I don't have to do anything in return for your dad."

"Just keep your integrity," she tells me. "Mark my words. Dad always invests in relationships early on. One day, he'll send you the bill. It could be a year from now or ten, and then you will feel like you owe him for the ten thousand bucks a month."

"Look, I promise whatever money your dad gives me to support the channel, I won't do anything that goes against my values, and I'll keep educating people on social rights and welfare policies."

"You promise?" Petra asks, squinting her eyes.

Letting out a quick chuckle, I look at the skyscrapers around us and say, "I do."

CHAPTER 26

Manhattan, October 17, 2020
Petra Van Gatt

The only issue with creating a financial growth plan for the next three years of my fund is to actually come up with a name for the fund itself. Since the fund doesn't belong to Gatt-Dieren Capital, it has to have another name to present to potential investors. Uninspired, I keep staring at my laptop screen and the first page of the template I downloaded. "Financial Plan of [insert company name here] 2021-2024"

What name should I put there? After all, Gatt-Dieren is an established brand among the media and capitalists. Maybe Dad would be okay with me using it and just adding "Art" after it. Giving it a try, I write "Gatt-Dieren Art Fund" as the fund's name. Not an original name for sure, but a safe bet. Then I realize the name "Dieren" is in it, and it'd be wise to get Alex's approval before using his surname on my financial plan… You know what? Fuck his approval. He never answers my texts anyway. "Gatt-Dieren Art Fund" is perfect. It's a safe choice and will make investors feel more at ease for years to come.

After deciding on a name, the second thing I need to do if I want to accept clients (aka investors) and grow the fund is create a website. Or at least some sort of online presence. Maybe just a subsection of the main Gatt-Dieren website will be enough though. Out of curiosity, I go to the Gatt-Dieren website to find some ideas for mine. The website is pretty responsive on my iPhone and is neat and minimalist. It starts with a full-width slide of featured images and titles. The first one is regarding an article about diversity and inclusion, the second slide is about principles and culture, the third one is about COVID-19 and how Gatt-Dieren is handling it, and the last one is about an interview Alex gave to the *Financial Times*. Scrolling down the home page, I find a bunch of testimonials about how amazing it is to work at Gatt-Dieren and how inclusive they are. I can't help but roll my eyes as I read them. *What a bunch of marketers…* There are even testimonials from Jess and Rach talking about their internships and how incredible they were. I huff instantly. They just did the internship, and they included them on the website? I see nothing about the performance of the fund though. And nothing about their types of investments either. Nope. Just articles about diversity, wealth inequality, their contribution to the LGBTQ+ community and women's rights organizations, and a statement from Dad standing against sexual harassment following the Me Too Movement. What? I am completely confused. Is this really the website of a multi-billion-dollar hedge fund? Is this what it is supposed to look like? Well, I don't think I need all this content on mine. Maybe just something focused on my mission to invest in art would be enough. Damn, this seems harder than I thought. It's almost as if Matthew and his team have taken care of their digital strategy. But I'm pretty sure this website has been around for quite some time, which means Dad and Alex must've hired a digital communication agency to take care of it. And I wonder if to play the game of Wall Street in 2020, I need to do the same.

"Do you have any idea what you want to wear to the investors dinner tonight?" Janine asks as she sneaks into my closet, her eyes most likely already scanning through the hangers.

"Anything really," I mumble as I stay focused on my financial plan. Then I take Peikoff's binge-worthy book about objectivism and underline my favorite sentence, "The artist is the closest man comes to being God." No wonder I have read this book several times. It's so moving and inspirational. I should actually put this quote on my fund's website and in my plan. Maybe a website focused on the artists will help the branding. One thing is for sure: I definitely need a digital agency to take care of the communication and marketing part. As I look at my financial plan, I can't help but smile at the growth projections. Being able to invest further in artists and their artwork feels like a dream come true. Then my mind starts fantasizing about having my own office with the name "Gatt-Dieren Art Fund" pinned on the marble wall behind the reception desk. Once the fund is big enough, I should rent one of those fancy offices somewhere downtown, hire a few associates, and have an art gallery on the ground floor where I can show off the most exciting pieces of art the fund owns. That would be so dope and alternative. Just like the fund.

"Jumpsuit or dress?"

Returning to planet Earth, I put down my book and find Janine standing in front of me with a formal white jumpsuit in one hand and a white cowl-necked slip dress in the other.

"Huh…" That's the most coherent answer I manage to give her. "Both look great."

But Janine isn't satisfied. "Miss, you have to pick one."

As I look more attentively at both of them, I notice that the dress, although it has a hem long enough for my liking, doesn't have sleeves like the jumpsuit, just spaghetti straps.

"Can I see the backs?"

Janine turns them around. The jumpsuit has a zipper on the back going all the way up to the neck, while the white dress is backless.

"The white dress," I tell her. I know this dress will piss off my dad. And I'm in the mood to piss him off.

"Perfect. Now jump into the shower," Janine commands. "Hurry up! Your dad will be here in thirty minutes to pick you up."

Rolling my eyes, I leave Peikoff and my laptop and go to the bathroom to get ready for the evening.

***

"Petra," I hear my dad calling from downstairs. "Are you ready?

"One minute!" I shout back as I look at myself once more in the mirror, while Janine applies hairspray to the high ponytail she just pulled my hair into.

She takes a portable mirror to show me the back of my hairstyle. "Do you like it?"

"I love it," I tell her, my tone filled with excitement as I clap my hands. I love how the ponytail pushes my hair up very high, showing off more of the backless dress I'm wearing.

"This dress looks absolutely fantastic on you," she praises.

"Thanks, Janine."

Now that I'm ready, I swallow a Xanax, then grab my clutch, the matte gloss I'm wearing, and my iPhone. *Let's do this*, I think to myself after drawing in a breath.

As I walk down the stairs, I notice Dad standing near the front door, wearing a tux, and impatiently waiting for me as he keeps glancing at his watch. Then his head turns in my direction, and his jaw drops. His expression remains totally dazed as he observes every inch of my dress as I come down the stairs. "What kind of dress is that?" he snaps.

"It's an evening dress, Dad," I reply snobbishly. "Haven't you seen *The Thomas Crown Affair*? One of the actresses even wears a similar one to a gala event in it."

"Yes, but—"

"And she is even a painter," I cut him off, a smile settling on my lips as I revel in his discomfort. "Shall we?"

"Petra," he says between gritted teeth, having none of it. "Do you see me showing off so much skin?"

"It's not my fault if men have to cover up," I snap as I open the door and walk outside. "Let's go. We are late."

I greet Anthony, who's standing in front of the car, before letting out a quick sigh of relief. At least this time Dad didn't book a limo. Anthony greets me with a big, bright smile and opens the door for me.

Once Dad sits beside me, I notice that his expression remains just as tormented at the outrageously immodest dress I'm wearing. Even though the dress falls below my knees, Dad can't hide his displeasure. And my smirk keeps rising.

His eyes finally leave my dress but then land on my left hand, which is resting on the middle seat. Dad keeps looking intently at it, before letting out an exasperated breath. Trying to hide his disapproval, he turns his glare to the car window, but I know him all too well.

"I won't remove it," I tell him. He doesn't say a word; instead, he just shakes his head. "I'll say it's a gift," I add. "Not an engagement ring."

"Whatever you tell them…" He turns back to look at me. "I don't want any improper behavior at the dinner. Are we clear?"

"What does that even mean?" I ask, my tone defiant. "I know how to behave."

I see Dad hesitating, before finally blurting out, "Your godfather will be there."

My heart freezes, and I have to close my eyes for a second. Those words. Those five little words. They have the power to crack and shatter me into a thousand pieces. After a month without seeing him, I don't even know what I'm supposed to say to him. That I hate him? Love him? Beg him to stay? Tell him to be happy in Singapore? No, I can't tell him that. I want him to be happy, yes, but not in Singapore, or, at least, not without me there. I know it sounds selfish, but I can't accept this fate. I can't accept this outcome. Oh jeez, I just want to throw up.

"So he is really attending..." I mumble feebly, still trying to figure out what I should say or do once I see him. "I didn't know he was in New York."

"He just came back for this event," Dad replies casually. "He'll make an official announcement about his departure and announce the new CEO."

A steep pain scorches my stomach, and I take a deep breath, taming the eminent desire to cry at the reality I'm destined to live. I cannot accept it. I can't. I have to do something. My mind keeps ruminating about how to persuade Alex to run away with me and leave it all behind. This is my only chance before he goes miles away once and for all. Then I remember Latifa, the Emirati princess who tried to escape from her family and run away from Dubai. But her father ultimately caught her, and we have never heard about her again. Looking at my dad, I know he won't hurt me, but I know if I try to run away, he'll find me and bring me back to New York. And Alex knows that too. I might not be the daughter of a sheikh, but I feel exactly the same— trapped.

This is the real world, after all, where princesses are caught and brought back to their golden prisons to live some sort of happily ever after they didn't choose.

Damn, how unfair life can be. Some people might not have money, power, status, or connections, but they have the freedom to be with whomever they want. Meanwhile, others have all the resources in the world, but don't have such privilege.

"Here we are." Dad's voice shuts down my thoughts, and, after blinking twice, my attention goes to his face. As I observe the wrinkles well-settled around his tired eyes, his short gray hair, and his tux, I feel nothing but pity—pity because his obsession for reputation and glory makes him the perfect victim to those who know how to exploit it. As Matthew would say, "We are all products and victims of the society we live in."

"Are you okay?" he asks.

I give him a side smile and just say, "You look great."

Then I stare through the car window at the entrance of Gotham Hall.

I can't believe he chose this venue again. How ironic, I think, shaking my head.

As the car stops, a valet opens the door and greets my dad. "Good evening, Mr. Van Gatt."

Dad gets out of the car first, then offers a hand to help me out.

"Ms. Van Gatt," the valet greets as I look instinctively around the entrance, already anxious and apprehensive.

Dad puts a hand on my back, gesturing the way to the front steps and door. "Shall we?"

Not surprisingly, as soon as we reach the ballroom, a thousand eyes alight upon us. But none of them are the ones I want. Dad smiles, and the crowd does the same in return.

He shakes hands, and I'm introduced to a few people, from longtime clients to partners of other funds. I try to remember names and faces, but as I glance around and listen to the jazzy music, all I can think about is how Gotham Hall is the place where I saw Alex again for the first time and how, in a few hours, it will be the last.

Between the laughter and champagne, it feels like the end of a chapter—a chapter I'm not ready to end.

Suddenly, two palms cover my eyes, and someone whispers in my ear, "I can't believe you came here without me."

A smile cracks my face, and turning around, I plunge Emma into a hug. A hug so tight that I hear her gasping.

"Oh, gosh," she says. "What's going on?"

"I'm so happy you are here," I tell her in a low voice, my arms still wrapped around her neck.

She hugs me back and says, "Me too."

We don't talk, but as we look at each other, Emma reads me like no one else. She strokes my arm, giving me an empathetic smile, and remains speechless. After all, there are no words to be said. No sweet "it's gonna be alright" kind of talk because we both know it'd be bullshit. It is what it is, her face tells me. Wow. Emma, my best friend, my big sister, the most adventurous person I know, giving me an "it is what it is" look. Did I expect something different from her? The idealist in me thought so. But as Emma smiles at my dad and kisses his cheek, I know there will be no escape plan hatched in the bathroom. And I know that at the end of the day, "it is what it is" is the only way everyone feels about it.

Except me.

"Petra!" I hear calling from behind me.

I instantly turn around, recognizing the voice. "Mr. Marques, how good to see you." Then I look at his wife, Anabela, standing beside him and greet her just as warmly. But as my eyes go to her dress, my heart tightens. "Oh, wow. Congratulations," I tell her. "How many weeks?"

"Thirty-two," she replies with a proud smile, putting a hand on her bump.

"I'm so happy for you." Then, for the sake of politeness and small talk, I ask, "Do you know if it's a boy or a girl?"

"It's a boy. But we are still struggling to come up with a name." And before I can ask anything further, my attention instantly shifts to the entrance, and everything stops.

And everything hurts, as I observe Alex greeting a few guests before walking toward us.

Yep, here he is. The man I hate and love the most in this world, looking sharp and elegant in his usual satin-lapel tux, a charming smile on his lips, with glowing skin and a perfect tan. While I have been undergoing therapy to survive my post-Alex breakup, this asshole seems to be perfectly fine.

"You don't say hi to your godfather?" Emma whispers with the most annoying sarcasm.

Surprisingly—or not—Dad gives him the warmest greeting, shaking his hand intently and patting him on the back. He then greets Anabela, Paulo, Emma...

"Mr. Van Dieren," I snap unsmilingly when his piercing blue eyes alight on me. I hate you, my glare says.

But my heart knows it's all bullshit.

"Miss Van Gatt," he replies, his voice irritably soft and mellow. His gaze goes up and down me, but his face doesn't give anything away. Then he takes a step closer to me, a step that makes my heart beat faster than I'd like to admit, and leaning close to my ear, he whispers, "You look absolutely stunning… in that white dress."

White dress.

Somehow those two words coming from his mouth bring back memories I shouldn't even think of. "Thank you," I reply with restraint. "It's actually very appropriate for the occasion." And to my surprise, I blurt, "It represents the end of a chapter in my life."

Why did I even say that?

"Well, I hope the next one will be better." He sounds polite and calculated.

"We share the same hope," I snap back, matching his tone.

A cold silence arises between us, and we don't smile or say anything else. We look like two strangers, with no past… and maybe no future.

He then glances over my shoulder, nodding at someone. "Excuse me, I've got some guests to talk to."

Of course you do. And just like that, Alex leaves me. If he is as broken as I am inside, then he's a fine actor.

"Petra, I've got someone to introduce you to." Dad seems overly excited as he takes me by the arm and ushers me to the other side of the ballroom.

"Who?" I mumble as we get closer to the stage.

"You will see."

There, I see musicians gathered around a female figure with blonde hair brushing her shoulders. I don't recognize her from the back, but as soon as she turns around…

"Oh my God!" I cover my mouth, but the words are already out.

"Petra," Dad starts, his excitement growing, "I'd love to introduce you to our singer for the evening…"

"Ms. Krall," I shout, not containing my emotion. My heart is thundering a thousand miles an hour. I just can't believe it! "I'm, um, it's, um…"

"Just call me Diana."

Of course. Why not?

"I'm one of your biggest fans." Sounds cliché as fuck, but it's true. I know all her songs by heart. I can't get enough of her music. "I'm so excited for tonight. I love everything about you. Your music is just fantastic," I end up saying.

"Well, thank you very much. What's your favorite song?"

"Um, there are so many… But 'The Look of Love' might be my favorite."

"Ah, that's a great one." Her gaze darts down curiously. "Beautiful ring you've got there. Are you engaged?"

"Not at all," Dad promptly interposes, clearly annoyed by the question. "It's just a gift, a keepsake. Petra prefers to wear it on that finger because it's more practical." Bullshit. "Let me take a picture of you two." Dad takes his iPhone out of his pocket and walks a few steps backward.

Standing beside each other, Diana and I wrap an arm around each other's waist. Then, as we both look at the camera, I can't help but notice Alex right behind Dad. A smile escapes me, but not the kind I want for a picture. Holding a glass of champagne, he seems to be happily chatting with Paulo and Mike. He doesn't even notice me. And it doesn't matter anyway.

Yeah, a keepsake from someone who broke my heart.

"One day I will be ready to take it off," I tell myself quietly, but loud enough that I know Diana heard.

One day…

My attention shifts back to the camera, and I put on another smile—the one Dad expects me to.

Click.

* * *

I'm not surprised to find out Alex will be sitting at our table. In fact, I'm not even surprised that he's been ignoring me the entire evening. Dad, Alex, Paulo, Mike, and two more execs have spent the whole dinner discussing how Asia is flourishing and how pharmaceutical and biotech investments have never performed so well. "The best year ever," they mention between giggles and sips.

"They could've done this in the boardroom," Emma rebukes in my ear. "I'm fucking tired of hearing about their plans for 2021. I'm even thinking of selling the info to BlackRock."

I can't help but chuckle at her statement. "And why BlackRock?"

"I've got some friends who work there."

"Friends?" I look at her with a side smile, and she cracks one even bigger.

"Friends…" she replies back, before burying her naughtiness in a sip of wine.

"Thank you for being here, Emma." I lay my hand on hers, and with all the sincerity in the world, I tell her, "I'm so lucky to have you."

Emma observes me without saying a word, then her eyes dart down for a second, as she thinks something through, before meeting mine again. "I know it hurts," she whispers in my ear. "But look at him. It seems like he's already moved on."

Oh, wow. Emma's words have just slapped me in the face and created a deep knot in my stomach. Indeed, Alex might be sitting in front of me, but I remain invisible to him. He hasn't said a single word to me during the whole dinner. I can't help but wonder if this is his way to grieve, or if, as Emma just said, he really has moved on.

Jeez, the idea terrifies me, and I have to close my eyes to calm myself down. My God, it hurts. It hurts loving someone you can't be with. And it hurts even more when that someone gives up on you. As I reopen my eyes, I see that Alex is looking at me. There is no smile on his face though, and I know it's easy for him to figure out how I'm feeling inside. Oh jeez, why? Is he enjoying seeing me in so much pain?

It is what is. Just accept it and move on, I keep telling myself.

Recognizing the first notes of the piano, my ears instantly perk up.

"The look… of love…" I hear Diana crooning.

I'm not sure if it's because of the music, but I give Alex a small smile as we both recognize the song. After all, it's the song we danced to at our engagement party and the one we wanted for our wedding dance.

"Ah! Alex will give his speech right after this song," Dad announces with a joyful tone.

What? I can't believe it! Dad knows perfectly well that Alex and I danced to this song at our engagement party. I bet he did this on purpose to ruin it for me. Maybe as some sort of revenge.

I look unsmilingly at my dad and ask, "May I have one last dance with my godfather before he leaves for Singapore?"

Neither Dad nor Alex say a word. And while everyone else at the table stares at them in amusement, Alex takes a sip of his water, speechless, before glancing at my dad.

"Sure," Dad utters, visibly conflicted.

Alex doesn't seem very enthusiastic either. After removing his napkin from his lap, he finally stands up. "What I wouldn't do for my goddaughter." His restrained, gentlemanly voice makes me hate him even more. Or not…

Nevertheless, I remain seated, waiting patiently for him to stand in front of me, and to extend a hand. Once he does so, I take his hand, and we make our way to the dance floor, leaving our table and my father behind us.

Hidden in the darkness among countless couples, I put my arms around his neck as Alex holds my waist, aiming to keep a safe distance between us. But I don't care, and I take a step forward—a step a bit too close for his taste, but perfect for me. With my body nestled against his, cheek to cheek, we start swaying back and forth while Diana croons in the background.

But then Alex mutters, "You shouldn't be so close."

"I love it," I reply in a low voice as our bodies keep moving together, following the sensual beat. "And I love everything about this song."

I hear nothing but a heavy grown. "Fuck…"

My lips curve up with pleasure and guilt at his discontentment. I can feel him growing hard under his pants as I keep my crotch pressed to his. "Indeed," I whisper. "That's exactly what I'd like to do with you right now."

His lips part with a ragged breath. "Petra, stop it," he insists. "This is inappropriate."

But I don't listen, and I stay just as close to him. Because this is what I want. This is what we want. Him here with me slow dancing to one of our favorite songs, feeling each other, and, most importantly, being with each other. Regardless of anything else, this is the life we want. And this is the life we deserve to live. "Don't move to Singapore," I plead, my tone low but shaky. "I can't let you go." My eyes shut at the immensity of my pain, thinking how, in a few moments, he will make it official. "I beg you, don't go."

Nothing but the instruments and my torment can be heard.

Then he looks me in the eye, his thumb stroking my cheek to calm me down. "I love you." My heart stops upon hearing him. I have missed those words so much. "Whatever you do with your life, I'll always love you." And he seals those words with a long kiss on my forehead just as the music stops and the magic of our dance disappears. It feels like a goodbye. I sniffle but make the conscious effort not to let the tears fall. I've cried too much and too many times for this man.

"Thank you very much, ladies and gentlemen," says Diana under a wave of applause. "It was a pleasure being here tonight. God bless you."

As she leaves the stage, Alex and I walk silently back to our table. And I know at this precise moment that nothing will make him change his plans.

Not even me.

Not even our engagement.

Nothing.

Dreams will remain dreams. And the nightmares I've had will actually become my new reality. I just never thought I wouldn't be able to prevent it from happening.

When we arrive at our table, we hear the presenter calling my dad onstage, and I see him leaving his seat with a big grin, more than ready for his speech.

I decide to take Dad's chair and sit beside my fiancé, or to everyone else, my godfather. I'm still holding his arm, but I don't care.

While my dad is already at the podium telling some dry joke and everyone is laughing hard at it, I remain quiet, staring at Alex and trying to memorize every single line on his face. But the harsh reality haunts me—tomorrow, he'll be flying back to Singapore, and we'll never see each other again. As I look down, I see my hand tightly holding his. A small smile settles on my lips, but it disappears just as fast when I hear Dad call him onstage. Alex gives my hand a kiss before releasing it. He then waves to the crowd, who are applauding him, and stands up.

This is it.

I close my eyes while my fiancé walks away, ready to embrace his new life in Singapore.

"Thank you, Roy, for the warm introduction," I hear him say into the microphone. "Good evening, ladies and gentlemen. It's indeed with the greatest joy that we are here tonight, not only to celebrate Miss Van Gatt's healthy return among us, but also to share with you some exciting news."

"Are you alright, Petra?" Dad asks when he returns, probably seeing my eyes closed.

I nod, and for the sake of politeness, I reopen them, giving him a smile as he sits beside me. I look at the stage, and, just like Dad, I wait patiently for Alex's announcement. But unlike Dad, I hope it never comes.

"Therefore, in order to accelerate our growth in Asia, we've decided that someone from headquarters should move permanently to Singapore and become the new managing director."

My heart squeezes tight at the word *Singapore*, and I feel it pounding faster and louder with every second.

"As CEO, it's my great pleasure to announce—"

I have to close my eyes again. I feel like I'm going to faint at any moment.

"That Mr. Paulo Marques, our dear CFO, will be the new managing director in Singapore."

WHAT?! I look at Paulo and Anabela instantly. They don't seem surprised. Then, at Dad. He, on the other hand, is under the same wave of shock as me. He is mute, gaping and glaring intently at Alex while everyone else is clapping and cheering for Paulo, who is now standing up to go onstage. I also look back at Alex, and that asshole has got the cheekiest smile on his face. I can't help but beam with joy, clapping my hands hard as hard as I can. "Congratulations, Mr. Marques!" I scream.

Paulo shakes Alex's hand, taking his place at the podium.

"Relax. It could have been worse," I tell Dad as I barely contain tears of joy.

"How? Just tell me. How?"

"Well," I lean closer to Dad's ear, lowering my voice, "he could've made a public announcement about our engagement."

Dad shakes his head in return, and, standing up in annoyance, he mutters, "I need some fresh air." And he leaves the table.

I also leave the table, but not for the same reason.

"Hey, Miss…" I grin at the man standing right in front of me. "Did you enjoy the speech?"

"Oh, it was…" It was perfect! "It was a great decision. Paulo has always enjoyed Singapore. And Anabela doesn't like staying alone in New York," I say as Alex keeps walking toward me.

"I agree." And then, reaching for my hand, he whispers, "Come with me."

Actually, I do want to come at his words right now from all the excitement. I follow him, holding his hand as we leave the main ballroom. We take the stairs up to the next floor, walk down the hallway, and Alex opens a door at the very end, rushing me inside. It's dark, but with a few windows lighting up the place, I can see it's another dining room. There are chairs and tables spread all over. Before I can look further, he snatches me up and shoves me against the wall, his mouth devouring mine and my hands already pushing his jacket off. With his help, I remove it, letting it fall to the ground behind us, but we don't care. Nothing else matters—just us. As he unfastens his belt, I remove my panties hurriedly, wishing they were never there in the first place.

Oh, he is not leaving. He is here. With me. He lifts my legs, wrapping them around his waist, and as my tongue plays with his, I grow desperate to feel him inside of me. I'm even sweating simply at the thought of it. Oh my... how much I missed him. His kiss is long, hungry, and passionate. "Ahh..." At the intensity of his first thrust, my mouth opens wide, but not my eyes. "Ahhh!" The deeper his thrusts, the deeper I feel how much he loves me, how much he missed me, and how much he needs me. Fuck! "Ahh..." This time I hear him too. I tighten my grip around his neck to hold on to while he mounts me eagerly against the wall. "Ah!" He becomes more insistent, his thrusts more hurried as he breathes in and out against my mouth. Then he moves to my neck, sucking it hard as he fucks me. And at that instant, with all the mixed emotions consuming me, I let the tears I was holding back all night fall. I have no shame in admitting it—I do need him in my life. Yes, I do. Like a terrible obsession. Like an addict with any vice, I don't want the cure—I can't even cure it.

"You really thought I'd leave you, huh?"

I can't reply. I barely have air in my lungs to breathe. He reaches my mouth again, kissing me lustily. And I know he knows I'm in tears. "I'll never leave you. Do you hear me?"

he scolds, searching my gaze. But I shut my eyes at the intensity of everything, sniffle, and nod. "I need you in every fucking sense of the word," he adds, emphasizing the fucking.

"Oh, Alex…" I rest my face against his shoulder, sniffling. "I need you so much." And then I suck his neck, inhaling his cologne. "Ahhh! Oh!" I feel my pussy throbbing, dopamine filling every inch of my brain, as I lean my head against the wall to moan, to breathe, to come. "Oh, fuck! Don't stop!"

Alex doesn't stop, no. He keeps going. He keeps going even harder. "Ahh!"

"Petra." His hand covers my mouth. "Don't moan so fucking loud," he scolds between clenched teeth as our imminent orgasms barrel toward us.

To my greatest pleasure, he keeps pounding me until he gives me the best part of him, the part I was missing the most. "Ahh…" he groans. Oh, there is nothing better than this. My eyes remain shut, as I moan against his palm at the warm sensation of him unloading inside me. I don't care if I'm loud. He knows how to fuck me, and I don't care if the world knows it.

Then, as we come back to our senses, we hear nothing but our panting breaths and our heartbeats. He plants a kiss on my forehead while remaining inside me, just as I like. We look at each other, and I find myself smiling quite proudly. "You know… I'm no longer taking the pill."

He lets out a chuckle at my statement, but the same smile settles on his lips. "I know."

And mine keeps growing until he steals it with a kiss.

As I feel his cum coursing down my thighs, I ask, "Do you have any tissue?"

He lets out a quick laugh, most likely in embarrassment. "They are in my jacket... which is lying on the floor."

I shake my head, beaming with joy. "We're gonna have to stay here forever, then."

"That wouldn't be such a bad idea." And I close my eyes to receive another peck on my lips. "Not having to deal with your parents would solve most of our problems."

"Do you think Dad will forgive you?"

"You mean, for betraying his trust and announcing publicly that I'm not resigning like I promised him I would?" he asks rhetorically. "Not sure. But it was worth it."

* * *

As we leave the venue, we don't see Dad around. Alex and I greet some guests at the entrance, and we find his driver waiting for us, standing outside the car. Alex invites me in, and we sit beside each other, my body nestled against his. "One-twenty Fifth Avenue," he instructs.

I smile immediately; that's not my address. "We're going to your condo, right?"

Our eyes lock, and we smile at each other. With an arm around me, he brings me even closer to him, and whispers, "Where on earth would my fiancée go if not to my place?"

This new reality tastes even better than my wildest dreams. While I know this is most likely just a temporary— or a weekend—move until he speaks to Dad, I couldn't care less. It's still way better than anything I expected for this weekend.

"Do you have plans for the weekend?" he asks.

I can't help but chuckle. "Yes," I reply, lost in his blue eyes. "You."

CHAPTER 27

Manhattan, October 18, 2020
Petra Van Gatt

For the first time in a month, I slept without nightmares, without waking up with a jump, and without screaming in tears. I wake up just like it should be—with the man I love by my side, placing warm kisses on my neck and nibbling the shell of my ear. "Good morning, Miss Van Gatt," I hear him whisper. "Breakfast is served."

Breakfast? Already?

"Mmm…" I mumble, stretching my body under the sheets. "What time is it?"

"Half past eleven."

Jeez, so late! My eyes open wide, and I turn to face him. Okay, he is already all dressed up, casually lying next to me on top of the sheets. "You woke up early, didn't you?"

He grins at me in response. "Just two hours ago." Given the fact that we made love until five a.m., two hours ago seems quite early to me. "You are so damn beautiful when you sleep."

"Oh, shut up," I tease.

"C'mon, let's go," he instructs, pushing the blankets down. "It's a glorious sunny day in Manhattan. Let's have breakfast and then go outside. You need a tan."

"The terrace is outside," I protest, still gaining the courage to get out of bed.

I look around for something to wear. And I realize this was my first time sleeping here in his condo, as I had only spent the weekends in Bedford Hills before. I find his white shirt laying on a chair, and, well, a shirt will do.

I drag myself sleepily to the terrace, waking up at the sight of my fiancé.

Fuck, look at him, with the sunlight beaming deliciously on the locks of his hair and his face as he's working on his iPad.

Then, as I scan the table, I can't help but say, "There are only two of us. Why so much food?"

"You said the same thing in Aspen…" And once his eyes are on me, a small smile charms his face, probably in amusement at seeing me in his shirt.

Letting out a quick chuckle, I say, "You did order too much food." Then I take a seat in front of him and grab some avocado toast.

"And what was my reply then?"

I swallow dryly as his blue eyes lock with mine. No matter how many times I have seen him, his face, his eyes, his smile, and his unbrushed hair falling on either side of his brow, I will never get enough of him. Blinking twice, I think

341

of the answer. "Um, that you didn't know if the food was good or not. Oh, so you ordered all of this?"

His lips curve up. "Do you see Maria around?"

And hope sprouts inside of me to the point that I can't contain my smile. "So does that mean we are gonna stay here, just the two of us?"

"For the weekend, at least."

I take another bite of my toast, my heart filled with joy. I still can barely believe he is finally back. "Did you manage to talk to Dad?"

"No, I didn't." Alex looks down before letting out a sigh. "I already left him two voice messages, but we have a meeting Monday, so we'll talk then." He pauses, pondering further. "Petra," he says cautiously, his eyes meeting mine. "What I did yesterday might have grave consequences for both of us."

I crease my brows at his comment, but I'm not surprised. "I know…"

Then he keeps looking intently at me, and all of a sudden, he asks, "Do you want to live with me?"

Oh my! My jaw drops at his question, and I remain speechless, blinking twice. As I observe him, I can tell Alex is damn serious about it. "Of course," I breathe, my heart pounding in excitement. "What a question."

"I'm not sure what your dad is gonna do next," he warns, his tone laced with concern. "But it's safer if you live with me and don't return to Park Avenue."

"I have always wanted to live with you," I say instantly. "And, um, whatever happens next, we are in this together." We remain quiet as we smile at each other. "Thank you for coming back." My tone is low but filled with gratitude. After all, I know how much is at stake.

After finishing my toast, I pour some matcha tea into my cup and drink it. Meanwhile, Alex remains engrossed in his iPad. Then, as I watch him, another question pops up. "Why didn't you reply to any of my texts?" I pause, gauging his reaction. "I know most of them were stupid, but…"

"Your phone is being tracked," he announces before putting his iPad down to revel in my astonishment. "And mine was too. I had to get a new one in Singapore."

"Oh…" Of course it's being tracked! Why didn't I think about that before? Jeez, I feel so embarrassed, realizing my parents have most likely read all my texts.

As he straightens his posture, he draws in a breath, pondering something. "I needed to make sure your dad knew we had really broken up," he explains. "If he had any doubts about it, he'd never have let me see you last night."

I frown, confused and troubled by his revelation. "But it was an investors dinner. You had to go."

"Me, yes. You, on the other hand…" And as he lets his words trail off, everything starts to make sense. That's why Dad suggested Matthew join us. "I needed to make sure you would be there."

"Dad wanted me to invite Matthew to the dinner," I disclose. "You know, the guy I texted you about."

"I know." And a wicked smile settles on his lips. "I'm glad he didn't come though. The poor boy would've been heavily disappointed."

Unable to deny it, I say, "Yeah, he had a crush on me last year. But he's a good guy."

"I'm sure he is." There's an ounce of humility in his tone that I wasn't expecting. Then we are quiet for a beat as I see him ruminating over something. "Petra," he starts, his face overly concerned and serious. "Your dad didn't give me much of a choice. After he came back from the Netherlands, I was forced to break up with you and leave for Singapore. The plane was there waiting for me. And your dad gave me just enough time to say goodbye to you. Our breakup was being monitored through our phones. Most likely to share it as evidence with your mom."

"What?!" I shout immediately, my mouth gaping at him. I'm so disgusted by my dad's behavior that I can't help but shake my head. Of course they were spying on us. Even if Mom wasn't physically present, she was nonetheless keeping track of my every move by proxy. "My parents are crazy. I mean, I should've known by now that they are. But I never thought my phone was being tracked, and that they were listening to our conversation."

I get up from my chair and go sit on his lap. It's cozier here. Then I wrap an arm around his neck, and, looking him in the eye, I mumble, "I love you." Alex observes me with the same tenderness, and after he takes my hand to give it a kiss, I can't help but tell him in a tone sadder than I intended, "But never leave me ever again."

* * *

It is indeed a glorious day in Manhattan. Alex and I have decided to do just what we used to do when I was seven: go to Central Park and feed the ducks and swans. Except now

we can no longer do so, as the guard is around and technically it's forbidden. But it doesn't matter. We are here, together, hand in hand, strolling through the park, our hearts
just as bright as the sun. Since we are not wearing masks, we
order two ice creams and sit on one of the benches. His gaze
is pinned to my mouth, observing me with amusement as I
suck on the ice cream, instead of eating it with a spoon like
he does. He lets outs a quick chuckle, and as our eyes lock, I
know he is thinking about if he should kiss me here in public or not. But he blinks and looks away.

"Alex?" I hear someone calling, and I look up. "What a
pleasant surprise to see you guys here."

Oh, it's Mike, the COO of Gatt-Dieren, with his girlfriend. Seeing him reminds me I still have to send him my
financial plan. We stand and greet them warmly.

"Congrats on your speech yesterday," Mike praises, giving Alex a quick pat on the arm. "Given your interview with
the Financial Times, I was getting scared you'd be the one
leaving." Alex returns the gesture but doesn't disclose anything further. And since Mike knows it, he looks again in
my direction, and says, "Ms. Van Gatt, what a pity we didn't
have time to talk yesterday. Are you still interested in the
second round of funding, or has your godfather already tak-
en care of it?"

Godfather. Fuck, when will he at least be my fiancé? I
smile, holding back the word on my tongue. "My godfather
hasn't been involved in it," I politely reply. "I'll send you the
financial plan. It's actually ready."

"Oh, that's perfect. I look forward to it, then." After the
usual small talk, Mike shifts his attention back to Alex.

"When are you having dinner with us? Have you been avoiding my invitation or what?" he asks, teasing him. "I'm inviting over some Swiss clients who are visiting New York. You know, that former exec who left Paribas, Laurent? He is dying to meet you. He just got his banking license approved and is opening a small private bank in Geneva…" Alex remains mute, pondering his request. "C'mon!" Mike gives him another quick pat on the arm as he notices Alex hesitating. "Just have dinner with us."

After letting out a breath, Alex smiles politely at him. "Sure. Why not? Which day of the week do you have in mind?"

And at that moment, I realize one thing: goddaughters don't go to dinners with their godfathers.

After all, why on earth would a girl like me go? A wife, yes. A girlfriend, maybe. But a goddaughter? What would be the point?

"Um, is Thursday evening good for you?" Mike asks, beaming with joy.

Alex doesn't reply immediately; instead, his attention shifts to me. "What do you think?" Me? "Is Thursday evening okay for you? If you want to fundraise, Laurent is a great contact to have." My heart can barely contain so much happiness. Oh, Alex. I press my lips tightly together to avoid kissing him in front of them.

"Sounds great, yeah," I reply in a nonchalant tone.

"Perfect. See you guys on Thursday, then," Mike replies, before leaving us.

I'm still trying to contain the urge to kiss him, but damn, I'm beyond excited. He notices and kisses my forehead, trying to contain the same urge. "Let's go home," he whispers in my ear. "I can't contain myself for much longer."

* * *

We don't even wait until we get home. While his chauffeur is driving, Alex's lips don't leave mine. Not even once. Nor in the elevator going up to his condo. And before he opens the door, he snatches me up against it, kissing me again.

"Did you miss my lips that much?" I ask, teasing him.

"I'll never get enough of them," he whispers, nibbling my bottom lip. "Never."

My eyes sparkle at the idea that we are finally going to live together, just like a normal couple.

Then he reaches for his key, and it feels like an eternity before we can get inside and make love. Maybe this time we could do it on the sofa, right past the entrance hall. As we pass the entryway, Alex closes the door behind us, and I shove him against the wall, devouring his mouth, already pushing his Henley shirt up.

"Sorry to disturb you." A male voice startles us.

"Dad!" I blink twice, but my jaw is already on the floor. It can't be possible! Then my gaze drifts slightly to my right. "Mom?" What? I must be dreaming! "What are you both doing here?" I cover my mouth with my palm, mortified at the sight. Oh jeez, my heart is stuck in my throat, and I can barely breathe.

"What the fuck, Roy?" Alex barks, already pulling me behind him. "You're crazy, you know that?"

I close my eyes, forcing myself to wake up from this nightmare, but as I reopen them, all I see is Mom and Dad standing in front of us, censoring us with their glares. Oh God, it can't be true! And yet my parents are literally here in Alex's condo with… two armed security guards!

"What a pathetic slut you are, Petra," Mom rebukes me in disgust, her head shaking.

"Fuck off, Tess!" Alex shouts. "Get the fuck out of here!"

"I don't think so," Mom replies just as stoically, her arms crossed over her chest.

Dad keeps his posture and glare as defiant as a murderer before killing his victim as the two armed men surround him. He paces slowly in our direction, his hands behind his back, and stands before Alex, coming quite close to his face. "What a terrible mistake it was thinking you could outsmart me."

His voice petrifies me, and I don't recognize him! Where is my dad? The one who was kind and supportive of my relationship with Alex? The one who even let us go to Aspen? Where is he now?

"Terrible mistake," he repeats, shaking his head.

"Roy, stop it," Alex snarls, barely containing his rage as they glare at each other. "This is twenty years of friendship you are throwing away. Don't be on the wrong side."

"Indeed, twenty good years." Dad lets out a breath, looking downward and then up at Alex. "I'm gonna miss them." He then turns his freezing stare at me. "Petra, these two men will be your bodyguards from now on."

"Fuck off, Dad!" I shout. "Just fuck off!"

Dad is about to grab my arm, but Alex steps forward, shoving him back. "Don't touch her!"

The two men rush over to Dad's rescue to protect him, and I see him so enraged, full of fury, that they trample toward Alex to do the same or even worse.

Oh God, they're gonna fight! "Stop it!" I yell through my tears, stepping in front. "Dad, please," I plead, trying to calm him down. "You guys are best friends. Stop it."

But as I face the darkness in the eyes of my dad, my mom, and the two bodyguards surrounding them, I know there is no mercy to be found here. And unless we want this day to end in a tragic accident, it's better if I just comply and leave.

"You don't have to do this," Alex mumbles, holding me by the arm.

Despite the difficulty of this moment and not knowing how long it will be until I'm able to see him again, I know this is the right thing to do. Alex can't win against two armed bodyguards.

I look him in the eye, memorizing the last look we exchange as well as I can, then I run a hand over his cheek, and with the back of my fingers, I caress it, enjoying how soft his stubble is. Leaning toward his ear, I whisper, "I will wait for you. As long as it takes."

CHAPTER 28

Petra Van Gatt

I never thought, not in a million years, that one day, Mom would be here on Park Avenue, sitting in our dining room beside my dad. I'd have never expected that she'd call me a slut either, and yet here we are. Yep, life can take some pretty unexpected turns.

Their faces are as frigid as the marble table standing between us. In fact, they haven't said a word since we got here. Not even when I asked them why there is a jewelry box on the table. Nope; nothing. It feels like those meetings where the child did something wrong and has to see the school principal, knowing all too well that some sort of punishment will be inflicted.

As we all remain mute, digesting the chaotic scene that just happened at Alex's condo, I can hear the swinging of the pendulum clock behind me.

Tick tock, tick tock...

But it's not only the pendulum clock that is behind me, no. The two bodyguards that my parents assigned to me are also standing there. And yet I haven't heard them breathing. Are they human?

Suddenly, I see Janine opening the door wide.

"My apologies for the delay." Dr. Nel makes her way in. I notice she's wearing her usual glasses and a fancy Hermès scarf around her neck, and is holding her briefcase.

After exchanging a few words with Mom, she sits beside my dad, who is now between those two witches.

Nel gives me her usual smile, but I don't reciprocate.

"Shall we start?" Dad asks.

They nod at him in perfect sync.

"Petra." I cross my arms at the sound of my name. "I know everything is my fault." His fault? I furrow my brows in total confusion. "And I take full responsibility for that." What is he talking about? What he did in the condo? "I should've never let you start this relationship in the first place. I should've protected you, and…"

"Bullshit!" I shout. "I'm not stupid! I know the only reason you had a change of heart is because Mom has got some dirt on you! Fuck off with your bullshit!"

Their jaws drop instantly—not sure if it's because of my language or that I know the truth.

"Enough!" he barks as he punches the table. A few beats of silence ensue as Dad recovers his composure. "In the beginning, yes." Ah, at least he admits it. "But after meeting and discussing your wellbeing with Dr. Nel, I understand how this relationship is not healthy for you." I can't help but huff at the crap I'm hearing.

"Your dad is right," Dr. Nel adds. "You have Obsessive Love Disorder, Petra," she announces. "This obsessive love you have for your godfather is very toxic and self-destructive. It will take time and a lot of courage, but it can be cured. And I promise you, if you give it a try, it will work."

"You can't cure love, Dr. Nel," I snap.

"You are sick, my poor child," Mom chides. "Sick and totally obsessed with that man. This is over once and for all." She taps her index finger on the table to mark her words.

Meanwhile, I keep shaking my head in total disbelief at the absurdities they are trying to feed me.

"Now…" Mom takes the jewelry box resting in the center of the table and opens it. "I want that ring and pendant in this box."

"What?" I touch my necklace instantly. "No! They are mine."

"Petra…" Dad insists. "Just remove them."

"I said no," I repeat louder. "They are mine, and I won't remove them. Get over it."

"What behavior! This is unbelievable!" Mom scolds. "Very well…" She then beckons to the two bodyguards, who slowly but surely move toward me.

"What the hell?" I ask her.

"At the end of the day, that ring and necklace will be in this box. We can do it gently… or not. It's up to you." Her icy tone is enough to chill the entire room.

"I won't remove them," I keep saying, but my voice is already shaking at the feeling of those two men now right behind me. I can't possibility fathom my dad letting them hurt me, but alas, today anything seems possible. I look at him and ask, "You will let those men hurt me?"

"Just remove the jewelry," he insists. "It's a simple request."

I glance at Dr. Nel, who is taking something from her briefcase, and as I pay closer attention, it looks like a syringe.

Now my body is starting to sweat, alarmed and in fear. My heart is even thundering at the thought of a forced injection.

"What is the syringe for?" I ask them, my blood pressure dropping with every second.

"Since we can't trust you…" Mom starts. "We have decided to implant a chip in you."

I freeze, totally mortified at her words. She must be kidding!

"This is illegal!" I cry out. "You can't do that!" Then I try to stand up, but I'm instantly restrained by two hands on my shoulders and pushed back down. I look at Dad, who remains silent and just as indifferent. "Dad, please…" I keep my anguished eyes on him, hoping he will say or do something—anything.

"Just remove them," he repeats.

I don't recognize him. With tears blurring my eyes, I beg, "Please, no chip."

As he doesn't seem convinced, my gaze remains glued on him, hoping he will reconsider.

After some beats of silence, Dad finally says, "Remove the jewelry, and there will be no chip."

Fucking jerks.

I look at the blue sapphire gleaming on my finger. A small smile settles on my lips thinking about the day Alex put it on me. He even cried when he said yes. Then he kissed my hand repeatedly and told me how much he loved me and asked me to never forget it, which I now understand why he insisted on that. With a heavy heart, I slowly take it off, leaving nothing but a white mark on my tanned skin. For the first time, I can see his family name engraved inside, and, as I put the ring in the jewelry box, I see my mom cracking a smile of satisfaction and victory.

"Don't forget the pendant," she says.

"This was a gift for my baptism."

"Petra," she presses on.

I know there is no point in arguing. After all, they had no issue taking it from me when I was seven. Why would they have one now?

I feel the first tears coursing down my cheeks as I open the clasp and take the fine golden chain off my neck. And as I look at the pendant now lying in my hand, I feel a bit dead inside, just like in my dream when I'd killed myself. Except now, I feel like I'm killing him too. Swallowing hard, I put the pendant in the box, right next to the ring. And in a sudden move, Mom closes the box and takes it away from my sight.

"What are you gonna do with them?" I ask immediately.

"Return them to whom they belong."

"They belong to me."

"No, they belong to a family you'll never be a part of."

I huff at her comment, and ask, "May I go now?"

"One last thing," Dad says. "Your phone is being tracked. If you try to plan anything with Alex or even to talk to him again, we will know it. So don't bother."

"I wouldn't have expected otherwise."

While I don't look surprised, the reality is that I never expected that he would confirm what Alex had just told me this morning. Damn! They have no shame whatsoever! Despite the harshness of the moment, I smile internally, knowing Alex never gave up on me, or on us. And I know that no matter what my parents have decided for us, he will come back.

* * *

I could've spent the rest of the afternoon locked in my bedroom crying with hate and anger over the most despicable parents on the planet, but for what? It'd just have been self-destructive. So instead, I lock myself in my atelier and decide to start a new painting. With some old tracks playing on my vinyl player, I stick with the same dark and gloomy abstract style. The first painting I do is very similar to the ones from the collection *Outrenoir* by Pierre Soulages that Alex and I saw last year, which makes me wonder if Mr. Soulages was also going through a dark period in his life. All of a sudden, I hear knocking, and confusion etches my face as I try to figure out who is at my door right now.

"Petra, may I speak to you, please?" I hear Mom asking after her failed attempt to come in.

Yep, it's locked. Thank God! "I'm painting!" I shout back.

"It won't take more than two minutes," she insists.

Since I'm not in the mood for any more bloody battles, I let out a breath, leave my painting, and go unlock the door. Then I lower the volume of the music and go back to my painting, focusing on it. If Mom wants to talk, she can do so, but she won't have my undivided attention. Oh no, that's a privilege I won't grant her.

As Mom steps in, the smell of fresh paint and wood is quickly replaced by a complex mixture of rose, vanilla, and amber. I'm surprised to hear nothing but silence though.

"What do you want?" I ask, since she doesn't say a word.

Mom stands still, just beyond the doorway. Then she finally closes the door behind her and says, "I'd like to apologize for what I said earlier."

My eyes narrow in confusion. "About what?"

Mom hesitates as she looks away for a moment. "About calling you, well, you know…"

"A slut?"

She takes a few steps in my direction, her expression just as embarrassed. "I had never seen my daughter kissing anyone before," she opens up. "Let alone a forty-one-year-old man who is her godfather." Mom draws in a breath, her eyes darting down, as she thinks something through. "Those images were… disturbing, to say the least."

"That doesn't justify your lack of manners," I snap back. "Dad didn't call me anything."

"I'm not him, Petra."

"Damn right, you're not." Mom widens her eyes, probably astounded that I replied back so fast.

As a cold silence settles in, the air between us gets tenser by the second, and my patience for sharing the same space as her is running out. "Can you leave me alone now?"

But Mom doesn't react. She seems to be on another planet as she glances around my atelier. "It's a beautiful place you've got here. This is where you paint?" Her tone is sweet and inviting, but I know what she is trying to do.

"Doesn't it look like it?" Since she is not leaving, I walk to the door and open it wide. "Can you leave now?" I insist.

If Mom came here just to apologize for her lack of manners, then it's done, so I don't see why she is not going away.

"Janine made a soup for you," she says very quietly.

But I reply just as fast, "I'll eat later on."

Mom hesitates for a second, but finally paces slowly in my direction, her posture composed and straight like always. Still consumed in her thoughts, she opens her mouth, but no words come out. Then, as she stands in front of me, she tries to stroke my cheek with her hand, but I move back before she can do so.

I pick up a brush and focus my attention once again on the canvas. "You may close the door behind you, please."

I don't know if she is still looking at me or not, but I hear her say in a whisper, "I love you," and the door finally closes.

CHAPTER 29

Manhattan, October 19, 2020
Petra Van Gatt

"It's Christmas! It's Christmas!" I shout, running down the staircase. Then I reach the hallway and go straight to the living room, where I see the Christmas tree standing beside the fireplace, covered with snow, stylishly ornamented with white and gold baubles, and gleaming with gold-colored lights. As my eyes drift down to the bottom, I see the floor covered with innumerable gifts, wrapped in gold-, white-, and silver-toned paper. My excitement is pounding hard in my chest, and I clap my hands, in a hurry to open them all.

"Dad! Alex!" I call, but in vain. They must be in the library—they always take their coffee there. I go back into the hallway, knock on the library door, and, after hearing a quick, "Come in," I turn the handle and open the door wide. My smile turns into a grin as I find my godfather sitting on the sofa. Without waiting any longer, I trot in his direction and pull on his wrist. "Let's go! Santa came already!"

"Petra, you can at least say good morning," Dad rebukes.

"Good morning," I mumble, continuing to pull on Alex's wrist.

Alex lets a quick laugh escape. "Good morning, Miss Van Gatt. Did you sleep well?" His voice has always been so warm and caring that it makes me feel special each time I hear it. It's very different from Dad's, which is usually cold and stern, even when I'm well-behaved and do nothing wrong.

Nodding at his question, I see that he is finally standing up, and I grin in triumph. "Roy, let's go," he says, giving my dad a quick pat on the arm.

"Will be there in a minute," Dad mumbles briefly, his eyes glued to his phone. The usual reply.

Alex takes my hand, and I lead him out of the library and into the living room. Once there, we stand still in the entryway, admiring the Christmas tree. "Look!" I point my index finger at the presents on the floor.

"Wow," he utters in admiration. "So many!"

I giggle, clapping my hands with excitement, before running toward the tree. Then I sit on the floor and take the first package. But I wait for Alex to sit beside me before starting to tear off the wrapping paper. Once he does so, I look behind me toward the doorway, but I don't see Dad coming. Shrugging my shoulders, I decide to open the present anyway. "Wow!" I shout, recognizing the wooden paint box I had seen at the store.

"Is that the one you wanted?"

I nod vigorously, totally mute as I open the box and find a complete set of oil tubes, brushes, and a palette.

"*Now you are officially a painter.*" Alex's joyful expression brings a wave of emotion through me, and as he strokes the back of my head, I open my arms and embrace him tightly.

"*Thank you,*" I mumble as I rest my head on his shoulder. It was the best decision to instruct Alex to hand my letter to Santa personally. I've heard stories of parents who never delivered their kids' letters to Santa because they were too busy, so of course the kids didn't receive the gifts they wanted. To make sure I'd receive mine, I gave it to Alex, and I also showed him the gifts I wanted in a shop to make sure he understood the importance of his mission. "*It's exactly the box I wanted.*"

His gaze goes to the doorway, most likely waiting for Dad to join us. After seeing no one there, he gives me a quick peck on the head and stands up. "*Let me check on your dad.*"

Blowing out a breath, I watch Alex leave the room with some sadness in my eyes and my lips twitching in displeasure. Not knowing how long I should wait, I start counting out loud the oil tubes in my box. One, two, three, four, five, six… Then I look again at the doorway, but there is still no one there. Seven, eight, nine, ten, eleven, twelve, thirteen… I take another quick glance, but still nothing. Fourteen, fifteen, sixteen, seventeen… There are seventeen oil tubes and no one around to share the news with.

"*Alex?*" I call, my eyes on the doorway. When no one replies, I repeat, louder this time, "*Alex?*"

My eyes open wide, as I wake up with a jump. Jeez, childhood memories are haunting me again. I briefly check the alarm and see it's six a.m. I think twice about taking another pill to sleep, but I better not. In three hours, I have Public Economics with Matthew and the group, so shutting my eyes, I remain lying in bed, ruminating… It's so strange how those memories with Alex are so vivid in my sleep. I didn't even remember that I'd given him a letter for Santa… I chuckle thinking about it. Then, I wonder if we'll still manage to get married on the fifth of December. One thing is for sure: if we do, then this year will be our first Christmas as a married couple. The thought of it brings me joy and warms up my heart. Despite living with the most horrendous parents, it's better to fill my mind with positivity and hope.

But two hours later, it's not Janine who walks in my bedroom with the intention of waking me up. Nope. I recognize her steps and her morning ritual by heart. As I turn the light on and prop myself up on my elbows, I see to my greatest despair that it's Mom.

"What the fuck are you doing here?"

Mom startles at the sound of my voice and stands still in the middle of my room. "I, um, I just wanted to wake you up…"

"I'm not a child, Mom! You don't come in my room without permission," I rebuke. "Only Janine can come in." Since Mom doesn't say a word, I add, "Even Dad knows that!"

"Alright, I'm sorry." She doesn't seem sorry though, just annoyed. "Um, do you have any plans for lunch? Maybe we could—"

"I have plans for lunch, yes." I can't believe after everything she's done to me, she still believes I want to hang out with her. "Can you leave me alone, please?"

Mom doesn't hide her disappointment, and her gaze falls to the floor as she thinks something through. Then she looks up at me again and tries to smile faintly, without much success. "Alright, um, have a great day. If you need anything, just let me know." And she mercifully leaves my bedroom.

* * *

Once the class is over, and not knowing if Mom is still here in the house or not, I decide to invite Matthew to have lunch with me at the same Japanese restaurant he invited me to last time. I'm not sure if we will have a table, since I didn't have time to make a reservation, but I hope they will recognize us and make an exception.

As Matthew and I leave the building, I see a woman smiling at me, blonde hair brushing her shoulders, Hermès purse hanging on her arm, wearing a gray coat and heels.

"Mom?" I forgot that this is my new reality now—stumbling upon my Mom when I least expect it.

"Hey," Matthew greets her with a warm smile. "So nice that your Mom's here."

"Fantastic…" I mumble as she slowly walks in our direction. Since it's the first time they've met each other, I make some basic introductions. "Mom, Matthew. Matthew, my mom."

"I'm Tess Hagen." Mom gives him a big grin and holds out a hand to shake his. "Petra has spoken fondly about you."

"Mom…" I rebuke just as fast.

But Matthew remains just as excited. "Ms. Hagen, it's such an honor to finally meet you. Welcome to New York."

Oh jeez, I can't help but roll my eyes at these two. And before this gets any weirder, I ask her, "What are you doing here?"

Mom simply gives me her sugary smile and says, "I'm taking you both to lunch." Did she ask me if I wanted to? Of course not. Why bother?

"We've got other plans, sorry." As I start walking, I notice that Matthew hasn't moved a foot. "Matthew?"

"We can invite your mom. It's alright, you know."

As I don't look very enthusiastic, Mom says, "We haven't had one single meal together. I thought maybe we could go somewhere, the three of us." Her tone is sweet and pitiful, but I'm used to it. I remain staring at her with total indifference. "Very well, guess I should keep going." *Yeah, you should.* She takes her iPhone from her purse and starts doing something on it. Probably booking a driver or something.

"C'mon," Matthew insists in a low voice. "She came all the way from Rotterdam for you."

Leaning toward his ear, I say, "She is evil personified on earth."

"Trust me, there is worse than her." I huff instantly at his words. *If he only knew...* "Ms. Hagen, there is no need," Matthew starts. "Petra and I would love to have you join us for lunch." *Liar.*

Mom gives him her usual enthusiastic smile, although she knows perfectly well that's not true. No wonder she's into politics—she can play with people's emotions like no one else. "How kind you are," she praises. "Do you have any place in mind?"

Matthew doesn't. I know him well. Until this year, he used to only eat at the canteen, and except for our lunch at Franchia Vegan Café, he normally eats either at my home or his. "Um, Petra?"

Shrugging my shoulders, I say, "I'm thinking Japanese." I know she hates it.

"Perfect. Do we need a car?"

"I've got mine," Matthew replies.

I instantly furrow my brows. "You drive?"

"Yep, sometimes." He then puts a hand on my lower back, leaning toward me. "Mainly if it's to take you to lunch." I can't help but shake my head in total disbelief. Matthew driving my mother and me to lunch. What world am I living in?

Damn, a few months ago, it would've been Alex who would be taking me somewhere. He'd greet me with a kiss, open the rear door to invite me in, and once inside, he'd remove my panties, unzip his pants, and—

"Petra?" My mom's voice brings me back to earth, and my heart tightens because those memories are nothing but distant ones, belonging to a reality I'm no longer certain I'll experience again. Jeez, incredible how life can change with the snap of a finger. "Shall we?"

* * *

After stepping into Franchia Vegan Café, I tell the waiter we want to have a quick lunch as we have class starting soon.

Fortunately, he seems to be a young college student too, so he nods in understanding and ushers us to a table, handing us three menus.

"I'll be right back," he tells us.

Good.

I sit in front of Matthew, with my mother beside us.

After a few moments checking out our menus, I feel a hand stroking my arm. Looking up, I see Mom smiling at me as she does so. "I'm so glad to be here," she whispers.

"I'm going to have the vegan sushi plate," I say, my attention shifting to Matthew. "And you?"

"Uh?" he mumbles, his eyes still glued on the menu.

"Matthew?" I call again. "Have you decided yet?"

"Not really."

I start shaking a leg impatiently under the table.

"Relax. I'm sure you will be on time." Mom is putting on her sweet, innocent tone today.

Doesn't she realize I'm impatient to leave her presence? "I have three books to read and a dissertation to give next Monday," I lie, but the truth will only create a cold and unpleasant atmosphere, and we have just arrived.

"What is it about?" And she keeps her mellow voice going.

Does it matter? But instead, I say, "How to respond in a financial crisis."

Mom nods, and as she feigns interest in my studies, she asks, "Are you managing to get back on track after all the classes you missed?"

"More or less," I tell her. "But Matthew and the group are helping a lot."

"Don't forget, after class you have your appointment with Dr. Nel." And I roll my eyes upon hearing her name. "Would you like me to take you there?" she asks, putting on her most caring expression.

"Anthony will do it." My stern voice has finally rendered Mom speechless. She lowers her gaze, looking absently at her menu, and after a beat of a silence, she stands up.

"Excuse me, I'll be right back."

As soon as she leaves our sight, Matthew puts down his menu and leans forward. "Why are you so cold with her?" he spits out. "She seems like the sweetest mom ever."

I huff at his words. "You don't know her. Believe me, she's malicious as a snake."

"Why? Just because she's against your relationship with that old dude?" *What the heck?* My jaw drops instantly at his vulgarity. "If I had a daughter, I'd do the same. Your godfather is fucking creepy. Glad your parents stepped in."

I lean over and snap, "That 'old dude,' as you put it, is my fiancé."

"*Was* your fiancé," Matthew replies back, glancing at my left hand.

And I'm not sure what is more offensive—the fact that he believes a ring is the deciding factor for my being engaged, or that he's siding with the woman who has made my life a living hell. Jeez, I can't believe I supported him when he became vegan, only for him to become a total jerk again. One thing is for sure: if there was an award for the most awkward lunch ever, this one would certainly be the winner.

Mercifully, the waiter steps in and asks, "Are you ready to order?"

Taking a deep breath, I say, "I will have the beans."

Matthew creases his brow at my answer. "You don't want the vegan sushi?"

"I'm no longer hungry. Beans are enough."

* * *

After the most pathetic lunch ever, Matthew insists on dropping me and Mom off at home. The fact that I have to share the same car as her twice is already bad enough, but as we get into the lobby of our building, Mom truly believes I'll also share the same elevator. *Wrong.*

As the doors of the first one open wide, I gesture for her to step inside. "You go first," I instruct with a fake smile.

After Mom does so, I press the button for PH and get out of the elevator just as fast. "We can share the same elevator, you know."

"I know," I tell her as I watch victoriously the doors close before me. *A small victory, but still a victory.* I take the other elevator on my right and enjoy a few seconds of peaceful solitude before it takes me to the highest floor.

As I step out, I don't see Mom around, but I do find one of the bodyguards standing beside the front door of the apartment. *What on earth?*

"You gonna stand here all day long?" I ask him, despite his stoic expression staring past me at nothing.

"Yes, Miss," he finally answers.

The more I think about it, the more I understand why—he wants to make sure I don't leave the house on my own, without my parents' permission. This is like a real prison after all, and he is the guard.

"You know I have to leave at five for my appointment with Dr. Nel, right?"

"Yes, Miss." He never looks me in the eye though; like a soldier in the army, he keeps his stare just past my shoulder. And as I step inside the entryway of my house, I wonder how long I'll remain a prisoner for. Heck, even prisoners know how long they will stay in prison. I mean, at least some of them do.

* * *

At five p.m, I receive a call from Anthony letting me know he's outside waiting for me. As I step out of the library, I pray I don't see Mom around to wish me a good session with Dr. Nel. Yeah, she'd be capable of saying something that stupid. I rush out of the house and see the bodyguard still standing in the hallway. Doesn't he get tired of standing there all day long? I brush away those thoughts, but it's hard to ignore the fact that my freedom is extremely restricted. On my way to the appointment, I put my AirPods in and listen to a pretty gloomy playlist, but I can't help it. It's such a horrible feeling, knowing your every move is being watched and you're just a little rat inside a cage, not able to break free. All of a sudden, I receive a text from Emma, and a smile spreads across my face as I read it. *Hey babe, how are you? It'd be great to meet up before I leave. Can I come by later on?*

And I reply just as fast. *Hey. Yes, come over for dinner.*

Once Anthony drops me off, I think twice about running away. But to go where? First, I need a new phone, and the only person I trust enough to get me one is Emma. I will ask her to get me a new one this evening. One thing is for sure: sooner or later I'll leave Park Avenue and the prison my parents built for me, and I will never ever return there again.

Letting out a breath, I go into my useless appointment with Dr. Nel. And just like usual, she welcomes me with a big, fake smile, inviting me in.

"Please make yourself at home," she says, seeing the skeptical look on my face as I slowly step into her minimalist office. Well, home is prison, so if that's what she meant, I'm already feeling at home. I sit on the edge of the chaise lounge, instead of lying on it like I usually do. Dr. Nel is the enemy, and I should've never been so comfortable around her. "How are you feeling today?" she asks, feigning interest in me.

"I'm alright," I say nonchalantly. If she believes I'm gonna open up and share my entire life with her, she's in for a big disappointment.

After she closes the door behind us, Dr. Nel goes to her briefcase and takes something from there. I can't really see what's in her hand, but as she stands in front of me and hands it to me, my heart falls to the ground.

"You can't be serious?" I ask in outrage.

"You're no longer on the pill, right?" Dr. Nel keeps extending her hand, holding a box containing the morning-after pill. "You had unprotected sex yesterday, so it's better you take one."

But of course, I forgot that my body also now belongs to them. What do I have left that can be considered mine?

Blowing out a breath, I know there is no point fighting Dr. Nel. If I try running away, the bodyguards will show up in record time and she will most likely insert that tracking chip under my skin. I can already picture the grotesque scenario: I'd be crying over my fate, kicking everyone as much as I could, but in vain, and she'd give me a little something to put me to sleep, then complete the injection without resistance. A shiver runs down my spine, and I feel like throwing up as I realize how powerless I am. Jeez, I am indeed a rat in a cage. *Breathe, Petra… Just breathe…*

I take the emergency contraception, put it on my tongue, and swallow. "Done," I tell her, showing her my empty mouth.

Dr. Nel gives me a sympathetic smile for my compliance. "Good…" Then she returns to her desk, where she takes her notebook and pen, and sitting in her armchair, she says, "Now we can start the session."

* * *

There isn't a single moment I don't think about running away. In fact, every time I step outside and onto the street, my heart begs me to ask for help, but my head reminds me how useless it is to do so. Then I see Anthony holding the rear door open and waiting for me to do what I'm supposed to do—get into the car and go home, without protesting about the lack of control I have over my own life. Actually, my parents and their minions expect me to comply at every turn. Otherwise… Jeez, I shiver, picturing what they are capable of doing. As I get into the car, my thoughts go to Dad and how naive I was to have trusted him to go to Rotterdam in order to talk to Mom… The faith and trust I had in my own father is forever gone. He sold his soul to the devil, and I'll never forget it. Fortunately, in a few hours, Emma will be here, and we will be able to prepare a plan for me to contact Alex and escape this nightmare once and for all. Incredible how a nineteen-year-old is more reliable than the man who's supposed to be my dad.

"Hey, how was your day?"

Mom's voice startles me as I step into the house. I'm so tired of her fake, sugary tone, but I prefer not to say a word about it. "I took the pill, in case Dr. Nel didn't tell you yet."

Mom doesn't hide her astonishment upon hearing my blunt answer. "I understand you're upset. If I were your age, I'd be hating my mom too." Mom walks closer and tries to reach for me, but I take two steps back. "Petra," she starts. "I can assure you that your dad and I did it because we have your best interests at heart. Even if you don't agree with it."

I can't help but huff at her pathetic excuse. And before going up the stairs to my atelier, I look her in the eye and say, "One day, I will marry him."

* * *

Three hours later, I thought Mom would have left the house and gotten a life, but alas she is still here, and she's again knocking on the door of my atelier. Jeez! She's the most persistent woman I know.

"Petra, Emma is here." *Oh! Finally!* The only words that could make me leave my painting in the blink of an eye and open the door wide.

"Emma!" I plunge her in a hug, embracing her as tightly as I can. Then I look at Mom and say, "Thanks, you may leave us now." But before I bring Emma into my atelier, I wait for Mom to leave the hallway and go down the stairs. Once I hear steps on the marble staircase, I invite Emma to come in, and lock the door behind us.

I put my index finger to my mouth, instructing her to stay quiet. In the silence, I close my eyes, trying to discern any noise coming from the hallway. Since I don't hear anything, I lead Emma to the other side of the atelier, as far away as possible from the door.

Without saying a word, Emma takes a brand-new iPhone 12 from her purse and gives it to me. *What? How did she know I needed a new phone?* But before I can ask her, she types in the passcode, which is 1205 and also my birthday, and I smile, immediately figuring everything out—it's Alex who gave it to her.

Then Emma goes to the Notes app and shows me a text. My heart picks up immediately upon recognizing that it's a message from him:

Petra, keep this phone away from your parents. I'll meet you Friday, 10 p.m., at Emma's place. Bring this phone with you and pack some summer clothes. Be careful not to get caught!
I love you, A.

Dear Lord! I have to put my palm over my mouth to contain my sobs. Emma pulls me into her arms to soothe me, and I quietly let the tears fall. Oh my… We are finally gonna be together soon.

"Thank you," I whisper in her ear. "You have no idea how much it means to me." I knew that Emma would always help me out.

As she releases me, her expression is filled with a seriousness I haven't seen from her before. She presses her lips against my cheek, and then asks in a low voice, "Did they do anything to you?" Her empathy and concern warm my heart. And I can imagine Alex called her immediately after I left his condo and told her what happened there.

I shake my head in response. For some reason, I don't feel capable of sharing with her my parents' threats of a forced injection.

Her fingers start stroking my cheek as she observes my untamable distress. "Everything is gonna be alright," she says, keeping her voice low. After all, we can never be too prudent. "Do you think you can manage to come over Friday night?"

"Yeah, I… I will talk to Dad and convince him."

And damn, I don't know what I did to deserve someone so special and caring like her, but thank God for sending me Emma.

CHAPTER 30

Manhattan, October 20, 2020
Petra Van Gatt

I didn't sleep well last night. But this time, it wasn't because of Alex, as I know it's only a matter of days until we meet again. This time, it was because of Mom. I totally screwed up yesterday evening when Mom wanted to have dinner with Emma and me. Yes, I should've been smarter and more pleasant, but the hate I have for her took over, and after a bloody battle, Mom had left the dining table in tears. *Just leave me alone and go back to Rotterdam*, I remember shouting at her when she wanted to sit with us. Even Emma asked me to calm down, but I couldn't. The disgust I have for that woman is too great. Then she asked me to stop, but I was too furious to even care, and that's when I spit out, *What a pity you are still alive.* Mom broke down crying and left the table, making me feel like the most horrible person on the planet. I have to admit, I'm not proud I said that. I hate hurting her, as it hurts me just as much, but I can't accept what she is doing to me either.

All I wanted was to be with you, she said before leaving the dining room, carrying her plate, most likely to eat in the kitchen—alone, miserable, and sad. I have to remind myself that Mom is just a manipulative bitch. She knows how to play with my emotions and make me feel remorseful. And damn, it's working pretty well. The truth is, one day, if I'm a mother myself, I can't possibly imagine my kids saying to me what I said to her. Maybe I should apologize for yesterday? No, she doesn't deserve that either. She's literally trying to destroy my relationship with my fiancé. Instead, maybe I should just please her and have a meal with her… Or at least behave civilly around her, despite everything she has done to me. Reaching the kitchen, I raise my brows seeing her already there.

"Oh, I'm sorry," Mom mutters, sniffling, her hands cupping a mug as she's sitting on one of the stools. For the first time, I see her without makeup, without her hair brushed, and in a long robe covering her pajamas. She looks barely recognizable without her daily makeup on. Then, Mom takes another sip of her tea and stands up. "I didn't know you would be up so early."

"It's okay," I mumble. "I couldn't sleep any longer." I give her a smile, probably the first one since she came here. "I'll try to be more polite," I tell her. "The toxicity in this house has become unbearable." She just nods, her gaze tired and sleepy. "Are you alright?" I ask her. "You know, Dad could walk in at any moment and see you like this." Not that I care, but I know she hates not being presentable.

Mom wipes her tears, and for once her voice sounds truly genuine and sincere. "Your dad didn't come home last night, so don't worry."

"Oh." Now I'm even more surprised. "And how do you know that?"

"Well, Janine arrived at my room at six this morning and told me his bed was exactly like she'd left it the day before."

Her tone saddens me, and for the first time in eighteen years, I decide to ask, "Was he like that during your marriage?" A question I've never dared to ask before. One, because their marriage has been over since I can remember, and two, because I know Mom hates to talk about it.

She just shrugs in return. "Nothing has changed."

"You must've felt very lonely," I point out.

"You get used to it," she says, before taking another sip of her tea. "And find hobbies to get over it."

Such as drinking? The question is on the tip of my tongue, but I decide not to ask it. I know the answer already.

"Mom?"

"Yes?"

"If I ask you something, can you be honest with me?" Not that I expect her to be, but one can always dream.

"Sure."

"Apart from the age difference and the fact that you don't like his family, is there any other reason you disapprove of my relationship with Alex?"

"Oh God…" Mom rolls her eyes just as fast. "Twenty-three years of age difference is reason enough, Petra."

"Mom…" I insist, letting the word trail off. She looks me in the eye, calming down, and I hope this time she will be sincere.

"No," she answers back. *Liar.* Jeez, for once I had hopes that Mom would finally open up and tell me what she has against him. But not surprisingly, she didn't. "The age difference is the main reason. As Dr. Nel explained to you, your brain isn't fully developed until you are twenty-five, which means you need seven more years to be able to fully weigh the consequences of your actions." She pauses, a disgusted expression settling on her face. "What Alex did to you," she says, shaking her head, "is beyond gross and shows a complete lack of any decency or respect toward you."

I can't help but protest, "You do realize we love each other, right? He didn't do anything I didn't want him to."

Mom chuckles. "No eighteen-year-old knows what love is." *Because she does?* "Believe me, what you have is nothing more than infatuation turned into an obsessive disorder." Her cold, formal tone has now taken over. "One day, you will understand."

The more I hear her speak, the more I wonder if Mom would've been against me falling in love with someone else, but of my age. Deciding to test the waters, I ask, "What if I were in love with Matthew? Would that be infatuation too? There is no age gap between us. I mean, unless you consider one year a significant difference."

"You are too young to develop those kinds of feelings," she says simply. "Love is a serious commitment that a teenager cannot fully understand. You may have a crush, but that's it."

Playing along, I keep inquiring. "So should I just fool around like Emma?"

"You don't have to fool around like Emma. I don't particularly fancy her lifestyle, but you can have a boyfriend and remain emotionally and physically safe."

My eyes widen at her comment, and I can't control the way my mouth hangs open. "What does that even mean?"

"Well, someone who respects your boundaries and understands that you are both too young to do certain things."

What? At that instant, I must have the most cringeworthy grimace on earth on my face. "Like having sex?" I'm about to crack. The infantilization she is into is borderline offensive. The more I think about it, the more I realize I actually never spoke about sex or kinks with her, only with Emma. Jeez, if Mom thinks I'm too young to have sex, I can't even imagine what she would think about the rest...

"Is that a requirement nowadays? You can have a boyfriend perfectly fine without doing it."

And here we go. I'd never have imagined she'd be so protective and strict about this until now. "It's not a requirement, but it's natural. And it feels even better when you do it with someone you love." I emphasis the word *love* to tease her.

But Mom is having none of it, and keeping her distant, formal tone, she says, "Of course it's natural. Teens are high on hormones. That's why it's our responsibility as parents to protect you until your prefrontal cortex is fully developed. The problem is that teens are stubborn, and think they know better." And she emphasizes the last word.

I can't help but shake my head. I want so much to argue back, but just twenty minutes ago, I decided to be more sympathetic. So, taking a deep, long breath, I just tell her, "I will have some matcha." And I leave the conversation there. No matter how much I try, Mom and I have fundamental differences. Differences that will never go away. I don't mind different opinions—Matthew and I are very different when it comes to philosophy, and Emma and I are very different when it comes to our lifestyles—but I do mind when those opinions are being imposed on my own life and the way I should live it.

* * *

As I blink my eyes at the screen of my iPhone, I'm not sure how I should reply to Matthew's invitation to spend the weekend in the Hamptons with the rest of the group to celebrate his twentieth birthday. After his disgusting attitude at our last lunch, he really expects me to join? What a joke! Anyway, I have to skip his event and go to Emma's, since Alex will be waiting for me there. But what if the body-guards follow me to her house? Jeez! That would be pure madness! This weekend is the perfect occasion to leave Manhattan and my parents behind once and for all though. I just need to make sure those guards don't follow me. How? As I keep ruminating, the ringing sound of my iPhone startles me. Not surprisingly, it's Matthew requesting a Face-Time. Damn! He sent me the invite, like, two minutes ago. What's the hurry? But curiosity getting the best of me, I accept his request, and when our cams are on, we clearly don't share the same enthusiasm at seeing each other—while I remain pretty stoic, Matthew gives me a full-toothed grin and waves at me in such a ridiculous manner that I wonder if he's doing it on purpose to make fun of himself.

"Hi," I say in response to his charade.

After exchanging the usual greetings and a little small talk, Matthew doesn't waste any time jumping right into the reason for his call. "Um, did you get my invite?"

"I did," I reply, reveling in his concern that I'll decline it.

"And?"

"And…" I let the word trail off as I ponder a proper answer to his question. But the truth is, there aren't a thousand ways to put it, so instead I simply say, "I'm not sure I should go."

Matthew's smile disappears just as fast, and I swear his expression has never been so grave. "Why not?"

Why not? Really? "Well, not sure if you remember, but you were pretty rude to me last time we went out."

"So you're mad at me?" It might come as a surprise to him, but I nod, not even bothering to argue my case. "Why? Oh! Because I expressed an opinion against your ex-fiancé or whatever he is right now?"

"It wasn't just an opinion, Matt," I snap. "You were rude and pitiful." Seeing Matthew blowing out a breath while he shakes his head in total disbelief, I add, "I thought you supported me. At least that's what you told me on campus, remember?"

He presses his lips together, looking past me at nothing. "It's not that simple…"

My brows raise at his statement. "You mean not being rude? I think it's pretty simple, actually."

Matthew runs a hand through his tousled hair as he keeps ruminating. "Alright, I apologize for that." Despite his words, I see no remorse whatsoever. I don't think he even means it. "Can you join us this weekend? Please, it's my birthday…" he insists, pressing his hands together like in prayer.

"It's the second time you've apologized for the same thing though…" I share my concerns out loud with him, not really convinced of his sincerity, which kinda sucks, since I truly believed in our friendship.

Seeing how skeptical I am of his claims, Matthew lets out a breath louder than usual, considering me for a moment. "Alright, you want the truth?"

Huh? His question makes me gape. "Yeah, that would be a good start."

Despite my welcoming his honesty, Matthew takes a few more seconds to mentally craft his answer, which leaves me wondering why. "I won't deny that meeting your mom, who is against the relationship, made my opinion feel validated."

"Validated?" I repeat, my eyes opening wide.

"Yeah, like, everyone else thinks your relationship with your godfather is okay, and I just don't share the same opinion."

"And that's why you decided to be disrespectful at lunch?" I ask, totally baffled.

"It was dumb, I know. What can I say? I'm only human." He might be only human, but the way he downplays his attitude toward me and my fiancé still remains problematic.

"Can you forgive me? I swear I'll never say a word about him again."

A part of me wants to give him another chance, but the truth is I've already done that before and Matthew hasn't changed. After all, friendship is first and foremost about treating your friends with respect—even when you don't agree with them. Despite knowing I can't go to his birthday weekend even if I wanted to, I remain undecided about what to tell him regarding the event, so I give him a polite smile and say, "Okay, I'll think about it and let you know." I will text him later on in the week and find an excuse to skip it.

Then I hear a knock on the door, and after ending the call with him, I shout for the person to come in.

Mom quietly steps into the library, her face unusually serene and calm. She stands still right past the doorway, her posture hesitant. "Um, your dad is not coming home tonight, so I thought maybe we could go out and have dinner together?"

And here we go again. I always thought Dad was the most stubborn of the family, but Mom has clearly dethroned him by now. Jeez, she really doesn't give up. But as I'm tired of our constant arguments, I simply say, "I'm still studying…"

"Oh, I know, sweetie. I'm just saying later on, maybe in two hours." Since Mom sees me hesitating, she adds, "Janine already left, so there is nothing prepared."

"I see…" My gaze drifts away as I try to think of another way to politely decline.

But since I'm not finding any, Mom says, "Um, maybe we can go to Jean-Georges. Your dad told me the food is excellent there."

"I'm sorry, but I don't go out during the week." I try this one, but she doesn't seem much convinced.

"We can eat here if you prefer."

Letting out an exasperated breath, I know I'm coming up against a brick wall. "What about me?" I ask, looking her in the eye. "Have you thought about what I want for once?" Mom is totally mute, blinking twice at my reaction. "Of course not, because all that matters are your own selfish desires." Head shaking, a chuckle escapes me as I think about how true this is. "Jeez, you're so selfish that it hurts." I pause, gauging her reaction. But there is none. "Not once have you asked me what I want in life, *not once.*"

"I don't think having dinner with my own daughter is asking for the moon."

My jaw drops at her remark. I just pointed out the fact that she doesn't care about what I want in life, but she's still focused on her damn dinner? "Wow..." Nodding thoughtfully, I let that reality sink in, and I say in the most distant way possible, "I'm sorry, but I don't want to have dinner with you."

"We didn't go ahead with the tracking chip, Petra." Her observation freezes my heart on the spot. We've now moved on to eventual threats? Is that what she means? "I've been very patient and kind with you. I even let you spend time with Emma last night." Oh, because the next step will be forbidding me from seeing my friends? Like those ultra-secured prisoners? It's clear as water that if I want to remain chip-free and be able to see Emma again, I've got to bow to Mom's desires. And since I can't risk not going to Emma's this Friday, I ask, "Where were you thinking for dinner?"

* * *

A wise man once said, "Keep your friends close, but your enemies closer." Okay, granted—this wise man might simply be Michael Corleone from *The Godfather II*, but his words have never resonated so well with me as tonight when I'm about to go and have dinner with my number-one enemy: Mom. Needless to say, she is over the moon about taking me to one of those fancy Michelin-starred restaurants on the Upper West Side. A restaurant I assume Dad must come to frequently.

"Was it Dad who recommended this place to you?" I ask as we sit at our table.

"Is it that obvious?" Her tone is particularly bright and jovial. Actually, I don't think I've ever seen her this happy before.

"A bit."

As I observe her, I must admit she's also made quite the effort this evening. Her short blonde hair is brushed back, showing off her beautiful black rose earrings, smoky eyes, and elegant black dress. But behind all the glam and smiles, all I can see is a control freak who restricts me and my freedom, a woman who truly believes that she's saving me from the evil grip of the man I love, without even realizing that the true evil is her.

"Ladies, good evening," greets the waiter as he hands us our menus. "Welcome to Jean-Georges. Would you prefer still or sparkling water to start?"

"Good evening. Still, please," Mom answers.

Then he takes the white napkin folded at her side, and lays it on her lap, before doing the same for me.

After he leaves, Mom leans closer to me and whispers, "What fine service, isn't it?"

A quick chuckle escapes me. "Yeah, it's okay."

She takes her glasses from her purse and puts them on before embarking on a long reading journey of the menu like it's some sort of fine literature. Despite hating her for everything she has done to me, her focusing on a simple menu makes my lips twitch in a smile, and as my gaze remains on her, I memorize every single feature of her face. Actually, she looks a bit like Megyn Kelly with her evening makeup on. And for some odd reason, I say, "You're really beautiful tonight."

Mom puts her menu down, her eyes never leaving mine, and gives me a smile that I will never forget. "You are very beautiful too."

She might not be in New York for the right reasons, and I might hate her for all the things she's been doing, but there is a part of me—a part that I don't know how strong it is—that yearns for a better relationship with her. After all, any daughter would love to have a good relationship with her own mother. And I don't think I am any different.

"Dad was such a lucky man." I reciprocate her smile, and it's full of empathy just like hers. "I'm sorry that he messed up."

"Life is full of ups and downs, darling," she brushes off. Mom is about to say something more, but the waiter steps in and asks, "May I serve you a glass of champagne?"

"Of course," Mom replies immediately. "Who are we kidding?" I can't help but laugh as the waiter fills our glasses. Then she raises her flute of bubbly and says, "To us, Petra."

It's not her voice that I hear, though, but Alex's. As if he's sitting in front of me and toasting with me. I close my eyes, trying to keep his voice from haunting me. And the more I try, the more I see him, hear him, feel him touching me... My mind starts recalling memories I shouldn't want it to, and I see him everywhere... in Rome, in his office, in Aspen, in Bedford Hills...

"Are you alright?"

Jeez, I look around, making sure he is not here. Indeed, I don't see anyone who resembles him.

Then, looking at Mom, I also raise my glass. "To us." And we clink our glasses.

As we remain quiet, looking over our respective menus, I decide to say, "Um, you know, Emma invited me to spend the weekend with her."

"Oh, she did?"

"Yeah..." My fingers are on my flute, playing with the base as I think of my next words. "She's having a dinner this Friday."

"But I thought Matthew invited you to the Hamptons this weekend?"

I'm about to ask her if she listened to our FaceTime call, but then I remember my phone is being tracked and she must have read his text instead. "Matthew has been an ass," I tell her. "So I prefer to go over to Emma's."

"I see…" Mom nods pensively, looking at nothing. "I'll have a talk with your dad and let you know."

Damn it! And I know in that moment that if they let me go, it's going to be with the bodyguards securing Emma's house like a high-risk prison.

I take a sip of my champagne, trying to tame my rising anxiety at the thought of it. Jeez, what a dumbass I was to have attacked Mom so fiercely. I should've just played along, swallowed my pride, and been a kiss-ass so she'd let me go. But the truth is, being nice to someone I despise so much is way harder than I thought.

CHAPTER 31

Manhattan, October 22, 2020
Petra Van Gatt

That Thursday evening, I should've been on the arm of my fiancé attending the dinner at Mike's place, but alas, Dad made it clear that he's got other plans for me, so instead, I find myself going to one of his many lobbying dinners. I have no idea why he insisted I attend, since he knows perfectly well I don't like politics, but he assured me I'll soon find out. As we arrive at the event hosted in a modern and spacious apartment in Greenwich Village, we're welcomed by a host who asks for our IDs, making sure we are on the guest list. Afterward, he thanks us and says, "No pictures or videos during the evening, please."

Not surprising.

As we step inside, we find a waiter handing out flutes of bubbly, so Dad takes one for himself while I scan the room for a waiter carrying soft drinks instead. After he takes a sip, Dad gestures for me to follow him toward the crowd that has gathered in groups around the open space that includes the living room and the dining room. I try to find a terrace, but I don't see any. The more I look around, though, the more confused I am, as I recognize absolutely no one here. Dad, on the other hand, is already smiling, greeting, and shaking hands, and despite the fact that he introduces me to everyone he knows, I can't find the will to feign interest in these people. They are friends of my dad's, allies, lobbyists, political influencers, and the longer I stay, the more they monopolize the conversation with their plans for 2021. Discreetly enough, when the group is engrossed in conversation, I sneak out and start strolling toward the quietest part of the house: the hallway leading to the other rooms. As I walk down the corridor, my eyes are drawn to the many frames hanging on the wall, featuring the same man in a suit, but posing with different governors, heads of state, and even US presidents. He must be the owner of the place. Then, standing still, my eyes squint as I focus on the last photograph, trying to figure out who he is.

"And yet not even a single photo with his family." A male voice startles me, and I turn around, recognizing it.

"Matthew?" I say in surprise as my gaze lands on him. Unlike the rest of the guests, I find him in casual attire though—gray sweater, a pair of jeans, and sneakers. What a contrast with everyone else. "What are you doing here?" He glances over my shoulder at the wall behind me. "Oh, so this is your dad?" I ask, pointing to the frame I was looking at.

"Yep," he answers, nearly in embarrassment. "That's when he became the attorney general of New York." Jeez, that explains all the pictures with politicians, then. And I'm pretty sure Dad knew who Matthew's father was long before I did. After briefly scanning the other photos, Matthew says, "Pops calls it his wall of fame."

The entire situation feels truly bizarre though, and I'm pretty confused about how Dad got invited here in the first place. "Was it you or your dad who invited us to come tonight?"

"Well…" A faint cheeky smile appears on his lips. "Let's just say I made some quick intros to get you here."

I cross my arms in amusement at his little game. "All of that just to see me?"

Matthew doesn't even bother to hide his smirk. "Guilty." I should be mad at him, but I simply laugh at the whole thing. "Let's be real—it was the only way to persuade you to come over so I could apologize face-to-face." He takes a step closer to me, his eyes still on mine. "I'm really sorry that I pissed you off." He breaks eye contact, searching for his next words. "Um, you are really dear to me." My lips part in surprise at how sincere he sounds. "Can you forgive me?"

With as much effort as he's put in to see me again, it's hard not to. "Your friendship is also dear to me," I tell him.

And before our talk becomes too awkward, we smile at each other, and Matthew takes me by the hand, ushering me toward the crowd. "Let me introduce you to my pops." We stop in front of a group standing in a circle, which also includes my dad. "Pops…" Matthew starts poking him on the shoulder. And as he turns, I recognize him from the photographs. He hasn't aged much, actually, and even his smile remains just the same. "This is Petra Van Gatt, the friend that I told you about."

"Mr. Bradford, it's a pleasure meeting you," I say, unsure how I should greet him.

To my surprise, he eagerly shakes my hand, full of admiration, it seems. "Please just call me Eric. What a pleasure to finally meet you, Petra." Eric seems way nicer in person than in the photos. "After showing such warm hospitality toward my son, I obviously had to invite you both over in return."

"It's always a pleasure having Matthew with us," my dad points out.

A bit embarrassed at so much attention, I just smile at Eric in return, anxiously waiting for all the gazes on me to go away. Fortunately, Eric notices and breaks our odd silence. "You are also going to the Hamptons this weekend, right?"

"The Hamptons?" Dad asks, feigning his surprise.

"Matt is turning twenty on Saturday." Eric wraps an arm around his son's shoulders as he smiles at him full of pride. "So he invited his closest friends to our beach house," he says directly to my dad.

"Oh, that's a great idea." It's impressive how Dad can fake the excitement in his tone and smile so smoothly. "Why didn't you tell me about that?"

As I think of an answer, Matthew takes over. "Petra declined my invitation to join us." What? I can't believe Matthew just said it out loud in front of my dad, his dad, and everyone else! My cheeks blossom with heat at the embarrassment, and I squint my eyes at him, trying my best not to kill him.

"Why on earth would you decline? Go to the Hamptons for the weekend. It's your friend's birthday after all."

How pathetic is he? Just a year ago, Dad considered boys nothing more than a stupid and useless distraction, and now he's playing matchmaker? Of course, Matthew Bradford is the perfect fit for me, according to him. After all, we are both studying economics, Mom likes him a lot, and his father is none other than the current attorney general of the state of New York. How convenient for Dad if only I would fall in love with Matthew and forget my fiancé. And as I look at him drinking his champagne and engaging in futile talks with Eric, I remain astounded by the swift change of his views toward the opposite gender when it comes to me.

I had other plans for the weekend, Dad, I think, but instead I say, "Sure, it'll be great." I know I'm not in a position to negotiate. It was obvious that my chances to go over to Emma's this weekend were close to none. In any case, I will just send my live location to Alex from my new phone, and we will leave this pathetic charade behind once and for all.

CHAPTER 32

Manhattan, October 23, 2020
Petra Van Gatt

As I finish preparing my backpack, my heart can't stop thundering in apprehension for tonight. Alex instructed me to pack summer clothes, which means we are most likely leaving the state of New York. And hopefully tonight, we will finally be together and leave this whole nightmare behind. I decide not to ask to Dad or Mom about the bodyguards. If they can just stay here on Park Avenue, all the better. It's a risky move, but the wisest. Once Matthew is waiting downstairs, I take my backpack and head out of my room. But before leaving, I take one last look around at the bedroom I spent my whole life in. After all, I have no idea if I'll ever return here. It's a horrible feeling, since I have so many dresses here that are truly dear to me, including the white dress I brought to Aspen, the red one I wore in Rome, and the one I wore to my engagement party, and my heart tightens at the idea of leaving them behind. Even though I have no space left in my backpack, I think twice about taking them. Maybe I should take a suitcase instead. No, my parents will find it suspicious if I take a big suitcase for only two nights. Glancing at my watch, I'm sure Matthew can wait an extra minute or two, so I go back into the closet, grab those three dresses, remove some of the clothes from my bag, and shove them in. Then, as I close my backpack, I heave a sigh of relief, knowing these three are coming with me. Afterward, I go to my atelier and double-check that the door is properly locked. Yep, at least no one will come here and take my paintings away.

I head to the entrance and find Mom and Dad waiting for me beside the main door. I'm shaking at the idea that they could send the bodyguards to follow me, but instead of showing it, I give them a broad smile and put on my most confident voice. "Alright, Matt is downstairs. See you both on Sunday."

"If you need anything, just call us." I give Mom a kiss for the sake of letting me go. And although her sugary tone is truly irritating, I have no idea if I'll ever see her again, and if I do, I doubt she'll use the same tone.

"Yes, Mom." Then I give my dad a quick kiss on the cheek, but before I can go, he holds me by the shoulders and looks me straight in the eye.

"Petra." His strident voice nearly makes me jump. "I hope you're gonna behave there." I have no idea what he means by that. Doesn't he know I have a fiancé?

"Matthew and I are friends," I remind him, outraged at his lack of decency.

"I'm not talking about that." Fuck! His stare goes right through me and leaves me totally exposed and mortified. At that moment, I know exactly what he is talking about. "Be wise." And he lets his words sink in as he presses his lips to my head.

After swallowing dryly, I say, "Alright. Have a great weekend." Then I open the door, walk outside, and smile one last time at the two tyrants I'm leaving behind.

Standing in front of my building, I find Matthew's car waiting at the curb. To my surprise, Katrina, Sarah, and David are sitting in the back seat, and I let a quick smile escape at the realization that Matthew reserved the front one for me.

"Hey," I greet as I get into the car, looking first at the group behind me. Then my gaze goes to Matthew, who's already smiling at me. His hair is just as messy as usual, which gives me an immediate urge to try to compose it. As I brush his hair a bit to the side and back with my fingers, I don't think I've ever seen him as happy as he is now. His eyes are gleaming, and his smile has never been so joyful.

"Is it better?" he asks as I observe his hairstyle.

"Not really, but it's fun to play with your hair." Not sure why I said that, even though it's true.

As he keeps his eyes pinned on me, he says, "I can't believe Ms. Van Gatt is coming with us."

Letting out a quick chuckle, my gaze drifts to my lap, a bit embarrassed at his comment, especially as he said it out loud in front of everyone else. "Miracles do happen," I reply in a low voice.

All of a sudden, though, Matthew reaches down and lays his right hand on top of mine, which is resting on my lap, and leans closer to me. "Thanks for joining us," he whispers near my ear, before giving me a kiss on the cheek. My heart might have sped up at his unexpected touch. Not knowing what to think of it, I just give him a quick smile in return. Then his attention goes back to the road, and he starts driving, putting two hands on the steering wheel.

After twenty-five minutes in, the car is filled with laughter, music, and playful chitchat, but I remain a bit aloof, looking pensively out the window as I think about what I'm about to do later tonight. I feel a bit sad for Matthew. Despite all our disagreements, he seems truly happy to have me here. And leaving tonight means I won't get to celebrate his twentieth birthday tomorrow with him and the group. Once I run away, not even telling him why, Matthew is gonna feel quite resentful toward me, and maybe even betrayed.

My attention shifts quietly toward his face. While his stare is pinned on the road, he keeps singing and dancing in his seat to a Katy Perry song that is now playing on Spotify. My lips twitch into a grin as I observe him. And I can't help wondering, would I have fallen in love with him if Alex had truly left forever for Singapore? The question terrifies me, and I mentally slap myself at having even thought about it. *No, Matthew is a friend, and he belongs in the friend zone, even if Alex had left*, I tell myself. A fatigued sigh rolls off my lips as I push those thoughts away. The uncertainty of what the future holds for me keeps my heart pulsing faster than usual. After all, not only am I leaving my entire life in New York behind, but I also have no idea where I'm going next.

Thankfully, I only have online classes for now, but what about next year? Will I be able to return to New York safely without repercussions from Dad or Mom? And what about Matthew? Will he ever forgive me for running away from his house on his birthday? I guess only time will tell.

***

The Hamptons, October 23, 2020
Petra Van Gatt

"Here we are," Matthew announces as we finally arrive onto his street. While everyone is praising the beautiful neighborhood and the direct access to the beach, I look discreetly behind us—fortunately, I don't see anyone. Maybe my parents decided not to send the bodyguards to the Hamptons after all. Or maybe they have been told to stay at a distance. But the road is really long, and I don't see any cars on the horizon. Maybe Dad decided it was safe enough and there would be no need to bring extra security.

Once Matthew stops the car in front of the gates, I take note how they open automatically when he presses a button on his keys. As we wait for the gates to open all the way, I see a pedestrian door with a doorknob on my right. When we get to the driveway, I notice a security cam perched on the front porch, recording the entrance. After parking the car in the garage, Matthew leads us inside and shows us our respective rooms. I must admit, I was not expecting the house to be so spacious and modern. It even looks pretty similar to Emma's. Matthew leaves the group behind and gestures discreetly for me to follow him down the hallway. He then opens a door, inviting me in.

"Is this room alright for you?" He turns the light on, and I take a few more steps, my lips curving up as I smell the fresh jasmine fragrance. My eyes marvel at the view of the beach from the floor-to-ceiling windows, but I'm particularly glad to see I have a private bathroom. I don't know why, but I've got a feeling it's the best bedroom in the house.

Pressing my lips tightly together, I can't stop thinking about what I'm about to do in a few hours. I'm nearly tempted to ask Alex to postpone until tomorrow evening, but that'd be so tone-deaf. After everything we've been through, I have to leave today. "It's great, yeah," I tell him, my tone not as enthusiastic as I wanted.

He strolls over in my direction and stops inches from me. "By the look on your face, it doesn't seem like it." But I don't dare look him in the eye, so my gaze remains down—it feels safer. "If you prefer mine, we can switch…" Then he brushes some hair behind my ear, forcing me to hold his gaze. Matthew pauses and simply stares at me for a few heartbeats. And as we look at each other, I feel a bit like a traitor for running away on his birthday without telling him why. The thought of it doesn't sit well with me, and I truly hope he'll forgive me. But I force a smile and say, "No, don't worry, this one is really nice. And the view of the beach is great."

But Matthew is still observing me attentively, like I'm some sort of puzzle he's trying to solve. "Are you still angry at me?"

I chuckle at his question. "No, I…" Pausing for a beat, I search for a proper excuse. "I'm just a bit tired because of the drive." *Bullshit.* "But I'm good." And feigning some enthusiasm, I brush his arm energetically. "So, how does it feel turning twenty?"

"Well, ask me that at midnight." And he gives me a playful wink, which makes me feel even worse. "Let's go. The rest of the group is already in the dining room."

We go to the dining room and find everyone already setting the table for dinner. As Sarah looks in our direction, her eyes shoot daggers at us. "Oh, finally," she snaps. "You guys thought you'd hide and not do shit?"

"Thank you, sweet Sarah." Matthew trots toward her and gives her a quick peck on the cheek, before taking the plates and putting them at each place setting.

Since I see everyone busy arranging the dining table, I ask, "Um, can I do something?"

"Don't worry, it's already done," Matthew mumbles as he finishes putting the glasses in front of each plate. Then he takes his iPhone from his back pocket and asks, "What do you guys want to eat? I'm thinking of ordering Thai. Is that okay for everyone?"

As the group gathers around Matthew to tell him exactly what they want, I excuse myself and quickly go to my bedroom. There, I take my new iPhone and send Alex my location, along with a text message: *Hey, I'm at this address. Be careful of the security cam at the gates. And I'm not sure if the bodyguards are around or not. Love you, P.*

"Petra!" I hear Matthew shouting from the dining room.

"Coming!" Glancing at my watch, I see it's only seven p.m., so I leave the phone in my bag and head back to the dining room.

* * *

After our Thai dinner, we get our coats and head outside to the beach where Matthew is lighting up a campfire, while David is already passing out beers for Sarah, Katrina, and himself. Then he shows me a bottle and asks, "You want one?"

"No, thanks," I tell him as I sit on one of the cushions. A smile settles on my lips at the fire already beaming on my cheeks, and I extend my hands to warm them up.

While everyone is sitting around the campfire, Matthew goes back inside the house without saying a word. As we wait for him, I discreetly pull out my iPhone and check the time: 8:30 p.m. I also notice Alex sent me a message in return, and I open it just as fast: *Noted. I'll wait far from the gates, then. See you at 10 p.m. Love you.*

Jeez, only ninety minutes to go.

"Here." Suddenly, I see Matthew standing beside me, offering me a mug.

"What is it?" I ask as I hold it and bring it to my nose.

He sits beside me, and I notice he's also holding a mug for himself. "Try it and tell me if it's good."

As curious as I am, I take a sip, and my lips curve up, recognizing the flavor. "I can't believe you made me a matcha latte."

"Is it good though?" he asks, still worried I won't like it.

"That's very sweet of you," I say in a low voice, quite in awe at his effort to prepare a beverage he told me he doesn't like. "And yeah, it's really good." As I see him also drinking a hot beverage, I ask, "Are you also drinking matcha?"

"Oh, no. This is a cappuccino. You want to try it?"

"Nah, I'm good."

Then Matthew glances around the campfire, and seeing that we are all here, he asks, "So, Sarah, you still want to play that game?"

Oh jeez, I had already forgotten the reason why we came here. I can't believe Matthew just reminded Sarah about it.

"Yeah!" she shouts, clapping her hands. "David, did you bring the shots?"

David shows us the beer-packed cooler resting behind him. "There is beer and tequila inside."

"Perfect." Then Sarah takes a sip of her beer and says, "Let's play, then!" Her voice has never been so joyful, which makes me laugh a bit. She then looks at Katrina, sitting beside her, and asks, "Katrina, truth or dare?"

Katrina presses her lips tightly together, pondering her options for a second. "Hmm, dare."

"Great!" And Sarah rubs her hands together, maliciously planning the dare. "Call Prof. Reich and tell him that his breath smells bad." While my jaw drops at Sarah's request, everyone else breaks into laughter.

"Are you insane? I can't!" Katrina yaps amid the laughter.

"Relax. Put your phone on private, and he won't know it's you," Sarah insists.

David takes her phone and helps her set it to private mode, then Katrina makes the call and puts it on speaker for us to listen.

"Hello?" My heart skips a beat recognizing Prof. Reich's voice. Everyone is containing a laugh, trying to keep quiet as much as possible.

"Prof. Reich?" Katrina asks.

"Yes, who's speaking?"

Jeez! It's really him.

"I was one of your students last year, and let me tell you, your breath smells terrible! Brush your teeth once in a while, for fuck's sake!"

Oh my gosh! I can't believe Katrina just told him that. She spoke so bluntly that I'm left blinking my eyes, speechless.

"What?" While everyone is breaking into laughter, the poor man remains just as confused. "Who's speaking?"

But Katrina then hangs up. "Done."

"Well done," David praises. "You might have saved his future students from that terrible breath."

Now being her turn, Katrina looks at Matthew and gives him a smirk. "Matthew, truth or dare?"

"Knowing you as I do, I will go with truth."

But Katrina blinks twice, most likely in surprise. "You know you're gonna have to do a shot first, right?"

Matthew keeps thinking for a moment and says, "Alright, I still prefer truth over dare."

Katrina raises her brows, still baffled by his choice. "Are you sure?"

"Go ahead," Matthew tells her.

Katrina takes the tequila bottle from the cooler, gets up from her seat, and goes to stand behind him.

Matt closes his eyes, tilting his head back, and opens his mouth wide for Katrina to pour some tequila into it. Everyone cheers and claps at the show while Matt tries his best to drink the tequila falling in his mouth, although most of it just lands on his chin. His facial expression twitches into a grimace as he keeps swallowing the distilled alcohol, and I find myself doing the same.

Once he drinks enough, Katrina goes back to her seat and then starts, "Matthew Bradford." Everyone remains quiet, patiently waiting for her question. "Is it true that you have a crush on Ms. Van Gatt?"

"Jeez…" David shouts at the blunt question.

And as I freeze on the spot, my cheeks must have turned a sharp shade of red. What an embarrassing question to ask. Damn!

Matthew looks at me, giving me an unbothered smile. "Yep, and I think she knows that," he replies in the coolest manner possible, his eyes on mine.

Wow. The way he dealt with such a delicate question couldn't have been better, and I return the smile, though a bit troubled that he still has feelings for me. *You are really dear to me*, I recall him saying in his apartment. Jeez, my chest tightens knowing how hurt he's gonna be when he finds out that I ran away.

"Oh…" Katrina utters. "That's so cute."

I'm not sure if I'm supposed to say something or not, but I break eye contact and take a quick sip of my matcha, anxiously waiting for the next round.

"Sarah," Matthew starts. "Truth or dare?"

Sarah doesn't waste any time, answering, "Dare!"

"Why am I not even surprised?" he asks with a chuckle, before thinking something through. "Alright, you're gonna lick Katrina's neck and then give her a kiss on the mouth."

"Really? That's it?" Sarah seems visibly disappointed, and we all laugh at her expression. "Sometimes I get the impression you are from last century." Without further ado, Sarah leans toward Katrina's neck and licks it in one go, which seems dumb to me rather than sensual, and I let a quick chuckle escape. Then the duo exchanges a quite intense kiss on the mouth, like they are used to it.

"Damn!" David's jaw drops to the floor as he observes the girls kissing in awe. And judging by his face, it seems like it's the first time he's seen this. I shake my head in amusement as I witness the whole thing.

"That was super hot," Matthew praises once they are done. "I didn't know you had practiced before."

"Ha ha," Sarah ripostes back. And her attention shifts to me. "Petra, truth or dare?"

Oh my… Why can't I just sit here and watch? I know if I opt for truth, I will have to take a shot, but I'm too scared of what Sarah will ask me to do if I choose dare, so instead I go with the safest option. "Um, truth."

"You know you have to take a shot of tequila first," Katrina says in a playful tone as she shows me the bottle.

"Can I at least drink from a shot glass?" Yeah, I'm definitely not going to put on the same embarrassing show that Matthew did. Plus, having tequila all over my mouth, coat, and shirt is far from ideal.

"Alright." Matthew rushes inside the house, and two minutes later, he brings out a shot glass. Then Katrina fills it and gives it to me.

Not wanting to waste more time on this, I take one quick sip, then force myself to swallow the rest just as fast. "Done."

I breathe slowly in and out, taming the urge to grimace as the alcohol goes down to my stomach.

"Is it true that your fiancé broke up with you?"

What! Her question is enough to startle me, and I blink twice, staring at her.

"Sarah!" Matthew warns.

I can't believe it! Did Matthew share details about my private life with her? Of course he did! That's the only way she could know! After all, I didn't share those details with anyone but him. That was confidential, for fuck's sake! I squint my eyes in annoyance and look at Matthew straight in the eye. It's clear he told her about my breakup, and most likely about everything else. Jeez! Letting the reality sink in, I stand up and say, "Well done, Matt." And I just leave this stupid game.

"You're not answering the question?" I hear Sarah asking as I walk away.

And Matthew yapping at her right after. "Fuck off!" Then I hear footsteps running in my direction. "Petra, wait!" As he reaches me, he grabs my wrist to make me stop. "I swear, I didn't tell her anything about your relationship."

Facing him, I cross my arms and shake my head at his blatant lie. "Stop lying. I didn't tell anyone about my breakup but you."

"I didn't say a word about it either," he insists. "Maybe it's because she noticed you haven't been wearing your engagement ring that she asked you that. I swear I kept my mouth shut."

My gaze drifts away, not wanting to face him anymore. I'm so hurt and mad at what he did.

"Petra, I promise I didn't tell her. Sarah is just drawing her own conclusions. You have to believe me on this."

I try to find the truth in his gaze, and although he sounds sincere, there's no way that's possible. But one thing is for sure: I'm done with this game. "Alright, um, I'm sorry, but I don't want to play anymore."

"I totally get it," he replies just as fast. "I'm sorry for Sarah's behavior, but I swear everything you told me has stayed between us."

I look to my left and see the pathway leading to the house, but I decide to sit on the bench first. Matthew sits beside me, and we keep quiet as we listen to the waves coming in and out onto the shore. I take a deep, long breath into my lungs, reveling in the cold air of the night. "It's a beautiful night." Then I look up and observe, amid the dark sky, some stars twinkling at me. "Cold, but beautiful." I rub my hands together to warm them up. What a contrast of temperature now that we're no longer sitting in front of a campfire.

Matthew slides closer to me and takes my hands between his to warm them up faster.

"You don't have to," I tell him, amusement thick in my tone.

"I know." And as he also knows that as soon as he lets them go, my hands will get cold again, he asks, "You want my coat?"

"Are you serious?" I shake my head in total disbelief, but he seems damn serious. "No!" And I just lean my head on his shoulder as he continues rubbing my hands to keep them warm. "But thanks, that's very kind of you."

And Matthew does the same, resting his head on mine. All of a sudden, we hear distant laughter and jokes coming from the campfire. Well, I guess David and the girls are still entertained, playing that game. We, on the other hand, remain quiet, simply enjoying the evening and each other's company.

"Do you think you'll ever forget him?" Matthew asks, out of nowhere.

The question squeezes my heart so tightly that I shut my eyes for an instant. I hate having to tell him the truth. Despite everything, Matthew is a good guy. "No, I don't think so." I pause for a beat. Then I lift my head from his shoulder in order to look him in the eye. "Matt, you deserve so much better than me. Someone who loves you as much as I love him."

But Matthew frowns a bit at my answer, most likely hurt by what I said. With a trace of a smile, he starts studying me, my face, my expression, my eyes, my lips...

I know he wants to kiss me. But he knows I don't want him.

"Petra..." he breathes, quite close to my face—too close, actually. "You have no idea how much I care about you."

And this time I know he's not only referring to friendship. "Don't say that..."

"I can wait," he interposes. "Unlike your godfather, I can wait. I have my entire life ahead of me." He then takes a deep breath and adds, "I'm sure one day you'll realize that we are meant to be together."

I close my eyes for an instant, wishing I could believe it. I wish I could forget the man who haunts my dreams every day. But even with my eyes shut, Alex is all I can see. There is no future for me without him in it. He is in my soul, my mind, my body, my dreams, my thoughts…

Then, as my eyes blink back to Matthew, I say, "I gave myself to him. I'm sorry."

"Um, what do you mean?" Matt frowns in confusion. "I don't mind if you're not a virgin. Like, I'm not a virgin either."

I can't help but chuckle in return. "Oh, Matt…" And I shake my head in amusement. "It's not about sex…" But how can I explain that to him? How can I explain to him that giving yourself to someone goes beyond intercourse? It's so deep, so transcendental… "He's my soul mate," I say, letting out a sigh. "I have to fight for him. He's worth it."

"I feel the same way about you, you know…"

Fortunately, our awkward moment gets interrupted by a beep from my iPhone. Looking at the screen, I see it's a new text, and after reading it, my heart explodes like fireworks and I beam with joy, leaping off the bench. "I'm going to rest. I'm tired."

"Um…" Matthew glances at his watch. "It's only ten p.m."

"Good night, Matt." I give him a quick kiss on the cheek and trot back into the house to grab my backpack.

He is here! Alex is here in the Hamptons, and he's waiting for me outside! Once I get my backpack, I close the door to the bedroom behind me, and head as fast as possible out of the house and toward the main gates. I run down the poorly lit driveway, my heart pounding like I'm in an action movie, and when I get to the gates, I unlock and open the pedestrian door and leave the property.

Fortunately, the streetlights are enough to give me some visibility as I look up and down the road, searching for him.

Oh God, there he is! I find his car parked at the end of the road, and his figure emerges from the driver's seat.

As I observe him now walking in my direction, all I can think about is how we are meant to be together.

Yes, my parents want us apart.

Yes, I should be with someone like Matthew.

Yes, for society's sake, we should remain goddaughter and godfather.

But to me, Alex and I are so damn meant to be together. My heart is pounding even faster as I run in his direction.

Once I reach him, I can't help but jump on him, my legs wrapping around his waist, and I welcome him with a never-ending kiss, my lips pressing tightly against his. "I missed you so damn much."

"I missed you too," he answers back, matching my low tone. And he kisses me again, as greedily as he does when we're making love. Then, our eyes locking on each other, cheekiness settles on his face and one corner of his mouth goes up. "May I kidnap you?"

The question makes me laugh, and I whisper close to his ear, "Only if you take me far, very far from here."

"I think I can do that." Then, looking over my body, his expression becomes more serious and worried. "Did they put anything in you? Any implant?"

Dropping my gaze for an instant, I take a breath before answering, "No, they didn't." I swallow nervously as I recall the moment they tried to though. "But I have a few body-guards. I'm not sure where they are."

"I know, give me your old phone."

When I give it to him, Alex turns off the phone and drops it on the ground right in front of the left tire, and I feel my heart dropping with it.

Once we get into his car, Alex drives over the phone, and I hear the horrifying sound of the screen shattering.

Crack!

Then he drives backwards, running over it again. And as we get farther away, I see my phone on the ground, totally broken. The sight of it leaves me a bit nostalgic. After all, every picture of us, video, and text are in there. And it was on that phone that I received his first message.

"Hey…" Alex mumbles, seeing my melancholic face as my eyes remain pinned on the broken phone. "You already have a new one."

"It's not about the phone…" Unable to disguise my sadness, my head dips a bit down.

Alex reaches out and squeezes my left hand. "I'm sure everything is on the cloud. We will transfer your data onto the new one."

I give him a smile in return, trying to bury my nostalgic feelings.

Then Alex keeps driving in the direction of East Hampton, more precisely to the marina and harbor, which spikes my curiosity. "Where are we going?"

Without taking his eyes from the road, he just says, "Far away, Miss Van Gatt."

As we arrive in the driveway of the marina, I see from afar a captain and crew members getting a modern sailing yacht ready.

"Is that for us?" I ask, barely containing my excitement.

And Alex seems to revel in it. "Yep," he mumbles as he parks in front of the dock. "We are leaving New York."

Oh jeez, my heart pounds faster and faster at the idea that we are going to sail away.

We step out of the car, and I can't help but gape as I observe the majestic sailing yacht, all lit up at night, with its sails the height of a tall tree already wide open. The sails are so tall that it seems like they could reach the sky. Now that I'm standing closer, I don't think I've ever seen a boat so large. Looking around, I see that we are lucky there is no one here but us. After all, this is the type of boat everyone would want to take a picture with. It's the perfect combination of contemporary and classic design, with its near vertical bow paired with a powerful yet sleek figure, and the dark hull contrasting seamlessly with the walnut color of the teak deck and the white tones of the sails.

Alex stands beside me and gestures for me to give him my bag. I do so, my head still tilted back as I can barely take my eyes off of the impressive design of our new "home." The closer we get to the stern of the boat, the bigger it seems to be. Then, we are welcomed by a set of two boarding stairs and the crew waiting for us at the base.

"Good evening, Miss. Welcome on board," greets the captain as we shake hands. He then introduces himself along with the crew members and explains what each one of them is in charge of. Afterward, while he shares a few words with

Alex, my eyes keep looking ahead to the stairs that will take us up to the deck.

"Petra," Alex calls suddenly. "It'll take five and a half days to arrive at our final destination—"

With excitement thundering in my chest and flowing through my veins, I cut him off and ask, "Where are we going?"

"It's a surprise," he answers promptly, gauging my reaction. "But I want you to be as aware as possible of what we are about to do here."

"Well, we are about to run away," I say, my tone cheeky. Then I wrap my arms around his neck, and as I come close to his deliciously kissable lips, I whisper, "Very far away."

But his expression remains just as stoic. "We are. And this will have serious consequences once your parents find out. You know that, right?"

Furrowing my brows, I press my lips tightly together and ponder his statement for a beat. "What kind of consequences?"

But Alex keeps quiet while considering me. As we look each other in the eye, I wonder why he's taking so long to reply. "I'm not sure if we'll ever be able to return to New York. Are you okay with that?"

Oh, wow. My heart falls to the ground as I let the severity of his words sink into me, but I try my best to appear unbothered. From my classes at Columbia to his home in Bedford Hills, a million questions are already running through my mind. And what about my paintings stored in my atelier? And his duties as CEO? Is he still working at the headquarters? With everything that ties us to New York, how can he believe we might never come back here? Does he truly mean *never ever*? But for now, and not wanting to ruin the evening, I silence my torments, and say, "As long as I'm with you, I can be anywhere."

CHAPTER 33

Petra Van Gatt

I had no idea that the first requirement once we stepped onto the boat was not only to remove our shoes, but also to have a full lesson on safety measures, especially during choppy waters and stormy weather. As Alex and I sit together on the sofa in the vast living room, I notice how the crew members are heavily invested in showing us the exits in case of emergency, where the tenders are, and how to wear a life jacket. Meanwhile, Alex wraps an arm around my shoulders, and it feels a bit like we are watching a private show.

"You have no idea what I'm gonna do to you later tonight…" he whispers in my ear as I watch out of politeness the steward wearing his life jacket and telling us about the weather conditions in the coming days. I try my best to contain a laugh, but my cheeks must already be as red as the life jacket he is wearing. "I'm gonna tell you…"

"Alex!" I rebuke, my tone filled with amusement, which makes Alex break into a chuckle. And his gaze is literally reveling in my bothered expression. "Are you paying attention?"

"Absolutely." He looks at the steward, giving him a quick nod, and the four crew members disappear from our sight just like that. Then Alex tries to pull me into his lap, but I give him a quick smack on his chest. "You were very rude." At least now my tone is more assertive. "They were giving us an explanation about safety measures." Why is he still smiling at me with those gleaming eyes? I thought my tone was steadier. "Why are you looking at me like that?"

"Like what?" he asks, unable to hide a full smile laced with pride, but I can't pinpoint why.

"Like…" Jeez, when I'm with him, my heart beats so damn fast that it's hard to even find the right words. "What were you thinking about?" I ask instead, since he most likely didn't hear a word of the presentation.

"You really want to know?"

I'm kind of apprehensive to find out, but I nod at him anyway. I'm just too curious. To my surprise, lounge music discreetly starts playing from the speakers, making the living room even more romantic.

"First, I was thinking about us later on, and then, when you started rebuking me, I was picturing how you would be as a mother."

I skip a breath, unable to keep my jaw from dropping at his answer. "Really?" That's all I manage to say.

Alex's smile stays just as big though. "Yep."

"And how would I be?" I ask, as he didn't disclose that part.

"Oh, absolutely horrifying."

Now my mouth remains wide open in shock at his stupid joke. "You!" And I'm torn between murdering him or kissing him, but Alex makes my choice easier by closing the small gap between us. He sinks into my mouth, kissing me long and deep, and I find my body following his as I straddle him. His hands go down to cup my ass, and mine come up to cup his jaw. Oh my goodness, I can barely believe we are sailing away. My pussy throbs at the thought, and I pour all my excitement into our kiss. His tongue is hot and demanding, flicking into my mouth and playing with my own, and Alex releases a little growl in the back of his throat, reveling in it. Then he pulls away to nibble my bottom lip and to whisper, "Let's go to our bedroom."

It's a pity we aren't already there. As we stand up, I can't help but notice the large bulge pressing against his jeans. *Oh my…* And the sight of it leaves me craving more—so much more. He takes me by the hand, and I follow him down the hallway, feeling the warm, slick ache between my legs. Then he stops in front of a door, and after pulling the handle, Alex swings the door open and invites me in.

"It's so beautiful," I praise, stepping into the vast modern bedroom with floor-to-ceiling windows, which offer direct views to the sea.

"So what do you think?" Alex asks as he stands right beside me. "It's not Aspen, but…"

"It's perfect," I tell him as I am mesmerized by the high ceiling, the large, comfortable bed, and the walnut floor.

Then I stand still in front of the floor-to-ceiling windows, watching in awe as the lights from the marina get smaller and smaller as we go farther away from the shore. Alex stands behind me, and without saying a word, he just wraps his arms around my neck.

"I'm so in love with you it hurts…" I tell him, as he presses his groin into my ass, letting me feel the ridge of his cock, hard and tempting.

Then he pulls my hair to the side and leans down just enough to kiss the edge of my neck. I let my head rest against his shoulder and close my eyes, reveling in his touch. "Mmm…" he utters, sucking and kissing my tender flesh.

Fighting against the rising heat, I add, "Dr. Nel even said I have a pathological obsession about you."

His hands go up to my shirt, unbuttoning my décolletage so that his hand can slide under and cup my breasts. "That makes two of us, then…" he whispers, his lips brushing against my temple.

My breath is ragged, and I'm shamelessly boiling beneath all these clothes. Fortunately, I see Alex pulling my shirt up, and all I do is stick my arms in the air, helping him out. Once shirtless, I turn to face him, my hardened nipples already pointing out. His eyes drift down to look at them, and I smile because it always feels like it's the first time he's seeing them. His fingers run over my chest and collarbone, giving me a little shiver down my spine. Then they go all the way down to the waistband of my jeans, where they unbutton them and pull down the zipper just as fast. And thank God I brought a pair of straight jeans, not skinny ones that are a hassle to take off. As I'm already shoeless, the jeans simply fall down to my ankles, and I step out of them, wearing only my white cotton panties now.

I'm about to reach for his sweater to do the same, but he stops me just as fast. "I need to ask you something first."

Oh jeez, I'm standing in front of him almost naked, my wetness coating my panties, but he still wants to play hard to get? "Now?"

All of a sudden, though, Alex takes something from his pants pocket, and I see him getting down on his knee.

Oh gosh! My hands are already over my mouth covering a gasp, and my heart explodes with excitement upon recognizing the small velvet box in his hands. I never thought my parents had really given him back my jewelry, and a million emotions take over me as I recall not only the day he put the ring on my finger but also the day my mother forced me to take it off.

"When your dad gave me this ring back, he asked me to forget you once and for all." He pauses, opening the box. And my eyes alight on the beautiful sapphire gleaming at me. "I know I'm risking losing everything, but everything is worth nothing if I can't be with you." With tears welling in my eyes, I sniffle in a failed attempt to push them away. "Miss Van Gatt, will you marry me?"

I nod, barely able to articulate any words. Then I take a deep breath, and despite my sobs and broken voice, I say, "Oh God, of course."

A big grin lights up his face as he stands up. And without further ado, Alex takes the ring and places it on my finger. As he does so, I know this time, he won't leave me. I know this time, we are the ones leaving. And I know this time, we are in this together until the end.

I try to calm down, but my heart is filled with so many emotions that all I can do is embrace him as tightly as I can and let the tears I was holding back fall in silence down my cheeks. His arms squeeze around my neck and back, and a million loving thoughts condense into a moment that I wish could last forever.

Afterward, I reach around to cup the back of his neck and kiss him. He doesn't hold anything back. And neither do I. My emotions turning into lust and desire, I pull his sweater up, and he helps me strip it off, revealing his wide shoulders and sculpted body. Jeez... My fingers travel down to unfasten his belt, and I take a deep breath in a failed attempt to tame my loud heartbeat. But my breathing is ragged, and my moves hurried. Fortunately, he helps me out and shoves his pants and boxers down in a wink, before pulling them off.

There is a bed somewhere, and that is where he's carrying me. As Alex lays me down on the sheets, his hands go to my panties, and he pulls the fabric all the way down my legs until he tosses it away. Then his body hovers over mine, and my mouth is on his mouth, craving more. Always more. The adrenaline of being here with him transcends everything. But in a sudden move, Alex flips us around, putting me on top of him. I look at him, a bit confused by the change in positions, but he gives me a smirk before saying, "You're gonna fuck me hard tonight."

Holy shit! My cheeks turn red at his demand. I'm used to him taking control, and except for that dry hump in Brazil, I can't recall any time I've found myself on top of him. Plus, the cachaça had given me some extra confidence and audacity then that I don't have right now. But I close the small gap between us and bury my insecurities in another kiss, claiming his mouth. His hands linger on my back so sensually that I shiver. Then they go all the way down to cup my ass, before squeezing my cheeks so tight that it makes me gasp. After breaking our kiss, Alex lifts his torso and sits up against the headboard. "Close your eyes," he says.

I do so, wondering what the hell he is doing. I hear him taking something from the nightstand, and I wonder if it's a condom. I hope not...

Then I hear a tube opening and liquid being applied to something. I feel his body moving, and it seems like he's lying down again on the bed. But my eyes remain closed as I stay mounted on his groin, straddling him. One of his hands is now on the back of my head, pulling me down to kiss him. My lips slam into his, and there is a small groan coming from the back of his throat at our climbing pleasure. Then I part my lips in excitement, feeling his hardness pressing beneath my thighs. My breath comes out panting as I reach down to angle his shaft at my entrance, before letting the head slide smoothly inside me. "Ah..." I roll my eyes shut, reveling in the pressure of his length filling me. His hips start moving back and forth, spreading me farther to accommodate him. This position is slightly more painful than the others, as I can feel him deeper than usual, leaving my body more vulnerable and exposed, but I start following his rhythm, and the pain quickly turns into pure, warm bliss. I'm about to lean down to reach his lips when I suddenly start feeling something at the entrance of my ass. Opening my eyes wide, I ask, "What the—"

"Relax…" Alex cuts me off. "It's just a plug."

"A plug?" I repeat, concern thick in my tone.

"Does it hurt?" he asks, pushing it deeper into my hole. With the amount of lube it seems to have, the plug goes inside me surprisingly easily. Oh dear… It's a weird feeling to have an object in there, but it's not painful.

"Um, no… it's just… weird." Then in a naughty tone, I say, "You love filling my ass, don't you?"

"Oh yeah," he shamelessly replies, before licking his lips. "And I'm gonna fuck it right after." What! And before I can protest, he kisses my mouth so hungrily that I'm left without air, and despite it all, my pussy throbs around his cock, enjoying these moments of pure lust. Our kiss is brutal and uncontrollable, my tongue twirling with his, pleasure burning under our skin, and I start to move, rolling my hips in a smooth, slow wave. "Oh yeah, that's it."

A burst of heat washes over me at his words. Jeez, there's nothing more satisfying than knowing I'm doing it right. Then my lips travel down to his jaw, and I nibble his stubble before pressing wet kisses all the way down to his neck, where I suck heavily, inhaling his fragrance. His hands are on each butt cheek, guiding the pace. And then I find myself sitting back so I can get a better look at him. My eyes are drawn to his swollen lips, so fucking delicious and kissable, then to the stubble covering his square jaw, and as I observe him, I can still barely believe that he's mine and mine only. Jeez, how lucky I am to have him here. His hands tightening, he pushes me back and forth over him with more insistence. My hips take over and start rocking into his, meeting each thrust. He shuts his eyes, his brows creasing from the pleasure while I keep the cadence, steadily moving over his cock. His hands leave my butt cheeks to cup and fondle my tits. His touch only makes me wilder, and I speed up the pace, bouncing my ass up and down his shaft, which slides so smoothly inside me now. And for the first time, I hear the headboard slapping against the wall. Jeez! My jaw drops at the sight, and I reach for my mouth to cover my gasp.

"Keep going…" Alex growls just as fast, throwing all my worries out the window. And I do so, each thrust bringing us closer to a shuddering climax. From my tits, one of his hands moves higher. And I can tell by the frantic way he grips my throat and the guttural sounds coming from him that he's getting closer. Fuck, I'm gonna make him come under me, and the thought of it drives me insane. There's something extremely sensual and empowering about it. He adds some pressure on my neck, but just enough to leave me in a trance, somewhere far away in the clouds.

"Harder…" His demand sounds nearly like a scolding, causing a flood of wetness between my thighs, and I speed up my pace, bouncing my hips more aggressively, consumed with the burning desire to take him to new levels of gratification. "That's it," he growls under me. "Fuck yeah." I shut my eyes, as I can't shut my mouth—I need it open to breathe and moan. His groans are the best melody and the best incentive to make me do things I'd never do sober. "Ahh…" They are nearly as loud as the sound of the headboard crashing against the wall with each of my thrusts. But I don't care, I keep riding him until he gives me what I want. "Ahh…"

I'm so high on lust right now that it feels like my pussy could break apart. "Oh fuck…" The words roll off my lips, and I realize they were loud enough for him to hear.

"You love riding my cock, huh?" he asks, loosening his grip around my neck, but his hips keep moving and matching my bounces.

My cheeks flush at his blunt question, and since I'm rendered totally speechless, I just nod in return. "Say it."

"Yes, I do."

"You do what?" And I know he wants me to explicitly say those words. Alex has got a morbid pleasure for making me say things I usually wouldn't dare say out loud. "Petra," he snaps, and my attention shifts back to him.

"I love riding your…" I don't think I have the strength to say the rest out loud, but he stops moving in displeasure, and I can't fathom disappointing him. "Your cock," I say it, most likely for the first time in my life. Jeez, my profs at Loyola would shake their heads in disappointment at my vulgarity. But better them than my fiancé. "That's the first time I've said the c-word out loud." I think that was worth telling him.

A pleasant smile charms his lips, and his gaze lingers over me before locking with mine again. "What a good girl you are when you comply." His hands reach down to cup my ass, and he starts pounding me deeper and faster, taking control over the rhythm and over me. "Tell me, little Petra, you want me to come inside you?"

"Oh jeez…" His questions are driving me to the edge, and I'm close, so damn close, to come. "Oh, Alex, please." I don't even have air to argue my case. My breathing is ragged, and my thighs quiver as he goes even harder. "Ahh…" My mouth remains wide open to moan, the sensation of his cock twitching and then throbbing taking me to oblivion, and my flesh tingles with rapture. "Ahh…" Then I hear him grunting in bliss, and I explode around his cock just as he releases his warm orgasm inside of me. Being able to make him come under me is so powerful, but also way more demanding. I collapse onto him, burying my face in his pillow. Despite his thick liquid oozing from me, I remain still, focused on regaining my breath. Alex leans over just enough to kiss my temple, while his hands rub my back in circular movements. Then I feel his hand reaching down to the base of the plug and playing with it. "How does it feel?" he asks, slightly pushing the plug.

Without even moving, I simply say, "Feels good, and different…"

Then he pulls the plug very slowly out of my ass, and I let out a quick gasp at the feeling. "I'll leave the plugs on your nightstand. Tomorrow morning, after your shower, you're gonna take the first one and put it in before going to breakfast."

I blink twice in confusion, and after pulling back to look him in the eye, I ask, "You want me to go to breakfast with a plug in my butt?" My tone comes off as outrageous as his request.

A quick laugh escapes him. "Yes, would you do that for me?"

"I think the question is more what I wouldn't do…" He doesn't say anything in return, as he knows that's the truth. Yeah, I'm possessed. Truly and utterly possessed by this man.

He's taking me to new heights, and all I can hope for is that he doesn't let me fall. For I know that this time, I might not survive it. We remain looking at each other for a few more heartbeats before he presses his lips against my forehead. Then they hover by my ear, and he whispers, "Turn around." And after ushering me to turn and face the mirror standing in front of the bed, he adds, "On your knees."

Oh jeez… As I do so, my ass remains up in the air, with my head down.

"Look at yourself in the mirror," he orders.

What? Look at myself in the mirror?

My first instinct is to decline, but curiosity gets the best of me, and I dare to stare at my reflection. But my attention goes to him standing on his knees behind me, wonderfully sculpted, his shoulders wide and heavy with muscle, his chest broad and flat. The light plays on every edge and corner of his abs, following the contours of the musculature below so that every striation is visible. I notice how vascular he is, especially on his arms, but two prominent blue veins bulge on each side of his abs and trace a pronounced line to his groin, disappearing below his waist. Oh gosh… everything about him is perfection.

"You're so fucking beautiful," he says just above a whisper as we look at each other in the mirror.

I laugh, thinking how he's just read my mind, and I let my head dip down.

"Eyes on me, Miss Van Gatt."

"Sorry." My heart keeps thundering as I see him reaching for his cock and placing it between my butt cheeks. Oh jeez,

I haven't done this since the hunt. My body tenses up, and I freeze instantly at the thought of having him inside.

"Shhh…" he says, stroking the lower part of my back. "Relax…" Instantly, though, my gaze drops again. "Petra." And I know he wants me to keep looking at him.

Taking a deep breath, I keep my eyes on his, and as I do so, there is a definite sense of his girth as he stretches me open to accommodate him. He thrusts slightly in, making me gasp at the feel of him. Oh fuck, I forgot how painful this can be. A plug is a total joke compared to him.

He cracks a side smile and pushes his head in a bit more.

"Ah…" I close my eyes for a second but reopen them just as fast.

"Breathe…" he says in a low voice while going deeper. "I know you can take it."

Well, yeah, but last time, I was not watching the whole damn thing in the mirror! I try to keep my eyes wide open as he thrusts farther in, but it's so hard. I want to close them, rest my head on the mattress. But I can't.

"Oh fuck," I hear him growling. "You feel so damn good." He licks his lower lip before moving his hips forward, this time harder.

Jeez, my cheeks flush just hearing his words.

"And you have no idea how much I love pleasing you." I don't know why I said that, but it felt like the right thing to say.

He holds me on each side of my waist, his eyes focused down there, and, in a sudden move, he rams into me, taking my breath away.

"Fuck…" I moan, feeling such a big part of him entering me.

But he doesn't stop there, no. He looks up at me again, and as we gaze at each other, he thrusts again. Deeper. Longer. Harder.

"Ah!" I whimper, my eyes never leaving his. I can see a smile of pride and satisfaction settling on his lips. And I smile too, knowing how much he is enjoying it. "Ah…" He thrusts once more, and I know in that moment that he is all the way inside.

"See…" he mutters, keeping his smile just as big. "I knew you could take it."

There is some sort of womanly pride in showing him I'm able to take him completely.

His hands leave my waist, going up to my hair to form a messy ponytail. Then he leans downs to meet me.

"Now…" he whispers, his lips brushing my ear, his cock teasing me inside, but his eyes still locked on mine. "I'm gonna fuck you so hard that you won't be able to sit tomorrow."

My jaw drops at his words, but not my gaze. I keep looking him straight in the eye, and in the heat of the moment, I utter, biting my lip, "I hope so."

"Keep looking at me," he demands, his hands holding my hair in a ponytail. "Even if you cry. Are we clear?"

I nod, my eyes never leaving his stare. My body is in a trance, trembling, sweating, my heart filled with anxiety and fear at his next move. How much rougher can it be?

He tightens his grip around my ponytail and my neck, and thrusts into me so hard that the only reason I don't fall on the mattress is because he is holding me. I've got to close my eyes for a moment to breathe. "Petra."

But I reopen them just as fast at hearing him call my name, only to see how wet they are.

"Ah…" he growls behind me as he keeps moving back and forth, propelling my hips forward with the intensity of each thrust.

Tears start blurring my vision, and I sniffle, trying to prevent them from falling. But he doesn't stop. No.

And as I look at us in the mirror, him holding my neck and hair, his cock deep inside my ass, his pelvis moving back and forth, and me on my knees, I can feel everything we are both feeling—the pleasure, the pain, the power, the submission.

"You're such a fucking good girl," he praises as we become one in that moment. And I can't help but smile at his words.

"Keep going," I tell him.

I have no idea why I dared to say that, but it just felt so natural to do so.

His intensity picks up, and with tears streaming from my eyes, I moan, feeling his cock spasm inside me with a spreading warmth of cum.

Then he closes his eyes for a second—the second he puts his lips on my temple. My heart melts at his tenderness, and I close mine too, losing myself in this heavenly sent kiss. I wish this could last forever. Tears keep falling, but not from the physical pain. I'd heard you could cry while making love, overwhelmed with emotions, but I never thought it would happen to me. "Hey…" he whispers. "Are you okay?"

"I'm sorry." I sniffle, feeling pathetic to be so emotional. "It has been a rough day."

Chuckling at my wordplay, he asks, "Should I leave?"

"No," I reply instantly before he can move away. "Stay inside me a bit longer."

As we remain silent, enjoying each other's warmth, I try to cherish this moment as much as I can. For some reason that I can't explain, a bitter taste settles in my gut, telling me the happiness won't last.

I can't help but get anxious at the thought of my parents' reaction once they find out we ran away. Are they gonna hurt him? Or us? Oh gosh! The thought of it makes me shiver instantly.

"Be careful with my parents," I tell him.

"I know," he replies, his tone filled with seriousness, as if he knows what I'm thinking. "I won't let them hurt us."

CHAPTER 34

The Hamptons, October 24, 2020
Matthew Bradford

"Are you sure about that?" Pops asks me once more, his tone coming off stern, as we remain on the front porch with Tess, Roy, and their security agents at one o'clock in the morning.

"Yeah, I swear. She received a text on her phone and then left," I tell them.

Pops had come as fast as he could and called Roy right after. When they arrived here, their faces were so grave that I thought Petra had died or something.

But one of the security agents standing beside Roy doesn't seem convinced. "We haven't intercepted any incoming messages though. Even the GPS tracking shows her phone is still here in this house."

And I'm not really sure what he means by that.

"So what happened here?" Tess asks him. "Do you think she received a message that you couldn't intercept? I thought the phone was fully traced, including calls." What? Petra's phone is being traced? So they heard my entire convo with her? Wow. They don't joke around.

"And it is," the agent insists. "We should've received this text too. We receive them all." He pauses, thinking something through, and then he asks, looking at me, "Did you see if she was carrying an extra phone with her?"

"Um, I didn't notice. I know she received the text on an iPhone."

"I've got the footage." With his iPhone in his hands, Pops plays for us the recording from the camera at the gates. We see Petra heading there with her backpack, but there is no car waiting for her on the other side. She then opens the steel door near the main gates and starts running away. Alex must have been waiting a bit farther down the road.

We all go outside to the driveway, trying to see if we can find any street cameras that would have a better angle to record the car and the plate itself.

We walk a bit farther down the street, and all of a sudden, I hear a *crack* as I step on something. Looking at the ground, I find an iPhone shattered in a thousand pieces.

"Well, that's why you thought she had never left the house," I tell the agents, pointing to what is left of her phone.

"It's him for sure," Tess snaps as she glares at Roy. Then she rubs her eyes tiredly, blowing out a long sigh. Her eyes landing on me, she asks, "Did she tell you where she would be heading, or anything at all?"

"No, she just said she was tired and was going to go to sleep," I tell them again. "And by the time I got into the house, she had already left."

"Roy," my pops puts a hand on his shoulder in order to appease him, "we will find her. I give you my word. And we will bring her back." Then he looks at the agents and asks, "Do you have a suspect in mind?"

"Yes, I do," I reply at the same time as everyone else.

"Alexander Van Dieren," Tess mutters.

"Okay…" My dad squints his eyes in confusion. "And who is he?"

"He's her godfather." Tess is the first to reply again, her face laced with disgust and rage. I can tell she truly hates the guy, even though she tries hard to stay as stoic as possible. "He's so obsessed with her that we had to keep him away from her for ten years."

What? That is something I wasn't aware of. Jeez! I always suspected there was something wrong with that dude though.

"Once he came back, he started grooming her again, so we asked him to move to Singapore and leave Petra alone, but this time it was too late."

Fuck! The more I hear Tess talking, the more I feel bad that I cooperated with that creep. Damn it! What a dumbass I was.

"He's a predator of the worst kind. And now… now he's kidnapped her," she says, trying to contain her rising tears.

I feel so damn guilty and even dirty to have helped him. And yet I knew he was a criminal since the first day I laid eyes on him. Fuck, I should've been wiser. That asshole literally used me. He had no intentions of leaving for good. Oh no, it was just for one single month to put a damn plan in place to kidnap Petra. And I, like a dumbass, cooperated with him... I shake my head at my own stupidity. Petra is really sick. And she needs our help, *my* help, now more than ever. This man is manipulating her, luring her into a relationship that seems pretty twisted.

"We will find her, Ms. Hagen," my dad tells her. "I'll put the best team in place, and they will find her and bring her back."

"Maybe we should call Emma..." Roy suggests to Tess.

But Tess just chuckles in return. "Emma? She will deny everything. Why even bother? She is a loyalist."

A loyalist? What does she mean by that? A loyal friend? Intrigued, I've got to ask, "Sorry, Ms. Hagen, but, um, what do you mean by 'loyalist'?"

"You may just call me Tess," she says, offering me a pleasant smile. "A loyalist is someone who stands for someone or something until the end, no matter what."

"I doubt that Emma wouldn't talk if she knew Petra was in danger."

"She organized their engagement party," Roy tells me.

Wow. Petra had had an engagement party? Knowing she hadn't invited me to such an important event in her life makes my heart squeeze even more. Fuck, I thought I was her friend. I try hiding my pain with an unbothered attitude, but it's easier said than done.

"Emma supports them. Tess is right, she'll never say a word."

"Maybe there's another way…" I look at my dad and ask, "What if you contact your colleagues at the bureau?"

"We don't need to get the FBI involved," Roy interposes, his tone pressing. "I will call Alex…" He takes out his phone, but instead of calling him, he says, "He just sent me a voice message."

"Play it," Tess snaps at him.

Roy remains undecided for an instant, but since Tess keeps insisting, he pushes play. He raises the volume, and we hear Alex's voice coming from the phone. "Hey, Roy…" His tone is not threatening or harsh, like I expected it to be, but rather tired and maybe even a bit melancholic. "It's me… your former best friend, you know, the one you built a business with, and the son of the man who gave you the opportunity of a lifetime." There is a pause while Alex takes a long breath in and out. "I suppose by now you are looking for Petra. Most likely with Eric Bradford, your new bestie."

What the heck? How does he know that?

"Rest assured, she's with me, and she's fine. But if you and Tess don't leave us alone once and for all, believe me, neither of you will ever see her again." Tess puts her palm over her mouth to contain a gasp, but I hear it even so. "Oh and save yourself the hassle of inquiring about where we are because no one knows. And I'll never tell you. Goodbye, Roy." And that's it. That's the message.

I put my hand on Tess's back, giving her some comfort, but I can only imagine what she's going through. She was damn right. He literally kidnapped her. Jeez, I boil with rage at not having seen it coming. I should've locked that door. But fuck, I never thought Petra would run away either. And as I look at my dad and he at me, we both know it's not the police or the bureau we need to get involved. It's his entire office. Then, looking at Petra's mom, I say, "Tess, you can trust us. My dad will find him, have him arrested, and throw him in jail."

CHAPTER 35

Atlantic Ocean, October 24, 2020
Petra Van Gatt

Sunlight beams through the floor-to-ceiling windows, casting light across the whole bedroom. Waking up, I prop myself up on my elbows and fill my eyes with the sight of the impressive blue sea blending with the sky. I didn't dream this; I'm really sailing away with my fiancé. Then I recall how I left Matthew's house yesterday in the middle of the night, and I wonder for an instant how he is doing. Maybe I should send him a text wishing him a happy birthday. Before doing anything, though, it's better to check with Alex, as I definitely don't want to do something that could compromise us. Since he's already left the bedroom—a terrible habit of his that I can't help but despise, I decide to get out of bed, and head to the bathroom. After showering, I go back into the room and stand in front of the mirror. There, I drop the towel and observe my naked body attentively, before applying some lotion on my skin. My neck bears four red hickeys from last night, and unless I put a scarf around it, I have no makeup that can cover this. Then I turn my lower back and bottom toward the mirror, searching for where the pain I'm feeling is coming from. I narrow my eyes at the dark mark at the end of my spine, right on my tailbone. Damn, it's a bruise! That's why it was hurting so much when I tried to move in bed. From the reflection in the mirror, I can see a black box resting on the nightstand behind me. I remember Alex's instructions about what I'm supposed to do before going to breakfast. Jeez, I can't believe I'm gonna have to stick a plug in my butt. I reach the nightstand, and as I look at the black box, there is a white envelope on top with four hand-written words: *Training for Little Petra*.

My cheeks flush at that simple phrase. Training? After blowing out a breath, I open the envelope and read the message inside.

Day 1: Size S for 3 hours. Rest for lunch if needed. Then 3 hours again.

Day 2: Size S all day.

He wants me to wear a plug all day? Holy shit!

Days 3-5: Size M for 3 hours. Rest for lunch if needed. Then 3 hours again.

Day 6: Size L for 3 hours. Rest for lunch if needed. Then 3 hours again.

My mind is blank, unable to process what I just read. I look again at the black ink on the white paper, and I realize these are clear instructions for the entire trip! I open the box and see three matte-black silicone plugs of different sizes presented inside with a small bottle of lube. I wonder which one I wore yesterday, but I take the smallest one, observing it attentively. *Must be this one.*

How am I gonna handle this for three hours straight? Let alone an entire day? And how can I even focus on my online courses with a plug in my butt? Jeez, leave it to him to make me wear one.

I rub the plug with as much lube as possible, and without further ado, I bend slightly down and force myself to relax in order to insert it inside me. Thanks to last night's intense session, the plug goes all the way in without hassle, but I still have to close my lips tight to restrain a gasp. As I stand up, I feel just a little something inside, filling me between my butt cheeks. It's weird, super weird. But not painful. Then I open my backpack and take out a pair of panties. I'm not sure what I'm supposed to wear here, but I opt for jeans and a striped blouse. Once ready, I walk into the living room, trying to find where breakfast will be served. One of the crew members greets me and leads me to the terrace, where I see a table with two place settings ready. I wonder for a minute why there is no wind, until I realize the terrace is surrounded by a sliding glass wall, which is pretty discreet.

"Matcha latte, right?" the steward asks, pouring some water into my glass.

"Yes, please."

I sit, feeling the soreness rising as the external part of the plug presses against the solid material of the chair. And if I was confident enough until now, this chair made sure to remind me of what I have inside me and how sore I am from last night. *Damn it.* The thought makes me want to break my water glass. But instead, I focus on the view and look out at the frothy sea that the boat leaves behind as it goes. I barely feel the yacht moving, and recalling what the steward told us yesterday, today we should have good weather and calm waters.

All of a sudden, I hear footsteps coming up behind me, and my lips curve up, recognizing the unmistakable fragrance that fills the air. I feel his hands reaching for the length of my hair and pulling the locks to the side so his lips can kiss my bare neck. His touch is enough to give me goosebumps, and I squirm a bit in my chair.

"Are you wearing your plug?" he asks in a whisper.

Oh my... A rush of heat booms in my cheeks at his bold question. "Yes, I am." I want to sound annoyed, but I come across as excited. *Pathetic.* "And I've got a bruise above my ass," I tell him, this time annoyance thick in my tone.

Alex just chuckles in return before kissing my neck once more. "Good." Then there's silence between us until he asks, "Can you lift your hair for me?"

My hair? I'm not sure why, but I do it anyway. A few moments later, I see his hands coming in front of me holding a golden chain. Oh! My pendant! He places the necklace around my neck and clasps it at the back. I reach up and immediately take the pendant between my fingers, a smile creasing my lips as I touch his family crest. It feels so good to have it back. It's like a part of me has finally been restored.

"Thanks for returning it to me," I say in a low voice, a bit overwhelmed with emotions.

"It's yours. There's no need to thank me." He then leans down, his arms embracing me from behind, and plants a kiss with a smack on my head. I giggle a bit at the familiar sound—he used to do that when I was younger. Then he goes and sits in front of me. "Have you had breakfast yet?"

"No, um, I just arrived."

The steward comes in and lays before me a plate of avocado toast with cherry tomatoes, grilled mushrooms, and my matcha latte.

"Do you want pancakes too, Miss?" he asks.

"Um, no, this is enough, thanks."

Then he takes Alex's order, and I take a sip of my matcha, waiting for him to leave the terrace. After he does so, I take a deep breath into my lungs, and knowing that we are all alone, I ask, "Can we talk about that box?"

"Which box?" I arch a brow at his little game. "Be specific."

Oh, now I have to be specific. *Great.*

Lowering my voice, I lean forward and say, "*Training for Little Petra?* Really?"

His lips twist into a smile full of pride. "What's wrong with Little Petra?"

The truth is, nothing is wrong with that part. He's always called me Little Petra ever since I can recall. "It's the training that's the issue. Or, more specifically, the daily plugs."

"Does it hurt?"

Oh dear, he's not making this any easier. I glance around, making sure no crew member is coming. "It's bearable," I reply promptly. "But why? Why do I need to wear this every day during our trip? What am I training for?"

Alex leaps out of his seat, and I wonder in that moment if I said something wrong. He goes around the table and takes the chair beside me, bringing it closer to mine. After sitting, he holds my gaze steadily, but he's not smiling. His lips are pressed into a straight line, his expression revealing nothing. "You want to know all the details, Miss Curiosity?" His tone is not even playful; rather, his words sound like a test.

I nod, uncertain about the outcome of such a decision.

He remains silent, considering me for an instant, then he leans closer to me, just inches from my face. "I'm training you to become more," he squints his eyes, a faint smile settling on his lips, "available."

My mouth gapes instantly, and I blink twice at his words. "Available?"

Alex bursts out in a laugh, amused by my constant inquisition. "Those plugs will loosen your little asshole for me, so I can go in more easily." And I realize how sexual this conversation has just become. My lips part to take some precious air into my lungs as my heartbeat quickens with every word coming from his mouth. "Yesterday I had to go very slowly to get in," he explains. "This training will make things easier for us."

"Oh…" I don't think we have ever had a discussion so intimate about my butt. But it doesn't feel as odd as I thought. Actually, I enjoy the attention he's giving to my body. It makes me feel desired, and I hope he'll always be like that. But I still have some questions. "And, um, I'm not gonna have any technical issues taking it out?"

He lets out a quick chuckle, but it's a legitimate concern after all. "It's gonna come out as naturally as any other. Don't worry." And he rises up just enough to kiss my forehead. "After a day or two, you won't feel the difference with it in."

He goes back to sit in front of me, right before the steward comes in and places his cup of black coffee on the table, along with an omelet, fruit, and an avocado. "For Monday, I imagine you will have online classes?"

Oh, I'm impressed how Alex can switch from butt talk to my studies so easily. "Yeah, and um, Tuesday I usually have a group session, as we are working on a study for Public Economics."

"You won't be able to have contact with anyone for now."

WHAT! "Why not?" I ask immediately. "Impossible. I'm in charge of the study. My name is on it."

"They can trace our location via satellite—"

"They are college students," I snap back. "Not the FBI."

"I know, but your friend Matthew can inquire about you and pressure you to give info about where you are. It's not safe."

"Speaking of Matthew…" Alex's brows pinch together as he observes me. "He's turning twenty today. And, um, I ran away from his house last night, where I was supposed to spend the weekend." Since he doesn't say a word, I add, "I need to at least wish him a happy birthday."

"Why do you even care about him?"

"Because he is my friend," I answer just as fast. "Is there a way I can send him a text safely?"

"A text can leave a trace, and the phone company can collaborate with your parents to track us. I don't think it's prudent."

My heart aches a bit at his response, and letting out a sigh in annoyance, I say, "I'm sure there is a way I can send it anonymously. Maybe from an app or online?"

Alex scratches his stubble, thinking something through. "I'll check into it."

Oh, he better do more than just check into it, as I won't let him leave the table without a solution. "Matthew deserves an apology for my running away on his birthday," I tell him, looking him in the eye, my tone serious.

His gaze remains steadily on mine, considering me. "Alright, I can ask my attorney to send him a message on your behalf. I think that's the most prudent."

"Your attorney?" I repeat, totally baffled by his suggestion.

"Yeah, he's the only one aware of the situation, since I'm pretty sure we will need him soon."

I hate the fact that I have to go through a middleman, but it's better than nothing. Plus, Matthew won't know the difference. "You promise he will deliver the message?"

"Of course. What do you want to tell him? 'Happy birthday and sorry for running away'?" Alex takes it as a joke, but I don't.

"It's not funny. He's really a good guy."

He shakes his head in amusement, until he finally blurts out, "Fine. I will take care of it."

* * *

Atlantic Ocean, October 26, 2020
Petra Van Gatt

If the first day onboard was sunny and the water calm, yesterday and today have been the complete opposite. The stewards warned the next few days we'd have "not so good weather," which must be a euphemism for terrible, seasick kind of weather. The unsettling imbalance of the yacht makes it nearly impossible to even stand up straight or walk. Fortunately, the stewards have been delivering our breakfast to our bedroom in a trolley cart covered with a white tablecloth. While Alex is already taking his morning coffee and reading the newspaper in the armchair, I'm still trying to gain the courage to leave the warm sheets and walk a few steps toward the cart, where my matcha latte is waiting for me. But each time there is a strong wave, I'm reminded how painful this is, and my head starts spinning horribly.

"Are you seasick?" he asks, seeing my resistance to get up. "You look nauseous."

"Yeah, this motion is horrible." And the only way to survive this up-and-down and side-to-side acceleration seems to be remaining in bed.

"Oh, poor you." He might be teasing me; nevertheless, Alex stands up and goes to take something from the cart along with a glass of water. Then he sits beside me and hands me a tray with pills and the glass. "Take one every six hours." As I do so, he brings me my matcha latte and the plate with my avocado toast. "And now you're gonna eat."

I take a bite of the toast, and I'm glad he's holding the matcha latte steady as the boat goes up and down, sailing through bigger waves. "Thanks." Then I check the time on my iPhone and realize I'm already running late for my first online class of the day. Jeez! Fortunately, my laptop is in my backpack, not too far away. I take a sip of my matcha latte, and after blowing out a breath, I get out of bed to grab my laptop. Once I've got it, I rush back and slide under the covers again. Then I put the laptop on my lap, turn it on, and connect it to a VPN before logging in to the class. The unsettling motion is not making it any easier, but I drink a bit more of my matcha, hoping somehow that will help.

"Petra, you barely ate…" Alex chides.

I notice he's still holding the plate with my avocado toast, barely eaten. "I know, but I have class starting soon. It's Monday, you know."

"At least finish your breakfast," he insists.

"After."

"You can't watch it later?"

"I wish, but this is an interactive class. Like, they see who's connected and who's not."

"This toast is to be eaten." It sounds like a command as he puts the plate on the nightstand beside me. Then he gives me a quick peck on the cheek. "Don't you dare not eat." And he leaves the bedroom.

* * *

While I wanted to spend the entire day sleeping, or at least taking a long nap, to avoid this terrible motion sickness, my online classes have taken all day long, throwing such a wish out the window. Even with the medicine I took, the imbalance has been very strong, especially during the afternoon, as it seems we are crossing a tumultuous part of the Atlantic. Jeez, I can't imagine how the European explorers managed to sail on their caravels for months and survive. Fortunately, by the evening, the sea has finally calmed down, so we take the opportunity to have dinner in the dining room rather than in bed like we did the past two nights. This time, though, I decide to dress a bit fancier. And by fancy, I mean wearing a summer dress instead of a pair of jeans. Once I'm ready, I realize I have been wearing the plug for more time than instructed, so I take it out before heading to the dining room. I wasn't expecting the dining table to be so formally set, like in a proper fine-dining restaurant. I also notice the bossa nova song playing through the speakers and the gold-colored lights coming from the crystal chandelier, all doing wonders to create an intimate atmosphere. It reminds me a bit of our dinner in Rome, but with a view of the ocean. Although, as I look out the windows, it's too dark to see anything outside.

"Oh, Miss Van Gatt dropped the comfy jeans tonight?"

I turn around and see Alex, always so perfectly dressed, sporting a slim white shirt and dark blue pants.

"Ah, yes, well, now we are finally inaugurating the dining room."

Standing still in front of me, Alex reaches down and takes my hand before pulling me to him. I feel his other hand slide behind my back, and as he starts slowly pacing back and forth, I know in that moment that we are about to dance and sway to the sensual beat of this Brazilian melody. Memories from our evening in Rio start running through my mind as I recall everything we've gone through to finally get to where we are now.

"Remember that dinner when Diana was singing?"

His totally random question confuses me. "Um, yes…"

"I'm the one who suggested to your dad to hire her."

My eyes widen in surprise at his revelation. "Oh, really? Wow, that makes more sense now."

"I wanted to make sure you'd have a good evening." Then Alex spins me around for the sake of spinning, and I'm all here for it. As our eyes lock again, he asks, "Would you like her to sing at our wedding too?"

"Yesss," I hiss just as fast. "And this time, my favorite song won't be ruined thinking you're leaving."

His lips curve up, a sparkle twinkling in his eyes. "I promise, this time I'm not going anywhere." The conviction in his voice makes me smile in return. Then, as I glance over his shoulder, I find the steward waiting for us with our starters in his hands. Alex follows the direction of my stare, and after seeing him, we stop dancing and go back to the table.

Normally, one of the stewards pulls out my chair for me to sit, but Alex is in the mood to do it tonight.

As the steward puts my plate in front of me, he says, "For the starter, we have a crispy tofu with marinated zucchini and cucumber gel." My face lights up at the harmonious colors and varying textures of the dish. I'm pretty sure Alex would've preferred anything but tofu, but his efforts to enjoy vegan food is really a big turn-on for me. "Enjoy." And the steward leaves us by ourselves.

As I cut a portion of the crispy tofu, my eyes lift discreetly toward him, and I can't resist watching Alex be entertained by his plate. When I think how he comes from a family of hunters, it truly amazes me what he has done for me.

"Thanks for doing this," I tell him.

His gaze comes up to meet mine. "Doing what?"

"This. Like, I know if you were having dinner with someone else, you'd be eating fish, lobster, or something from the sea, but you are eating tofu…"

Letting out a quick laugh, he knows exactly how true this is. "I don't mind eating something different once in a while. I've been eating fish, lobster, and everything in between my whole life."

After he takes a bite, I can't help but ask, "Is it good?"

He observes me for a moment, a smirk rising on his face. "Well, I'd rather have steamed lobster with lemon and herb butter sauce, but it's edible." And I knew there would be a joke coming.

"Very funny." I take a mouthful, and to me, it's absolutely delicious, packed with light and fresh ingredients, including a taste of citrus, which complements the Asian flavors in the tofu glaze.

"By the way, did you manage to watch your classes with the VPN?" he asks. I know how much he stressed about it. I had to download a VPN on Sunday, and Alex told me multiple times to connect it to an IP address in Switzerland.

"Yeah, it was alright. A bit slow sometimes, but it was okay." And remembering that tomorrow I have Public Economics with the group, I say, "Um, you know, I'm gonna have Public Economics tomorrow. And, um, Matthew and the group will be connected…"

"Can they chat with you?"

"Um, no, they can't, but they will know I connected to the class, and I wanted to make sure we don't run into problems if I do so."

Alex starts ruminating over my question. "If you want me to be honest, I don't think you should attend that class." I was kinda expecting that answer myself. "I'm already worried enough about any tracking information you are leaving behind when you connect to the others."

I nod pensively, knowing that, in the end, we can never be too prudent. "Okay, um, maybe I can skip that one. It doesn't count toward my grades anyway…"

His face lights up with a smile. "That's the wisest decision." And he picks up his glass of wine, taking a sip. "Thank you."

We're both quiet for a while as we finish our respective starters.

"Petra?" he asks suddenly.

"Hmm?"

"Now that you are no longer living with your dad, are you getting this degree because you want to, or is it still to please him?"

The truth is neither one nor the other. "Um, actually, it's one of the requirements in the inheritance contract I signed with him," I tell him.

His eyes widen in astonishment. "An inheritance contract?" he repeats, quite baffled. And I nod at his question before taking a sip of my water. "Why do you have one?"

"Well, because he threatened to disinherit me if I moved out and lived elsewhere."

Alex puts down his cutlery, his jaw clenching for a moment before he bursts out, "That's insane."

"Yeah, and getting my degree at Columbia is one of the requirements. Dad is totally obsessed with that. I don't know why…"

His eyes drift away for a moment as he ponders it. "I think he's very emotionally attached to that school. It was a dream come true for him when he moved to New York to study there."

Oh, I shouldn't be surprised that Alex knows so much about my dad's life. Quite curious to know more, I ask him, "Do you know how he ended up there?"

"My father paid for his scholarship," he says casually.

And my jaw drops at his answer. "Hendrik Van Dieren?" Alex just nods in return. "He paid for my dad's tuition?"

"To be precise, our family office paid for it."

"Oh… I didn't know that." I lower my gaze, a bit dazzled by the revelation. "You know, I never met my grandparents. Dad has always been so mysterious about them," I tell him.

His lips curve slightly up, but he doesn't say a word. After all, I'm probably not saying anything he doesn't already know. As I keep my eyes glued on him, he utters, "Your dad comes from a modest background."

"Did you know them?"

"A bit," he says as the steward comes in to remove our plates. "They were farmers from the northern part of Rouveen."

I try to appear unsurprised, but I've got to ask him what is on the tip of my tongue. "So Dad was closer to Hendrik?"

"Well, my father was his boss and mentor." He pauses for a beat, staring at me for a moment. "And then your dad followed me when I decided to do things on my own."

I narrow my eyes in confusion. "But why? I mean, why did he follow you and not Hendrik?"

But the steward is now placing our main dishes in front of us. And stealing our attention, he says, "For the main course, we have mushroom risotto with truffles and vegan parmesan."

The sight and smell of it makes my mouth water. After all, this is one of my favorite dishes ever. I'm sure Alex told the chef. There is no way he would've known himself.

Once the steward leaves, Alex is already holding his fork, ready to take a bite, but I remain patiently staring at him for an answer. "So? Why did he follow you and not Hendrik?" I ask again.

Alex looks up at me, holding his fork halfway to his mouth. "Because we both wanted the same thing—to build something of our own."

"And how did your dad react?" I ask, before he can taste his food.

He heaves a sigh of annoyance. "Why are you so damn curious?" But he finally brings his fork to his mouth.

And I can't help chuckle in return. "I'm just trying to understand how my dad ended up trusting you so much, leaving his mentor behind."

He picks up his white napkin to wipe his mouth and then drinks some of his water. "What about you?"

"Me?" I ask, blinking twice.

"Why did you end up trusting me so much?"

As I don't have an immediate answer, I simply say, "Shouldn't I?"

"Why do you trust me?" he asks again, our eyes locking.

I thought I'd need more time to find the right words, but no, my instinct already knows why. "Because you showed me I could."

"See? You've got your answer."

CHAPTER 36

Atlantic Ocean, October 29, 2020
Petra Van Gatt

Alex was right, and I hate him for that. I recall how the first day over breakfast, he'd told me I would get used to wearing a butt plug. Well, it's impressive and terrifying what our bodies are capable of. But even though the size M has been manageable, I don't intend to switch to the bigger one. *Absolutely not.* It looks terrifying to me. He hasn't checked which one I have been using anyway. As I get dressed, regardless of his instructions, I again put in size M instead of the L. Then I put on a pair of comfortable jeans and a top, and head outside for our breakfast on the terrace. To my surprise, I find Alex and the captain talking in the living room. As their eyes alight on me, they both greet me, and Alex doesn't waste any time announcing, "We will be arriving at our destination around five p.m."

My lips twist into a smile full of excitement, and I can't wait to see where we are heading. Then, as I reach the terrace, I feel a light breeze touching my hair and skin. And as I look around, I notice the sliding glass is wide open. The breeze is warm though, which is not usual. Once Alex steps onto the terrace, I can't help but ask, "How come it's so warm and sunny today?"

"Well, that's the beauty of sailing. Yesterday was cold and gray, and today is the opposite."

I pass by the table and chairs and cross the terrace to go out onto the deck. There, the strong sunlight beams on my face and on the deck floor. "It's getting really warm outside," I tell him, squinting my eyes at the brightness. Then I look ahead, seeing the frothy water the yacht leaves behind, and I wonder if the water is also just as warm.

After breakfast, knowing I'm running late for my online class, I grab my laptop and my iPhone and head outside to the main deck, where I lie on a lounge chair by the pool. The devices recognize the Wi-Fi provided by the satellite and connect immediately. Suddenly, though, a notification pops up on my iPhone with a new voice message. That's weird though—no one knows my new phone number. Since I have zero contacts saved, I only see it's from an American number. And without waiting any further, I press play and listen to it. The first sound I hear is a loud breathing out in exasperation, but then my heart jumps, recognizing the voice.

"Petra, it's Emma, I hope you are doing well and that you are happy and safe wherever you are." A flow of emotion rushes through me at hearing Emma's voice. She sounds worried and way too serious. "Um, your parents came to my house with your friend Matthew and his dad."

WHAT! They are insane! My heart can't stop racing in apprehension. I swear, if they did something to her…

"He's the attorney general of New York, in case you didn't know. Yeah… it's pretty fucked up. Um, they asked me if I gave you a phone and if I know where you are. I denied everything, but I've got the feeling there is an investigation going on, and I don't think it's safe for you guys to come back." There's a pause while Emma takes a deep breath in and out. "I overheard them talking about a tracking device or something." Oh gosh, my body freezes at her words. "Be careful, babe. Love you." And the voice message ends.

Oh my goodness. I feel the urge to call Emma straightaway and ask her if they did anything to her. But I force myself to stop. Alex was clear I couldn't reach out to anyone, as it could leave traces of our location. But what if they threatened her? What if she is in danger? What if they locked her up? My parents are beyond crazy. But I know it's mainly Mom who is the driving force behind all this. Indeed, behind her sugary voice and sweet little smile, that woman is pure Machiavellian evil. Blowing out a breath, I play the voice message again, and force myself to analyze every word coming out of her mouth. This time, though, the first thing I notice is that Emma doesn't mention even once if she is okay. The Emma I know always starts a message talking about herself and how amazing her life is wherever she is. Not hearing that is a huge red flag. I keep listening and pause after she says, "Yeah… it's pretty fucked up."

There is a lot of hesitation in her voice as she talks about Matthew's dad. Like she is apprehensive to reveal something. What is she afraid of though? The Emma I know is blunt, direct, and doesn't shy away from anything. The more I listen to her voice, the more I feel the urge to call her. Decision made, I run back inside the boat, searching for Alex.

I find him in the living room, sitting on the sofa, a bunch of papers spread out on the low table in front of him.

And without wasting any time, I say, "Emma sent me a voice message."

"What?" he utters almost automatically as his gaze meets mine. "How does she even have your number?"

"You didn't give it to her?" I ask instantly.

"No, I just gave her the phone and told her to give it to you." Alex pauses, thinking something through. "I guess she called herself from it to save your new number." And he lets out a loud rush of air in annoyance. "Damn it."

"It's okay. Um, my parents went to her house along with Matthew and his dad." And I think it's best to disclose the rest. "His dad is the attorney general of New York, by the way." I pause, gauging his reaction, but Alex doesn't seem surprised. "Did you know that?"

"No, I had no idea."

"Oh, okay. Um, Emma told me there's an investigation going on." Words are hard to get out amid my racing heartbeats. "I need to call her to find out more."

"Petra, you know the rules."

"I have to talk to her," I insist. "I need to make sure she is safe."

"I'm sure Emma is doing alright."

"How?" I snap back. "How can you be a hundred percent sure? From her voice message, it doesn't seem so."

"Getting in contact with anyone is dangerous," he says mechanically. "If there is an investigation going on, the first thing they want to do is trace our location. If you call her, her phone records will show where the call has come from. We can't risk it."

"I can't stay here without knowing how she is doing," I tell him, my emotion stuck in my throat. "We have to do something."

"I'll call my lawyer in New York. He's the only one I trust there, and he will reach Emma on your behalf. Alright?"

The idea that again I have to go through a middleman, especially to talk to my best friend, doesn't sit well with me. But I guess for now I don't have much of a choice. The last thing we need is for my parents to find us. And knowing how stubborn my mom is, she is most likely searching every single corner on earth to find me.

"Alright. Can you give him a message for her?"

"Sure."

Then I grab my iPhone and start typing relentlessly in my Notes app the first things that go through my mind: *Emma, I'm fine and safe. I miss you so much, but unfortunately Alex said it's not prudent to call you. Please tell me if you are safe. Are you still in New York? Are they blackmailing you? Do you know what Eric is doing? Please be careful and run away from my mother! Do not believe a word she says. She's manipulative, and her sweet little voice sounds like she's harmless. But she's crazy! She tried to implant a tracking chip in me! I love you, P.*

"Hey…" I peer up and find Alex standing in front of me, rubbing his fingers over my cheek to calm my apparent nervousness. "I know it's hard, but we need to be as diligent as possible."

I find myself staring into his piercing blue eyes, but a sudden wave of panic flashes through me. Images of Dr. Nel taking the syringe out of her briefcase along with a little flask containing the tracking chip fill my mind. And I recall how Dad didn't even blink. He just stood there, assisting in one of the most horrific moments of my life, totally indifferent. It's unbelievable how he has changed so much with the threats and influence of Mom in New York. And I'm scared, so scared, that Emma will find herself in the same situation.

"When will I be able to call her?" I ask him as I send the message to his iPhone through AirDrop.

Alex takes a quick glance at his screen, acknowledging the receipt of my text. "When I'm sure it's safe to do so."

The uncertainly in his answer makes my heart ache. "If something happens to her…"

His hands hold my arms, and he looks steadily at me. "I'm gonna make sure Emma is safe, okay? No one is gonna hurt her."

Taking a deep breath, my head dips down a bit, anxiety blurring my thoughts. I know Emma is a big girl, but still. I can't imagine something happening to her and not being able to prevent it. Then, my gaze goes up to him, and looking him in the eye, all I can say is, "Make sure she is safe."

***

Throughout the day, I try my best to focus on my online classes, but Emma's voice message is all I can think of.

Leaving her in New York with Eric, my parents, and Dr. Nel terrifies me. *Maybe I'm exaggerating*, I tell myself. After all, Emma knows how to get herself out of any difficult situation better than anyone else I know. Plus, she's a Hasenfratz, which means she's pretty much untouchable. And unlike my dad, Mom can't threaten to ruin her reputation, since she's not a public figure. I look at my laptop screen as the prof speaks, but I can't process his voice. I can only hear Emma's. *He's the attorney general of New York, in case you didn't know. Yeah… it's pretty fucked up.* Those words play again in my head like a broken record. And they don't seem to stop. Does Eric know things about Emma that could compromise her? *Impossible.*

"Ms. Van Gatt?" I peer over at the stewardess walking in my direction. "Your fiancé is calling you. He's upstairs on the flybridge."

As I look behind her, I see land from afar. Land! Finally! I close my laptop, leap off the lounge chair, and trot toward the staircase that goes to the flybridge.

"Wow," I utter as I take in the panoramic sea view. Being on the highest part of the boat, the breeze is much stronger here, and the sunlight too. Standing beside Alex, my eyes alight on what seems to be a distant long sandy beach that stretches for miles, with vast green scenery behind it. Looking a bit more carefully, I can spot a small dock on the beach, which gives access to a villa with a white-tiled roof perched right there amid the lush vegetation.

I feel Alex peering discreetly at me, probably to look at my expression as I stand admiring the view. "Welcome to Bermuda." And he takes my hand, giving it a kiss.

Squinting my eyes, I notice there are a few people standing on the dock and waving in our direction. I look around but don't see any other boats nearby. "Who are those people waving at us on the dock?"

"My dad and his staff," Alex replies.

My jaw drops instantly. "Your dad is in Bermuda?" *Let's say Hendrik is far away*, I remember Julia saying at Christmas. "Wait, that's where he's been living since the separation?"

Alex gives me one of his irresistible smiles. "Not too bad, huh?"

My jaw remains hanging open as I realize something. "So, he already knew we were coming?"

"Oh yeah, he has got an entire reception planned for us."

And I keep gaping at his comment. "But what if my parents find out?"

"No one knows we ran away. If anyone asks you, just say we came here to pay my dad a visit, alright?"

We hear footsteps approaching, and as we turn, we find a steward who says, "Mr. Van Dieren, the tender will be ready in about twenty-five minutes."

"Thanks." The young man nods before going back downstairs. "Let's go. It's a white party. We should get ready."

Oh, there is even a dress code? "How many people will be there?" My heart starts racing as I think about crowds, inquisitive eyes, noise…

"Relax, just a few close friends of my dad's." Alex tries to appease me with a quick peck on the top of my head, but all I can think about is if I have a spare box of Xanax in my bag. Then, we leave the flybridge and go to our bedroom, where I start wondering if I also brought a white summer dress for the reception.

After closing the door behind us, Alex goes to the closet, where he takes a gift box from the shelf and a hanger with a long asymmetric linen dress.

Oh, I forgot how he plans everything ahead. He lays the dress on the bed and gives me the box.

"What is it?"

There is a trace of a smile settling on his lips as he says, "Your underwear for the evening."

Oh boy… It reminds me of when he asked me to wear the black lace thong at his family estate and then the red corset for our night there. "You really love lingerie, don't you?" As he cracks a quick chuckle, I pull off the ribbon and open the box, and I can't help but raise my brows in total surprise. "You bought a white lace set?"

"I should've brought it to Aspen, but…"

Oh, he's had this since Aspen?

"I think it'll go well under your dress."

After we shower, I realize it's the first time during our trip that we're getting dressed together. I really love seeing my fiancé putting his shirt on and closing every button one by one as he looks at himself in the full-length mirror. There is something extremely intimate about it.

"Um, this lingerie does everything but cover my skin." I note, checking out how the lace bra has a lot of transparent fabric, which barely covers my nipples. Alex turns to face me, and his gaze travels from top to bottom without saying a word. He remains speechless, but his eyes are still glued on my body. At this point, I feel like I'm a Greek sculpture in an art museum.

"That set was really made for you."

"Really?" And just when I thought I was looking bland in it. After all, I have very fair skin and small breasts—I never would have thought a white floral lace bra with no push-up would look good on me. All of a sudden, Alex takes me by the hand and brings me in front of the mirror. As he stands behind me, he kisses my shoulder and observes me in the mirror. "Lingerie is not meant to cover your skin…" Then his fingers linger softly around my right nipple in circular movements, and I shiver a bit at his touch. "It's meant to enhance it." His gaze then drifts all the way down to my butt. "Are you wearing the L?"

Uh, oh…

A blush comes over my cheeks at his question. "Um…"

"You are still wearing the M?" he asks with censoring eyes as he observes my expression in the mirror. "Today is the last day."

"I know, but I'm just…"

"Scared?"

"Well, that plug is big."

Alex turns me around, and I'm now looking him in the eye. "You've had way bigger inside you. What are you afraid of?"

I just shrug my shoulders. "It's not the same."

"It is. Remove your plug." He moves to the nightstand and opens the box, where he takes out the biggest one—the one I have no idea how it'll feel inside. Jeez, when I thought I could get away with just wearing the S and M…

As I see him holding the big plug in his hand, I can't help but ask, "Why do you want me to wear the big one at your dad's party? Are you insane?"

"Petra!"

"I prefer to keep the one I have in now. This one I'm used to, and it's better to wear in public," I press on.

Without saying a word, Alex beckons to me.

Fuck… Letting out a breath of annoyance, I take a few steps in his direction before coming to stand beside him.

"Remove it now," he insists. "Or else I will do it myself."

Squinting my eyes, I consider his request for a second. Since I prefer to do it myself, I bend slightly, a hand on the nightstand, and force myself to pull out the plug that has been inside me since this morning. I press my lips tightly together and close my eyes, as I'm not used to having him watch me. Once I take it out, I see Alex applying a lot of lube on the new plug, and my heart starts pounding anxiously as I watch him doing so.

"Why are you insisting on this one the day I'm meeting your dad?" I ask him once more, nerves running through me.

"I'm sure you're gonna be just fine." He rubs some more lube in between my butt cheeks and then in my hole and starts pressing the tip of the plug inside me. "Now, just take a deep breath in and out." His voice soothes me, and I focus on my breathing as much as I can. "Relax…" The lube helps greatly, but the girth of this plug is something else. Jeez! I can really feel the difference. "Ah…" I let out a quick gasp as it slides all the way in.

"It's inside. See? You managed." I remain bent over, still focused on my breathing as I get used to the new size. Meanwhile, Alex starts rubbing my back and leaving a trail of warm kisses from the lowest part of my back all the way up. "Is it that bad?" he whispers close to my ear.

"Um, it's really… filling." And it is. Of course, it's not like having him inside me, but it's not like the smaller plugs either.

"Good." He gives me a quick peck on the temple. "Now get dressed." And then a sudden smack on my butt before walking out of the room.

"Ah!" I flinch a bit at the blow but stand up and take the dress laying on the bed.

As I put it on, I can't help but feel the pressure of the new plug filling my hole. Jeez! How am I supposed to walk normally with this in my ass? Then I take a quick glance at myself in the mirror as I wrap the ribbon on the dress around my waist. I must admit, Alex does have an eye for finding dresses that fit me well. I put some gloss on my lips, brush my wavy hair, and head outside.

I find Alex waiting for me in the living area, dressed in white pants and a white linen shirt, sleeves casually rolled up to his elbows.

"Hey…" I greet as I stand beside him.

His gaze lands on me, and his face lights up immediately. "That dress…" He lets his words trail off while observing me. "You are a vision." And he takes my hand to give it a kiss.

I smile at his compliment, and I can only hope that this plug won't make any difference during the evening. Then I take his arm, and we are escorted to the tender boat, which will take us to the dock on the beach.

As we sit inside, I take in my surroundings and realize we are right in time for the sunset. With my eyes set on the horizon, I watch the glowing sun, already half bathing in the ocean's meek waves, while painting the sky and its wispy clouds in a palette of oranges and reds.

Then, reaching the dock, my eyes alight on the tall, old man dressed very similarly to Alex and accompanied by a younger woman at his side. His eyes are a crisp blue, surrounded by tired lines, his light gray hair just as tousled and thick as that of my fiancé, and while his beard is longer, his charm is just as unmistakable. A smile pulls at my lips when Hendrik runs a hand over his wild hair, the locks falling on each side of his temples.

"You guys are so alike," I whisper to Alex before we arrive.

Once the tender is tied to the dock cleat, Alex gets out of the boat first, taking a quick jump, then offers me a hand to help me out. In that moment, I'm glad my dress is long enough and that my panties cover the base of the plug enough for me to take a big step and leap onto the surface.

"There he is," Hendrik greets, his arms wide open to welcome his son.

"Dad."

Hendrik gives his son a quick pat on the back before they exchange a few words. Then his eyes go in my direction, and I hear him say, "Ms. Van Gatt…" I wonder how I should greet him, but Hendrik just takes my hand, giving it a kiss, and I giggle a bit as he does so. *They are just the same. It's incredible.* I must confess, despite his age and the wrinkles on his face, Hendrik is just as charming as his son. And most likely, also a well-known heartbreaker on the island. "What a pleasure to finally meet you." His deep, husky voice is joyful and magnetic, just like the vibe of this place, and a big grin settles on my lips.

"The pleasure is all mine," I tell him. "And please just call me Petra."

"Petra, what a beautiful name. And I'm Hendrik, the father of the luckiest man on earth."

A quick laugh escapes me, and I'm so glad that I can call him by his first name. After all, I've called Alex by his last name so many times that it'd be awkward for me to do the same with his dad.

Then Hendrik looks at the woman standing beside him, and putting a hand at her back, he says, "And this lady here is Mona, my best friend and the angel of my life."

Mona shakes her head in amusement. "Hi, Petra, welcome to Bermuda," she greets me with a broad smile before we exchange two cheek kisses. "Is this your first time here?"

"Yep," I reply. And as I glance around the sandy beach and take a deep breath of the fresh sea air, all I hope is that we can stay here long enough to explore the whole island.

We start walking back to the pathway that leads to the villa, when Alex leans closer to me and whispers, "I'm gonna have a quick chat with my dad. Mona will show you around. She's really trustworthy. I've known her for, like, eighteen years." And he presses his lips to my head as he always does.

CHAPTER 37

Bermuda, October 29, 2020
Alexander Van Dieren

The last thing I wanted is to be here at my dad's place asking him for help. But alas, he's the only person I trust enough to fight against Roy and Tess. And if I recall correctly, Roy still values my dad a lot. He invites me to his favorite part of the house—his study. Despite the windows being wide open, there is still a lingering smell of sex and cigars. And as I glance around at the Chesterfield armchairs and sofa, I wonder if there is any surface that hasn't been fucked on. Glad he followed my advice and got a vasectomy before leaving the Netherlands. One bastard in the family is already insulting enough.

"Well, I don't think I need to tell you this, but damn! What a fine woman you brought with you." Jeez, at seventy-two, he still talks like he's twenty.

"Thanks." I pace slowly around his office while Dad serves us some whiskey.

Then I stand still in front of an oil painting that hangs above his sofa. Holding two glasses in his hands, he walks toward me and gives me one. I take a first sip, my gaze steady as I continue observing the nude portrait. "Mona?"

"A gift for my birthday," Dad replies, a smile on his lips as he gives it a quick glance.

"She treats you well."

"I can't complain." Then he gestures for me to sit in the armchair behind me, while he takes a seat on the sofa. "So, what brings you all the way from New York?" And I knew he wouldn't waste any time asking me just that.

"I told you. I just wanted to introduce you to my future wife. Sounds reasonable, no?"

"Bullshit," he replies just as fast. "What kind of trouble are you in?" I can't deny that he knows me well.

"It's Roy…" I start cautiously.

His eyes widen instantly in shock. "Don't tell me you proposed to his daughter without his blessing?"

"Well, I asked him last year, and he was okay with it then." I pause for a beat. "But not her mom, and now she's blackmailing us."

"Ah," Dad just utters right before taking a sip. "Her mother is that politician who denounced Julia on TV, right?" I'm impressed he even knows that. Dad doesn't watch TV, and Julia doesn't even talk to him. It must have been Sebastian who told him.

"Tess Hagen, yeah. Julia told me she enlisted with the CDA for the elections next year, and I don't think it's to become a member of parliament."

Dad tries to contain his laugh. "She hates Julia, doesn't she?"

"And me, and Roy, and everyone involved in that incident."

Dad's gaze drifts away, knowing exactly what I'm referring to. "Does she have evidence?"

Letting out a sigh, I say, "Mom said she does."

He nods pensively, his eyes staring at nothing, before they land on me again. "You are in deep shit, son."

Classy.

"Well, I wouldn't be here if I wasn't." I shouldn't have been so blunt with him, but the words came out of my mouth before I could even do anything about it.

Dad crosses his legs, an ankle resting over the other knee. "So, let me see if I've got this straight: you steal my best employee, vote me out of my own company, force me to leave my country, and now you come here all the way from New York with your barely legal fiancée because you need my help?"

I take a quick sip before blurting out, "Pretty much, yeah."

Blowing out a breath, he starts shaking his head in disgust. "What a son of a bitch you are." And yet I can't stop laughing at his comment. Coming from him, it nearly sounds like a compliment. "It's gonna cost you a fortune."

And that was expected. "How much?"

"Oh, this is not about money." He pauses, his smirk growing. "This is about family."

I observe him attentively, my brows pinching together. "What do you want from me, Dad?"

He keeps the smirk on his lips as he revels in my situation. And after a brief silence, he says, "Your indisputable… loyalty."

Yet he knows perfectly well my answer. "I'm afraid I can't afford that. Anything else?"

Dad thinks something through then promptly demands, "I want to attend your wedding."

But I protest just as fast. "Mom will kill me if I let you come."

"She doesn't need to know." He pauses, studying me. "I can just… invite myself." And since I don't appear convinced, he adds, "Just give me the details, and I will take care of the rest."

"I don't think that's a good idea," I insist.

"I won't miss my son's wedding." His voice carries a severity that moves me. After all, Dad wasn't invited to Maud's or Yara's weddings. And I know how much it affected him not being there.

"If I tell you the details, it stays between us, are we clear? Not a single word to anyone, including Mona. No one can know you are attending the ceremony."

"I give you my word." Dad raises his glass, as if holding his whiskey up gives him more credibility.

I ponder for a moment as I look at him. His tired blue eyes are craving what he lost a long time ago: love and acceptance. Love and acceptance from us—his children. For a long time, I was the only one who would send him photos and videos of his family and the birth of his grandchildren. Until I managed to persuade Sebastian to get back in touch with him. "It's the fifth of December, on Petra's birthday, at the St. John's Cathedral in Den Bosch."

With raised eyebrows, he asks, "Where Julia got married?"

"Yep."

"Oh, so the bishop of Den Bosch is marrying you?" His tone remains just as surprised.

"Do you have a problem with that?"

He cocks his head to the side, uneasiness written all over his face. "Sebastian is behind it, huh?"

"Julia suggested it," I point out. "And he endorsed it just as fast."

"Be careful with them."

"I know." Blowing out a breath, I say, "Sebastian made it clear if Tess steps out of line, consequences are to be expected."

"Does Petra know about it?"

The question leaves me just as uneasy as he is. "To a certain extent…"

But Dad seems to be determined to know all the details inside and out. "Does she know what you and her dad did?"

"Of course not," I promptly snap. And I hate Roy for not keeping his mouth shut about that incident to my dad. Jeez! He had been thirty-five, and yet he couldn't stand not telling the truth to his dear mentor. "She just knows her mom is blackmailing us."

"And she's okay with that?" Dad seems surprised, and I must say, I'm also surprised that she is.

"So far," I add. "Petra trusts me a lot."

"And once her mom decides to press charges against you?"

Another question that makes me tense up. "I hope it doesn't come to that," I tell him, but I can't hide the concern in my voice. "But I hope she will stick by me even then."

"For better or worse, huh?"

And I can't help but say, "That's the idea."

* * *

Petra Van Gatt

As Mona shows me around the house, I must say, what a nice refuge Hendrik has built here in Bermuda. His villa is not only spacious and cozy, but it also has an impressive backyard, with a large pool, terrace, bar area, and gardens. The only thing I didn't expect is for the place to already be full of people. Mona invites me to the bar, and we pass through a big crowd that is now dancing to the rhythmic music of the live band, lit by a string of gold-colored lights hanging above them.

"What do you want to drink?" Mona asks over the noise.

"Um, any nonalcoholic cocktail is fine," I tell her. Then I look around at the live band, the singer setting the crowd on fire as she remakes a classic of Charles Bradley's, "Ain't It a Sin," and the crowd shouts and applauds in excitement. It reminds me of my dad's galas and his old vinyls that are religiously stowed in my atelier. Reveling in the funky energy of the evening, I can't help but say, "This place is surreal."

"Yeah, it's pretty nice." As we wait for the cocktails to be served, Mona is the first to break our silence. "What brought you here by boat? We have an airport, you know."

I crack a laugh at her question. "Um, sailing is pretty nice too. And it gave Alex and I five days filled with great memories."

The waiter puts the two drinks on the bar counter; a margarita for Mona and a nonalcoholic mojito for me. We take our respective glasses, and Mona raises hers in a toast. "Well, to your stay in Bermuda." And we clink our glasses.

After taking a quick sip, I decide to get to know her better. After all, Alex mentioned he's known her for over eighteen years, and Hendrik literally said she's the angel of his life. "Who did you meet first?" I ask. "Alex or Hendrik?"

"I met Hendrik first. I used to work as an interior designer for properties and hotels. Hendrik wanted to change the decoration of his villa, and I took on the project. We got along pretty well, and um, he was such a charmer, you know…"

I love seeing Mona slightly blush as she talks about him. And I can't help but agree with that. "Yeah, he and Alex are so alike, it's frightening." Then another question comes to mind. "Have you ever met the rest of his children?"

"No, just Alex. He's the only one who ever comes here."

I try my best not to gape, but damn, after living here for nearly twenty years, no one has ever come to visit him except Alex? While I don't know much about Hendrik, it must be pretty tough not seeing his daughters and to have never met his grandchildren. "Oh, um, I didn't know that." I switch to a less sensitive subject, focusing on her. "Have you always lived here in Bermuda?"

"I've lived a bit of everywhere. As an interior designer, I used to work for many international companies, so I lived in New York, London, Sydney, Hong Kong... Despite now living here with Hendrik, the world is still my playground." The great energy that radiates from Mona is so contagious that I can't help but smile at her.

"Wow. Your life must have been so exciting." Then I squint my eyes and wonder, "But wait, um, how old are you, if I may ask?"

As she returns the smile, she leans closer to my ear and says, "I'm fifty-six, my dear."

What? I mean, she's nearly my mom's age. Yet I wouldn't have said more than thirty. "Oh, wow. Well, that's really inspiring. Is it just good genes, or is there any recipe for your perfect skin and toned body?"

"I guess a fair amount of good genes, and discipline too."

The ringing sound of an iPhone breaks through our conversation, and in a quick move, Mona puts her phone against her ear. "Yep?" As she takes her call, I let myself revel in the current music and electrifying vibe. My eyes are on the singer, fully invested in the moment, her vocals drifting into a soaring soul groove. And while I usually hate parties, especially the ones I have been to in New York, the energy of this one is so authentic, genuine, and unpretentious that, to my greatest surprise, I can truly enjoy it without my anxiety kicking in.

Mona hangs up and looks at me. "Hendrik would like to talk to you." *Hendrik? Did I hear her correctly?* "Shall we?"

Sounds like I have no other option. "Sure…" I finish my mojito in one sip and leave the glass behind.

Mona leads me into the villa, and as we cross the long hallway, I look both ways, but I don't see Alex. Then my attention alights on Hendrik, who's standing in the doorway of a room.

"Petra," he greets me with a warm smile. "Are you enjoying the party?"

"Oh, it's amazing, yeah. And the singer is fantastic."

"Ah, yes. She has got a great voice," he promptly replies with a pleasant tone. "May I have a word with you?" He's already gesturing for me to come in, regardless of my answer.

And I barely mumble a quick, "Sure" as he welcomes me into a traditional study—Chesterfield sofa and armchairs, polished wood floor, walls filled with books, and a decent-sized rug in the center, resting below a low glass table. My gaze turns to my right, and I raise my brows at the nude portrait hanging there. It looks like Mona, but I don't dare ask him about it.

"Have you met some people already?" His question makes me blink, and I turn my head in his direction.

"I was just chatting with Mona," I say, a smile on my lips. "She's such an inspiration."

"True, she's a wonderful woman. We have known each other for eighteen years. Her aunt is also here. She's a soothsayer. I mean, I don't believe in those things, but the girls love it."

My lips part in astonishment. Is it just a mere coincidence? Jeez, that reminds me of my mom's friend. And anything that reminds me of her is not something I have any interest in.

"I'm gonna serve myself a drink. Can I get you something?"

"Oh, um, just water if you have it."

Hendrik gestures for me to sit in the armchair while he goes to the bar. I quietly take a seat, my mind already ruminating about the soothsayer. What is the likelihood of Mona's aunt being one? Does Hendrik know things I don't know? If I remember correctly, I've never told Alex about my experience before.

"You know, after ten years, I really thought Alex would settle down with Amanda." His totally unexpected revelation startles me, making my heart squeezing tight, and I wonder if he said that to get something off his chest or to provoke a response from me. But I keep my lips in a flat line, indifferent. Hendrik's directness shouldn't surprise me. After all, Margaret is just like that.

"Oh, you know Amanda?" Not sure why I asked him that. If Margaret knows her, obviously Hendrik does too! What a dumb question.

"Of course I do. She is Mona's daughter."

WHAT! My jaw drops immediately, and I can't hide the astonishment on my face. Why didn't Alex tell me that? Oh my God, that means Amanda is like family to Hendrik. And he and Mona were most likely looking forward to a wedding between their children. Oh jeez, and Amanda must have told them that I called her a witch. I swallow dryly, feeling like an intruder. Ironically, at the same time, Hendrik extends a hand toward me with a glass of water. And as I take it, I force myself not to drink it all at once.

"I mean, they seemed to be very happy together. I even asked him, 'Son, why haven't you proposed yet?'" I give him a polite smile as he sits beside me on the sofa. "Oh boy, I'll never forget his answer…"

Curiosity tickling my tongue, I ask, "What did he say?"

"Well, Alex said…" Hendrik takes a sip of his drink while my heart pulses faster with every second. "'Because she's not my soul mate.'"

And my heart tightens hard upon hearing this. I press my lips together, picturing that moment in my mind and Alex's voice.

"I cracked up laughing. I took it as a joke, you know. I mean, c'mon, after ten years together? So I asked him, 'Then who's your soul mate?'"

I breathe slowly in and out, doing my best to tame my emotions and remain as stoic as possible.

"And that's when he told me about you." Hendrik pauses, observing me, and a smile escapes him before he takes another sip of his drink. Not sure if he can tell the state I'm in, but I hope not. "I was seriously worried. I mean, the fact that he gave his heart to his once seven-year-old goddaughter was freaking me out. But I guess he's good at keeping his promises."

"Promises?" I squint my eyes in confusion. "Um, what promise are you referring to?"

"He didn't tell you?" Since my eyes keep squinting at him, he says, "That he'd never love or marry anyone but you."

Huh? He promised me that? But… if I recall properly, except for the fact that Alex was extremely embarrassed by my request at the time, no one had ever mentioned that he had actually agreed to it. So, wait! Does that mean Alex actually said those words to my dad and Amanda? Letting out a quick chuckle, I act like I already knew about it. "Ah, yes, he did."

Hendrik keeps smiling at me, most likely reveling in my uneasiness with the whole conversation. "I'm sorry to tell you all this, but I thought you had to know." *Liar.*

I might be young, but I'm not that naive. There is an underlying reason why he's sharing these stories with me out of the blue. He either wants to create friction between Alex and me, or he wants something in return. There is no free ride. Obviously, Hendrik was truly looking forward to his son's wedding. But it was not with me. Jeez… If Margaret made me feel nervous, Hendrik makes me feel like a total intruder. I have no words, no answer to offer him in return. I genuinely thought he liked me, and my disappointment makes me want to throw up. My mind is totally blank. After a few more seconds, though, I take a deep breath, hold his stare steadily, and ask, "Why are you telling me all this?"

He blinks twice, taken aback by my question. "I just think it's important to be frank with each other. I'm sorry if Alex didn't tell you that himself." And he ends his comment by taking a last sip, finishing his drink.

So apparently Hendrik wants to create tension between his son and me. That's his goal. But why though? Is it some sort of punishment for Alex leaving the family office to start his own hedge fund with my dad? Or is it because he left

Amanda? "I…" My mind keeps searching for words, any words. "It belongs to the past anyway. And, um, I believe Alex has got his own reasons for not telling me who Mona was and how close you are with his ex-girlfriend."

"And you still take his side no matter what," he states, not sure if it's praise or not. But he seems genuinely surprised. "You do really trust him."

"I do, yes." And I don't really see why I wouldn't. "Doesn't Mona trust you that way?"

There is a sly smile growing on his lips, and a few beats of silence ensue. It seems like his answer is not as straightforward as I thought it would be. "I hope this little talk can stay between us." He doesn't even bother to reply to my question. It seems like the truth was too harsh to face.

***

After leaving Hendrik's office, I'm still baffled at everything we discussed. From his relationship with Mona and Amanda, to Margaret, I feel like I was his confidant, but I can't discern why he would confide in me so easily. Is it because of my loyalty toward his son? If that was the case, though, then why did he ask me to keep our conversation strictly between us? The fact that he never answered my question about Mona, who he's known for eighteen years, is quite surprising to me.

As I walk down the hallway, I follow where the noise is coming from and find myself in a vast dining and living room combo filled with only unknown faces. Some are having dinner, others are sitting on the sofa chatting, and still others are standing around in circles.

"That was a long meeting."

Alex emerges from nowhere among the crowd, and my lips curve up instantly upon seeing him. As I look at the man standing in front of me, I can't help but be drawn to him. No matter how many times I have seen him, he always makes my heart pound faster when he is around. In that moment, I realize that if I had met Alex for the first time right now, it would've been love at first sight.

"Are you alright?"

"What would have been the chances of us meeting each other if you were not my dad's associate?" I ask casually.

His eyes widen a smidgen at my unexpected question. "That's what you are thinking right now?"

"Yep…" I step closer to him and run a hand over his open collar, fondling his skin. "Do you think we'd have ended up meeting at some point? Or do you think you would've married someone else?"

Alex just chuckles in return. "Alright, I see. My dad told you who Amanda is."

Wow. Am I that easy to read? But I don't want to talk about Amanda, so instead I say, "You didn't even answer my question."

Alex keeps his gaze steady on mine, his face glowing as he says, "I don't want to think about a world where I'd have never met you. Sounds way too terrifying."

I know he's speaking from his heart, and I feel exactly the same way—a world without him is too terrifying to even think about. Because I know it all too well.

"Thank God you are here." His hands go up to cup my face, and my eyes shut tight as he leans in and presses his lips to mine. Finally! The first kiss since we arrived in Bermuda… gets interrupted with the ringing sound of his iPhone.

Alex reaches down to his pocket, and after a quick glance at the screen, he says, "It's my attorney." I feel a bit anxious as he takes the call, moving a few steps toward the door to avoid all the surrounding noise. After a few seconds, though, I hear Alex calling me over and saying, "My attorney is with Emma."

Emma? I immediately trot over and take his phone just as fast. Then Alex leads me down the hallway and to a quieter part of the house, where I can hear her properly. "Emma?"

"Hey! How are you?"

"Oh my gosh!" The sound of her voice sends a wave of emotion bursting through me, but I force myself to calm down. "How are you?"

"I'm good, um, just planning my next trip. I received your message, by the way. And, um, regarding your mom, with all due respect, I kinda felt during the meeting that she was a manipulative bitch."

A chuckle escapes me at her usual bluntness, but I'm glad she saw through my mom. Then I promptly ask, "What about Eric? Did he say or do anything against you?"

"Ha, that lil motherfucker…" She lets her words trail off, leaving me anxiously waiting. "That dude, I swear…"

"What happened?" I promptly ask, my curiosity mixed with fear and nervousness rising.

"He struck a nerve…"

"Gosh, tell me!"

"Well, when your parents showed up with your friend Matthew and his dad, I invited them in for a quick chat in the living room. You know, they were polite, super worried about you, so they asked some questions that I answered, and it was all good. But after our meeting, since no one got the info they wanted, Eric requested to speak privately with me."

"What?" I can't contain my outrage.

"Yeah, I was so stunned by his question. Like, what the fuck? Where does he get off? I swear, that dude was out of his mind. Obviously, I refused and even chuckled, then I simply instructed them to leave."

"And then?"

"He didn't appreciate that. And while everyone was leaving the room, he stood there like a pitiful dickhead and asked the same questions, but without your parents and his son around. I said I was done, and that's when he crossed the line…"

My heart is racing with every word coming out of her mouth, and my nerves are boiling. "What did he do?"

"I was gesturing for him to leave, but he was stepping closer to me, and he was, like, 'You know lying to a public servant is a criminal offense,' and then he asked if he should call the cops to make me tell the truth."

My mouth remains wide open in total awe. "What the hell?" I can't believe this is the same man Matthew introduced me to. He seemed so polite and well-behaved.

"Yeah, that dude is insane. So, at that point, I was losing my shit, and I asked him to leave before he would regret it."

Now I'm blinking twice. "You really said that?"

"Of course! He's a fucking idiot who only got into my house because he was with your parents."

"And then?"

"He left, but he said I would hear from him soon."

"Oh jeez…" Well, if Eric got his little ego smashed, no wonder he might want to avenge himself in some way.

"I'm not sure what he is up to. But my parents already made a few phone calls to put him in line."

"You think he will get fired?"

"I dunno. It's not easy to fire a state attorney general. But we have some people tracking him, and they will find a way to get him to resign."

"Damn, Emma. I'm so sorry for this…"

"Babe, it's all good. Um, I'm gonna head somewhere warm and have fun." I smile, thinking how that's exactly where I am right now. "And then I'll see you in December for the wedding." I let out a quick sigh, realizing we are only a month and a half away from it. "Still happening, right?"

"Of course," I reply just as fast. "Emma, be careful. There's only one Emma Hasenfratz in this world."

"I know. My parents told me exactly the same thing." She then pauses for a beat. "By the way, um, can I be your maid of honor?"

My brows raise at her question. Since Julia said she'd take care of the organization of the wedding, I hadn't even thought about it. "Yes, of course." I've got no idea what it means to be a maid of honor, but why not if that makes her happy?

"Perfect, well, I'm gonna have to go. Alex's lawyer has been patiently waiting for his phone. Thank Alex for me."

"I will."

We say goodbye to each other once more. And thank God I got to speak to Emma tonight.

After hanging up, a huge weight slips off my shoulders, and I blow out a breath, more relaxed and calm now knowing my Emma is safe.

"Is she alright?" I turn my head in his direction, and I see Alex has been behind me the whole time.

"Yeah, she is fine." I give him his iPhone, before putting my arms around his neck and whispering, "Thank you for that." I pause, smiling at him. "I know how much is on the line, but I'm really glad I could speak to her."

"Hey! Finally, there you are!" We hear a female voice, and I see Mona walking toward us. "There's someone I would love to introduce you to." Oh gosh, don't tell me Amanda is here! "Have you ever met a soothsayer?" she asks with excitement in her tone.

"Oh, um, no. I haven't." Jeez, I don't want to talk to a soothsayer. I've got no interest in knowing what the future holds for me. Honestly, after my mom's friend foresaw my death, I prefer to know nothing and live in peace.

"Oh, you haven't met Auntie Louise yet?" Alex asks.

The fact that he calls her Auntie Louise bothers me more than I'd like to admit. After all, she's not his aunt, she's Mona's aunt. I shake my head in response, but it's hard getting used to the fact that Hendrik has a new family here—

Mona's. And even though they are not married, after eighteen years together, it's normal that Hendrik—and consequently, Alex—knows her family well. I'm at least glad her daughter is not here. It'd have been such poor taste.

"You should. She's really a sweetheart," Alex insists. A sweetheart? Maybe, but she's also a soothsayer!

All of a sudden, though, Mona takes me by the hand and drags me to the other side of the living room. There, I see an older lady with very short gray-white hair, glasses, cherry lipstick, and silver hoops in her ears sitting on the sofa, surrounded by younger women. She seems to be the oldest of them all, but also the wisest. Her smile is so kind and warm that it's obvious to me that, as Alex just said, she's a sweetheart. We stand a few steps away from her, and I observe how this lady, with her enigmatic presence and warm energy, is describing what she sees in the palm of the woman she is talking to. Then she gives her a hug like a grandmother would to a granddaughter.

"Do you want to try?" Mona asks me. And before I can say anything, Mona is already calling, "Auntie?" As the soothsayer looks in our direction, we step closer, and Mona says, "Petra is Alexander's new girlfriend. Can you read her lines, please?"

All the women glare at us like we should wait in line. And I just want to run away from here, hating being the center of so much unwanted attention. Damn, I don't even want to do this. Louise's gaze lands on me with real genuine empathy, and she slowly takes my hand between hers.

"I know you are going through a lot. It's alright, don't be afraid."

I'm left speechless, totally gaping at her words. How does she know that? Then she gently turns my hand over, looking at my palm.

"Mmm, I see money and love are in abundance…" Her voice soothes me, and I give her a warm smile in return. "But deep troubles with family and acceptance." Well, that couldn't be truer. And I wonder how she'd come to that conclusion? Her smile then quietly vanishes, and her face turns into something more sinister and gloomier.

"Is there something wrong?" I ask immediately.

"Um…" And I can tell she's not comfortable telling me the truth in front of all these people. All of a sudden, though, Louise just stands up, excuses herself, and silently walks away. Everyone starts whispering among themselves as we all remain in shock at her behavior. I hate to be the center of attention, and right now, with all these women staring at me and wondering what I have done to make Auntie Louise leave, it feels like I'm living my worst nightmare. And although I didn't want her to start reading my palm, now I can't help but wonder what she saw and why she left. I decide to follow her as she crosses the living room, then the entryway, all the way outside to the parking area.

"Ma'am, please," I plead, before running in her direction.

But Louise doesn't react; instead, she keeps walking toward her car, ignoring me.

Speeding up my pace, I get close enough to reach her shoulder, and say once more, "Ma'am, please." As she turns around, her face is stern, yet laced with torment that petrifies me. "Please," I plead. "Tell me the truth." Then I extend my right hand once more, showing her my palm lines. Her eyes dart down for a second, observing them briefly, before looking up at me. "What do you see?"

After a beat of silence, she finally exhales a loud rush of air and says, "I only see death and misery, Miss." My heart stops at the sound of her voice, and my eyes widen in shock. "I wish I could tell you otherwise. I'm sorry."

She turns again, taking her car keys out of her purse, but I have more to ask. "Why? I... I don't understand. I had an accident earlier this year, but I survived."

Her head lowers for a moment, and while I can only see her back, I know her eyes are closed. I remain still, patiently observing her. Louise looks over her shoulder and mutters, "This relationship..." She pauses, shaking her head. "It won't end well. Now, I must go. Good night."

Her words were said with so much conviction that I remain baffled and barely breathing.

I hear the sound of her car engine, but I don't dare look at her and wave goodbye.

Returning inside the house, I'm left with not only a wave of shock but also a big mental mess. This woman doesn't even know me, yet she said the same thing as the one who spoke to my mom. Then I wonder why Mona insisted so much for me to meet her. Was it just in good faith? Or did she know what Louise would tell me?

"Hey, I was looking for you." But I don't even look at Alex coming in. "Are you alright?" he asks, rubbing my arm in a failed attempt to soothe me.

"Yeah, I was just speaking to Louise." I force myself to put on a smile and brush that incident from my mind.

"What did she tell you?"

"Oh, nothing that matters. Don't worry about it." My ears perk up, recognizing one of my favorite songs now playing. I put on a joyful expression, and, grasping his hand, I try to lead him to the outdoor terrace, where everyone is dancing to "Sway" by Michael Bublé. "Shall we? I love this song."

"Petra…" But Alex doesn't even move; instead, he just pulls me closer to him. "What did she tell you?" he repeats, this time a bit slower.

Lost in his blue eyes, I contemplate if I should tell him the truth or not. Since lying again doesn't feel like a good option, I say, "Well…" Then I clear my throat as I think of the best words to say it. "She said as long as we remain together, my life will be filled with death and misery." He widens his eyes in surprise. "But my mom told me the same thing last year. And yet here we are, happy and healthy."

His face remains unreadable, but not his gaze. "I will never let anyone hurt you or us." Cupping my face in his hands, he stares intently into my eyes. "No one." I give him a quick smile in a failed attempt to silence my torment. "Look, from now on, I'll always introduce you as my fiancée, and I'll never travel again without you by my side."

"Really?" Now that's something I wasn't expecting!

"Yeah, I have no idea how far your parents would go to tear us apart, but I do know they are capable of going pretty far to do so."

My encounter with the soothsayer might not have been the most joyful moment of the evening, but knowing that from now on Alex will no longer introduce me as his goddaughter, but rather as his fiancée, certainly is.

* * *

The party seemed to last forever, but fortunately, at midnight, the music finally stopped and most of the guests started to leave. Then Mona apologized to me for her aunt's behavior, which I insisted wasn't her fault regardless of how badly she felt about it. Even after the party ended, Alex and I stayed to chat with some of Mona's friends, and I must say, everyone was incredibly polite and friendly, which kinda surprised me, since they all knew Amanda had been Alex's girlfriend for ten years. But no one brought it up—not even Mona. After saying good night to everyone, Alex finally leads me to his bedroom. As we step inside, my eyes immediately go to the wall on my right, which consists entirely of floor-to-ceiling windows with a sliding glass door leading to a private balcony and then to the beach. Turning my gaze to the bed, I can't help but hear Hendrik's voice echoing in my mind, *I mean, they seemed to be very happy together.* And my heart tightens horribly knowing they fucked there. Yep, they did. Jeez, I shouldn't think about it, but it's a reality that's hard to swallow.

"Is everything okay?" I hear him asking.

I flatten my lips and cast my eyes down. "I'm sorry, um, it's just… it's just weird knowing you slept here with someone else."

Alex doesn't say a word as he lets my answer sink in. Then he just stares at the bed and again at me. "Do you want to go back to the boat?"

"No, it's fine." I never thought I'd admit it, but I miss Margaret's rule that didn't allow him to sleep with a woman he didn't intend to marry under her roof. Pity Hendrik was not like that. "It's okay, really."

But Alex doesn't seem convinced. "I'm sorry. I should've thought about it." His soft tone makes me feel even worse that I give a crap about it. "If it makes you uncomfortable, we can go back to the boat…"

"No, it's okay." And deciding to open up, I say, "I just didn't know Amanda was so close to Hendrik."

"I didn't want to make you feel more anxious or apprehensive to meet him. And I didn't know my dad would tell you about it. I'm sorry."

I soak up the sincerity of his words. It's not that I'm mad at him, but the truth is, I never expected his relationship with Amanda would affect me like this until I realized he had shared ten years of intimacy with her, to the point that Hendrik, Mona, and everyone else thought they'd get married. It might sound silly, but I feel like an intruder in their lives. Like I'm the one who stepped in and messed up their relationship and their happily ever after.

As I remain lost in my thoughts, Alex stands before me and starts stroking my hair. Then our eyes lock, and he says, "She belongs to the past. You are my present and future. You know that."

"I know, I just…" I pause for a beat, pursing my lips together. "I just feel bad cause I can tell she loved you. Like, a lot." Or at least that's the impression Hendrik gave me. And I wish I'd have ended the conversation there. Curiosity getting the best of me, I add, "Why did you spend ten years with her if you didn't intend to marry her? It sounds so selfish."

He chuckles, before shaking his head in displeasure. "I was always honest with her about what type of relationship she could expect from me. Marriage and kids weren't part of it." And meeting my gaze again, he just says, "She was okay with it until she wasn't."

"Well, after ten years together, I guess she thought she could change your mind…"

"But she didn't."

And I obviously know why. It's a pity that Alex had never told me that he'd promised the seven-year-old me that he'd never marry anyone but me. Why did I have to learn it from his dad? Is he ashamed to have said that? But I'm just too tired to ask any further.

Wanting to lighten the mood, I slide a hand under his open collar, and, after wetting my lips, I say in a whisper, "You know, I should get some kind of reward for tonight." My voice is sweet and innocent, and Alex smirks in return, his blue eyes gleaming with satisfaction. "After all, I spent the whole evening with a big plug in my butt." He heaves a rush of air in amusement, but I keep going. "Don't you think?"

CHAPTER 38

Bermuda, October 30, 2020
Petra Van Gatt

The sound of waves swaying back and forth on the shore is the perfect morning melody to wake me up. As I timidly open my eyes, the amount of light present in the bedroom makes them sting, and I shut them again just as fast. Jeez! It must already be so late. I blink my eyes a few more times, getting used to the strong brightness. Then, I instinctively look around to find where the light is coming from, and that's when I notice the sliding door that leads to our terrace is wide open. I look beside me to the empty side of the bed, and it doesn't take a genius to figure out where Alex has been. Grabbing a bikini and a pair of denim shorts, I put them on in a blink, slide my iPhone into my back pocket, and head outside to meet him. Standing against the baluster railing, I rest my forearms on the surface and bend slightly to observe the most handsome man swimming far out to sea, like he's competing in speed and performance against himself. I didn't know he was such a fine swimmer, but I've come to the conclusion there is still a lot about him I don't know. As Alex leaves the water and returns to the shore, I observe him like he is moving in slow motion. The way his hips sway, his eyes surveying the white sandy beach, his hand running through his wet hair, his presence, his body, everything about him demands attention in every sense, causing my heart to hammer against my ribs. As I observe him walking through the beach, his muscular body covered in the salty water of the Caribbean Sea, I can't help being drawn to him. There is so much beauty in him that I grab my phone and discreetly take a few pictures of him to keep selfishly to myself. I'm too far away for him to notice any-way. A silent breath escapes my lips, and I chew my bottom lip. Loving him has been quite a hard battle. A battle filled with so much pain and suffering, but now, it seems like it has all been worth it.

His gaze travels to the terrace where I'm standing, and as our eyes lock, I see him picking up his pace to climb the stairs that connect our terrace to the beach.

"Hey," I greet as he stands before me, my eyes lingering a bit lower than they should.

"Sleep well?" The sound of his voice makes me bat my eyes twice, bringing my attention back to his face and pulling me out of lusty land.

"Yeah, pretty good. How is the water?"

His lips twitch into a naughty smile. "Let me show you." And in a sudden move, Alex lifts me off the ground and car-ries me like a baby from the terrace.

"Alex!" I barely have time to hold on to his neck before a shiver shoots down my spine and goosebumps coat my arms in enthusiasm. Then a rush of adrenaline begins beating through my veins at the realization that he's gonna drop me into the water… along with my iPhone and my newly taken pictures! "My phone!" As he carries me through the sand and toward the sea, I manage to throw the iPhone in the beach cabana that stands beside us. Not the best place, but still better than in the water or sand.

"Ahh…" A quick sigh escapes me at the contact of my warm skin with the fresh water. Alex keeps walking deeper into the water until our bodies are totally immersed.

"I'm not too heavy?" A stupid question, but I couldn't help but notice how he managed to carry me all the way from the terrace to the water without straining or breaking stride.

Alex doesn't restrain his loud chuckle. "You? Heavy?" Shaking his head in amusement, he then asks, "So, how is the water?"

"It's perfect." My voice comes out nauseatingly sweet as I let myself float in his embrace. Then, as I release him, I realize I can no longer stand here like he can. So, keeping my arms wrapped around his neck, I press my lips hard to his and put everything into our morning kiss. And as we look into each other's eyes, I tell him, "I can't believe I'm here with you. It feels too good to be true."

He kisses me in return, and after smiling at me, he says, "Thank you for not giving up on us. Even after I had to leave."

"I just couldn't," I tell him sincerely. Then, as I observe him attentively, I notice that Alex already looks so much tanner since we left New York. It's incredible how he doesn't get burned in the sun like I do.

Following our lazy swim in the warm waters of the Caribbean Sea, we go to the beach cabana, where I find two towels and two cushions for lounging, and my precious phone—alive and well. I remove my soaked shorts, and after Alex lies on the mattress, I lie on top of him and start kissing and sucking his sun-kissed neck. My chest heaves, blood pumping rapidly through my heart as I trace a line of soft kisses from his collarbone down to his torso and abs. A little grunt escapes him once I press my lips against his belly button, and I feel his hands on my hair, stroking it while my mouth keeps going down. His skin tastes just like the sea. As I reach his pelvis, I'm about to push the waistband of his swim shorts down, but Alex stops me instantly. "Petra, not here."

Raising my head up, I look at him and ask, "Why not?"

He lets out a rush of air, before saying, "My dad or his staff could come out here." He pauses, regaining his breath. "It's not as private as you think."

Oh, dear! The last thing I need is for Hendrik or his staff to witness what I had in mind! Jeez, what an embarrassment that would have been. I guess I will have to content myself with some cuddles. I move up again, and nestle myself against him, just like I'm so used to doing. As we both rest quietly on the mattress, my fiancé starts stroking my leg, my waist, and any skin he can lay his fingers on.

"Your dad truly lives in paradise," I mumble, as I keep listening to the waves coming in and then slowly leaving the shore.

"That doesn't mean he is happy."

"Why wouldn't he be?" I ask, raising my head up to meet his gaze. "He's got everything here."

I hear nothing but his breath. Alex seems to be ruminating about something as he stares absently out into the void. After a few seconds, though, his eyes finally land on me. "Except those he loves."

It reminds me of the chat I had with Mona yesterday, but I ask him like I know nothing, "You mean, your sisters never come here?"

"Nope…" And the truth seems to bother him. Or maybe even hurt him. "He's dead to them. I'm the only one who ever comes here to visit him."

Alex might disguise his pain with a smile, but as I observe him saying these words, I can tell how much this has impacted him, so I reach for his hand, holding it tight.

"My dad can laugh, dance, and drink, but at the end of the day, I know he feels dead inside."

His words squeeze my heart just as if they were about my own dad.

"Family means a lot to him. Much more than he'd like to admit."

Despite all the grudges I hold against my dad, the more I think about Hendrik's fate, the more I'd love to forgive him, so he never feels like Hendrik does. A part of me still wants to believe I'll be able to, someday, somehow. After all, Dad was the first person to tolerate our relationship. He was even the one who came with me to the Van Dierens' and gave Alex a chance. I'll never forget that. I guess most parents would've behaved just like my mom. The truth is, without his initial support, I have no idea what would've happened to Alex and me.

"Does anyone know you still visit him?" I ask.

"No one, except Sebastian." Throwing a smile at me, Alex then adds, "And that's a secret, Miss Van Gatt."

"Mr. Van Dieren?" We follow the male voice coming from our left, and see Jason, the butler, approaching in our direction. And I've never been happier that Alex stopped me from going down on him a few minutes ago. Once Jason gets close enough, he says, "My sincere apologies for the intrusion, but, um, your dad would like to talk to you two. He's at the main terrace. And it sounds like it's urgent."

"That serious?" Alex presses on.

"It seems so."

I squint my eyes, perplexed and already quite curious. "Alright, let's go, then." After standing up, I check to see if my shorts are dry enough to wear them, but since they are still pretty damp, I leave them on the mattress to dry, and just take my iPhone with me. We follow Jason back to the main terrace, and as we enter, we find Hendrik sitting at the table with two other men I don't recognize.

"Ryan?" Alex asks in surprise. "What are you doing here?"

I lean toward my fiancé and ask, "Who's he?"

"My attorney," he replies.

"Alex," he greets in such a serious tone that it makes me shiver. What a contrast between them in suits and us in swim attire.

"Ryan came as fast as he could," Hendrik notes.

Alex seems confused, just as I do. "But why?"

The two men exchange a stare, before Ryan announces, "Roy is accusing you of kidnapping his daughter. It's in the *New York Times*."

"What?!" we both shout at the same time.

"Yep, so I figured you might need some help." Ryan hands me today's newspaper, and my jaw drops as I read the headline, "Wall Street Titan, Alexander Van Dieren, Kidnaps Young Girl and Leaves the Country."

"Kidnaps?" I snap, out of breath as I see our pictures printed next to such a ridiculous headline.

"Eric Bradford is leading the case," Ryan tells us. Oh my God! Emma told me he was going to do something. But I never thought his revenge would be against me! "And they have his entire office looking for you both."

"Fuck," I hear Alex mumble as he starts looking at the article more closely.

I also read a few lines, enough for me to ask, "How can I be abducted by the man I love? That doesn't make any sense."

"Well, according to the story, he abducted you to isolate you from your family and to prevent you from recovering from your OLD and depression."

"I'm an adult," I remind them. "I can be with whomever I want. This OLD is bullshit."

"It might be, but they will use your current illness to claim you couldn't consent and most likely to become your legal guardians."

I freeze at the word guardian. "How can they do that? What kind of guardianship is that?"

"Most likely guardianship of an incapacitated adult under the Mental Hygiene Law," another man sitting beside Ryan says.

I chuckle at the absurdity. "That is not possible, right?"

"I'm afraid it is," Ryan replies back. "Under New York law, if the court decides you are mentally ill based on enough evidence, the judge can appoint a legal guardian to prevent you from doing anything that they consider, um, well, harmful."

Evidence. Oh my God! I went on a hunger strike and confessed my suicidal thoughts to Dr. Nel. Could that be enough?

It feels like a nightmare, or in this case, a loophole for possessive families to keep controlling their kids when they reach adulthood. Trying to strip my freedom away as soon as I make one damn decision on my own? Breathing becomes harder as I look again at the headline, but I try to keep my composure. I hold myself up against the back of the first chair my hands land on and focus on inhaling and exhaling.

"Are you okay?" Alex asks.

But I focus on my breathing as I feel my blood pressure slowly coming down.

Closing my eyes, I nod, but I don't have the strength to talk. The palpitations in my heart are jumping off the chart at the idea that a judge could strip my freedom away. A judge my dad or Eric could know perfectly well.

Then, I hear Alex ordering fresh water with lemon, and I find myself in his embrace, with his lips pressing against my forehead. "Hey…" he whispers. "It's gonna be alright." I force myself to remain calm, breathing in and out and fighting the growing fear of what the future holds for us. "Can we have a moment, please?"

I hear everyone standing up and footsteps leaving the terrace. Alex takes me by the arm and makes me sit in one of the chairs.

"Here, have some water." Opening my eyes, I hold the glass and bring the fresh water to my mouth.

After taking the first sip, I say, "You know that story of Latifa, the Emirati princess who tried to escape her controlling father, but was caught and brought back to Dubai?"

"Um, I heard about it, yeah."

"Her father said the same thing to the media, that she had been kidnapped," I tell him before finishing my lemon water in one gulp. "My dad is becoming very good friends with Eric Bradford," I tell him. "And Emma told me Eric was up to something." I pause for a beat and say, "I have to talk to Matthew."

But Alex cocks his head to the side. "Petra, I doubt your friend will be of any help."

And while Alex might be right, a part of me sincerely hopes not. Matthew is a close friend after all, and he can talk to his dad and persuade him to drop the charges against my fiancé. He knows perfectly well that it's all bullshit. "I have to try and talk to him."

"You know the rules…"

"Don't you get it?" I snap back. "If we don't fight back, my freedom is at stake. Use a fake number, a VPN, or whatever, but I have to talk to him."

Alex takes my phone and does something on it. "I'm gonna connect to a VPN and set your number to private, but we're taking a huge risk."

Then he gives me back the phone, and as I look at the screen, I force myself to remember Matthew's number and type in the digits, hoping they are in the correct order. I put the phone against my ear and wait…

I draw in a breath upon hearing a male voice answering, "Hi?"

"Matthew? It's me, Petra," I reply with excitement.

"Petra? Jeez, how are you? Are you okay?" His tone is laced with worry.

"I'm fine, yes. Um, I just saw the article in the *New York Times*—"

"Where are you?" he asks, cutting me off.

"I can't tell you that. Look—"

"Fuck, is he holding you hostage?"

My jaw drops at his question. "No. I'm fine," I repeat. "Please, tell your dad to drop the charges against my fiancé. I don't want to be found."

But Matthew releases a loud breath in annoyance. "Is he asking you to say that? Petra, you are being manipulated," he replies, sounding condescending. "He's cutting you off from everyone and everything. That's how abusive relationships start."

"Matthew," I call, trying to calm him down. "We are here because my parents were tapping my phone, imposed bodyguards on me, and nearly implanted a tracking chip in my arm. They are the ones who are abusive."

"Your parents have common sense!"

I huff immediately at his answer. Since when is this common sense?

"You are so sick. Like, you have been diagnosed with OLD, depression, and PTSD, but you are still in total denial. They did it to protect you."

I can't believe after everything my parents have done to me, Matthew is still protecting them. What about me and my happiness? Don't they matter? Jeez, he's beyond crazy. Since Matthew doesn't seem to understand I'd rather be free and with the man I love, than unhappy and trapped under the guardianship of my parents, I know at this point I have to dissuade Eric to drop the charges myself. "Matthew, please, may I speak to your dad?"

"Um, what do you want to tell him?"

"I need to know what's going on," I lie. What I want is to persuade Eric to leave us alone. "I just need five minutes to talk to him, please."

After a few seconds of silence, Matthew finally says, "Alright, one minute." I heave a sigh of relief as I wait for Eric to take the call.

"Yes?"

"Hi, Eric, it's Petra Van Gatt," I greet as politely as possible.

"Ms. Van Gatt, thank God you managed to contact us. Where are you? Did he harm you? Did you manage to escape?"

Damn, his questions are beyond absurd. "Don't worry, I'm doing great. Um, I read the article published in the *New York Times*," I inform him. "I'm not sure how my parents managed to get this article out, but may I remind you that misinformation and defamation are serious offenses?" I keep my tone cold and calculated, but not aggressive. "I suggest you drop all the charges against my fiancé. There's no need to engage in a judiciary battle over such nonsense." My heart keeps accelerating as I anxiously wait for his answer.

"Petra, my job as a prosecutor is to go after those who abuse their position and show predatory behavior toward younger girls. I'm afraid only a judge can decide now." What the heck is he talking about? "We have laws in place to protect people who have been incapacitated due to mental illness."

His comment is so condescending that I feel the urge to hang up, but instead I say, "I appreciate your concerns over my mental wellness, but I'm fine. I'm perfectly capable of making decisions on my own. If my parents want to ever see me again, they better drop the charges."

"Alright, I will transfer the message," he says dryly.

"Thank you." And we hang up.

Jeez, I shiver at how disgusting the Bradfords have become. Matthew has always advocated for individual rights and freedoms, and yet now he has sided with my parents, who would gladly take mine away. What a fucking jerk! Why is he doing this? For the Patreon money my dad has been giving him every month? For the sake of having a good relationship with him? Unbelievable how he threw his integrity out the window for so little.

"Alex?" Ryan comes out, holding an iPhone. "Roy is on the phone."

"Put it on speaker," he says.

But Ryan gives a quick glance at me first. "Are you sure?"

"Yes."

Ryan walks toward us and puts the phone on the table, before pressing the speaker button.

"Hi, Roy," Alex greets, his tone more restrained and severe than usual.

"Alex…" I haven't heard my Dad's voice for so long that it feels strange and foreign to hear it again.

"First off, you are on speaker. And there's my attorney here and Petra," Alex announces.

"Good to know." Dad's tone is so cold and clinical that he sounds totally unrecognizable. "Petra, how are you?"

"Dad, please stop this nonsense. Why are you doing this?" I ask, taming my anger, rage, and all the other boiling emotions inside, trying to keep them from taking over me. "You know perfectly well that Alex didn't kidnap me."

But Dad doesn't reply to my question, and instead he says, "You guys are also on speaker, and the entire board's here with me. We are having a meeting to vote you out."

"What?" I ask, immediately looking at Alex. I can't keep from gaping in outrage at my dad's move. "They are trying to fire you?"

But Alex doesn't give anything away. "HR was perfectly aware that I'd be out for fourteen days. I'm taking my leave."

"HR, yes. The board, not really," Dad snaps back.

What a freaking monster he is! I'm glad I saw through him since the day he threatened my inheritance. As I notice Alex's hand resting on the table, I decide to take it and hold it tightly. It might be a simple gesture, but I hope it's enough for him to know we are in this together until the end.

"Roy, you know you can't fire me. I own as much of the company as you do. Stop this freaking nonsense," he tells Dad, aiming to bring some common sense to this useless fight against us.

"Correct, we both own forty-seven percent, and our dear investors the remaining six. And they are here, at the table, quite alarmed by your actions."

"You need more than that to fire me. Any evidence that my actions are hurting the company financially? It's our best year so far, so I highly doubt it," Alex points out. "You are actually the one who is putting the company in jeopardy by publishing defamatory articles about me."

"Me?" Dad asks rhetorically.

"Yes, you know this is just to destroy my reputation, which makes no sense, since this can also hurt our company."

"My daughter is sick, and you abducted her to prevent her from being treated! It's the least I could do!"

What? I can't believe what I'm hearing. Dad's totally lost his mind! "That's a freaking lie!" I shout. "I'm going through depression because of your abusive and controlling behavior! I should be the one pressing charges against you and Mom."

"Petra, stay out of it," Dad scolds. Not a chance!

"Alex?" I hear a calm, serene female voice on the phone. And thank God she piped in. I was ready to blow a fuse. "We don't intend to vote you out. Your performance this year has been excellent. But tensions between the chairman of the board and the CEO are never good for business. We expect you to be back in New York to fix this mess."

Before any of us can respond, Mike, the COO, steps in. "Yeah, the story published about the kidnapping and the attorney general being involved is not reassuring our clients. Your credibility took a big blow, mate." My blood pressure is climbing with every word coming out of his mouth, and it takes everything in me not to refute his statements. "We don't want this to get worse and then have to put you out to keep them."

"Mike, no one is gonna pull their investments because of this nonsense," Alex presses on. "This is just a poorly calculated move by our chairman and his ex-wife."

"Some clients are seriously worried," Mike confesses. "You know, these kinds of stories can spread quickly. A young woman, barely legal, who is the daughter of our chairman…" Mike exhales a rush of air, trying to remain as politically correct as possible. "Our clients are not happy with your lack of ethics."

Alex shakes his head, knowing all too well that it's all bullshit. "I will make some calls, don't worry."

"Are you gonna come back to fix this mess, yes or no?" the female voice asks again.

"Look, I can't promise I will be back in New York, but I promise I will fix this from where I am. I will contact our PR team and issue a press release and call our clients."

"Alright, you better fix this mess and fast," she adds. "We don't need any more bad publicity."

"Will do, bye." And Alex hangs up.

Now that it's just the two of us and his lawyer, I say, "I can't believe Dad was trying to fire you." Shaking my head, I look downward in disgust at what he just did. "You guys are best friends."

"He's being pressured by Tess. Your dad is innocent."

And I blink twice, totally baffled at how Alex is still trying to protect him. "Dad is an accomplice; he's not innocent," I correct him. And, drawing in a deep breath, I ask, "Ryan, may I have a moment alone with Alex, please?"

"Sure…" Ryan walks off the terrace, closing the door behind him.

Once we are left totally alone, I look my fiancé in the eye and tell him, "You know that my loyalty toward you is unconditional." A sincere smile tugs on his lips at my statement, and we keep our hands just as tightly entwined. "But I need to know the truth." He cocks his head to the side in confusion. And knowing that I have to be a bit more specific, I say, "What does my mom have against you two?"

But he breaks eye contact just as fast, pulling his hand away from mine. "You know I can't tell you that."

His words hurt me like a knife to the chest, rendering me totally speechless. Then, nothing but a dense silence fills the air between us. "Damn it," I let out. Dragging some precious air into my lungs, I exhale loudly. "They are attacking me, trying to strip my freedom away, and you can't even tell me the reason why they are doing all this?"

His expression is just as stoic, cold, and unbothered. "My attorney is gonna defend you properly. You have nothing to worry about."

I can't help but huff and shake my head at his comment. "So you won't tell me what's going on? Even after everything I'm going through because of you?" I repeat, making sure that's what he intends to do.

"You know what's going on," Alex responds, confirming my thoughts. "What your mother has against me and your dad is totally irrelevant."

"Until the day she blows it up in court," I rebuke.

"She won't," he snaps back. "She's smarter than that."

I clench my teeth and dip my head slowly in disgust at the bitter taste of the exclusion I'm being subjected to. And although I trust him deeply, I have the sharp sensation that it is not mutual. "So you don't trust me enough to tell me the truth?" My eyes meet his again, and I hope he can see the disappointment they bear.

"It has nothing to do with trust," he replies, sounding quite sure of himself. "It's just something that belongs in the past. We have to focus on the present, on us."

"It's because of your past that our present is how it is," I snap back. "It's because of your past that I'm gonna have to fight for my freedom." Taking a breath to calm myself down, I finish by saying, "A past I know nothing about."

"Petra, stop."

But I'm too curious to even consider it. "What are you so afraid of, huh?" I ask, staring right through him. "That I'm gonna call the cops on you?"

As our eyes lock, his brow creases, either hurt or confused by my question. "Of course not."

"So why don't you tell me the truth?" I ask again. But his gaze drops to the ground, searching for an answer. "Fuck, I need to know what's going on."

"No, you don't!" he barks, his piercing blue eyes defying mine. The sharpness in his voice tears my heart in two. "You don't need to know shit." And a thick, toxic tension fills the space between us as he blows out a breath and adds, "I love you, and I'm ready to go to court and face a lot of backlash for you." He pauses, letting my anxiety and torment hammer against my ribs. "But you have to accept the fact that I won't share certain things with you."

And hearing this, my heart stops. I press my lips tightly together to prevent a sob of agony. I'm so hurt by his lack of trust that I need to focus on my breathing to avoid losing my mind and shouting things that I'd regret later on and would only carve a deeper hole between us.

"Now, if you excuse me, I've got some calls to make."

Alex doesn't even try to kiss or embrace me. Nope. He just rushes back inside the house and leaves me alone, ruminating on my own fate and on everything we just went through. One thing is for sure: whatever my mom has against my dad and Alex seems to be dark and serious enough to put them in jail for a long, long time.

And while I knew something was off, I always hoped that one day or another, when the right moment came, he'd open up and tell me the truth. But now that he's made it clear he'll never do so, how am I supposed to trust him when I know nothing about his past? And that alone is enough for me to wonder, what kind of man am I marrying? And most importantly, how far should I go for him when he doesn't trust me like I trust him? Without knowing such an important part of him, it seems impossible to answer.

THEIR STORY CONTINUES IN
LURED INTO LIES

ACKNOWLEDGMENTS

A big thank you to all of you for continuing this journey with me. The saga of *Blossom in Winter* is a dream come true and I'm so grateful for the amazing support, positivity, and excitement you've shown since the very beginning. Thank you so much to every single one of you!

Thank you to my editor, Tiffany, for being with me since the beginning of this journey. You are not only an amazing editor, but also an incredible person. I'm so happy to have you in my life.

To all the influencers and bloggers who have spent their free time reading, reviewing, and sharing this series online and offline. I love you guys!

To those who inspired me for the second book:

My life partner, best friend, and *compagnon de route*, Diogo, thank you for always standing by my side and trusting my craziness. Ten years with you feels like ten minutes.

My Roy Van Gatt—my dear friend Roy, thank you as always for all your support, loyalty, and kind words. You are the only friend I annoy so much about my work, and honestly I wouldn't do otherwise. Your life and work ethics are a true inspiration. Oh, and I promise I will visit you soon, and congratulations for your newly acquired castle in Scotland.

Mona, I told you I will put you in the saga, and here you are! You are just as beautiful and also living your best life in a sunny island, partying and drinking fancy cocktails as always! I miss you a lot and hope to catch up soon in one of our favorite lounges this summer.

Now working on the third book of the saga, *Lured into Lies*, which will also be released in 2021. I'm so excited for the judiciary battles, secrets, and revelations, I can't wait for you guys to read it!